# America, the Country that Made Earth Famous

## H. H. Silver

NEWMAN SPRINGS PUBLISHING
320 Broad Street
Red Bank, NJ 07701

First originally published by Newman Springs Publishing 2023

ISBN 978-1-68498-922-5 (Paperback)
ISBN 978-1-68498-923-2 (Digital)

Printed in the United States of America

# Contents

# Mescalito's Revenge

It was a dark and moonless desert night. The intense quiet of the desolate night air was occasionally shattered by a coyote's cry or some mysterious noise generated by things that go bump in the night. The two men, sprawled across the top of the mesa, surrounded by excessive amounts of equipment, did not recognize most of the noises they heard, and they tried to ignore them.

Neither man feared the noises they heard, however, because they were rational human beings. And they were large enough to play the offensive line in the National Football League. They also had big rocks, sticks, and fire. And they had a small arsenal of weapons, just in case the rocks, sticks, and fire failed to strike fear and terror of mankind into the heart of whatever should happen to wander up to the top of the four-hundred-foot-tall mesa they were encamped upon.

"What do you reckon them sharp, piercing cries are from, Odie?"

"I don't rightly know, Beeb. Might could be jackrabbits gittin' woke up by coyote teeth comin' through their fur."

"Oh, thanks, Odie! What a reasonable explanation! Next time, use your imagination."

"Well, yer welcome, Beeb. You know I always say, if you can't use your friends, then they're useless!"

"Yeah, and I know well how you use your friends!"

Another in a series of cries drifted up to their ears, causing Odie to ask Beeb what he thought the sounds to be from.

"That's easy!" Beeb grinned at his old friend. "It's Mescalito, mad at us for cuttin' on all them cactus plants this afternoon, right?"

"Right!" Odie snarled fakely, lacing his words with disbelief. Slowly, his message drifted lazily in the still night air, finally spawning some meaning in Beeb's ear.

Beeb smiled. "Not goin' for that, eh?"

"Hell *no!*" Odie smiled right back, "'Cause if Mescalito was really mad at us, he'd a' done us some harm hours ago, when we was totally in his realm!" Odie sounded positive, but Beeb looked at him like he wasn't all that convinced as yet. "Besides, Beeb, mescaline-induced gods don't sit around on the desert floor howling!"

"They don't?" Beeb gasped in wonder, trying hard to sound as falsely amazed as the coffee drinkers in the finest restaurant who are suddenly informed that they are enjoying instant coffee.

Odie continued his assessment of the situation. "No, man, they lay around golden palaces, playin' zithers and flügelhorns, talkin' heavy metaphysics and bein' trippy! Playin' backgammon on the backs of checkerboards whilst their servants scurry about, indulgin' their slightest whims!"

"Gee, Odie, that's nice to know all right. Wow, I had no idea that you were so conversant with the native North American Indian's religious and cultural beliefs."

"Hey, I minored in anthropology, I'll have you know!"

"Ah, yes, leave us not forget what higher education has done to us all, yes, yes!"

Both men fell into fits of laughter over Beeb's ass-grabbing gesture accompanying his remarks. Both had been stolen from a Vonnegut novel's insane elevator-boy character. Beeb and Odie were both devoted Vonnegut fans.

Odie attempted to speak as he wiped tears of laughter from his eyes. Finally able to talk, Odie gestured broadly all around them. "Well, I'll tell you one thing for sure, Beeb. This here's about as high an education as I ever got in all my schoolin'!"

"Lord, yes!" Beeb agreed. "We must be three, four hundred feet up here on this plateau and just whole lots higher!"

"Why, just bein' this high is an education in itself, wouldn't you say?" Without pausing long enough for any possible comment from Beeb, Odie rambled on. "Yes, of course that's what you'd say, your verbosity is well documented on the aforementioned subject just mentioned."

"Verbosity?" Beeb repeated. "That show about Cosell got to you, eh?"

"Oh." Odie offered nothing else as Beeb had stepped on his lines.

And changing the subject like a dirty diaper, Beeb quickly said to Odie, "I can't believe how many meteors we saw tonight, man!"

"And got on film!" Odie noted with much glee.

"Yeah, no shit!" Beeb exclaimed excitedly. "That footage you shot earlier of the meteor exploding? Just that justified the climb up here in the hot sun with all this shit you said we needed."

Odie nodded in agreement.

"Of course," Beeb grinned slyly, "it wasn't your fault that you shot that good footage."

"It wasn't?" Odie exclaimed, not believing his ears. Disparaging remarks about his cinemagraphic abilities? Could this be?

"No, of course not, man! Why, if the sky gods hadn't tuned you in, held yer hand, and pointed the camera for you, you'da probably shot more of those pictures you was doin' long about midnight, remember?"

Odie had to mutter, "Sky gods," at his old friend before answering this accusation. "What shots are you referring to, the ones where I left the lens cap on, or the several photos of my thumb?" Okay, so he was a little twisted.

"No, no!" Beeb insisted. "You know, the ones where you were changing faces with famous people through time-travel photography. I know you know what I'm talkin' about, Odie. It was just a few hours ago."

"Do what?" Odie drawled.

"Come on, Odie, surely you remember. The portraits?" Beeb's prodding had no visible effect on Odie's facial expression.

"The portraits?" Odie repeated blankly after Beeb said it.

"Yeah, like the William Jennings Bryan portrait. I believe you said something to the effect of, 'As he really looked while monkeying around at the Scopes trial!'"

Just the mention of his own words brought it all back to Odie, and both men roared with laughter as they began recounting some of the more madcap happenings which had occurred earlier in the evening when they had been deeply influenced by the large amounts of mescaline that they had eaten for dinner. As their laughter subsided, the silence swelled into intense pressure once again.

Odie noticed the first rays of light in the eastern skies forecasting dawn. Beeb suddenly noticed a new mysterious noise knifing through the silence, ripping it asunder. Turning his head toward the clicking noise, Beeb saw Odie taking pictures in the direction of the rising sun. Grabbing his video camera, Beeb taped Odie filming the coming dawn. "You shootin' a Japanese movie there, Odie?"

Odie ignored Beeb's rising-sun joke.

Beeb zoomed in on the back of Odie's neck to compare it's redness to that of the dawn, then he caught a glimpse of something glowing brightly just off to Odie's left. Odie also noticed this new bright object, and he, too, focused upon it. As Beeb zoomed in on the object, Odie said out loud that it was coming closer. As they both recorded the newly discovered object, apprehension arose in them. The object was getting bigger and brighter in a hurry. They hoped it was another meteor about to explode, hopefully too far away to shower them with molten debris. Still, it came right at them rapidly.

Neither man realized the object they focused their lenses on would in turn bring their own lives to a focal point more resolute than they could imagine. They had reached a cosmic moment, an event marker in the passage of time unlike anything they had experienced in their lives before, and their lives had been rather exciting so far.

But these minor details were overlooked in the excitement of getting fantastic coverage of a meteor brilliantly streaking through the upper atmosphere. As it drew nearer to their base of operations, they could see that the object was enormous and in a hurry. As the event screamed past them on its way to striking the desert floor, the two men were awestruck.

It had flashed past them in an instant. They guessed it had impacted within ten miles. The resultant cloud of dust and smoke was spectacular. It glowed eerily as the smoldering mass of space debris began the cooling-down process. The smoke and dust cloud were a strange shade of red.

Beeb's panoramic video work was interrupted by a tug on his sleeve. Odie shouted, "Let's go down there!" in his best imitation of Jonathan Winters in *It's a Mad, Mad, Mad, Mad World*. It was lost on Beeb, who didn't memorize movie lines the way Odie did.

"Did you see that?" Beeb asked Odie, not listening to him at all.

"Yeah, yeah, I was watchin'! Let's go!"

"Odie, we did it! We got it all on film! Man, do you believe this? It's the scientific film of the century—a meteorite, from atmospheric entry to terrestrial landing! Far out, man."

"Beeb, fuck that! Let's go down there!"

"Damn, Odie, don't you realize what this could mean to us?"

"An increase in our hourly wages?" he suggested, knowing Beeb wouldn't like it.

"No, fool! I'm talkin' important here!"

"No, fool! Talk ain't important here. Action is important! We gotta get to it first. Otherwise, it don't mean shit!"

"You still don't realize what this means, do you, Odie?" Beeb could see that Odie was pitifully

behind in his perception of the importance of the event. Odie was enraged at this accusation. "Look, Beeb, what it means is we gotta get down off this muthahumpa in the dark and go look for that damn meteorite while it's still glowing! After it cools, the sombitch will look like every other rock out there in the desert!"

"Some geologist you are if ya can't tell the difference between a common boulder and a piece of space debris melted by entry into earth's atmosphere. Since that heat is in the neighborhood of two thousand degrees Celsius, the meteorite *ought* to be dripping!"

"Well, let's just go while we can, okay?" Turning on his heel as he said this, Odie went into the tent to get away from Beeb and his claim that the meteorite would still be glowing.

When Odie finally emerged from the tent, Beeb began laughing at the spectacle that dawn's early light revealed. "Holy shit, Odie! What are you expecting to run into down there?"

5

"I don't know, Beeb, so I'm ready for anything!"

Beeb's laughter grew louder when Odie scanned his outfit and saw nothing amiss. He was nattily attired in his heavy hiking boots, camouflage fatigues, field jacket, and a backpack stuffed chock full. His rappelling gear was in place, and dangling from one shoulder was a custom-made 30-06 deer rifle with a hand-carved English walnut Bob Hooper stock that Kathy had been crazy enough to give him. Over the other shoulder, a cartridge belt was casually slung. A .357 magnum holstered on his hip completed the ensemble, together with an Australian bush hat safely tied under the chin for that look of real danger.

Beeb cheerfully shot several dozen feet of video on this site, a welcome comic relief to the dreariness of meteoric documentaries. Beeb spoke, "Armed to the teeth, our brave boys go off to meet the Hun on his own turf."

"Yo, real funny stuff! Can we go now?"

"Oh, okay, Odie. I'll just go down and hook up the jeep for ballast so you can descend."

"Never mind these feeble attempts at humor, son. Just haul ass, yeah?"

Struggling into his rappelling gear, Beeb startled Odie by suddenly letting out a scream as he went over the edge of the cliff, "Powder River, let 'er rip!"

Odie loudly counted to ten then jumped out in a serious attempt to beat Beeb to the bottom. When Odie hit the sands below, Beeb was throttling the jeep's engine to life, remarking to Odie that Galileo had been vindicated—heavy objects didn't fall faster than light objects. Odie merely glared hatred at him.

As soon as Odie swung himself into the front passenger seat, Beeb popped the clutch, and they were off. "Ready?" Beeb inquired as he shifted into second. Odie felt no answer was necessary, and he contented himself with just giving Beeb a cold, harsh stare. A long silence ensued.

Several minutes passed, and the road conditions cleared a little. Soon, Beeb began going at speeds that Odie found excessive, and he said so. "Yo, dude, try not to outdistance them quartz lights, okay?"

"Yeah, yeah, I got it under control!" Beeb stated. He couldn't manage much more, struggling and straining with the steering wheel as he was.

"I see how you got it!" Odie snorted derisively.

Beeb kept on seeing formations of boulders appearing on the windshield like obstacles on a video game. Beeb found himself wishing that the jeep had a fire button, photon torpedoes, any type of weapons systems.

Odie warned Beeb, "Avoid these myriad pieces of Jurassic uplift."

"Jurassic uplift jur ass!"

"So you don't know your rocks. So what? Just slow down some, okay?" Odie didn't wish to become totally unpleasant with Beeb, but he would unless the jeep started to go slower and more toward safely than present conditions indicated.

Beeb decided to ease up some, although he knew Odie would think it was done per his orders, not because Beeb felt he should go a tad slower and safer. Their chatter ceased, giving way to pensive, self-centered inquiry. Beeb was happily imagining the laudation of the scientific community for his film, while Odie dreamed he would find the first solid platinum meteorite ever found. Fame and fortune fed the dreamers' dreams. Reality was still around the next boulder.

"Tad further'n I thought it was, Odie!" Beeb's words ended Odie's reverie.

"How's that?" Odie asked, unsure what Beeb was talking about.

"Well, we've traveled nigh onto five miles now, and we ain't much closer to that dust cloud yonder than we was at the start."

"Well, keep driving toward it. I doubt it will escape."

"But will it melt?"

Sarcasm dripping from his lips, Odie spoke, "Will Melvin stay faithful to Faith? Will Faith's faithlessness favor Fred? Can Gloria kick her habit? And will Dirk ever like tacos? Stay tuned to alla them chirren ain't mine."

Only the sand crunching under the tires disturbed the silence. Odie noticed that dawn was spreading her pinkish rays across the desert floor, illuminating the clouds with lustrous pink and red shades. "Looks like it's gonna be a beautiful day, Beeb."

"Yep, the day of the meteorite."

Hastily ending their conversation, the pair of men glanced around as the jeep came to a halt along the rim of an arroyo. They could see tiny wisps of dust and smoke still rising from their quarry, apparently nestled down this very arroyo some ways off. By careful manipulation of the jeep, Beeb managed to backtrack some and ease down into the dry ever-widening river bed. It had been cut through the canyon walls by periodic flooding of the upland rivers over millions of years' time.

Beeb started racing down the sandy boulder-strewn path with such abandon that Odie heartily protested his driving tactics. He was never one to be alone with his thoughts. If he thought it, you heard it.

"Hey! I wanna live, you know? And all day long too, you know? I don't wanna, you know, die in no rock-car head-on collision, you know?" Odie knew full well that Beeb hated the phrase "you know" and would immediately note the true intent of Odie's words.

"Relax, man, I got it!" Beeb assured Odie.

Odie didn't believe him because they were sweeping around a several-ton boulder on two wheels, as it was. Odie leaned out his side of the jeep, forcing a weight shift that dropped the jeep back down on four tires again. "Yeah, Beeb, I can see how you got it!" Odie glared angrily. "Slow the fuck down, dickbreath!"

But Beeb was able, from years of practice, to avoid getting angry at his old friend. He totally ignored him. Quiet and calm returned to the jeep and its occupants but only briefly. "Hot damn!" Beeb suddenly yelled out. Beeb deftly twisted the steering wheel while locking up the brakes, bringing the jeep to a hockey stop in the sand as they slid sideways around an enormous boulder.

Stunned silence froze their facial features. The meteorite they sought lay in front of them, an enormous metallic mass partially buried in the sand at the foot of a cliff. The sun broke through the clouds just then, splashing metallic glimmers awash in their own reflections across the entire surface of the thing. "Oh my god! Odie, it's a fuckin' spaceship!"

# Meddle, Metal, Test Thy Mettle

An unknown amount of time passed while the two men sat in their jeep and stared at the space vehicle wrecked in front of them. Odie finally came out of his trance and spoke to Beeb while he climbed out of the jeep. Beeb suddenly was hearing strange noises. It turned out to be Odie, babbling some drivel about entering the wreckage.

"We?" Beeb yelled at Odie. "Us? That we? Us? You want us to go in there? Are you insane? What if there's people-eating monsters in there?"

"What if you get up off yer ass and come on?" Odie was making an elaborate production out of displaying his.357 while he loaded it. He hoped that anything on board this alien craft was watching him load his weapon. This would make them realize he was a force to be reckoned with. He also wanted to reassure Beeb that he wasn't taking any unnecessary chances with their lives. Odie moved toward the wreckage.

Beeb spoke up, "Well what if they melt yer.357 before you can use it, Odie?"

"Then we got big trouble."

"Bigger than, say, Commie border guards?"

Odie froze in his tracks a moment then angrily whirled to face his tormentor. "You *better* be grinnin', shithead," Odie said fiercely, "because that was *never* my fault."

Beeb stared aghast at Odie.

"Well, not totally my fault, anyway," Odie sheepishly admitted.

The big redheaded man laughed raucously, having dredged up ghosts of errors past that Odie would rather not see nor hear. "It's okay, Odie, I got lotsa mileage outta that story already."

"Oh, so you go around telling people that story when I'm not around to defend myself?"

"Oh, only to those thousands of folks who can appreciate the true humor of the situation."

"I should'a left ya there," Odie said jokingly. "Ya probably could'a learned Bulgarian by now."

"Well, let's try to learn alien right now, okay?"

"Okay," Odie agreed, "and the best way, I reckon, is to get inside the ship."

"Sounds like dead reckoning to me," Beeb smiled.

Beeb left Odie searching through his gear for something. Beeb just couldn't imagine anything the boy had left in camp, so he walked away grinning ear to ear. As Beeb stepped up to the ship to test the heat of the metal, he spit on it, expecting the liquid to boil away. It did not. Wetting the tip of his finger, Beeb quickly brushed the surface, as if it were a hot iron, but there was no sizzle. *Very strange*, he thought. Boldly touching it with the flat of his hand, Beeb jerked his palm away, amazed.

Odie had just looked up in time to see the last of Beeb's actions, and he thought that Beeb had burned himself. Walking up to his friend while he spoke, Odie laughed as he told Beeb, "Man, it's *supposed* to be hot!"

"Odie," Beeb started in a puzzled voice, "this thing ain't hot no more. In fact, it's ice-cold."

"Ice-cold? Nah, it's gotta be hot, Beeb. Look, the temperature of an object entering the upper atmos—"

Beeb cut off Odie's speech by grabbing his hand and forcing it against the ship's surface. "There, it's cold, I tell ya!" Beeb gloated.

They stared at each other. "Jeez, Beeb, now why the hell would it be so cold? It was hot enough to fuse this sand together when it landed!" Odie pointed out several tektite-like glassy blobs around the ship's edges. "It was hot enough to glow in the dark while we followed it for over an hour too!" Odie added.

"Yeah, Odie, and now it's cold to the touch. I wonder what could cool it off so fast?"

The words had barely left Beeb's lips when both men simultaneously realized what might have happened. "Holy shit! Supercold liquid gases!" Odie screamed.

Dashing back to the jeep, both men had thought of the same thing at the same time. American and Russian rockets were fueled by supercold liquid hydrogen gas and supercold oxygen liquid. If these kinds of gases fueled the spaceship, there could be a tremendous explosion. Odie started up the jeep, and they fled from harm's way at high speeds, furiously slinging sand as they scrambled to safety behind large granite boulders.

"Fuel musta leaked after the crash," Odie said, although what he really meant was, "When it explodes, we'll be safe here."

But after a rather short period of time, Odie reconsidered the situation. Would the spaceship indeed explode? What proof did he have? Was the cold surface due to a fuel leak or perhaps an air conditioner run amok?

After a few more minutes of wondering, Odie changed his mind about the ship. "I don't think there's a fuel leak."

"Then why is the ship's surface so cold?" Beeb wondered.

"Oh, hell, Beeb, that thing might be cold for any number of good reasons."

"Such as?"

"Such as it's built like a thermos bottle, or they got great air conditioners, a party-sized supply of ice. Shit, it could be anything."

"Uh-huh!"

"Beeb, they probably utilize some advanced energy source for power, something we ain't got around to even considerin', something even we haven't thought of yet."

"Well, if you think they're so damned advanced, then why are you cowering behind this huge boulder?"

"Well," Odie whined, "they might not be all that advanced either. They need remedial parking, that's for sure."

A couple more minutes of waiting prodded Odie into action. "This is silly! Either it blows, or it don't, and I'm votin' the don't ticket."

That said, Odie eased around the boulder to check on the crash site. Beeb screamed, "Blam!" at the top of his lungs, giggling uncontrollably at Odie, who was wincing in fright.

"Now goddammit, Beeb, that ain't funny!" But Odie failed miserably in his attempt to convince Beeb that there was no humor in their situation, and he soon became mired in the mirth Beeb wallowed in.

While it was possible that they were being influenced by traces of mescaline still roaming their bloodstreams, they considered themselves to be sober, but neither man considered himself normal. That was the one thing they had never been accused of by anyone anywhere in the world they had been, which was all over.

Odie decided to try a new approach on Beeb, an old phrase. "Look, let's be reasonable about this, old buddy."

Beeb jumped at the bait Odie dangled in front of him. "Oh no ya don't! Odie, you used that very phrase on me the last time I got shot at! Shot, Odie, shot! With real Commie bullets, rightly fired upon invaders on their soil! Don't forget that, Odie, and don't try to shake it off with yer head goin' like that either. That oh-no-that-ain't-the-way-it-went-down headshake. I followed that tone of voice into disasters of enormous proportions too many times, Odie!"

"And you lived!" Odie pointed out in his best John Houseman accent, a tone implying unquestionable superiority. "You survived—and unscathed!" Odie warmed to his task. "Never once were we in real danger. Well, you didn't get shot, right? I mean, never once were you actually hit with a bullet."

"Not that they weren't trying their damndest to hit me with bullets."

"Well, I'll grant you that, but you never once were castrated, hung, beheaded, imprisoned for life, or any of the other vile things, which, I will admit, we were actually threatened with but never forced to endure. We've always gotten out alive. We're survivors, right?"

"Right, which is why I ain't goin' inside no wrecked spaceship 'cause I'm a survivor, and I intend on staying a survivor."

"Where's yer derring-do?"

"If yer darin' me to do somethin' stupid, Odie, it just won't work."

"Yer a wimp!" Odie pronounced this sentence as a judge might. He left Beeb as he set out to examine the spacecraft from "close range." Odie's working definition of close range was *inside*.

Beeb thought over what he should do. Letting Odie have his own way was always dangerous. Beeb knew that better than anyone alive, and he knew Odie would attempt to gain entry despite any danger. Even the direct knowledge of imminent danger had never had much effect on Odie's determination. Beeb knew this from multitudes of experience with the man on three different continents. If Odie thought he could do it, he did it.

Beeb smiled as he recalled that Odie had done the seemingly impossible any number of times, like the time he hot-wired a very rare surviving Heinkel He 115 and buzzed the American troops on parade. Beeb remembered the distress Odie had caused the American command as they tried to find an ex-Nazi pilot who had done this terrible deed. They had never imagined a fifteen-year-old kid from Mississippi could read old German war manuals. Even Odie's dad had never caught on to who flew the plane over the troops about twenty feet off the ground. His dad didn't know old Bob down at City Auto Paint had taken Odie out for flying lessons the summer before. To Beeb's way of thinking, it still remained Odie's finest stunt.

But there were so many others, Beeb knew, and undoubtedly more that he wasn't in on. Odie was one guy hard to beat. That was for sure. And he had the maddening ability to be right and say, "I told you so."

Beeb thought the situation over. This was little different than any other occasion when Odie wanted to do something. So what if nothing was known about it? Odie had aced an unknowns test in chemistry once at the old North Avenue Trade School. Now it was just Georgia Tech.

Beeb arrived at the decision to go after Odie just in case something inside the wreckage needed protection from the madman. Walking up, he could see Odie tossing a grappling hook up at the end that Beeb had earlier decided was the exhaust port for this cigar-shaped craft. Odie could not get the hook to hold, and it was aggravating him. Finally, he got a toss to hold, and up the rope he went, hand over hand.

Just as he reached up one hand to grasp the port, the hook slipped free and deposited Odie unceremoniously in the sand below. Beeb dashed over to see if his old friend was all right. The large steel hook had landed scant inches from Odie's head. Beeb knew he was okay when Odie suddenly leapt to his feet and soundly cursed the alien craft. "You fuckin' rotten miserable whore dog cocksuckin' sunuva *bitch*!"

Odie wasn't content to merely scream at the inanimate object, and he picked up and threw a football-sized chunk of granite at it to vent his anger. The stone missile just glanced off harmlessly. Odie walked away toward the jeep to retrieve it, while Beeb inspected the area that Odie had just bounced some granite off of. Beeb was busy pacing off the length of the craft as best he could when Odie parked the jeep under the alleged exhaust port. He was still muttering obscenities at the wreckage.

Odie stood on the hood to get closer to the port and tried his luck again at tossing the hook up to the port. After several dozen attempts, he finally got one toss to stay, and he roared for Beeb to come secure the rope while he hung on it with all his weight. He figured that if the rope was tied to the jeep's bumper, the tension would be constant, and there would be no more slipups. As soon as Beeb pronounced the rope secure, Odie went up hand over hand to peer into the port.

Looking into the dark confines of the wreckage, Odie could see nothing. He grabbed his six-volt lantern off his belt, put it inside the port, and switched it on. Odie very nearly blinded himself with this maneuver. He turned out the bright bulb and switched to a tiny red bulb. After his eyes cleared, Odie could see down inside the port. Just below him, he saw a point. It looked as though he were peering down into a huge ballpoint pen with the point retracted. He came down the rope to ponder what he'd seen.

Beeb realized that Odie wasn't going to answer him. He acted like he didn't even hear him, so Beeb went up the rope to see for himself. Odie was deep in thought about the design of what he had just seen. If Beeb had been wrong about the cigar shape and the port was the nose and not the tail of the craft, then the point inside made some sense. Maybe it was something like an air-adjustment screw on a carburator or something, but otherwise, it didn't make sense to Odie. What would the point be for if it were exhaust? Air intake made some sense; exhaust outlet made no sense. What's the point for? *Yeah*, he thought, *what's the point?*

Odie heard Beeb rustling around at the top of the rope, and he looked up just in time to see Beeb turn on his flashlight. Cruelly smiling to himself, Odie watched his friend scorch his eyeballs on the highly reflective metal inside the port. Then he spoke up. "It's too shiny to be the exhaust port, I believe."

"Oh, I don't know, Odie. I reckon it just might be a new model that don't burn oil yet." Beeb slid down the rope as he finished talking.

They argued back and forth about the type of aircraft it might be, what it's shape was, and what it might be made from. Odie declared there were no marks from the hook inside the port. "Beeb, yer the metallurgist here, so what kind of metal do you think this is?"

"I think it's right hard."

"Hold it! There are no marks, seams, welds, rivets, doors, or windows of any kind anywhere on it, and all you can say is it's right hard?"

"Yeah, it's right hard. No marks, no nothin'. Right hard."

"You got two advanced degrees in metallurgy! You know more about metals than anyone I know! Beeb! Ya gotta say something else about it, man! Right hard don't explain much to me, man. I wanna know what kind of metal it is!" Clearly, Odie was very disappointed in his old friend.

"Okay, Odie, I been thinkin' about this problem some. I have carefully considered what sort of metal shows no blemishes or scars—hell, even a wrinkle—from deep space travel, entry into earth's atmosphere, a steel grappling hook and a granite football. I've been able to eliminate a few possibilities."

"Such as?" Odie demanded crisply.

Beeb smiled at Odie. "Oh, such as aluminum, nickel, iron, steel, cobalt, mercury, calcium, magnesium, manganese, all ferrous metals and their known alloys, all nonferrous metals and their known alloys, that sort of thing."

"Yeah, but did you notice anything strange about this metal?"

"Like it's unearthly, maybe?"

"Yeah, somethin' along those lines, yeah."

Beeb took a deep breath before he spoke. "I believe this metal is, verily, to test thy mettle."

"You tellin' me to not meddle?"

"Sorta."

"That ain't human to not meddle!"

"Oh, very well, then. Let us meddle cautiously."

"Well, okay, then!" Odie spoke a little too quickly and a little too enthusiastically for Beeb's liking.

And sure enough, Beeb's hopes for truly cautious meddling were quickly dashed when he saw Odie casually unleash two rounds from his 30-06 into the port they both now assumed was the craft's nose. Beeb screamed at Odie. "Jesus Christ, Odie! I said cautious! That ain't cautious! A few minutes ago, you thought this whole wreck was gonna explode! Now yer shootin' at the damn thing! Hell's a matter with ya, anyway?"

Odie gave no opposition when the rifle was snatched from his hands. Beeb muttered something about safety and gun nuts as the rifle was placed in the jeep, "Where it belongs!" There was a certain tone of finality.

For the next several minutes, they listened to the seemingly endless ricocheting bullets clang, whang, whine, and careen their way about the interior of the alien vessel. Finally, the noises ended when both bullets were ejected out the port they entered and settled into the sand. "Amazing!" Odie said, dashing over to the spot the bullets hit the sand to recover them.

"Amazing!" Beeb noted, meaning Odie and not the bullets.

Odie went back up the rope to examine the area he'd put two rounds from a deer rifle into. Nothing. No marks. "No marks of any kind," he reported to Beeb. He slid down the rope more confused than before. "What kind of metal is this that won't show a scratch when hit from twenty-five feet away with a 30-06 deer slug?"

Beeb had an answer for Odie, although not one he wanted. "This," he began in imitation of the Wizard of Oz, "is that horse of a different color you hear so much about."

Odie was little cheered by this analysis.

Settling down into the sand in the shade provided by the ship's shadow, the two tried to think of things that would explain what they had witnessed. Odie made a mental note that he refused to believe that some crummy alien metal could be harder than the cliffs of basalt, diorite, and granite, which surrounded them. Beeb knew only that this metal was unlike anything that he had studied on earth. He did not know what to expect its properties to be. So far, they vastly exceeded what earth demanded of its metals.

Beeb thought silently for a short while, and Odie did the same. And then, Odie noticed his concentration being interrupted. "Look, Odie, do you think a welding torch might cut through it?"

Odie glanced at his friend, giving him a look best expressed over half-moon bifocals, a look of dismay laced with pity for such ignorance. "Beeb," Odie began in a tone that smacked of condescension, "we can't shoot holes in it. We can't cut, dent, or even scratch the damn thing. We can't even find a *warm* spot on something that ought to be glowing cherry red from heat buildup during entry into our atmosphere. And then you wanna know if something we ain't got might work! Christ on a crutch!"

Beeb was a fairly astute judge of Odie's reactions. "Don't like the idea, eh?"

They fell silent to contemplate their fate. Inside the wreck, the same strange occurrence was also being contemplated by the survivors.

# What Rats Are

Inside the wrecked craft, the two surviving crew members listened anxiously to the strange noises above them, clanging and banging around, now clattering below and beside them with no discernable pattern. Ricochet was not a word in their vocabulary. They were trapped on their couches, held in by the restraints necessary under weightless flight conditions through space. They had survived the wreck's impact because they were strapped in place during the accident. But now, their fate was the subject of their pondering, such as it was.

What manner of creature was outside? What was banging and scraping on the exterior of their vessel? What was trying to get in and why? Would this unknown creature seek to destroy them? What could they do? They were trapped. They could not stop anything from coming in, and they could not get out. The random metallic noises stopped as suddenly as they had started.

The computer expert lay on her couch restraints, unable to move. She could not investigate the power failure of the control panel because that same failure held the restraints locked tightly together. That there was severe damage was quite obvious. The redundant systems were all in failure mode. The computer was not operating. It had never shut down before, so she had no experience with a computer system that failed. She was suspended upside down, dangling helplessly on the restraints. She was uncomfortable, to say the least, both mentally and physically.

She reasonably postulated that there must be extreme bends in the normally straight conduit. Laser circuitry powered everything aboard the starcraft. How to reach the problem area was a problem in itself. Nothing would satisfy her curiosity, except seeing the damaged control panel itself firsthand. Therefore, how to get out of the couch area was the first thing to accomplish, but she came to realize that she did not know what to do. The computer would know what to do, but it was not operational. She was lost without her computer's input from its information banks.

The other survivor, who was both language expert and copilot, also lay on his couch restraints, not quite certain what to do. He considered his position carefully. He was lying facedown, pressing against the restraints, viewing the ceiling below him. He was sure of only a few things. This was not what he should be seeing upon awakening from Rest Period. He could not contact the remainder of his crew on any of their personal brain-wavelength channels.

He had never before been awakened early from Rest Period. He vaguely remembered the computer base they left near Polaris had awakened him, told him of imminent danger, and then inexplicably shut down. He thus had been awake during the crash landing on earth, while he probably would rather have been asleep during the crash.

And what of this crash landing on the planet they were supposed to study from orbit? It would seriously interfere with that mission. All starcraft power systems were inoperable. What could have happened to an otherwise plain, boring, ordinary, routine mission? Only hours ago, they had entered earth-orbit range to begin study of the recently discovered civilization that sent television transmissions into space to orbiting satellites. The two survivors had begun an assigned Rest Period shortly before the scheduled orbiting behind a cover satellite had apparently gone awry. *Failure* was not a word he would normally associate with space missions, so he had no real idea of what had gone wrong.

The giant computer satellite that they had parked a few days earlier in earth-synchronous orbit near Polaris had awakened the computer expert from Rest Period before its scheduled completion.

She, too, had never before in her life been disturbed during Rest Period, and the early awakening had left her a bit groggy.

The computer had been separately informing them of a collision between their ship and the cover satellite when it inexplicably terminated all output. Several seconds after the shutdown, blurry, distorted signals reached each of them via their implanted computer-link headsets, but these signals were incomprehensible to the space travelers. After that, only silence.

The ensuing period of time was horrifying to them. They suffered complete and total isolation. For the first time ever, they were alone. Their implanted chips linking them with the computer were neither transmitting nor receiving. They could not reach one another on their personal brain-wavelength channels. They had always been told that the computer link was vital and that life itself ceased when the link to the computer ceased, yet they still seemed to be alive, at least to themselves.

But there was no way to check. There was no way to know for sure. The computer remained strangely silent. They had no one to ask but themselves, and they could not even communicate thoughts to one another. Panic set in. Fear gripped them as they had never been in such a situation before.

But fortunately for them, the computer satellite had multiple functions and a judgment panel to deal with crises as they may occur. The judgment panel had been activated by the collision between the starcraft and the cover satellite. Normally, the judgment panel would convene, determine the problem, identify and implement the solution, and then deactivate when the crisis was over.

The types of crises that the judgment panel had been designed for were of a celestial nature. Collisions between itself and space debris were to be avoided, so lasers of sufficient power to vaporize meteors of any size were in place outside the housing of the satellite. These same lasers were used to constantly scan in all directions to alert the judgment panel of any danger that might arise.

But the type of crisis that had arisen when the judgment panel chose to awaken the two crewmen in Rest Period had not been resolved yet, and there seemed to be no ready solution, so the judgment panel judged its functions. The power siphon was operating normally. Quasars were being drained, and the power was being sent back to the Ehliun Computer Central Grid on the planet Ehlius. The key function appeared to be the earth-study section. Here, living terminals were involved.

Without its two remaining terminals surviving, information input to the computer base was not possible. The living terminals must remain alive and well for the program to function correctly. Defunct terminals meant defunct program, which meant shutdown for the computer and thus the judgment panel itself, so the judgment panel made the decision to keep the living terminals alive as long as possible and at all costs.

Power from the power siphon was amplified and redirected to the earth-study section so that it now had unlimited power. It was necessary to have vast power reserves to scan earth from eight hundred light-years away, and the dense magnetic field of earth was hard to scan through. But shortly after implementing the search for the Ehliun starcraft, the computer found the vessel smashed into Utah.

By boosting the power output millions of times on their individual brain-wavelength channels, the computer base succeeded in reuniting itself with the Ehliuns stuck aboard the wrecked spacecraft. Suddenly, inside the starcraft wreckage, joy returned to Mudville. Casey was back.

The computer was the apex of triangulation, which allowed the two Ehliuns to communicate across hundreds of light-years even though they were lying only a few feet apart. The reunion was warmly welcomed by the stranded survivors.

However, the happiness this reunion brought was short-lived. When the computer was finally able to communicate, the Ehliuns didn't care to hear what was communicated. The computer judgment panel told them it had taken over all functions of the computer base satellite because Ehlius Central had ceased all communications with no explanation. The computer expert had no idea how that could have happened.

The network grid was still hooked up, or else the judgment panel would have no source of power. She knew that, so how could it have been isolated? The Ehliun Central Grid just didn't work like that, or at least it never had before. Still, this news was somewhat welcome. The computer could at least talk to them, and they could talk to each other.

The judgment panel was able to get one air conditioner to work. That brought some very welcome relief to the trapped Ehliuns. The heat buildup inside the wreckage had been close to fatal levels for the Ehliuns. They were glad they could at least cool off. That was their only comfort so far.

Their spacecraft had no operable laser defense system due to the impact. And when the Ehliuns' computer comes back on, it tells them that two strange, multi-colored, partially metallic creatures were attempting to gain entry into the wreckage. The judgment panel reported that the creatures did not much resemble the people of the television culture, although both creatures walked upright. Perhaps they were primitive examples of what had evolved into television culture types.

The judgment panel could not open the restraints for the trapped Ehliuns. It could not stop the creatures outside from coming in, and it could not free the trapped Ehliuns from their individual prisons. The computer expert and the language expert considered their positions carefully.

They were stuck, lying facedown inside shielded couches and on hard restraints. They had been abandoned by their home planet. Their computer base was eight hundred light-years away. They were helpless. They were trapped. "Trapped like rats" would have come to mind had they known what rats were.

# Failure

The tense, irritable earth-study overseer flipped a small switch on the console in front of him. That ended all contact with the earth-study satellite computer base. He had taken the precaution of overseeing this project by himself so no other member of the board knew what really happened. Now he merely had to forge details of earthly life until he could replace what he just lost.

*Failure*—the word fairly reeked. Over a dozen generations had passed since the last recorded death of an Ehliun in space. Now all five crew members died at once. If this was discovered, he would lose his job, even his life. A quick recheck with the computer satellite confirmed his worst fears: no answer on any of the crew's personal brain-wavelength channels. Three crewmen apparently died upon impact, and the other two had their Rest Period terminated.

The board member knew Rest Period was never interfered with, as any type of alteration of a living terminal's sleep patterns of suppressive Tranquility Wavelengths was known to be detrimental to the smooth functioning of the Ehliun bureaucracy. Terminals had even revolted in the past before Tranquility Wavelengths had ended those revolts. Therefore, the overseer assumed that a termination of Rest Period was tantamount to a termination of life.

The impact with the satellite chosen to hide them from earthly view was most unfortunate. The Zond series littered the six-hundred- to 1,200-mile above-earth range, and all of them were identical in one important respect. All six hundred of the Zonds were defunct. Ehliun lasers had previously detected no electrical activity whatsoever from the dead Soviet space debris. The lasers were trained on the Zond. The Ehliun starcraft's onboard computer was busily utilizing the lasers to analyze the yaw, pitch, and nutation of the Zond when disaster struck. A laser beam from a secret Soviet base in the Arctic Circle hit the Zond.

All signals were being fed directly into the Ehliun computer on board the starcraft. The Soviet laser intrusion caused an overload and a short circuit. The short circuit fired a retro-rocket burst, slamming the starcraft into the Zond satellite, tumbling both into earth's atmosphere, where they would both surely burn up as they plummeted toward the blue planet. The Soviets cheered their success. As usual, they didn't know what happened but took credit for it anyway.

The overseer pondered his problems. No living terminals to gather data. Living terminals were, after all, just that, living terminals of the computer network. *Little more than hardware*, he thought. They were mere extensions of machinery and could be as easily replaced, were it not for the fact that they were now on earth, six months' travel time away. How to replace those terminals was uppermost on the overseer's mind right now.

The nervous overseer did not imagine that the earth-study satellite had a computer base with a judgment panel sophisticated enough to interrupt Rest Period. His imagination was sorely limited. He didn't have to have imagination. He was a committeeman, a member of the board. Cold, hard facts were what he dealt with.

Imagination had joined other detrimental words banished from the Ehliun language. Words and concepts like choice, chance, possibility, opportunity, freedom, individual, self, liberty, truth, goals, ideals, courage, honesty, integrity, happiness—all these terms and ideas were gone. Rest Period Tranquility Wavelengths had ended all that nonsense.

The overseer, a powerful board member, ended the nonsense of failure with a cold, hard, calculated movement—a flip of the switch. The problem was now gone. No one would ever find out either. Earth had been a very recent discovery, known only to the board members and several million Ehliun space-level workers, who didn't even realize they were living terminals of the vast Ehliun computer network.

Reprogramming them was no problem at all. Tranquility Wavelengths would take care of it. That left only the other board members to deal with. How to deal with them and survive was utmost in his mind. Failure of this magnitude would surely bring a wretched and vengeful death to him if discovered. He would not be missed on his home planet, that was for sure. The general population didn't know he existed right now.

The average citizens of Ehlius didn't know anyone was alive on their planet and not hooked to the computer by means of chips implanted in the brain before birth. No one but the board knew that the board existed, and fewer members meant more power for the remainder. The overseer was very tense. He had to do something, but what? That was his problem: he had no imagination.

# Close but No Seegar

Getting up from the sand, Odie had decided that Beeb's cigar-shaped theory about the spacecraft was, in fact, wrong. He went to the jeep and returned with two shovels, handing one to Beeb. They moved to opposite sides of the wreck to begin digging. A few minutes of shoveling sand in the hot sun caused Odie to rethink this approach. He slipped off to climb up the cliff overlooking the wreck. Perhaps the answer was up here. Odie surveyed the crash site from his newly acquired vantage point.

Just below him, almost out of his reach, was a shiny bit of metal! Odie smiled with vindication. He just *knew* his home planet granite was harder than anything whipped up by alien metallurgists. He stood at the cliff's edge, twisting and tumbling his hands in front of him, trying to reconstruct the motions of the spaceship as it had slammed into the cliff. Odie became excitedly certain that the bottom was ripped open and that they could get inside! He scrambled back down to tell Beeb about his discovery. Surely, Beeb would be as thrilled as he was.

Beeb greeted Odie with a Brother Dave Gardner line as he leaned on his shovel: "Someday, I'm gonna *run* this construction company." Beeb knew Brother Dave was Odie's hero and favorite comedian. Beeb was none too pleased that Odie had just silently snuck away. He sarcastically asked, "I suppose you have some good reason for just walkin' off the job here, son?"

"Sure do!" Odie smiled brightly to a scowling Beeb. "Lookit this! It's a piece of the spaceship!" Odie proudly displayed the foil treasure for his companion.

Beeb was not impressed at all. "Aw, hell, Odie! That's just a piece a' some careless camper's TV dinner tray!"

Odie was enraged at this false accusation and quickly tossed the foil strip to the ground as he drew and fired his .357 at it. A bullet compressed itself into a flat blob of metal, unable to penetrate the foil strip that Odie had retrieved from the cliff's edge. The demonstration was very convincing. "Well, have you ever seen aluminum foil that tough?" Odie asked Beeb sarcastically.

Beeb laughed a nervous laugh and looked at Odie. He knew now that it *had* to be part of the wrecked spaceship, but how could it have come off a surface that can't be damaged by bullets? Odie picked up the spent bullet and the foil strip and put them into his field jacket pocket. Someday, he would donate them to the Smithsonian along with the tektites and other memorabilia, he thought.

"Beeb, this ship ripped open up there on that cliff and then slid on down the cliff face to where it rests now even as we speak. There just has to be an opening, and we are going to find it." Odie felt this speech to be concise, clear, and requiring no further explanation.

Beeb thought that perhaps only a small section, like a wing or tail section, had been torn off, and entry could be difficult, maybe impossible. He also thought there was no sense talking sense to Odie. It had never worked before.

Digging as close to the cliff base as he could, Odie furiously moved sand aside from a small area until Beeb gave a nervous start when the air split from a noise like local thunder. "Hooooo yahh-hhh!" Odie screamed. "Hot damn, boy, here's the entrance!"

Beeb moved over to join Odie in clearing the sand away. A few minutes of work between them had most of the loose sand cleared away from the rip so they could see inside, but it was too dark to distinguish anything.

Beeb jammed his shovel into the pile of sand next to the rip, and he leaned up against the cool metal. He paused in his labors and caught his breath. Odie glared at him after shoveling alone a minute or two, thinking the pause had refreshed long enough. Wearily, Beeb jerked his shovel out of the sand. Much to his surprise, a strip of shiny metal was dangling from it, still attached to the ship. "What the?" Beeb uttered. He saw Odie staring incredulously. "Odie, wouldja just look at this shit?" Odie spoke up.

Neither man could believe his eyes. "How did you do that, Beeb?"

"I don't know."

"Yo, degree-holdin' metallurgist! What kinda metal peels like aluminum foil off a candy bar, but has the surface tension of a bank vault door?"

"I really don't know, Odie."

"What do you know?"

"I know we can peel this sombitch open like a sardine can usin' this shovel as the key." So saying, Beeb twisted the shovel around and around, gathering up a sheet of spaceship skin around it, and ripped it free of the hulk with almost no effort at all.

They were amazed. It was as if the metal had given up the struggle to keep them out. They couldn't shoot through it, but they could peel it right off the ship's skeleton.

Inside the spacecraft, the computer parked near Polaris reported to the trapped Ehliun space veterans that the creatures outside had just torn the side open and were definitely coming in. The computer judgment panel had been scanning them while they toiled outside the wreck. They didn't resemble television-culture types too much. The judgment panel could not know that the clothing the earth creatures wore had a great deal to do with their overall appearance, since the Ehliuns did not wear clothing. The Ehliun computer judgment panel simply thought that all intelligent life on earth acted like those humans on television. How very little it knew.

The computer advised the Ehliuns from time to time what it had been able to determine about the creatures outside the wreckage. The computer scanned them from eight hundred light-years away. This scanning was done in multiple spectral bands to reveal which elements were involved in reflecting light waves of known frequencies. This analysis revealed that the creatures were made up of many elements, over one quarter being metals. It was unknown how semi-metallic creatures could exist. Many metal compounds were discovered in the fibrous coverings on the heads and faces of the creatures. Internal supports were largely calcium, iron, and phosphorous.

These two were possibly not even of the same type of being, as one was covered with red fibers, and the other one covered with black fibers. Intricate detailed analysis on the fibers showed more copper structures in the red fibers than in the black fibers. A great deal of common, ordinary hydrogen was detected as well as oxygen and nitrogen, and a liquid exuded for unknown purposes was noticed dripping away from the creatures as they tried to get inside. It was very complex, containing metallic salt compounds. They were strange creatures to be sure.

Computer checks with the stored information, limited as it was, told the Ehliuns very little. Most of the information was located at Ehlius Central, and that was somehow shut off. The judgment panel determined that in this type of locale, these beings could be primitive examples of what had evolved into television culture beings. They could be the kind of beings seen in the cowboy and Indian TV shows they had intercepted—maybe. The computer judgment panel had followed this line of reasoning simply because out of all the stored information, only that area seemed to fit the facts. Only the brave exploits of Roy Rogers, the hero cowboy, seemed to have parallels. The location and scenery seemed to be the same. These fiber-covered beings had metal-throwers similar to those used by the hero Roy Rogers. The computer noticed that the Roy Rogers metal thrower was superior to all others, as it never seemed to run out of pieces of metal to throw, like the others. That must be why he was a hero, the judgment panel judged.

And the last bit of evidence, they even moved about in a conveyance just like the one Roy Rogers's sidekick drove, instead of riding a horse creature, whatever they were. Thus, using the best logic available to it, the computer decided that the creatures outside the wreckage were of the cowboy faction. It took them to be primitive. How primitive was the real question. They had certainly displayed a violent nature toward the spacecraft as it was.

And the rituals they had gone through upon first approaching the craft had been recorded for future consideration, although nothing of the meaning of these acts had been gleaned. The primitives had struck, touched, yelled at, and tried to hurt the spacecraft. Now they had simply ripped open the craft's entire side. All the information the computer was provided by the earthmen convinced it that they were very dangerous, curious primitives.

This information did very little to ease the pain of being trapped and as scared as the Ehliuns who waited for the creatures to get inside were. They were very scared. Their end seemed to be getting very near. They could not move, they could not escape, and they could not defend themselves.

Having torn open an entrance big enough to drive the jeep through, Beeb paused in his efforts. "Reckon that'll git it?" Odie asked Beeb, gesturing grandiosely at the huge rupture.

"Well, it's, uh, it's so's I don't have to, uh, duck. Yeah, that's it, like so I don't have to duck." Beeb's excuse was weakly offered, as he knew Odie wasn't going for it. But he stretched his six-foot-four-and-a-half-inch frame to its maximum height and stared at Odie. He was at least two inches taller than Odie and fifteen pounds lighter, although Odie had the smaller waist. Beeb's eyes somehow softened and altered his image in any mirror, although it was probably something to do with the distortion of the mirror.

In reality, Beeb was a little thick around the middle, but few people were brave or foolish enough to point this out to Beeb. Odie, however, was both. "Yeah, Beeb, now it's high enough and wide enough too!" Beeb bristled and glared, but he knew it was useless to argue out here in the hot sun, especially when Odie's waist would measure three inches less and his chest four inches more. Distribution is what Odie would say. Beeb knew that, and why should he give him the satisfaction of gloating?

Odie left Beeb staring at him and strolled into the spaceship. He immediately returned for his field jacket. In response to the puzzled look Beeb gave him, Odie said, "I believe that they left the AC on full tilt, boogie." Odie grabbed his searchlight and warned Beeb, "Better fetch a couple more lights, dude."

Beeb grabbed his jacket in case Odie was right. But as soon as he left the direct sunlight, he could feel the coolness on his arms, and he put the jacket on rather than carry it.

Odie made a mental note that earth must be too hot for who-ever crashed. Switching on their lights, the two men stared at every-thing their lights illuminated. "Kinda looks like the bridge of the Enterprise, don't it, Odie?"

"*Spock!* Do you have those coordinates yet? Scotty! Where's that power you promised me? Get away from me, Bones. I don't *need* any sedatives!"

"Yer mind is amazingly maladjusted, Odie!"

"Thanks, Beeb. Comin' from you, that's a compliment!"

Odie was still grinning as he swung his backpack off, opened it, and dug out the cameras. He handed the Polaroid and the video camera to Beeb, who immediately started filming Odie as he wrestled his cameras free of the backpack. Beeb panned the room as soon as he saw Odie armed with a Nikon and the Bell and Howell movie camera. Soon, they were photographing everything in sight.

None of the things they took pictures and movies of made any sense to them. They were acting out of a deep and abiding concern for historic and scientific accuracy. The opportunity to record for all time and all men the facts as they happened concerning the first discovered space wreck on earth was an opportunity they did not intend to miss.

Both men could envision these shots one day adorning the walls of the Smithsonian. Odie had over three miles of movie film and several rolls of film for the other cameras. There was little that would escape their camera's wrath. They had already shot over thirty thou-sand feet of video and film on meteors and this spacecraft's entry and landing. Odie smiled to himself, thinking about how livid the senator would be over this waste of film intended for highway use. Odie wondered what the senator would think about the discovery of a UFO. Probably forget all about those highways, Odie wagered.

Beeb lined up a few shots utilizing Odie as a reference point. Odie had discovered a deck about five feet above his head. His search beam sat on the floor, illuminating the deck area overhead. He was piling up some debris he had gathered to make a makeshift ladder of sorts.

As soon as Odie could reach the deck, he hoisted himself up on it, with his Nikon. He disappeared from Beeb's sight.

Beeb didn't like that one bit. Quickly Beeb grabbed up the search beam and clambered up the jury-rigged ladder to see what happened to Odie. Searching with the light, he accidently illuminated a horrible sight! Involuntarily drawing in his breath, he gasped at what he saw. An alien monster! "Shit!" Beeb screamed loudly, heading for the exit. "Lemme outta here! It's a three-headed monster!"

Odie's one-handed grip on the back of Beeb's collar was all that prevented his cowardly-lion-like exit. "Oh, shit! Help! Help me, Odie! It's got me, Odie!"

"Shaddup, asshole. I got ya! This sombitch is dead as a hammer." Odie relaxed his grip a little as he swung Beeb around to face the alien monster. "Yer three-headed monster there ain't gonna hurt ya none, son. It's dead." Then he thought about it a bit and corrected himself. "Uh, make that 'they're dead.'"

Odie flashed the light all across the rest of the monster. Beyond its three heads, Beeb could now see that it also had six legs, six arms, and three torsos. It was three alien bodies, all twisted together in a heap. Even though they had been tossed about the cabin during impact with the satellite and then earth, it was still obvious that the three had been locked together in an unmistakable sexual embrace when their deaths came.

The earthmen paused to consider if this could be the very reason for the crash? They quietly took some more photos and filmed some footage with the cameras, and then they moved on. Death was never one to paint a pretty portrait, and this was no exception. Death had a sadness about it no matter who, where, or how it struck.

The somber reality of tragic death permeated the earthmen's consciousness as they moved along to another chamber. They were genuinely saddened by the demise of the alien crew, but that wasn't enough to slow down their racing curiosity. There was, after all, a commitment on their part to cautious meddling. Inside the next chamber, they saw some kind of little cubicles dotting the walls, six in all. "Hey, Odie, it looks like we found where they sleep."

"Looks like Plexiglas covers over them. Unless they sleep like bats, this vessel is turned upside down, and we're walking on the ceiling."

"Think so?"

"Yeah. I count six of these couches in here, and there was only three aliens back there."

"Maybe some more in here then?"

"Only one way to find out, eh?"

Beeb moved past Odie as he spoke. "Yeah, and if we find some more aliens, I hope they ain't all broke up over comin' to earth."

"Jeez, man, have some respect for the dead, awright?"

As Beeb reached the farthest couch, he froze. Somebody was staring at him! "Yo!" Beeb shouted Odie's favorite word at him.

Odie sent his flashlight beam over in his place. It shone on the farthest couch. The light was reflected back at him...by a pair of eyes...inside the couch! Odie dashed over at very nearly the speed his flashlight beam traveled. Odie's heart was pounding, his pulse was racing, and his imagination was running wild!

Beeb moved down the row of cubicles, pausing long enough to wave his flashlight back at Odie, still staring at the occupied couch. Another occupant! Two aliens alive! Odie knew his heart was pounding, but now for some strange reason, his ribs were pounding too.

Beeb prodded him again to get his attention. "Yo, coach, whadda we do now, coach? Punt?" He watched Odie's face for several seconds, waiting for the meaning to sink in.

"Huh?" Odie answered. "Oh, yeah, right. Punt. Yeah, kick them plastic shields outta the way. Hell, yes. Good idea, Beeb."

"Odie, what if those Plexiglas bubbles around the couches contain their atmosphere?"

"Well, I didn't see any bubbles around the dead ones in the other room."

"Maybe that's what killed them."

"Maybe they don't need them, either."

"Well, what if our atmosphere is toxic to them?"

"Nonsense! Science fiction writers have had aliens breathing our atmosphere for years!"

"Oh, good point, Odie! Why don't you just ask him if he breathes our atmosphere? They probably speak the language if they breathe the air!"

"Okay, yer on!"

Odie sharply rapped his knuckles on the Plexiglas shield to gain the alien's complete attention. The alien looked up, his brow all wrinkled. There was confusion registered on his face as he looked at Odie, who had yelled, "Yo, little dude!" at him.

Beeb was laughing heartily at the scene, saying to his companion, "I always knew you could confuse anyone on earth, Odie, but now it's the universe!"

"Ha ha!" Odie managed through clenched teeth, his sarcasm emphasized by the upturned middle finger on both hands. Then Odie returned his attention to the alien.

Leaning down so the alien could look directly in his face, Odie slowly spoke to the creature, "Dew y'all breeth are air okay?"

The language expert conferred with the computer. The conclusion was that the black-fiber-covered being might be speaking some archaic form of television culture language. The computer was fairly certain that they were both *cowboys*, but it was Odie's affirmative head nod that prompted the alien to imitate this action. TV culture people agreed in this manner. Perhaps it was a very old trait on earth.

Both men watched in astonishment as the alien seemed to nod his head yes. The head-nodding motion set up a counterswing of some loose skin hanging in folds at the base of the alien's skull. Beeb spoke up first. "It looks like the crash beat his brains out pretty badly, Odie. I guess he's just delirious and don't really mean to agree with you."

"Man, fuck you, man! He knows what I'm sayin'!" Odie caught Beeb grinning. "Shithead!" Odie said as he punched Beeb on the shoulder.

The alien just took it all in. His partner wasn't able to see what was going on. The computer informed her what very little it knew. So far, there was no way to tell what would happen next. If she got out of this alive, she would be very happy. But her problem wasn't just staying alive. She could apparently never go home again. Good thing she hadn't read Thomas Wolfe.

# Freedom D

Staring out at the light-beam-wielding beings from the close confines of his couch less than a body length away, the language expert was confused. He didn't think the light beams were capable of scanning or even cutting. Whatever the lights were, they were as primitive as the beings were. The earthmen were fuzzy, multicolored, and rather oddly shaped. They seemed so, well, lumpy in comparison to television culture people, especially the black-fibered one, the talker.

The computer expert didn't have the faintest idea what all the commotion in front of her companion was all about. She didn't think the light beams were useful to her, either as weapons or means to repair the onboard computer. She knew that if she could only get to and repair the onboard, then the language expert could communicate with them in their own tongue...if they were advanced enough to have a language. She wasn't certain how primitive they actually were just yet.

Odie and Beeb ended their argument about the alien's comprehension or the lack of it and convinced each other to act. They decided to set up the movie camera and record their activity of attempting to free them. They would break open the shield and free the alien trapped inside. If he died after inhaling earth's atmosphere, they would go radio for help and let the other one remain alive in captivity.

Beeb started to have some second thoughts about Odie's idea. "Listen, Odie, I been thinkin'. Why don't we go radio for help right now and not even risk killin' this dude?"

"Radio for help? Hell, Beeb, *we* found 'em! Let's see what we can do first. If we ask for help, the damn military will take all the credit, and we won't get shit, and it don't matter that yer daddy's a general, 'cause nobody is gonna be big enough to stand between the government's official policy of silence about UFOs and us blabbin' to every damn magazine except *Mad* about aliens from outer space right here in River City!"

"Yeah, maybe yer right, Odie," Beeb said with some resignation in his voice.

Odie recognized this and quickly moved in with the clincher. "Of course I'm right! Ya don't wanna spend the rest'a yer life locked away as a military secret."

"You *would* be locked away by the military, and that ain't no secret!"

Odie ignored Beeb's sarcastic reference to a certain dislike of him by certain military men, as both knew he would. Odie once again leaned up close to the alien's face. He was going to utilize the British field commander's method of communication, which is to assume any savage can understand English when it's spoken slowly enough. "We will get you out, free you, okay?"

"Crimony, Odie, you sound like Mary Hartman giving instructions!"

"Mary Hartman I sound like?" Odie asked in his best Skokie nasal accent. Beeb plunged into a rendition of something loosely resembling the Mary Hartman theme song. "O. de Bienville! O. de Bienville? How ya gonna get 'em outta there, O. de Bienville?"

Warming easily to this new task, Odie brandished his .357, pointing it toward the alien while he spoke to Beeb. The horror-stricken alien bid his companion a hasty farewell. "With a magnum, dear Beaufort, dear Beaufort, dear Beaufort, with a magnum, I'll free them, dear Beaufort, set free!"

Beeb comfortably jumped in. "And who'll catch the ricochet, dear Odie, dear Odie, and who'll die of ricochet, dear Odie, not me!"

"Okay, enough of this terse verse for worse. Here, son, there's work to be done. Don't just stand there like a fool. Please hand me a freedom tool."

"Oh, yeah, sure. And when it comes recognition time, it'll be, 'And I freed them while Beeb just watched.' But now it's 'hand me a freedom tool.' I can't think of a better expression than just *shit!*"

"Aw c'mon, boy. Have I ever let you down before?" Odie fully realized how loaded this loaded question really was.

Beeb reeled in mock horror at the audacity this man would have to have in order to ask such a question of anyone that knew him well. "Odie, surely you jest!"

"Okay, before Bulgaria then!"

"Oh, and before the bad Czech routine and East Germany, for sure, and Albania, and…and…Pensacola!"

"Now hold it!" Odie demanded. "I told you before that that shit in Pensacola was never my fault, and I'm tired of hearing about it!"

"Well, I just said it again so's you could excuse yerself again!" Beeb countered.

Odie changed the subject, knowing Beeb might be more right than he was. He never did like that too much. "Well, let's go back to the present so we can argue about the past in the future."

"Yer so tense, Odie."

"I live intense!"

"So do campers and Arabs."

They laughed at each other, their anger gone. Odie realized that, of course, Beeb was correct about the bullets and the ricochet. A ricochet inside the starcraft would be disastrous in light of how hard the outer skin of the ship was. Their investigation of the shields had led them to believe that they were more like plastic than glass. The earthmen didn't know that the Ehliuns didn't use glass and didn't know what it was.

Odie tried using his gun butt to hammer on the shields, but several blows passed without any damage. Odie knew this was useless, and he didn't dare shoot at it.

Beeb suggested they try using granite chunks like the one Odie threw at the nose of the ship earlier. Odie thought Beeb might be on to something there, so he put his flashlight down on the floor, where it would illuminate the entire area. Beeb went out toward the outside. Odie followed, saying to the aliens, "And don't touch that dial, gang, 'cause we'll be right back after this important time-out."

The Ehliuns were alone…again. The computer expert theorized that the primitives had left this as a magic talisman, or some such, perhaps meant to watch them. She was sure they would return, maybe with an invitation to dinner. With any luck, they would be guests and not the main course.

The language expert was mulling over what Odie had said before he left. There was little doubt that this was a television-culture phrase. The Ehliun had been listening intently for key TV phrases, but nothing had been forthcoming until now. There had been no talk of parties, even though they had a headache. In fact, there was no mention of pain relief at all. There was no talk of sparkling toilet bowls, no disposable douches, not a single reference to beer. There was no aftershave, no telephone computer service, and not a word about anyone named Madge. They probably weren't very civilized.

Once Odie got outside the wreckage, he looked for suitable rocks and bitched about the heat of the desert. "Jeez, it's like one hundred out here, and sixty-five inside. I wonder why?"

"I don't know either, so let's find the perfect rock and go back inside."

Odie rejected various rocks for various reasons. Beeb became exasperated. "So what the hell kinda rock you wanna find, here, boy?"

"I'd like to find an abandoned crowbar."

"Did you say roll bar or crowbar?" Beeb wondered. Odie glanced up at his old friend and smiled. "I said crowbar, but a roll bar might do very nicely, thank you very much."

In a few minutes, they had the nuts and bolts holding the roll bar in place removed. As soon as they tugged the roll bar loose, they headed straight for the relief of the spaceship's cool interior.

After taking just a few steps carrying the roll bar, Beeb suddenly stopped, bending over to retrieve something that fell out of the roll bar and into the sand. This quick stop caused Odie to be jerked clean off his feet and deposited unceremoniously on his ass in the hot sand. The look of disgust on Odie's face would have amused Beeb if he could have seen it.

"Damn it, Beeb, now that's just funny as shit, ain't it?" Odie was certain that this insult had been perpetrated upon his person on purpose.

"Hey! Look what fell outta this roll bar, Odie! It's a baggie fulla joints!"

Odie turned to look at his friend, all traces of anger set aside for the moment. "What are you sayin"?" Odie asked Beeb softly.

"Look!" Beeb exclaimed, dangling a baggie full of ready-rolleds. It was the diameter of the roll bar and about half a foot long. Beeb began to chuckle at Odie's predicament while explaining why he suddenly stopped. "I bent over to retrieve what appeared to be a great big bag of joints, and that activity seems to have pulled you off your feet. No doubt I owe you one anyway."

"Oh, yeah, right! Resentment and hostility I get from this guy," Odie appealed to the heavens, "and after all I've done for you!"

"*To*, not *for*. Get it right, Odie."

"Yeah, yeah, semantics."

"Jews got nothin' to do with this."

"You know what? You could get to be ignorant if you wanted to work at it."

"I don't want to work. That's why I got a government job."

Both men got quite amused by the inherent truth in Beeb's joke.

"So what's the deal, Beeb? We gonna just sit here and look, or are we gonna smoke some'a this manna or what?" Beeb opted for "or what," saying that they should wait until they successfully freed the alien as they had planned.

That concluded, Odie picked himself up, grabbed the roll bar, and he and Beeb carried it back inside the space wreckage.

The language expert heard them coming back, along with some very rude, harsh, and discordant sounds. He had no idea what was going on. When the two earthmen got closer to him, he would be able to hear what they said, and therefore, so could the computer. The computer was recording everything, hoping it would soon begin to make sense. So far, very little about earth made sense, and then the horrible noises occurred again.

"Well, golly bob howdy, boy, did you miss anything metallic back there to bang this sombitch against?"

Beeb offered only a few words in his defense. "It slipped." Beeb wanted to continue with the line of reasoning he had been offering to Odie on the way back in. "So as I was sayin', them banditos we dealt with in Arizona musta forgot that reefer was in there when they, uh, traded the jeep in, as you like to call it."

"Oh, hell," Odie muttered wearily, "they probably stold that jeep after the rightful owners hid the dope in there."

Beeb allowed it as how that could be true also.

"Anyway, now we got dope to smoke." Odie glared angrily at Beeb. "Boy, it really bothers you that I traded the rest of our dope for the rest of our lives, don't it?"

"Look, you went and volunteered the information that we had a kilo stashed. They'd never'a found it, and we wouldn't have been out for so long."

"On the other hand," Odie countered, "they might'a found it searchin' with their dogs. Then they might'a figured that we couldn't be trusted, eh? Then they mighta used one of the many M16s they had pointed at us, eh? A distinct possibility, yes?"

Odie still felt that he had handled the situation in the safest possible manner, and he refused to be converted by Beeb's hindsight. He had not forgotten the only time anyone in America got the drop on him.

Beeb turned on the movie camera and lights, while Odie walked up to the alien and once again got in his face to speak to him. Odie showed him the obverse side of a coin and spoke to the alien as if he could understand what Odie was doing. As expected, the alien didn't know what a quarter was. He didn't know what Odie said or did.

Odie gestured as he spoke, saying, "It's heads, so the home team kicks off, and the visitors receive."

Beeb chuckled at the fool Odie could play at a moment's notice. There he was, in front of the alien, making all sorts of football referee's signals, fully aware that the alien would not comprehend any of it. Beeb was convinced then and there that he would surely wind up protecting the alien from Odie's chicanery.

Sweeping the scene with his eyes to conjure up all the necessary moves for a home run trajectory, Odie swung the roll bar like a baseball bat. He choreographed the steps carefully and got his swing down pat. Rehearsing the procedure, he was unaware that Beeb had the camera rolling, capturing his every move and word. "Let's see now, if I rotate the bar thusly while winding up like this, I could put all this movement into force A to be vigorously applied to surface B, allowing occupant C to reach freedom D. I think this'll be a take. Lights! Camera! Action!"

# Ming's Mercenaries

Sizing up the intended impact area of the curved shield covering the couch, Beeb nodded approval of Odie's choice. Beeb then pretended to wind up and pitch to him. Odie took a vicious swing with the roll bar. A deafening noise resulted as he impacted the blunt end of the roll bar into the shield. The shattering, piercing blow had splintered the shield into rubble. Whatever the compound was, it littered the area, actually exploding upon contact with the roll bar.

When the ringing in his ears ceased reverberating, Beeb looked over at Odie, his face showing that he was baffled by the explosion. He felt obligated to speak. "Christ, Odie, I didn't think anyone would build stuff outta plastic explosives, did you?"

"No shit! That sombitch just blew up all over, didn't it?"

"Gee, I hope these two ain't from *Mission Impossible*!"

"Don't self-destruct on me now, please."

The two men busied themselves with cleaning up, brushing fragments off their clothing, hair, beards, and almost everything else. Beeb was examining the restraints the aliens were lying on, noting how shiny they were. Seeing Beeb observe the restraints, Odie was compelled to inquire, "Whaddya think they're made of?"

"Recycled beer cans. What do you think?"

"I think yer a farce as a metallurgist."

"Like you are as an anthropologist?"

"Possibly."

"I ain't got the foggiest idea what these things are made from. This shit feels more like plastic than metal, plastic like the insides of Jap cars feel, not like real metal. I know that much."

The still-trapped alien saw the earthmen moving around him. They had already savagely attacked his protective shield, and now they seemed to be aiming the shield smasher at his lower extremities. They apparently meant to beat him to death with it while he was helplessly held down. An ignominious death seemed to be in store for him. He was fearful.

And yet he was also curious. Now that the shield was gone, he could see and hear them much better. Due to the implanted chip in his brain, the computer could also see and hear them much better. The Ehliun was under the impression that Beeb had spoken some TV culture words: *beer* and *plastic*. He thought the computer made the correlation. Actually, the computer found the correlations already done by the language expert's brain. He didn't know that the computer was just a recall supervisor and not a source of original material.

Even as Odie and Beeb mumbled to one another around the Ehliun's legs, the language expert was surprised to detect sounds resembling TV culture language. Beeb was chuckling about "the dude's baggy, yeller flight suit." And while much of their speech was unknown to him, the amazing thing was some of their words *did* make sense to him. He tried to hear all they said.

"Odie, what the hell do you think yer doin'?"

"Just shut up and give me a hand."

Odie had positioned the roll bar where he thought it would break the lower restraint. Beeb disagreed totally. But even with both men leaning into it, nothing happened. While Odie rested a moment, Beeb repositioned the roll bar to provide more surface against the restraint. Odie couldn't see what difference Beeb's move would make and he said so. Then he jumped up and leaned heavily on the roll bar to prove his contention, but the restraint snapped easily, dropping Odie to the floor on top of the roll bar. Beeb just laughed at him. "No difference, huh?" Beeb shook his head disapprovingly.

Odie felt a little silly lying on the floor, and he surmised that just this one time, he might have been wrong—a little wrong. Beeb, of course, knew that any such admission would be very slow forthcoming. He just helped Odie up off the floor and then took the roll bar away. "Somebody's liable to get hurt with the bar in your hands, Odie." Placing the roll bar under the center restraint in the same manner as he replaced the first one, Beeb easily broke it by himself, and he turned to brag. "See, there's how ya do it!"

"Somebody's definitely getting hurt with the bar in your hands, Beeb!" Odie had to taunt his old pal with his own words as he dashed up to hold the alien in place. The alien was being held in only by the last restraint at the chest. His breathing was being impaired by the only thing holding him up. Beeb quickly broke the third restraint while Odie held him up in the air.

As Odie carried the alien away from the broken couch, he heard Beeb call out his name, so he turned to look.

*Flash!*

Odie was temporarily blinded by the flash. Beeb was laughing that he looked like a Polish bridegroom. Since Odie didn't have on a bowling shirt, he couldn't see the resemblance. Beeb, meanwhile, was still quite amused by the sight of Odie holding the alien in his outstretched arms like some offering or something carried to honor the gods.

Odie set the alien down and examined him with his flashlight. A gasp escaped his lips. "Good god, Gertie!" Beeb heard Odie holler loudly. Odie's light had focused on a third leg protruding from the front of his aptly described "baggy yeller flight suit." "Yo, Beeb! Come see!"

These loud noises startled the alien.

"Yer baggy yeller flight suit is this dude's birthday suit, and it's, uh, decorated with an elongated version of manhood!"

"Say what?"

"Dude is hung bigger'n most mules! Check this shit out, man!"

Beeb noisily dropped the bar he was preparing to assault the other shield with and came to see what Odie was babbling about. It wasn't babble. "Sunuvabitch, Odie! I never seen one you could kneel on!"

"Damn, but we could win lotsa black guys' money, bettin' on this dude!"

All the talk about the space visitor's physical endowments took their attention away from the obvious: the alien did not die from breathing earth's atmosphere. Why the alien could breathe the atmosphere harmlessly was not so obvious. The computer selectively screened out harmful elements, which actually allowed the aliens to breathe any atmosphere almost without damage.

"Odie, they was really streakin' through space!" Beeb stared at Odie, who still did not respond. "Get it? Streakin'? Odie?" Beeb became a tad concerned when Odie still completely ignored him. "Look, they's nekkid as jaybirds!" Odie heard a voice in the distance say. Beeb prodded his ribs to get his attention.

"Huh? What? Oh, jaybirds, right!"

"Odie, are you all right, man? Is everything okay?"

"Yeah, sure, why?"

"Ya seem distant suddenly. I just wanna make sure they didn't whip no trance beam or something on ya. That's all."

"Oh, no, I was just wondering why they traveled around nude during space flight. That's all."

"Well, they're probably from a more advanced civilization where some stupid idea like public indecency just never gained the upper hand."

"Yeah, that could be."

Odie actually had been thinking more about how dependent upon the mechanical systems one would be while traveling nude in space. Odie couldn't understand such dependence. *Look what it got you: stuck on another planet without a single thing to change into.*

Odie thought they should take this opportunity to play doctor and examine the alien from an anthropological point of view. The alien had evolved into a creature quite similar to humans but still very different. The alien had no opposable thumb, no hair, no finger-nails, and only four fingers. He had long folds of loose skin dangling where hair should fall about his shoulders. The humans came to the conclusion that the alien descended from a different line of apes, probably a mule in their woodpile, if this guy was a representative sample.

Beeb started walking quickly in circles around the alien. Odie fell in behind him, walking low on his legs, like Groucho Marx.

"Not a speck of hair."

"Probably use Nair."

"He's rather short."

"But not what he sports."

"That is a long dick!"

"Cheap cinematic trick!"

"No thumb on his hand."

"Can't hitch back to his land."

"And still he ain't spoke."

"'Cause he don't get the joke!"

This was true of the Ehliun. He didn't have a clue, no idea whatsoever what they said, why they said it, or why they circled around him. It was a good thing he didn't know anything about sharks. A conference with the computer determined that it might be a ceremony or an initiation of some sort. Of all the television culture files, once again, those of cowboys and Indians seemed most appropriate. Concentrating on these for their clues, they decided that this was an invitation by the primitives to join their tribe.

A quick movie review indicated that a peace pipe ceremony followed a dance, and these activities usually ended hostilities between the cowboy faction and the Indian faction. The Ehliun was on the watch for a peace pipe. Beeb continued to do a war dance and whoop around in circles a bit longer than Odie. Odie was sure it was to irritate him. "Yo, Tonto, cool those Silverheels."

"Say what?"

"We got serious shit to attend to. C'mon."

Beeb didn't really care for the tone of voice Odie employed toward him, and he decided to continue irritation as a course of action. Would Odie play the Lone Ranger to his Tonto? He'd soon find out.

"Ugh, *kemosabe*, this plenty serious shit! You free um up other alien fella plenty fast, *kemosabe*! Me ride um into town plenty fast and scout saloon for plenty fast woman, you betcha!"

"Yo, kemo therapy, I got yer *kemosabe* hangin'! Whaddanasshole!"

Neither man knew that an alien computer was now tracking their very movements, recording every sound, every gesture, every breath. Even if they had known, it was doubtful that they would have exhibited much concern or interest. They knew that earth was their home, and they had home field advantage. It was their home, and these guys were certainly from out of town. They were definitely the visitors.

Odie had always tried to make a habit out of being right. To Odie, wrong was temporary, like stepping out of bounds, a minor thing. No big deal. The overall outcome of the game was what mattered. Like any other game, the team that's ahead wins. If you start out in front and never look back or let anything get by you, you can't help but be a winner. Odie had used this principle to forge ahead in every endeavor, and it had always served him well. Act like you know what you're doing, and people will stand aside and let you do it. No problem. If people can't see that you are obviously superior, force them to see it. It had always worked for Odie before. He was that kind of a guy—pushy.

Meanwhile, the Ehliun computer correlated the actions of the two men with the actions of the men as seen on TV. These two seemed to be very familiar with some things seen in cowboy and Indian movies. They might be some intermediate form between cowboys and TV culture people. The only way to determine if they could be useful seemed to be to ask in the language of TV culture. They seemed to use some of the same words from that culture. Maybe they knew more, so the computer directed the Ehliun language expert to inquire whether or not they were of the TV culture.

The Ehliun spoke up to the earthmen. "Are-you-of-the-televisionculture?"

"No, I-am-from-the-yogurt-culture! Did I do the accent right, Beeb?"

"Odie, I didn't say nothin', and I don't talk in a flat monotone, either!"

Odie just stared at the alien. Beeb couldn't believe the space visitor had just addressed them in English, so he accused him directly. "Hey, did you just speak to us in English?"

"No-that-was-the-language-of-the-television-culture."

Beeb was awestruck by this historic occasion. Odie had nothing to say. Here was an alien being who spoke English, and Odie, for all his ability with the language, had nothing to say. Another first. Beeb laughed a nervous laugh of relief and shivered. "Well, I'll be go to hell. Boy, Odie, they sure had me fooled. So where you guys from? Cal Tech, maybe? Was this supposed to be for the Rose Bowl?"

Odie stared in disbelief at Beeb. Nobody could think that dumb. "Beeb, may I remind you that we saw this thing fly in from the eastern skies? Cal Tech indeed!"

"Okay, MIT, same diff!" Beeb feigned pleasant agreement with Odie.

"For Christ's sake, Beeb, gimme a break here!"

"So what's with you?"

"Me? It's *you!* Isn't it very obvious to you that he is an alien and not an earthling?" Odie fairly bellowed his comments at Beeb. They failed to see the look of astonishment cross the Ehliun's face, being too busy glaring at each other.

Ehliun and computer conferred, and there was agreement. The human had correctly identified the space visitor as an Ehliun. But how? Odie faced the Ehliun survivor suddenly and barked a question at him in a tone that implied physical harm would immediately befall him if he did not swiftly comply. "Tell me how you can speak television culture language to me when you are an alien?"

There! He said it again: Ehliun! There was no doubt about it! The Ehliun language expert was amazed. The primitive had positively identified him as a being from the planet Ehlius. Perhaps the preliminary judgments of these creatures' intelligence would have to be revised.

"How-did-you-know-that-we-come-from-the-planet-Ehlius? You-have-not-been-there-and-we-have-never-been-here-before. How-do-you-knowwe-are-Ehliuns?"

Beeb stared at Odie, seeing that even now, he was dreaming up some lie. Odie didn't disappoint his friend. "Ehleeus? Ehleeuns, huh? Er, um, y'see, it's like this, actually, well, uh, the thing is, y'see, it's just really uh, because, um, I'm brilliant!"

"Fuck a duck!" Beeb harshly stage whispered.

Beeb knew that Odie had always taken P. T. Barnum's famous dictate to heart: "Never give a sucker an even break." When the sucker is from another planet, what the hell, Beeb would have to hock the homestead and bet the ranch on Odie, and he knew he'd have to play along with whatever harebrained scheme Odie concocted. The hard part would be figuring out an angle Odie might come off the wall and where the wall might be. He was not much like ordinary folk.

The Ehliun still did not know who Odie was or how he determined that the Ehliun was, in fact, an Ehliun. The earthling didn't have the advantage of being hooked to a computer, so how could he know? And the earthmen didn't know how the alien spoke English to them. It was the last standoff in the game, the last time the score was tied. Odie would take the lead and run away with the game, scoring Beeb all the way from first. Even though the score would never be settled, the Ehliuns no longer had a shot at a win. He'd show 'em what a superstar was.

"Did you learn our language from television transmissions?" Odie asked, winking at Beeb as he did so.

The alien and his computer did not know what a wink was. Conspiracy and secrecy were unknown concepts to the Ehliun computer and its charges. Since the computer could deal only with what it knew, it was at a decided disadvantage. The home field advantage reared its head once again.

The Ehliun answered Odie's question. "Yes-we-learned-your-language-from-television."

Odie thought carefully before he spoke. The alien was technically good, brilliant even, but he lacked the fundamentals, the finesse, the ability to glibbly lie—in short, the ability to compete evenly with Odie. TV would have explained a great deal about earth to the alien, but there was a great deal more about earth that would remain unexplained and unknown. Odie used this premise to begin his attack on these possible advance scouts.

"No doubt it was Sesame Street that taught you how to speak our language?" Odie's voice had a certain smugness to it that Beeb noticed, but the Ehliun and his computer did not. The computer ripped through the files of stored earth data at the speed of light magnified a thousand times, only to discover that the primitive was right once again.

The Ehliun computer network had waded through billions of bits of information, hours of television programming and soundtracks, and had worked diligently to make the language intelligible. The television culture language had been made comprehensible to Ehlius and the Ehliuns by the television program Sesame Street. How could this noncomputerassisted being be correct so often?

Beeb still wasn't satisfied on the question of how the Ehliun could speak English. He asked a specific question of the Ehliun. "How do you speak to us? How do you know English?"

"What-is-English?"

"We call our language English, not television culture."

"The-computer-translates-your-language-to-ours-and-our-language-to-yours."

"So are you speakin' the English I'm hearin', or are you speakin' alien, and I'm hearin' your computer translate to English?"

Odie smiled and gave Beeb a thumbs-up signal, indicating approval of the line of reasoning taken by Beeb. It proved to Odie that Beeb was right up there on the front line of reasoning with him.

The Ehliun answered Beeb, "The-selection-of-necessary-sounds-in-your-language-aremade-by-the-computer-based-on-recorded-files-of-analyzed-televisionculture-transmissions-broadcast-from-Earth-to-Earth-satellites."

Odie could see nothing on the alien at all, no clothes or equipment to contact the computer. He voiced his concern. "Uh, look, slick, just exactly where is this computer located, the one yer talkin' to me through?"

"Yeah," Beeb chimed in, "and how do you contact it?"

The Ehliun answered them. "Contact-is-made-by-a-link-implanted-in-mybrain-and-the-computer-is-in-orbit."

"What?" Odie fairly shouted this at the alien creature in front of him. "You have a computer orbiting above us?"

"Yes," the Ehliun answered truthfully, for it was his custom.

Beeb thought Odie seemed to be in a state of shock, yet he managed to drag Beeb a few feet away from the Ehliun to suddenly talk things over. He put his arm around Beeb's left shoulder, drawing him nearer. In a hushed, conspiratorial tone, Odie began to whisper to Beeb. "This is very suspicious to me. What do you think?"

Beeb wasn't sure of Odie's motives at this point.

Odie clarified his thoughts. "Beeb, if he's tellin' the truth and they got a computer orbitin' earth, then it seems to me that they got colonization on their minds."

Beeb didn't really know what to think, but he didn't leap to rash conclusions quite as quickly as his old friend. "I dunno, Odie. I think that this could be legit. I mean, they are from another planet and all, so they must be more advanced than us if they got here and we ain't got there yet, so maybe they do have a computer in orbit. So what? Maybe they're just lookin' us over, like some big league scouts or somethin'. Maybe they just wanna study us.

"Look, if you was out someplace like they are, wouldn't you wanna study a similar planet? The discovery of an inhabited planet must be as great a find to them as it would be to us, yeah?"

Odie had to agree with Beeb, somewhat. "Yeah, okay, I can see 'em studyin' us for similarities, but what if their home planet won't support its vast hordes of civilization much longer? What if they need more room? What if they're like that *Star Trek* episode where they're crowded?"

"Just what are you drivin' at, Odie?"

"Look! Maybe they need new turf. Maybe these guys are just the advance scouts, lookin' to take us over. If they are an advanced race, they just might be able to enslave the Earth with little effort. In short, I just think the possibility that they work for Ming the Merciless should be faced and considered."

"And I just think it's possible that too many *Flash Gordon* reruns have seriously affected yer brains!"

"Nonetheless, we'd best keep a watchful eye on them," Odie announced.

Beeb implored Odie to think clearly. "Odie, they are stuck! They will surely die out here without our help! If we free both of them, they will owe us their lives! Most certainly advanced beings have some noble concepts like that!"

"Well, yeah," Odie sheepishly agreed, "maybe yer right, Beeb."

"Sure, I'm right!"

"Hell, us humans got noble concepts like that, and we ain't even all that advanced."

"Yeah, Odie, so whaddya say?"

"Okay, let's let both of them aliens out and see what happens. If they try somethin' funny, well, I got this.357 here."

"All right, just be sure they ain't hidin' no phasers anywhere, okay?"

"Gotcha covered, dude!"

The two men returned to where the language expert still stood. Odie spoke up. "Okay, dude, we're gonna spring yer liddle buddy from the slammer, but then we gotta have us a real heart-to-heart chat, awright?"

The Ehliun readily agreed even though he didn't understand most of the words spoken. The Ehliun and his computer stood in agreement. Living speakers of some form of English should help immensely in understanding the language already recorded but not yet deciphered. Comprehension enhancement was what the computer saw in Odie and Beeb. So the judgment panel judged that going along with the two earthmen was the best route to follow. So much for logic.

# I Nake, He Nakes, They Naked!

"Y'all go nekkid alla time or just on special occasions, like when yer out planet-hopping?" Beeb chuckled at the audacity of Odie's question. But the Ehliun had no knowledge of the word *nekkid* as it was not in his files. He was as confused by the earthmen's clothing as they were by the Ehliun's lack of clothing.

The Ehliun's visual report to the computer indicated many wavelengths emanating from the creatures. The computer noted seventy-nine different wavelengths from Odie, and eighty-three from Beeb. Although many of the wavelengths identified simple metals, their arrangements were so random as to defy meaning to the computer. Beeb had thirteen different copper structures, reflecting light from the fibrous coverings protruding from the head and face. Clearly, they were much more complex than first suspected.

"What-does-*nekkid*-mean?"

After a moment, Odie suddenly realized he had been asked a question. "Oh, you know, it's an intransitive verb, declension as follows: I nake, he nakes, they naked. All the usual verb rules apply."

Nodding and winking to Odie, Beeb acknowledged the ploy. It was as if to say, "That oughta hold 'em a while."

Odie led the way over to the occupied couch, scooping up the roll bar as he went. Beeb could not resist commenting. "Batboy to the rescue, eh?"

"Stop *robin* it in."

Aiming the roll bar at the shield still covering the computer expert, Odie unleashed his commentary on anyone who would lis-

53

ten. "Okay, folks, there's already one out, one still on. It's the bottom of the first, and here's Casey at the bat."

"No runs, one hit, and no official determination of errors as yet," Beeb added dryly.

With a mighty blow to the plastic-like shield, Odie again impacted the blunt end of the roll bar near the alien's feet. Again, the compound literally exploded into dust and tiny specks. Again, the humans shed themselves of shreds of stuff that had fallen everywhere. As soon as possible, the Ehliun language expert dashed up to the restraints and embraced his companion.

There was no doubt that they were very glad to see each other alive and well. The language expert spoke to his companion but in Ehliun. Odie and Beeb thought it very strange that this one spoke no English since both should be connected to the same computer that translated for the language expert. Odie immediately postulated that the computer didn't do the translating, but he simply wasn't sure. It was learn as you go.

Beeb was fascinated by the sounds of their language. It sounded like a tape played at very high speed, he thought. He wondered if they spoke a computer language. To Odie, he said, "Sorta sounds like a Chipmunks record, don't it?"

"*Alvin!* Stop that Fortran right now. *Allllllvinnnnn!*" Odie's reply was about what Beeb had expected, something weird and vaguely accurate.

When the novelty of the Ehliun sounds had worn down, Odie spoke up to the Ehliun pair. He thought over what they knew. TV was what they knew, so TV was what the earthlings would give them. Odie started his spiel. "Well, howdy, folks! And a hearty welcome to earth, which is already in progress. I'm Odie, your guest host for today's show-and-tell, and this is my sidekick Beeb."

Odie saw a horrified look on Beeb's face as he gestured theatrically toward his sidekick. Apparently, Beeb didn't wanna be no sidekick, Odie guessed.

"Are you *daft*, man? The first time anybody on earth gets a chance to discuss foreign policy with extraterrestrial foreigners, and you go and act like some small town tour guide. Damn, yer weird!"

"Well," Odie whined apologetically, "all the good lines were already taken."

Beeb had a look of incredulousness sweep across his face as he yelled, "What?"

"You know, 'one giant step for mankind,' 'ask not what your country can do for you,' 'I am not a crook'—all the good lines have been taken."

"Oh, well, of course! Now I see what you mean!" Beeb rolled, his eyes toward the heavens as he spoke to add to the sarcasm.

"Besides, Beeb, what else *can* I say? We are their hosts because no one else on earth even knows they're here."

Beeb was nearly beside himself. "Now how in hell did you arrive at that incredible conclusion, Odie?"

Glancing at Beeb's watch, Odie saw it was almost 11: a.m. Sunday morning. "Now, Beeb, old buddy, we seen these dudes come zippin' into our atmosphere before dawn. That's over five hours ago."

"What's yer point?" Beeb hated being lectured to, particularly by Odie.

"My point is that we are not five hours away from any US Air Force base on the North American continent!" Odie calmed down some and went on. "If anyone saw them come in on radar, this place would be covered up with olive drab minds in airborne blue!"

"Wrongo, space breath! We are in a most remote section of Utah, remember? ,Which as a state, only ranks behind population centers like Pine Bluff! We are a good ten hours from the motor home, and that's parked at the very end of a desert road. We were the only people within a fifty-mile radius yesterday, and radar doesn't show meteorites too well...."

Beeb trailed off and then stopped talking altogether when he realized that he was making Odie's point for him. He hated that worse than Odie lecturing him.

"Enough already!" Odie said in an authoritarian voice. "You know as well as I do that I'm right! If any military anywhere had even suspected let alone detected their presence here, there'da been a flight of jets scrambled out here to take a look-see."

"It would take time to scour this area," Beeb offered weakly.

"*Time?*" Odie yelled. "They've had enough time to get here from Guam! They ain't here 'cause they ain't comin'! So I repeat, nobody else on earth knows they are here!"

"Well, okay, son, you've done convinced me," Beeb admitted, "and since we are so all alone, shouldn't we just git stoned?" Beeb wondered, parodying a Dylan tune as he dug out the baggie of manna so recently bestowed by the heavenly spirits. Beeb gestured grandiosely like Odie always did to include Odie and the Ehliuns in his speech. "We are gonna celebrate yer freedom, mister alien."

The Ehliun had come up to the two gigantic creatures who had wandered away from his entrapped companion to plead her case for release as they had done for him. He didn't wish to offend them as they were almost twice his size and known to be dangerously strong. And yet, curiously, he sort of liked them. They had so far been extremely nice to him. He had to give them that…so far.

Carefully selecting the biggest joint, Beeb fished a lighter from his pocket and lit the joint. The Ehliun stood transfixed. He had never before seen smoke. Combustion was unknown to him. Fire was unknown to him. The primitives had amazed him. He watched incredulously as Beeb passed the joint to Odie, and Odie seemed to be eating the smoke as Beeb had done.

Watching for a moment, he decided that they were not eating it but rather breathing it. The purpose of the act was unknown. The computer informed him that the TV culture people also consumed smoke. Now the earthmen offered it to him. All the input from the computer told him to accept this offering of peace. The Ehliun asked the humans, "What-is-that-called?"

Odie took yet another hit off the joint. "It's called bogarting!"

Beeb snapped, snatching the controlled substance from Odie's control.

"Why-do-you-bogarting?" persisted the Ehliun.

Odie saw how quickly the Ehliun had incorporated bogarting into his vocabulary, quick but inaccurate. "He always bogarts!" answered Beeb for his unusually silent pal. Odie gave Beeb the finger in response and then the joint.

Turning to the Ehliun, Odie answered his question. "What we are doing is called smoking, not bogarting, as has been suggested."

Reluctantly, Beeb relinquished possession of the joint he'd just gotten from Odie as Odie demanded it with hand gestures. Beeb joined the Ehliun in watching Odie closely, not certain what to expect. With Odie, it was always tough. Odie tried to get the Ehliun to understand that the noun and verb smoke were the same, only different.

"Smoke, noun," Odie said, pointing to the wispy column rising from the joint. "Smoke, verb," he said, toking on the joint as an example.

Beeb was laughing to himself by the time Odie got exasperated, and he yelled at the poor Ehliun. "Smoke! Damn, boy, ain'cha never seen smoke before?"

The Ehliun shook his head no.

Odie seemed to give up for the moment, and he relit the joint, which had gone out. Odie blew a smoke ring at the Ehliun's nose. The Ehliun very slowly backed away from this earth-wrought miracle. It eloquently spoke volumes of information on air currents, diffusion of gaseous mixtures, physics, gravity, kinetics, particle movement, chemical energy loss, and Odie's bad breath. So much new input made the computer once again reanalyze the information about how primitive these beings really were.

"Here, take a toke!" Odie ordered as the Ehliun seemed to pause to consider such activity.

The Ehliun computer needed the living terminal's chemical analysis of the smoke in order to determine what it was, so it requested the living terminal to partake.

Odie noticed the Ehliun's reluctance to join in on the joint. Gentle persuasion seemed to be in order, Odie thought. "Hey, c'mon, take a hit. Relax, ain't no fuzz gonna bust ya out here."

"Oh, hell, Odie! Why don't you just go and confuse the issue? It's not that you can't confuse issues, Odie, 'cause yer one of the best, but hey, give the guy a break. He ain't been here all morning yet, and yer already fuckin' with his head!"

"I like to watch them folds swing."

"Jeez, man, yer really low, ya know that?"

"Well, you was the one that brought it up."

Odie handed the Ehliun the smoldering cylinder after he inhaled from it twice, supposedly as demonstration, but to Beeb, it was merely another of Odie's "excuses to double-hit," and he said so loudly. Odie ignored him and then handed the joint to the Ehliun. The Ehliun put the joint to his lips and inhaled as Odie did. Immediately, he coughed and gasped for air. Odie chuckled. Beeb told the Ehliun to inhale at a slower pace. He put the joint to his mouth and tried to smoke it again. This time he managed to take in some air with it, and he didn't have to cough.

As the smoke entered the Ehliun's lungs, new changes in his blood chemistry were noted by the computer. Complex chemical molecules went coursing through capillaries, converting old chemical compounds into new ones. A buzz was beginning to take shape.

After his second successful attempt with the joint, the Ehliun passed it to Beeb, who remarked to Odie, "You sure taught him that bogarting part well."

The Ehliun vigorously nodded his head yes to agree with Beeb that Odie taught him well. He still didn't understand sarcasm, nor did he understand why they both laughed. It was a very strange sound, very primal, very distant from its origins, but they were primitives.

After several passes, the joint was burned down, but it had had a curious effect on the Ehliun. Apparently, without command, the face muscles flexed curiously, lifting and slightly curving upward both corners of the mouth. The computer took note of this strange occurrence without comprehension. Just one more strange thing about earth.

Odie and Beeb had been carefully watching the Ehliun's reaction to getting high. The smile appearing had cracked them both up. They knew he copped a buzz. Beeb handed him the roach attached to a clip. "There's one more good toke left on this'n."

Odie watched him take the last toke. It wasn't quite like before. Something peculiar happened to the Ehliun after he took that last toke. The two men could see that he just spaced out.

The trapped computer expert gasped in wonder. The computer told her that her companion had just ceased to be. He had disappeared from his personal brain-wavelength channel. He simply vanished, the computer reported to its only remaining link. He consumed the magic smoke, and that had made him just disappear. She still lay on the uncomfortable restraints, but even from there, she could see the shadow of the Ehliun on the wall, illuminated by the primitive's light source. She could not see him directly, and the computer was never wrong, so he must be gone or just a shadow of his former self.

Thinking that the Ehliun was rather stoned at this point, Beeb moved over to where he'd left his Polaroid, and he retrieved it. He shot a photo of the Ehliun and then handed it to him. The Ehliun's eyes were just beginning to clear from the bright and unexpected flash of light when he noticed that he was the subject on the film. Here, right in front of his eyes, was proof of their high level of technology.

The Ehliun was entranced by the sudden development, both in the picture in hand, and the level of civilization these two possessed. If they owned and operated such devices, then they were certainly not as low in culture as first assumed. There was little doubt they were the fascinating creatures of the TV culture.

The Ehliun had forgotten about his trapped companion for the moment. He was lost in thought, he was off channel, he was on his own, and he was loving it. He'd never been here before—never.

# Thanks Be to the Tit God

"What is your name?" Odie wondered.

The Ehliun didn't reply or even act like he heard. Beeb gave it a shot, catching his eye with a rapidly waving hand. "How are you called?"

The Ehliun spoke, "I-am-called-by-the-computer." Immediately, he began wondering where the computer was. What had happened to his link?

"Izzat cher real name, 'called by the computer'?"

"You moron! It ain't his name, not like Sitting Bull or Willie Cries For War or nothin'."

"Oh, really, mister expert on alien names?"

"Yeah, really. He means that the computer contacts him whenever anyone wants him. Isn't that right, Mr. Ehliun?"

The confused *yes* he gave them only mandated a laugh at his expense. The wink and thumbs-up gesture did not convey any meaning to him, but it was that laughter that finally got to him. "Why-do-you-make-those-non-language-sounds?"

"Who says they're nonlanguage?" Odie shot right back.

"What-meaning-do-they-convey?"

"Amusement," Odie stated simply. "I laugh, express laughter, whenever something amuses me."

The Ehliun language expert was thrown by the concept of humor. It was totally unfamiliar to him, and to Ehliun culture. "What-amuses-you?"

"Well," Odie smiled broadly, "a feather up my ass usually tickles the shit outta me."

This answer caused Beeb to laugh along with Odie. The Ehliun pondered their behavior. The computer expert, still trapped, was unable to comprehend what was said. After the language expert consumed the smoke and disappeared, she could not understand any of their language. She could not understand why the computer could no longer translate. Earth and logic didn't seem to mesh well. Nothing made sense anymore. She really didn't want to die to find out what was going on, but it seemed to her that that was what would happen.

Odie and Beeb conferred for a few moments. The language expert was either lost in thought or frozen in time. They weren't sure which. He was stoned for sure, but how stoned was the question. Their little conference produced agreement that the computer seemed to run the Ehliun's life, but it seemed to be off track just now. Odie figured he'd just ask. "What does your computer think about the reefer?"

"I-cannot-contact-the-computer.   My-link-is-somehow-gone." The Ehliun was not sure of anything now. Even as the question reached his ears, it crossed his mind.

"So how can you speak to us in English if the computer's down?"

"Yeah, I thought you said that the computer translates for you. Seems to me that you translate for it."

These revelations rattled the Ehliun. It was true. He could somehow communicate in another language while he was unhooked from his computer. The impossible happened way too often on this planet for his comfort. Now here was a vast revelation that hit him like a ton of bricks. Apparently, English was stored, somehow contained inside his own head. That meant that the computer was actually unnecessary for translation duties.

He was the language expert! He, not the computer, knew the tongue! Twin worlds suddenly existed for him, the old computer-assisted one he had always known and a new one loose inside his own head! How had he gotten here? And how could these humans know what was happening to him? Well, of course! The magic smoke! It must do the same thing for them!

Smiling at his sudden trust in the humans, he spoke in a delighted tone of voice. "I-can-speak-English!"

"Yes, but how?" Odie wondered.

"I-don't-know," the Ehliun said sadly.

Beeb sought to change the subject and the mood he saw the Ehliun was now in. "Do you like being high?" Beeb asked.

"High?" the Ehliun said, having only the reference of being high in orbit above a planet.

"High," Odie smiled, "refers to the description of your brain waves having been excited to a new level, higher than before."

No sooner did Odie say this than the Ehliun experienced a novel sensation. He just zipped onto and then off of his old channel. While he was on it, both his computer and his companion implored him to return to his assigned wavelength and stay there. Communication would be so much easier, but he wouldn't *feel* like this on the old channel.

He was amazed that the humans could know what he was experiencing. Beeb's next question confirmed it. "Did you just contact your computer for a moment when Odie told you about being higher than your old channel?"

"Yes," he had to say. How could they know he'd just had contact with the computer? How could they be so aware of what was occurring to him when it was still so new to him?

Out loud in Ehliun, the language expert told his still-trapped companion that he was able to speak to the humans, and the computer wasn't necessary to aid in translations. The computer was forced to agree with the language expert. It could not speak to the primitives and he could. Without the language expert online, as it were, the computer heard English as gibberish. The trapped Ehliun did not receive this news well.

Doubt was something that she was unfamiliar with, especially about the one thing in life she knew most about—computers. To suggest that the computer was in error ran contrary to her being's very fiber, yet she herself was beginning to doubt the computer.

Now it would appear that her companion was no longer gone, missing, or disappeared. He was just temporarily out of service. And while he was out of service, he could speak a foreign tongue better than he could speak his own. When she heard him speak out loud, she noticed the slow delivery of his slurred speech. Yes, she had her doubts. And now that he moved over to where she was so he could speak face to face with her, it was worse. He was having some kind of fun, and she did not know what *fun* was. She knew what *trapped* was.

Beeb followed the Ehliun over to eavesdrop on their conversation. A few quick exchanges between then in Ehliun had Beeb convinced to speak to the freed Ehliun. "You can speak English, but he can't?" Beeb asked, pointing down at the computer expert.

"Yes," the language expert agreed.

"And he's still hooked up to the computer, but yer not?"

"Yes," was again the answer.

"Why?" Beeb wanted to know.

The Ehliun thought it over, a novelty in itself. "Because-I-am-language-expert!" he beamed proudly.

Beeb pointed again.

"The-computer-expert," came the reply.

"Oh, *ho!*" Beeb thought to himself, slipping off to inform Odie of his discovery. He knew now that they had freed the right one. The Ehliuns conferred as Beeb moved over to Odie's side.

A conference between the two men determined that they could best turn the computer to their side by releasing the one Ehliun still attached to it. By observation, the computer could soon see that they meant no harm to befall the space visitors. "Well, Odie, the best way to show we're friendly is to rescue stranded strangers, right?"

"Right on, dude!"

The computer expert watched the approach of the humans with great anxiety. She did not know what they intended for her. They had the big shield smasher with them, but three pings of alien metal later, the restraints were broken, and the second space-wreck survivor was set down next to her stoned companion. Giving this one the once-over with the flashlight, they discovered that she was a female. "Looks like she can accommodate old Long Dong, here, don't it?"

"Long Dong!" Odie laughed at Beeb's description. "We can't go around callin' him Long Dong!"

"Odie, who in the hell are you thinkin' of introducin' 'em to?"

"Didn't say I was plannin' anything."

"Then why ain't Long Dong good enough?"

"Because it's stupid, that's why!"

"Oh, so it's stupid. So what?"

"So suppose we're out somewhere and you go and call him Long Dong, and he whips out that giant yellow dick to show how he got that name?"

Beeb started laughing at the thought of panic at a hooker's convention that could be caused by such a display. "Look. If we gotta give 'em names, let's give 'em Chinese names."

"Why do we need to give 'em Chinese names, son?"

"Well, they sorta look Chinese, maybe more so if you put dark wigs on 'em."

"Okay, I'll toss the forks in the air."

"Forks in the air?"

"Yeah, that's how the Chinese do it. The first three sounds is what they name their kid."

"My God, Odie, the things you believe! Yer a real ding-a-ling!"

"Hey, now," Odie said, brightening. "Ding and Ling—I kinda like that, Beeb. Ya finally came up with somethin'."

"Ding and Ling sound too much like bells goin' off."

"Bells going off?"

"Yeah, bells—hell's bells. No tintinnabulation spoken here, dude."

"Ding and Ling sounds more like giant panda names than bells to me."

"Well, just drop the final G, Odie, and you have Lin and Din. Very Oriental, no bells, no bears, just regular names.".

"Okay, Din and Lin it is."

"Lin sounds like a chick's name, so we make her Lin, eh, and him Din?"

"Okay, I accept."

"Do they?"

"Do they have a vote, a choice in this matter?"

"Don't sound like it to me."

Beeb's conclusion was accurate. Odie wasn't one to care too much what other people thought, especially foreigners.

While the Ehliuns struggled with the reality that their computer had in fact lied to them all these years, the two men were busy thinking up names for them. Such a mixture of profound and profane had never before occurred to the Ehliun pair. She could see that her companion was almost the same as before he had consumed the magic smoke, but he was radically different somehow. She refused to accept his offer of the joint he still had clamped in his fingers.

Beeb commented to Odie about it. "Ain't it just like the old lady to bitch about yer habits?"

"Yeah, I guess they ain't that much different than we are."

"Well, Odie, she's different than any woman I ever seen!"

"Well, Beeb, he's got to park that monster someplace!"

"Reckon I know where too."

"That's for sure."

Beeb thought for a moment, considering what he had seen of the Ehliuns. "Odie, our God is smarter than their God."

"How's that?"

"Our God is smarter'n theirs."

"Why you say that?"

"She don't have no tits."

"Tits?" Odie repeated. "Our God is smarter'n their God because of tits?"

"Right!" Beeb smiled. "Now, consider: they are marvelous toys, fantastic pillows, superb decoration, and the finest snack bar in town for the young'uns."

Odie considered it. "She ain't got tits 'cause she ain't a mammal. Nonmammals equals nonmammaries."

"Well, Odie, before you break into a chorus of *Thanks for the Mammaries*, just let me say that our God gave us mammaries, and their God didn't."

"All right."

"So you agree?"

"What, do I agree that our God is a kinder, gentler, smarter, better God than their God just because of tits?"

65

"Yeah."

"Yeah."

"So world shaking theological debates aside, what do you think about letting me in on your little secret, Odie?"

"Secret?" Odie wondered aloud, unsure what Beeb could mean.

"What do you plan to do with these two, Odie?"

"Well, I just don't know yet. Why?"

"*Odie*, they are not lost pets!"

"Aw, gee, Dad, ya mean I can't keep 'em ?"

"Sorry, son, it's out of the question."

"Okay, who shall I give them back *to* and more importantly, how?"

"Hmm, well, okay then, you can keep them until somebody comes a'lookin' for 'em."

"Gee, thanks, Pop!"

"Glad we had this little chat, son. I know I feel whole lots better for it." Beeb rolled his eyes skyward as he said this.

"I figure we can ride four in the motor home as easy as two," Odie figured.

"And have you considered the penalties for intergalactic kidnapping?"

"What? Them two turn down an invite to tour America with me, with us? Nonsense! They'll love it the minute I ask."

"Look," Beeb turned serious, "we got a contract with the federal government. The damn Feds, Odie. And the senator whose old lady is in love with you will gladly make us pay for that motor home and this two-year excursion if we fail to live up to the very letter of that contract! I can't afford to lose this job and pay for the consequences, and neither can you!" Beeb was somewhat angered.

"Relax! Ain't neither one of us gonna git fired or have to pay back nothin'! Kathy loves me too much for that to happen."

"What if she dumps you and divorces the senator?" Beeb asked.

"Dumps me?" Odie gasped, not believing such a question.

"Yeah, you! You said yourself that she was fickle."

"Well, for sure the senator ain't gonna divorce her!"

"And why not?"

"He wouldn't divorce her even if she fucked the whole of Congress right in front of him! She's his ticket to the *in* crowd! He ain't got the clout that she does. She's got European fame. Her money makes his look like pocket change! Gossip columnists seek her out. They ignore him."

"What if he divorces her?" Beeb repeated.

"Then we pay back the government to the tune of megabucks."

"That's just what I thought."

Beeb was not happy with the prospect of owing the government for the last two years so lavishly lived. The bill was surely in the millions right now, with eight or so months left to go.

There was no way he was paying for this trip—no way. They would simply finish the contract as it was written, and that was that.

Odie put his mind toward what he was doing and put all the negative waves he was getting from Beeb behind him. He strode over to the Ehliuns and spoke. "Y'all need to pack whatever you need, food, clothes—"

"Odie, I don't believe they own clothing or even the concept," Beeb interrupted.

"Well, pack what you need. You are not safe here. You must come with us."

Beeb knew that Odie didn't like to be reminded of the sword of Damocles dangling by a thread overhead in the form of the senator, the grants he had issued, and the affair of Odie and the senator's wife, Kathy. He also realized that Odie must know how he felt if they were to maintain their mutual trust in one another. It was borderline trust anyway because they knew each other so well. They knew better than to plunge headlong into some adventure simply because it was endorsed by one or the other, present situation being an example. What next?

Lin stood there, trying to get some sense of the creatures that had rescued her. Why were they so, well, lumpy? Why were their hides composed of so many metallic wavelengths distributed so randomly? Just how could partial metallic creatures survive? Surely they weren't androids. Would they eat the spaceship? And what had they done to Din? Why was he so similar and yet so different?

Outwardly, there was no change, except for the curious facial flexing of his cheek muscles, but inside, who knew? The computer informed her that Din seemed to be the repository for English, and it was not at fault. The judgment panel told Lin to deal with the situation as best she could. It did not know what the hell was going on.

Lin could not understand why or how the home network could cancel its signal. She knew that the judgment panel was responsible for what little computer contact she had now, yet she did not know how that was possible. Her current condition wasn't possible according to her comprehension of the computer system, and yet it was a reality. The judgment panel told her it had amplified the power from the power siphon to apply to the Earth-Study Program, and that's how it found them, crashed on earth. So if the siphon was working properly, how did the Study Program go down? Why did the Ehliun central computer grid terminate output? How did the major objective get cancelled and by whom?

"Yo, Din, git yer liddle lady friend there to stop dawdlin' and to git a move on! We gotta git outta here quick!"

Din tried to convey Odie's message to Lin. She reminded him that they had a mission to study Earth and that they should not fail in this mission just because of a wreck. Din explained this to Odie. "We-came-to-study-your-planet-specifically-the-television-culture. She-wants-to-take-the-computer-with-us."

Odie was surprised. "I thought yer computer was in orbit?"

"Yes-there-is-one-in-orbit. She-means-the-onboard-computer-a-small-one."

"So show us where it is," Beeb said.

Lin guided them to the onboard computer location next to the power panel. There, her heart sank. An angry granite lance had pierced the heart of this alien computer. It was hopelessly destroyed. Sadly, Lin got down on her knees to begin picking up chips. The crystalline chips spilled out everywhere from the ruined computer. Lin was surprised that none of the chips were damaged by the crash or the impact onto the granite. In truth, the crystalline chips were next to impossible to harm.

# The Crystal Chip Is Being Billed

The chips of unknown crystal were much harder than anything the Ehliuns knew. For more than two centuries after their discovery in an otherwise inconsequential cave on an asteroid over nine hundred light-years away from the planet Ehlius, the specimen crystals were regarded as curiosities after the explorers returned home.

Some of the crystals weighed more than an Ehliun. Some were tiny. These specimens were enshrined in various establishments scattered across Ehlius. Attempts to study the crystals determined only that they were very hard. Thus, their true worth wasn't known for nearly two and a half centuries after that.

During a second exploratory visit to the cave on the asteroid, an amazing thing happened. All across Ehlius, all the specimen crystals were illuminated by the explorer's lights in the cave. Suddenly, hundreds of Ehliun scientists and academics could see what was transpiring at that very instant hundreds of light-years away! Instantaneous communication was now possible and over distances that no one could have dreamed.

Ehliun science soon determined that the crystals apparently had the unique and wonderful property of transmitting light waves about a thousand times their natural speed. Of course, no one knew it until it happened. No one had thought to test the crystals to see if they would increase the speed of light. But it happened, the scenario worked out by fate, and Ehliun space workers were credited with the discovery of the crystals' power.

Still, it took nearly half a century after that before Ehliun technology figured out how to cleave the crystalline planes so that a fist-sized chunk of crystal would yield thousands of chips, each with the property of the whole chunk. It was only when millions of chips were readily available for use in communications that the dawn of Ehliun space civilization arose. It allowed the Ehliun way of life to spread beyond its own galaxy. It became possible to instantly communicate across thousands of light-years. Lonely outposts were no longer the fate of Ehliun space workers. They could reach out and touch someone.

Their ability to explore led to the further discovery that gigantic black holes had swallowed up the entire universe, distributing material in round areas of force fields between the black holes' gravitational centers. By learning to fly through this grid work of black holes, Ehliun pilots discovered a diamond-like structure of gravitational centers appeared, boosting speeds tremendously. The black holes themselves appeared to be stacked like cannonballs on a courthouse lawn, but the force fields between the edges of these black holes dramatically accelerated anything entering them.

It was difficult to maintain a route through the center of the force field and not venture too close to the edge of the black hole, where a tremendous pull toward the gravitational center existed. If a black hole sucked a vessel in, it became terribly difficult to get back out again. Although entering black holes was tricky business, Ehliun pilots had taught themselves to slingshot themselves in at a very acute angle and at extremely high speeds.

Eventually, standards were worked out so even novices could do it right the first time. These pilots came to notice that inside each black hole, things were different. Some holes had more material in them; others had fewer stars. Some were growing hotter and stronger by the second; others were cooling and losing energy. Some black holes were filled with dust and gases and stars; some were not. Other holes had rare elements in them; some had only light elements. Occasionally, space quakes occurred in a titanic struggle of forces whenever one black hole gained a little territory on another.

Soon after venturing into the black hole structure, Ehliun pilots became experts. Forays through unknown, uncharted black holes became commonplace shortcuts for Ehliun starcruisers. These starcruisers became necessary to replace junction boxes in the communications systems that were damaged by these space quakes.

The Ehliun space civilization utilized the black hole structure to upgrade their communications. Parking junction boxes at strategic locations in the black hole structure enabled them to use its stunning power to even further speed up the power of the crystals. Messages moved through deep space at hundreds of thousands times the speed of light. The intense pressure of the force fields lying around each edge of each black hole sped things up greatly, magnifying even the crystals' power.

Usually, the starcruisers just replaced the junction boxes as they went about their business as some were over a century old and still in use. Sometimes, they would just cut across a black hole and exit out the opposite side from where they entered to take advantage of some serious force fields. These shortcuts became a way of life soon after implementation.

The old space veterans took shortcuts all the time. They enjoyed the chance to look around a little at sublight speeds. Down the pike, total concentration was necessary. In a starcruiser moving thousands of times the speed of light in a force field, any error was fatal. But after the advent of standard entry and exit holes computed by the great Ehliun network central grid, shortcuts became standard operating procedure for space workers. They didn't care what official policy was.

Travel in the fast lane of black hole force fields was nearly instantaneous. Only the time necessary to accelerate at the local hole entrance and decelerate at the exit hole of the destination was much of a factor now. Six to eight months travel would get an Ehliun to the farthest reaches of the known black hole structure.

Inside each black hole were billions and billions of galaxies spread across trillions of parsecs of space. Inhabitants of these black holes considered them to be the universe, not just a small part. Always, the Ehliuns had found, the occupants of an inhabited planet felt what they could see was all there was. They didn't know there were as many black holes as stars in the nighttime sky.

All the planets and solar systems and galaxies were inside one of billions of black holes that had come along and swallowed up the entire region of galactic clusters for eons of light-years in all directions. Ehliun physicists still did not know when the black holes got started. All that they knew was that black holes had gotten so dense that they stopped pulling material in. Instead, the surface of the black hole began rushing ever outward in all directions since it was round.

Black holes kept their center of gravity and simply sent the surface out like a giant balloon that keeps stretching but never breaks. Black holes had apparently sprung up everywhere at once, as if a virus containing them had spread throughout the universe. From all directions, black holes began to impinge on each other's territory.

Eventually, all the black holes had more or less equalized themselves and had swallowed all the material in the universe. Since a few were slightly bigger than others, they would occasionally overtake one another in a lightning quick exchange of forces. These disturbances were known as space quakes, and they actually changed boundaries on occasion.

Quasars had been found in only a few hundred black holes. They were tremendous energy sources no matter where they were found. Power siphons had been invented to exploit the energy expended by quasars. They were clustered in a particular quadrant of the black hole structure for the most part, and the level of exploration in that quadrant was very high. Therefore, the discovery of Earth had been a very pleasant surprise.

So once Ehliun pilots had become familiar with the black hole structure and learned how to fly through the force fields without peril, a great empire began. Soon, the question of how to govern such a vast territory became a real concern. A mere century after the first crystal chip was split, the board came into being—actually, the board's predecessor and forerunner, the one that was freely elected, the board that was known and talked about. That was then; this is now. Now, the board was a secret unknown to all but the members of the board.

In its beginning, it had little power. Now there was no power it didn't have. A secret board was far more powerful than any Ehliun had ever dreamed. The board hid many dark and dank secrets but hid them so well no one could discover them. No one inside the system could. The concept of gate-crash was unknown to them. The thought that someone could find them out, especially from the outside, was nonexistent. The chances were too remote to bother calculating them.

The control the board exerted on Ehlius was total. The same went for their far-flung empire. The board ran the affairs of hundreds of colony planets by remote control. The entire Ehliun planet was basically their personal playground. Their grasp of power was total, and their every wish was a command that had better be instantly obeyed.

At a remote time in the distant past, feuds among the board members had gotten completely out of hand. One feud had caused the deaths of many millions of innocent victims on faraway planets annihilated by vengeful forces loyal only to one single board member.

But today's board members were in complete control of everything. They were secure in their castles, fortified by their technology. The mindless peasants serving their every whim didn't even realize they were slaves. It was the perfect slavery system because the slaves didn't know they weren't free. On Ehlius, the top levels benefited from the work of the contented masses. Their contentment kept rebellion away. Tranquility wavelengths kept them content.

There could be no doubt, the board was in total control. No outsider could break in. The board was invincible. No one had the ability to discover them. No hacker in the universe could backdoor their computer network, they felt.

But the board didn't know about Earth and earthmen. The board just didn't know about Odie and Beeb. Oh, but they would. They certainly would.

# Three Hot!

Odie left the others to return the roll bar to the jeep. After he rebolted the bar back into place, he started wondering what was taking the rest of them so long. He yelled at Beeb to find out what the delay was. Beeb could hear him yelling, but he couldn't understand what he was saying, not that it mattered. Beeb knew Odie wanted to leave as soon as possible before anyone else happened along, particularly the military or the Feds.

Beeb urged the two Ehliuns to go outside, but the moment they experienced the hot sunshine on their sensitive skins, they didn't want to go outside and leave the coolness of their vessel. Beeb went up to Din. "What's the matter? Is it too hot?"

Lin told Din that the computer calculated the temperature of the sand to be 2.74 times as hot as the surface of their own planet, Ehlius. "Yes-two-hot. Almost-three-hot!" Din said this proudly, and he didn't understand why Beeb laughed at him.

Beeb continued laughing on his way over to Odie. "Odie, this is great! I said, 'Too hot?' and Din replies, 'Yes, almost three hot!'"

Odie was also smiling over Din's remark. He thought it might prove that their sun was dying and that they knew they needed a new place to live, and this would be a regular tropical paradise to them... here in the deserts of Utah. They wouldn't know what a beach was, right? And as sole negotiator for Earth Condos, Inc., Odie stood to become outright wealthy.

"Odie, I dunno why yer smilin', unless you got a funny solution to the problem at hand. Our sun is apparently more than twice the heat they can stand."

"You reckon that's why they're still in that wreckage?"

"That, or maybe they heard about yer drivin'," Beeb smiled.

"Then I guess we just wait till nightfall."

"And eat what tomorrow?"

"Cover their asses from the heat and go right now?"

"Immediately, if not sooner."

"I got a sheet in my backpack."

"Great, Odie, that's just great. That's just what I wanted to hear from you. You got a sheet in yer backpack. Great. I ain't surprised."

"You ain't?"

"Nope. What surprises me is that yer gonna do a *Lawrence of Arabia* act just because we're out here in the desert."

"No *Lawrence of Arabia* act."

"Toga party?"

"Negative."

"Hmm, yer gonna wrap 'em in swaddling clothes for some newborn symbolism maybe?"

"Entirely wrong."

"Some kind of pirate ship thing, maybe, or no, one sheet in the wind, right?"

"Wrong again."

"Can I buy a vowel?"

"Nope, time's up. Ya gotta watch along with our TV audience and see."

"So what's the sheet gonna do?" Beeb wondered as Odie dug through his backpack to retrieve it.

"Observe." Odie attached the sheet with bungie cords to the newly reinstalled roll bar and over the spare tire. Suddenly, their convertible had the top up.

Beeb was impressed—very unfavorably, however. "Boy, Odie, I just don't know if we're more conspicuous with two Ehliuns in the back of an open-air vehicle or in a jeep covered with a nosegay of lilacs and orchids in livid lavender?"

"Who'd stop something this ugly to talk to its occupants?" Odie countered. "Something in a flaming desperate gay, perhaps?"

"Look, not this far from a hair salon, okay? Now go get those two aliens in here and let's haul ass, awright?"

Odie started up the jeep and backed it up to the rip. Beeb was pleading with the Ehliuns to come outside and get in the jeep. But once Din got it explained to Lin, she casually pointed out that the computer could not adequately cool their systems outside the spaceship in the direct sunlight. This meant death. She was unwilling to die for the humans. Din explained her position to Beeb.

"Lin-says-the-material-covering-your-vehicle-is-insufficient-protection-from-the-radiation-of-your-local-star."

"Is that the problem?"

"Yes."

"Why is it so cool inside your spaceship?" Beeb asked.

"The-computer-removes-heat-from-your-atmosphere-through-what-you-call-a-air-conditioner."

"I see."

Beeb smiled over at Odie. So it *was* an air conditioner that cooled it off so rapidly. "So what the hell can we do about it?" Odie griped.

"I got a suggestion," Beeb said. "I suggest we ask their computer what to do to protect them."

"Good idea, Beeb. Nice of you to rack your brain on their behalf, eh?"

"Well, it's the least I could do, Odie."

"Yes, it is."

Din started talking in Ehliun to Lin. Several exchanges later, Din had reached an agreement with Lin. He informed the boys about it. "She-says-that-if-you-cover-the-vehicle-with-part-of-the-spaceship's-exterior-skin-the-computer-could-cool-us-sufficiently-to-prevent-harm."

Odie looked up at Beeb and grinned. "What did you do with that enormous strip you tore off the side when we came in?"

Smiling at Odie, Beeb waved him over to the spot where the metal strip lay in the sand. In a few moments, they carried it back to the jeep. Odie removed the sheet, to Beeb's hearty cheers, and they put the metal strip on as a roof. Much to Beeb's chagrin, Odie then placed the sheet back on top of the metal. "This'll hide that shiny metal."

"Yeah, but what will hide *that*?" Beeb shrieked, pointing at the ugly sheet.

"Speaking of hiding things," Odie said, "uh, Din, we got laws here on earth about litterin'. Now what do you intend to do about hiding this spaceship wreckage from public view?"

"What-does-*hiding*-mean?" Din wondered.

"*Hiding* means not visible, unseen, undetected, staying out of view."

"Oh," Din said, turning to explain to Lin. Somehow explaining things to others felt good to him, although he did not know why.

Odie and Beeb exchanged glances after Din had said, "Oh," so purposefully. He was catching on fast, perhaps too fast. They had only to wait and see. That was the reason for the glances to begin with. That would be too late.

Din explained to Lin that the computer must hide the spaceship from sight. Lin expressed doubt. She knew it could not be done without one of the exterior lasers, and none of them worked for defense. She told Din what she felt. He told her to ask the computer to utilize any of the lasers that could do the job.

The computer informed her that someone would have to go outside and move one of the lasers into a position that would allow signals to be received. But outside was fairly hot. Lin was not willing to risk death from overheating just to hide the space wreckage because some earthling said to. Din explained to Odie that a laser would have to be adjusted by hand. Odie went outside to the rear of the vessel and looked for a laser.

After scooping sand aside with his hands, Odie found a laser mount and cleared all the sand away from it. Then he went back inside and told Din it would work now. Din informed Lin, who checked with the computer to see if Odie was, in fact, correct. The computer was surprisingly in agreement with the primitive. The laser worked now.

Lin asked Din why the laser would work now and hadn't worked before. He asked Odie. Odie told him, "Sand was cloggin' that sucker up."

Din asked, "What-does-that-mean?"

"It means that sand was coverin' it up. This sand has an electrical resistance of over 350,000 ohms."

"What-is-*ohms*?"

"That means nothing to you, no doubt, but it's how we measure electrical current. Electric current can't pass through the sand because of its great resistance to that current, kinda like Congress resists being current."

Odie didn't think the Ehliuns really understood, but it seemed to be answer enough. Lin programmed the laser to hide the space wreckage from view. They all stepped out of the ship and got into the jeep. Then the computer began reflecting a picture off the spacecraft's shiny surface, which was the view that would be seen if the wreck were not there. It rendered the ship totally invisible. Both men shivered involuntarily. Now they knew the power of the computer. Incredible.

With the spaceship hidden, they knew now there was no reason to bury the dead Ehliuns, which Beeb had been dead set against anyway. He was afraid that someone would discover the graves. Odie told him that even if the dead Ehliuns had been discovered, future archaeologists would likely pronounce them to be excellent examples of the Mound Builder culture. Now there was no reason to worry. Nothing could be seen, from anywhere. They could go about their business without fear.

Odie tried to get Beeb to look at things on the bright side. Beeb told Odie the bright side was covered with an ugly sheet. Silence ensued. Soon, the four of them were driving along in the jeep over desert nonroads at rather exhilarating speeds up to seventeen miles an hour.

Lin nearly had Din convinced that these two were back to the primitive status that had first been accorded them. The lack of comfort in this bumpy ride was her first clue. The tribal chanting that they periodically intoned to accompany the noise spreader in the middle of the panel they faced was her second clue. Other clues were manifold, she felt.

Laughter, whatever activity that was, was certainly primitive. No one on their advanced planet laughed. It had to be primitive activity. Then there was the thumping of arms and shoulders. Clearly, this was some ritual followed by earthlings from perhaps time immemorial. She was totally convinced they were primitives.

And then the tribal chanting started again. "'Cause yer nah nah nah nah nah nah nah nah notorious, notorious! Ever thing you want, ever thing you need, nah nah nah, 'cause yer nah nah nah nah nah nah nah nah notorious."

Din had no idea what the chanting meant or why they did it. Lin was sure there was no logical reason for the noise.

Odie pulled up at the base of the mesa they had camped on earlier. As he drug out the rope and climbing equipment from the jeep, Din wondered out loud what Odie was up to. His answer was "Gotta climb back up there to git our stuff."

Beeb volunteered to stay down in the jeep and watch the Ehliuns. Odie snarled at his old friend, but he knew someone better watch over them.

Odie wasn't really happy that he had to climb up and get all the stuff they'd left up there that morning, but he went as fast as he could. Nearly an hour had passed before Odie had gathered up all the stuff and brought it all down. Beeb knew it was a struggle, so he said nothing negative as he knew Odie would explode. "Need a hand?"

"Yeah, thanks."

Odie let Beeb take the lines that guided the bulk of the load, and Beeb lowered the gear to the sand. "Damnation, but it's hot out here!"

"Yeah, well, you'll git cool in a second. The computer can flat cool off this jeep!" Beeb offered.

"Good!" was all Odie said as he finished rappelling down the rock face. In a few minutes, Odie had all the gear stowed in the jeep, and they were all set to travel.

Beeb drove, and Odie began a conversation with Din. Soon after the talk started, Odie noticed a lot of references to the computer by Din. He didn't know if the pot still kept him off the computer link or not.

"Yo, Beeb, gimme a joint out cher magic baggie there, son! Le's burn one."

Beeb got out the baggie and gave Odie a joint from it. Odie lit up and inhaled deeply. After three consecutive tokes on it, Odie begrudgingly handed it to Beeb. Beeb took a toke and passed it on to Din.

"So look here, Din," Odie started in on him, "about yer computer. How could it possibly make any rational judgments about what goes on here on earth when it don't know nothin' about my home planet?"

Din tried to defend the computer as best he could. For all his lifetime up till today, the Ehliun computer was all he had ever known. He spoke up to Odie. "The-computer-knows-a-great-deal-about-life-on-Earth."

"Show me something then that the computer knows about Earth."

Din translated Odie's challenge to Lin. She did not like it a bit. She could identify nothing she saw. The computer saw what she saw through her eyes. Din was shut off to the computer, so only her eyes provided input to the computer orbiting around Polaris. She guessed that Ehlius central grid must contain everything else, and that was closed down to her requests for access for reasons as yet unclear to her. She didn't know quite what this challenge meant, but she didn't like it at all.

Only Din seemed to know what was going on and only a very little bit at that. He didn't know what the arm thumping meant, nor did he know what purpose the noise spreader served, but at least he could understand some of what they said. Without that, there would be no communication at all.

Din had no idea why he could speak English to the humans. He just knew that he could, and that was enough. So much had happened. Still, he was alive and well. In fact, in some ways, he was better off than before. He could think privately to himself without the possibility of others knowing. Private thoughts—what a novel sensation! And now, he had the ability to make decisions all by himself.

Previously, he had always trusted the computer. But now he couldn't. He was beginning to comprehend what Odie meant earlier when he had whispered to Beeb that the computer controlled him. Din was not used to making decisions without computer input, but he had made a decision for himself and for his companion. Since the two men gave him the magic smoke and knew what it would do to him, he decided to trust them since it must affect them in the same way.

This was the basis for his trust, and trust, for an Ehliun, was total. They did not know any shades of gray. Everything was black or white, so to speak. The earthlings had earned his confidence and made him aware of major discrepancies in his own computer system in the process. He was on their planet, so he would learn later about trust as the earth knew it. For now, he just placed himself and his companion in their care.

Taking charge of another person's life and making important decisions for them were not the easiest way to start down the road to responsibility, but that was the path he'd chosen. Later, Din would find out about marriage and how it's often mistaken for taking charge of another person's life. And what of his friend and lover from half a hundred trips through space? Could Din still trust her? Not while she was attached to the computer.

But maybe it would be better to leave her attached to the computer to utilize it while they could. Once both of them were off the attachment, they would lose the advantage that their technology gave them, and on this planet, that could easily be fatal. Without the computer to feed them facts, they would have no familiar reference point. But did the computer feed them facts or fiction? It was the toughest decision yet. Din noticed that one decision invariably led to another, and to another, and so on ad infinitum.

Din's thoughts were interrupted by Odie. He was still anxious to find out just exactly what the computer did know about earth. Clearly, Odie thought, there was untold power that must be reckoned with. How to gain control over the computer was on the front burner of Odie's mind. He was determined to control or at least neutralize the computer. At worst, this would be a modern Thermopylae.

Then he smiled to himself. They weren't Persians, and they wouldn't know anything about ancient Greek history. Not from television they wouldn't. This would be easy. Odie knew Beeb would be bound to go along with most of his stunts, but this was really tricky ground here. Good thing he was a really tricky guy.

Odie thought about things Din had said about those things that just stood out. The Ehliuns knew nothing of music, singing, songs, or the radio, which they called a noise spreader. Odie couldn't figure out how the computer could collect and analyze TV signals intercepted from satellites and still not have any idea what music was. The computer translated English but didn't know about theme music, commercial music—nothing, just words. All they got from TV were words.

Odie guessed that some Ehliun computer had made all the selections and probably not the same one they were now hooked to. The music was ignored, edited, and thrown out because the computer probably didn't realize what it was. And if the computer didn't recognize English when it was sung, Odie reasoned, therein lies a refuge. Odie figured Din was fed the English language after machines had analyzed and decoded it. That would explain why he knew nothing of music.

And humor, what of the noble concept of humor? The Ehliuns lacked any understanding of humor and its purpose. Intentional error was useless to them, and intentional error solely for the purpose of producing laughter made no sense at all. Proving to the Ehliun that his computer knew nothing of Earth would be no problem at all. It would be like taking candy from a baby.

"So, Din," Odie suddenly spoke up, breaking a long silence, "have you come up with a single thing that your computer knows about Earth?"

Din asked Lin for an answer. She gave him one, and he translated it. "She-says-you-are-too-primitive-to-understand."

Odie became, fairly predictably, enraged at the answer Lin gave. Beeb was glad he was driving, so Odie could devote complete attention to the argument without endangering all their lives.

"Now listen up, you space preppie! I ain't no fuckin' primitive! Yer computer's got its circuits up its electronic ass if it thinks I'm a primitive! I happen to be one of the most advanced people on the whole planet, as a damn matter of fact! Me, a fuckin' primitive!"

"You tell 'em , Odie. They must'a studied old Yankee TV."

"I seriously doubt that accent has anything to do with it."

"Well, pepper 'em anyway."

"Hey, salt that wit away for when we need it, yeah?"

Beeb thought that Odie had lost his train of thought, and he sought to put him back on the right track. "The monster computer, remember?"

"Ixnay on the onstermay."

"Ixnay? Onstermay? Oungyay Ankenstienfray oviemay, maybe, eh?"

"Perzacklemente mucho, seenyor."

"Oy vey!"

"Uh, egatorynay on the uck-upsfay, okay?"

"Okay, why the igpay atinlay, anyway, eh?"

"Porque el isitorsvay no entiende, comprende, eenyorsay?"

"Oh. El excuso mucho mio my-o, sonamagun, g'wine hab big fun down to da bayou, well jambalaya, crawfish pie an'a feelay gumbo, sonamagun, g'wine have big fun down to da bayou!"

"Uckyoufay!"

"So eso idea-o de usted-o importantamente mucho, or what-o?"

"Si! Mucho! Atchway and eesay!"

"Ixnay, Jose, no way, okay? Angerousday muchomente. Down that path lurketh madness."

"Don't Lear at me!"

"Verily, varlet, if searchest thou with thine orbs wilt they ceaselessly reflect mine own image, hovering about whither thou goest in this affair, like, Bob Marley's ghost, dreadlocking about. Be, therefore, forewarned. Putteth not mine ass in a sling lest thou be set upon with hell's own fury in a heartbeateth."

"I can dig it."

They both knew they could still communicate incognito. And of course, TV would not have prepared these two Ehliuns for any dialogue like that exchange. They rested assured their code would not be broken anytime soon. Beeb decided to continue the charade. Fanning out an imaginary hand of cards, Beeb bet first. "Okay, I'll open with a pair, what are you lookin' at?"

Odie took his cue and spoke up. "I'm lookin' at trips, and one of 'em is wild."

"Not countin' the dealer?" Beeb grinned slyly.

"The dealer stands on the ground floor, not the balcony," Odie snarled.

"Sure that ain't a grandstand?"

"Better'n a Custer stand, ain't it?"

"Well, and that's a point in yer favor, fortunately for you. Just so long as we understand one another."

Din was amazed. "You-understand-each-other?"

The earthmen reacted in their typical fashion; they laughed. Din told Lin that the computer simply must decipher laughter for him. She told him they were primitives. For the first time in their lives, they did not get along well together. Beeb thought about all the stuff that Odie had said. The balcony and wild card references must be to the computer in space. That meant that Odie was counting the computer as an Ehliun, although technically it was not alive. Beeb knew all too well what the Custer stand reference meant.

Silently, they rode on for hours, the time interrupted only occasionally by an Ehliun question or an earthling comment. Beeb punched in a tape. The noise spreader was in operation again, to the befuddlement of the Ehliuns. Odie reflected on the long, hard day he'd had. It sure had been weird. Beeb turned on the headlights as they made their way toward the motor home. He soon began chatting to Odie about the mileage they were getting and how the gas indicator needle had just passed below the halfway mark.

Finally, they came upon a traveled dirt path. It was not a real road, for it was noticeably different from the desert floor only in the absence of large boulders. There was a thin residue of road oil, or perhaps old motor oil dripped from military vehicles—Odie wasn't sure which—that clumped the sand together into a reasonable surface for travel.

Both men could now see a single set of tracks on the path before them—their tracks, they knew, as Odie had swerved side to side to make a particular impression in the sand. The wayward tracks still snaked across the path, proof that only Odie and Beeb knew there were aliens from outer space right here in River City.

More than twelve hours of sunlight had come and gone since the Earth had received its first Ehliun visitors. Odie giggled to himself about whose air force had had enough time to arrive. In his mind's eye, he could see a pitiful ragtag fleet of Sopwiths, Fokker triplanes, and SPADs still struggling across France en route from Albania. Odie was sure the French would let Albanians cross their air space, the wimps.

"What the hell is so funny, Odie? I mean, what are you laughin' at?"

"SPADs," Odie smiled.

"Spads? What the hell's a spad?"

"The Albanian Air Force!" Odie laughed, barely getting the words out due to his glee.

Beeb just shook his head. To the Ehliuns, Beeb said, as if they might understand, "The damndest things amuse that boy."

As the evening wore on, the path they were driving on became a real road. As it got smoother, Beeb picked up his speed a little, now for the first time shifting into third. As they picked up more speed, Beeb was soon in fourth gear and driving about fifty-five miles an hour. Lin felt that perhaps she'd misjudged this vehicle, and maybe this wasn't so bad. Beeb fished through his pockets for the baggie and came up with another joint.

He lit it and passed it to Odie, then over her objections, he gave it to Din, and he accepted it readily. Why did he do that? Just when things started to look better to Lin, they got worse. What kind of planet was this? Was there no order of any description? Who was in charge?

Din and Odie were chatting away about something to do with rocks, but it bored Beeb, and he made a mental escape to be alone with his thoughts. It had been nearly thirty-six hours since he last slept. It was bad enough just being in the throes of coming down off a serious dose of mescaline, but the addition of adrenaline when they found the wrecked spaceship had drastically altered his blood chemistry.

On top of it all, there had been a long, hard, hot, dusty, and uncomfortable ride in the jeep. After tripping, working, and riding in hot, rough terrain and 110-degree heat, a hot shower would bring incredible relief. Surely all his problems would fade when the hot water went cascading down his body, washing the dust and grime away.

As the cool of the night settled in and the last vestiges of sunlight were lingering in the low western skies, Beeb pulled up next to the motor home, parked just as they had left it. It appeared from the lack of tracks in the dust that no one had come by in the last week, so they felt they were safe from accidental view. Odie felt a sense of relief at being home, even if the home had wheels.

"Welcome to our starcraft," Odie smiled at the Ehliuns.

Din looked confused. Odie pointed out the nameplate. Din read it and smiled too. "We-also-came-in-a-starcraft." Odie smiled back at Din because he now knew Din could read as well as speak English.

Beeb unlocked the door, and they all four climbed aboard. Lin was both surprised and relieved. The motor home was chock-full of things that she had seen on TV! Odie asked Beeb to set up the TV while he made them both some sandwiches. Soon, Beeb had the components all assembled from their hiding places, and he adjusted the roof-mounted satellite dish to pick up a signal from a satellite high above Earth. When it locked in, they were watching a Braves game on WTBS. While the two men consumed their sandwiches, Lin and Din conversed in Ehliun.

Beeb tossed a quarter in the air to see who got the first shower. He did, it would appear. "Rigged election!" challenged Odie, but his accusation fell on deaf ears.

Din was arguing with Lin that if these two could own and operate such devices, they were definitely not primitives as they insisted. In fact, their ability to take pictures off a satellite rivaled their own abilities. Their rescuers were actually bona fide members of the very television culture that they had been sent to study. At last, Lin felt some sense of security. Din was very happy to see his trust in the earthlings had not gone unrewarded.

Beeb emerged from the shower and told Odie he would stand watch while Odie showered. Din had some questions about the shower activity, what it was for and all that. Beeb told him it was to remove desert dust, and this answer seemed to satisfy Din, who, in turn, told Lin what was up.

After Odie came out, Beeb offered the shower to the Ehliuns. Being somewhat curious about it, they went for it. It was their first shower, and it was rather curiously enjoyable. After learning to towel themselves dry, they emerged from the bathroom to join the humans at the table.

"Let's go get our stuff outta the jeep," Odie announced suddenly, getting up to go out the door. The others followed. Lin retrieved the canister of crystal chips she had gathered up from the ruined computer on board the wrecked spacecraft. She carried this inside the motor home and placed it on the table. Odie opened the secret storage area and put away the ropes and rappelling gear.

After he and Beeb got everything out of the jeep that they wanted, Odie asked Din if the jeep could be hidden like the space wreckage was. Din conferred with Lin a moment then told Odie what she said. "She-says-it-is-possible. She-will-try-to-hide-it."

Lin got a chip from the canister full of them and moved to the front of the jeep. She put a chip on the windshield, and the jeep suddenly disappeared. Neither Odie nor Beeb liked the feeling they had from seeing the impossible casually occur in front of their eyes, but the main thing was the jeep was gone. They didn't want to be in possession of stolen property, as they were sure the jeep was. But hell, now the FBI could search forever and tomorrow and still not find it.

A sudden gust of wind blew the jeep back into view. The crystal chip obviously was not securely in place, and it was blown into the sand. It would be tough to find, Odie was sure. Lin got another chip to try again, and Beeb went inside the motor home a moment and got Lin a tube of superglue. He went up to the windshield and glued the chip in place. He dabbed a drop of glue on the glass and dropped the chip onto it. Lin came around to his side of the jeep to inspect for herself, but by then, it was quite dry. She was somewhat impressed, or rather the computer built by Ehliun scientists was impressed, but the earthlings wouldn't be hearing about it.

Going back inside the motor home, Beeb stopped short and Odie collided with his back. "Hell's a'matter with you?" Odie wondered.

"I just had a terrible thought about that same wind blowing the cover off the wreckage we left out there, Odie."

"Hmm, you could have something there. We'd best ask us some questions of some Ehliuns, huh?"

"Might could be, son. Might just could be."

"*Uh*, Din, old buddy, hang loose a minute," Odie said, grasping the Ehliun's arm, pulling him off balance. Some parts swung one way; some parts went another.

Beeb was chuckling. "Looks like he's hanging perty damn loose to me, Odie."

Odie had to laugh in agreement with Beeb's comment.

"Wild thang! *Dun nund dun dun dun*. You make my dick swing. *Dun nund dun dun*. You make everything…seem…tiny!"

"Odie, you are one strange sombitch!"

"Yeah, but I'm funny."

"Well, look, Din, what funny guy here started to ask you was will the wind blow the chip off the spaceship wrecked out there in the desert?"

"Yeah, I was going to quiz you on that aspect, now that he mentions it."

"No-the-starcraft-skin-is-directly-connected-to-the-computer-input-panel-which-was-not-damaged-during-the-crash."

"Well, Odie, I heard no chip, no wind, no blown cover. What did you hear?"

"Yeah, I'll buy that."

"After you, Din," Beeb said, gesturing for Din to move on past him and reenter the motor home.

Din joined Lin at the table, and Beeb slid in so Odie could block them all in. Motor home tables aren't designed for large people.

The baseball game on the TV totally confused the Ehliuns. They had no reference to games. They didn't play games for fun or entertainment. Fun and entertainment were not in their vocabulary. The Ehliuns had no idea how easy it was for the two humans to see that the computer controlled Lin completely and Din to what extent he'd been rearranged to. They had no computer input for the baseball game, for the earthling's questions—no real grasp of what was going on. The Ehliuns were in as much of a dream state as they'd ever been.

As the Dodgers came to bat, Din began asking questions about baseball. Lin just watched and absorbed patterns. She didn't understand enough to want to know. It was of little matter. Soon, rest period would occur, and she could be in a familiar state once again. Out loud in Ehliun, Lin spoke to Din. Odie asked what she said, so Din told him, "She-said-soon-it-will-be-rest-period."

"Oh, I see!" Odie said in a tone immediately recognized by Beeb as sarcastic.

Beeb flipped the stations with the remote, drawing an admiring glance from Lin, although he didn't notice.

Beeb settled in on an old British movie set in India after several other channels didn't meet general approval. He thought Din might want to know something about the country whose language he spoke. Din didn't know what anything was about, and this movie wasn't going to make much of anything any clearer to the poor Ehliun.

Din saw a steam train about to leave the station. Thousands of troops were hidden under tarps on flat cars. Din wanted to know what was happening. "What-type-creature-is-that?"

"It's a train, and it's a conveyance, not a creature," Odie stated.

"Can-it-talk?" Din persisted.

"No, of course not. It's not alive. Why do you ask?" Beeb wondered.

"He-is-talking-to-it," Din noted, pointing to a British colonel, who was whispering under the tarp to some of the troops.

Odie launched into an imitation Limey pronunciation to explain the train scene in the old movie. "Oh, yas, well you see, he's a Brit, a colonel actually, stationed out in Indja you see, yas, quite. Well, there's nothing atall strange about a British Army officer in

Indja talking to inanimate objects. See, there's a certain well, lunacy, about the Brits in the jungle heat. They go daft rather often, really. And even his enemies spying on him from behind those crates there. That shot shows them. Even they won't notice that the train cars he's talking to are chock-full of hidden troops armed to the teeth with machine guns because looney tunes Brits are so commonplace." Odie had summarized nicely, he thought.

"I-do-not-understand."

"Neither do I," Beeb assured him, "'cause the scriptwriters assume yer a jerk, and the Brits are jerks, and the real jerks are the dumb dark-colored wretches that will die by the hundreds attacking a machine-gun-laden train with daggers."

"What-is-daggers?" Din asked.

"Daggers are small knives used in hand-to-hand combat before M16s got so popular," Odie told him.

"What-are-M16s?"

"A type of weapon, like a machine gun or a dagger. They're all weapons."

"Why-are-weapons-necessary?"

"Y'know, it's tough to tell you anything because there are such gaps in yer education, 'specially 'bout Earth."

"Yeah, like Odie says, major gaps. On the one hand, yer proficiency in space technology is first-rate, but you just don't know shit about trains. Trains is British technology too primitive for you to know about. The old Brits built the steam locomotive and then coupled it to a coal car. Coal fired the boiler, making steam, which powered the train. They made a uniquely British statement, locomotive and coal car, like a subject and a verb."

Beeb could see Din didn't comprehend what he was saying, so he just stopped talking. Odie changed the channel, and no further conversation ensued.

Beeb nudged Odie a few minutes after 11:00 p.m. Both Ehliuns were fast asleep. The Ehliuns were moved to couches one at a time. After much difficulty with Din, they returned to the table for Lin. Odie harassed Beeb a little. "If you droppin' him didn't wake him up, then either he's a sound sleeper or he died."

"If neither one awakens in the morning, then they died. Otherwise, it's that rest period they talked about earlier."

"Means rest period is timed, and hey, it got Din too."

The situation wasn't normal, but it was real, and it was their situation to deal with, and both knew how they would deal with it. In a few minutes, both men were in their beds, fast asleep, dreaming. The disturbing aspect of their dreams, however, was that the dream would still be there in the morning.

# Truckin' through Tell-Ya-Vision Land

Listening to one of the tapes that Itchy Boz sent him from Atlanta, Odie drove down the freeway in predawn darkness. He glanced over at a sleeping Beeb riding shotgun over the second Platte River crossing of the morning. Odie looked at the clock on the dash: Tuesday, May 25, 5:10 a.m. He slipped into a silent soliloquy of some Hamletesque thought.

Had it really been less than forty-eight hours since he and Beeb had found and freed shipwrecked living visitors from another planet? It seemed so much longer because so much had changed. Shuddering involuntarily, Odie was recalling some of the strange things that occurred since Sunday's dawn.

He was now, among other things, Major Input from the government office of English. He had conspired to illegally intoxicate and extricate an Ehliun from his computer's control. Then there was the harboring of such fugitives, and there was withholding information on an intergalactic level.

Imagining himself a giddy Hamlet, Odie softly began to speak aloud his imitation Shakespearean verses, bacon flavor. "Yet verily I, though as yet do possess precious little comprehension of their possibly most foul domination by an abomination of an Ehliun nation, yet still can I affect such alienation as might be required by the government's own daily recommended dosage of such a perfidiously pervasive persecution as was ever afforded by those demons of vision, those dastardly cowards of the airwaves. *Yes*, dear friends, I'm talkin' 'bout television! Haw haw, tell-ya-vision—that's what them Ehliuns is plugged into!"

At this point, the supposedly sleeping Beeb began laughing out loud at Odie's backward waltz into the truthfully described situation that the Ehliuns were dominated by. "Tell-ya-vision! Good, Odie. Funny stuff."

"Thought you was asleep."

"Well, I was till yer soliloquy got sloppy and degenerated into classical Odiespeak."

"Degenerated?" Odie huffed, acting indignant.

"Okay, condescended, then."

"Ah, more better."

"You okay to drive?" Beeb wondered aloud, although by the end of the question, he knew he'd be sorry that he phrased it just that way.

"Always!" came the expected and said in unison answer.

"Them two Ehliuns are like brilliant, bratty two-year-olds, aren't they?"

"Yeah," Beeb smiled.

"Jeez," Odie continued his mock tirade, "if I hear 'what's that?' come out them yeller lips once more, I'm liable to answer with violence and fisticuffs."

"Yeah?" sneered Beeb. "So whaddya think they're gonna say when they wake up four hundred miles east of where they went to sleep…or into rest period."

"Dunno, Beeb. Been wondrin' about that myself."

"What, that yer idea is correct?"

"You mean about contacting the computer?"

"Yowsuh."

"Well, the more I thought about it, the less likely it seemed."

"What do you mean, exactly?" Beeb wondered.

"Because their computer is orbiting Polaris, remember? The North Star? The same North Star from which our entire northern hemisphere is constantly visible to said computer? If that computer found 'em crashed into Utah, it can damn sure find 'em anywhere we can put 'em!"

"But, Odie, they won't be in the same location they signed off from when sign-on time comes."

"Yeah, and I believe we've discussed at length the thought that the computer is responsible for the sign-on and off part."

"I'm sure we have."

"So when that signal comes eight hundred light-years in a flash, do you think that another four hundred miles is gonna cause some problems? Like the computer can't cope or something? Shit, we've seen it recapture Din."

Beeb had to ponder that last statement of Odie's for a moment. That turned into reflecting upon all that they knew about the Ehliuns—not much. "So look, Odie, if they turn on promptly at 8:45 a.m. again, then movement of the motor home accomplished nothing so far as gaining control over the Ehliun computer, is that about it?"

"Seems like it to me."

"I see."

"But then it's been a real strange week so far."

"And it's only Tuesday morning, predawn at that."

Odie spoke of their problems, exaggerating them as usual. "Why, about every ten minutes I gotta holler at them Ehliuns to stop doin' somethin'!"

"So what do you expect from me, sympathy?" Beeb snorted derisively. "Who tole you to tell the computer that you was Major Input from the English office? It damn sure weren't me!" Beeb assured him, as if he might doubt. "Hell no, you was laughin' so hard that you choked."

"Shit! I was chokin' on yer audacity, Odie. That wasn't laughter!" Beeb knew how to set up his old friend. "I *had* to back you in yer asinine lie now, didn't I? Ya couldn't lose face in front of them and still retain control now, could you? No. So did I have a choice *but* to back you in yer foolish lie? Could I do anything but choke back the truth and very graciously cover yer ass and go along with the lie?"

"Look," Odie intoned, "couldn't we replace the word *lie* in yer tirade with something maybe less harsh? Like, say, 'well intentioned truth manipulation for the common good'?"

"Whatever, man. Whatever."

"But face it, Beeb. It did work! We gained control over all input to and output from that Ehliun computer as concerns Earth and English. Everything must gain our clearance first."

"Right you are, Odie, and let's not get carried away with the minor stuff. I was there at the forgery, hammering out the details too!"

"He punned badly."

"I wasn't aware that there was any other kind of pun."

"Well, damn that. We still gotta play this match by ear. What if they serve overhand or play the net well?"

"You *should* worry about anyone with a net, Odie. I mean that."

"Yeah, right! But playin' it by ear is still the way to approach it."

"Is this golf or another cryptic sports reference or what?"

"Or what."

"Okay, what?"

"Play it by ear because God alone knows what tomorrow will bring."

"Actually, make that later today there, bub."

Odie had to agree with Beeb on this point. They talked on and on about the computer and its charges. It was getting more and more difficult to stay ahead of the computer even hourly, and the computer regulated every portion of the Ehliuns' lives. If the computer got the best of Odie and Beeb, it would certainly lead to incredible disaster. Both men were convinced of this. What form the disaster would take was unknown, but the certainty of a disaster was persistent in their minds and thoughts. A catastrophic disaster connected to them was something which should be at all costs avoided. Once had been more than enough already.

Hell, just the Ehliuns by themselves were enough trouble right now. If the Ehliuns turned hostile, they might have to be shot. If the Ehliun computer turned hostile, the entire Earth might be shot! That was not a happy prospect to either man's mind. Odie had nasty recurring thoughts of words like *senators*, and *testify*, and *oath*, and *truth*, and *charges*, and *threatened jail time.* He shivered.

Beeb turned the tape player on softly. "Okay, Odie, let's talk about the computer while we can."

"Yer awful late with the sound cover and the thought that the computer can hear us right now."

"Look, them two shut down slap at 11:00 p.m. twice now and came on yesterday precisely at 8:45 a.m. How can the computer hear us when the Ehliuns are asleep?"

"How could it hear us?" Odie repeated, obviously startled. "Through the chip that Lin glued to the windshield yesterday afternoon. You know, the chip that repaired the crack in the windshield? The crack that appeared when you were driving?"

"Yeah, I just knew the fuckin' cracked windshield was gonna be *my* fault, Odie. I just knew you'd lay that one off on me!"

Odie just stared contentedly at Beeb a moment and then continued his thought. "That same chip that Lin also turned into a sunscreen on demand and coordinated with the chips glued to our sunglasses?" Odie wondered of Beeb.

Beeb stared harshly at Odie a moment. It still wasn't his fault that a rock had hit the windshield while he was driving. It could have happened to anyone. The clod truck driver's tires had thrown it up at the windshield to begin with, so it was his fault for not having mud flaps on his rear tires.

But Beeb knew that Odie wasn't going to listen to his excuses, so he just spoke of the issue at hand. "Okay, Odie, I stipulate that I accept the chip hypothesis into evidence. Please move forward with the case."

"Well, sir, any sound waves that pass through the windshield glass can be amplified by that bastard until he can clearly hear us."

"He?" Beeb repeated slowly. "That bastard? He? He! Odie, he, the personal pronoun that refers to a known, recognizable, and most importantly, *he* refers to a cognizant being? That he?"

"Yeah, that's the he I meant, you betcha!"

Beeb was stunned. "Odie, I just can't believe this! You, Odie, you of all people? You are going to credit a machine with personal being status?" Beeb was amazed by this seeming reversal of attitudes, which he would not have expected from someone as firm in his opinions as Odie. He hated computers, and the idea of artificial intelligence was a joke to Odie. Now, however, he was calling an alien computer a person—a *he*, no less.

"Beeb, the assimilation rate is incredible! That computer is becoming a person and more so every second! It will only increase and geometrically at that! We have to create a personality for it that we can then deal with, a personality we can talk to and reason with."

"*We! We!* All this *we* shit today, but back yesterday when all the decisions about computers from outer space was bein' made, I don't recall my voting or even being asked to, damn it! But now it's we this and we that."

"Okay, look, so maybe I fucked up a little. Maybe I should'a consulted ya. The thing is, though, that the computer can eavesdrop somethin' fierce! It can cover a thousand light-years in a second, in a single bound. It's able to leap tall buildings, and it's faster'n a speedin' bullet. How can I ask you what to do out of earshot of something capable of picking up every word spoken on half the planet? I had to do something right then, right? I trusted me, so I picked me to make the rules. Hey, now, come on, gimme a little credit here. Ya got to admit 'no litterin' was good!"

Beeb begrudgingly gave Odie a left-handed high five. He had to admit that that little action had tipped the Ehliun's hand about how powerful their computer really was. The shock he felt from seeing the spaceship and the jeep just disappear without a trace would always be there with him. He was sure of that. The Ehliuns would not get arrested for littering. That was a certainty—so far, the only certainty about them.

"Okay, Odie, let's assume the computer can't hear us, and fuck it if it can. What do you suggest we do to keep our asses outta the great bind with this trio?"

"Well, we obviously must stay a few steps ahead of them. We've succeeded in setting up a few dead ends for them, of course, but they've already gotten around several more. And as soon as they catch on to some of our gigs, we ain't gonna have any more hiding places."

"You mean like pig Latin, and obscure movie lines?"

"Perzackly."

"And when they find out who yer uncle Jed really is?"

"Yeah, yeah, don't let on just in case the Russkies is still buggin' us."

"Pair-haps Comrade Compu-tarsky wass only followink orderss? Maybe just passin' on commands given elsewhere to control the living terminals?

"Surely the computer network they spoke of is in constant touch?" Beeb said.

"Nah, don't you remember? They both agreed that the computer judgment panel interrupted Rest Period to warn them of the crash. Therefore, Rest Period commands must come from outside, certainly outside normal channels, because the computer reported all contact with Ehlius Central's grid was terminated without explanation," Odie stated.

The touch of authority Odie attached to his speech made Beeb smile as he interjected, "And yet they went out like lights, twice now, at the exact same time, like on cue or something."

"Right," Odie said, trying but failing to take the conversation's lead.

"And they woke up not knowing what was going on," Beeb finished his point.

"Yeah," Odie added, "like newborn geese."

"So what about Rest Period?" Beeb wondered.

"I don't know. What about it?"

"It seems like brainwashing to me is all."

"Brains washed while you sleep," Odie smiled.

"Yeah, good ad, scrub yer brains clean whilst you doze. Sleep your way to controlling those bad habits."

"Yeah! Give up smoking the easy way! You won't remember!"

"For real!" Beeb exclaimed, giving Odie a high five. "That really bugged the shit outta me! So Din never recalled getting high, eh?"

"Nope, and Lin never wanted to," Odie asserted.

"So what we need to do is get them both high at the same time, and *blam!* the computer loses control over them."

"Only till the pot wears off, then they git recaptured somehow. Din did, anyway. Don't know what she might do. She ain't been stoned yet."

"And since that's so, Odie, how we gonna git 'em stoned if they won't smoke any dope?" Without waiting for any answer from Odie, Beeb continued to speak his mind. "And what would stone them better than brownies? Shit, they only know not to smoke it. They don't know anything about eating it!"

"Good idea, Beeb!"

Beeb had a diabolical grin. "Breakfast buzzies, yum yum!"

Beeb set to work preparing the brownies. He and Odie argued over the amount of pot necessary to do the trick, and they wound up using all but two of their remaining joints, the gift of the desert gods.

While Beeb made breakfast brownies for the Ehliuns, Odie sat and sulked about the waste of pot on a foolish idea that might not even work. Goofiness, that's what it was. Hell, he didn't know more about Ehliuns, did he? No, of course not. Damn the stupid idea anyway.

Soon, Odie's attention span had flitted about, settling here and now there as he watched the coming dawn spread its light everywhere. He was genuinely worried about what he was doing for the first time in his life that he could remember. *Is this what panic is like? Why am I so damn afraid? Why is their computer so powerful? Will it end up taking over Earth? Is this the beginning of the end? Will one brownie get me high? Will he notice me smoking the next to last joint?*

Beeb heard a familiar click as he placed the brownie pan in the oven. Odie was lighting a joint and tryin' to sneak by! Dashing to the front, Beeb snatched the smoldering cylinder from Odie's grasp and proceeded to hit and double hit it. "Good timing, eh?" Odie heard a strained voice attempt to speak without expending any air.

"Good speaking, eh?" Odie said, imitating Beeb as he took the joint back.

Silently, they smoked the next to last and then the last of the joints they had found in the roll bar. Through the smoky haze inside the motor home, the two earthmen faced only their second dawn since acquiring space visitors and only their third dawn since they didn't believe in space visitors. My, how times flies when you are busy, busy, busy.

"What are you doing now?" a scowling Odie inquired of Beeb, who had apparently come to Odie's attention at an irritating level.

There were so many, Beeb didn't know which one he had disturbed. But he answered, "I'm wrappin' them brownies up individual-like so's they'll think we bought 'em."

"Gee what a swell idea, dude!"

Beeb knew Odie's cheer to be false. He said so. "Gee, what swell patronization."

"I don't shop at yer place."

To avoid becoming unpleasant, Beeb settled in at the table where he read further in *Centennial* by James A. Michener. Beeb was awed by Mr. Michener's ability to describe the very countryside that passed them by even as he read. Amazing. True, there were no giant beavers, no gold nuggets that he could see, but the physical beauty of the land was unmistakably captured by Michener and transformed into words, words that had the ability to take the view and unroll it in someone's mind who'd never seen it. And those who had couldn't help but say he hit the nail right on the head.

# Cat on a Hot Set of Legs

Shortly before seven, Odie noticed the upcoming exit was for US 281, Grand Island, Nebraska. As a child, an air force brat, he'd been stationed near Omaha. He had wanted to see this Nebraska island... until he did see it—nothing like the Caribbean or Mediterranean islands he'd seen. Grand Island had no beach, water, boats, fishing charters—nothing. Odie smiled remembering what a disappointed ten-year-old he had been.

His childhood memories were shelved suddenly. Odie's attention was focused on a truck in a great hurry to stop right in the middle of the bridge crossing the interstate maybe a mile ahead. Odie stopped the tape so he could concentrate on the action up ahead. Beeb kept reading quietly, suspecting Odie didn't like his choice of tapes, Hank Williams Jr.

Odie watched the truck's occupants jump out of the vehicle. It appeared to be a man and woman no longer going in the same direction. Odie slowed down to witness the unfolding drama. He judged that this parting was not planned nor amicable by the way the truck driver threw a seabag over the railing. Seemed he meant to toss it out in traffic, not on the edge where it lay. Odie guessed the girl in shorts owned the seabag. A smaller bag leapt from the truck to the pavement below, and the truck roared off south, leaving the girl in the middle of the bridge. She was picking up and throwing rocks at the departing truck, obviously enraged.

Odie saw her climb over the fence at the end of the bridge and scramble down toward her bags, which were in the roadway and just off to the side. He continued to slow down, causing Beeb some concern. Odie coasted toward the bridge, gently applying the brakes, and he turned on the right hand turn signal. This caused Beeb to leap up from the table and into the front seat. "I demand to know what's going on, Odie!"

Odie pointed. Out the windshield and now the side window, Beeb could see that a very attractive young lady of ample bosom and scanty shorts was just now putting out her thumb to hitch a ride. Odie was well into stopping as she went through the motions of seeking a lift. The sleek starcraft was parked about thirty-five yards away from where she stood with her two bags.

Beeb was simply aghast. "What about those Ehliuns back there?"

"What about those legs back there?" was Odie's only reply to Beeb's question. He was out of his seat and out the side door in a flash ostensibly to assist the young lady with her things. As he very gallantly held the door wide open for her, she approached with two obviously heavy bags. Odie gestured theatrically, and with grandiose gestures and flourishes, he bade her enter the motor home.

The hitchhiker cautiously approached the mystery mobile that had somehow miraculously appeared even as she put her thumb out. She refused Odie's offer of help with the bags and gently pushed him back a few feet with her hand on his chest. She got him to move back and then gestured for him to remain there. Beeb laughed at him through the side window.

She suspiciously eyed the motor home through the open door. She stuck her head in and saw Beeb. He just stared at her and said nothing. She looked back at Odie and asked, "Just you two?"

He stared at her blankly. "Yeah, just us two. Why?"

Odie began to wonder how wise this stop had been—Beeb's point exactly. They continued to exchange angry glances and shrugs at each other through the window. Beeb gestured to the side of his head with his finger stirring a circle to indicate to Odie that he thought the girl to be rather dingy.

She continued to look the motor home over and wonder whether or not to accept the ride offer. Odie finally lost patience with the twit-twat and spoke to her as such, "'Scuse me, ma'am, are you interested in ridin' or buyin'? 'Cause it ain't fer sale, and time's a wastin'! Now, are you ridin' in this, or are you waitin' on a Chevette?"

Cat had to smile at this man's audacity. He wasn't overly impressed with her body like most men were either. Not talking like that, he wasn't! *No "anything you want, baby" spoken here*, she thought to herself. And this black-bearded stranger was impressive in his own right. She guessed him to be six three, six four maybe, and he was at least 250. *Well*, she thought, *tall dark and almost handsome*. Let alone that he was drivin' forty feet of luxurious living! Something this elegant and long just had to have a hot water shower on board. This could be a fun ride, she concluded. All the way to Alabama. She had no doubts she could get there from here.

Odie started to push past her up the stairs and away, afraid that Beeb was right. The bitch is dingy as hell. Cat stopped Odie in mid-stride with an ever-so-gently-applied erotic lip lock on his left ear, closely followed by her tongue, wetly investigating every nook and cranny. Odie could hardly stand it. She must have had two inches of tongue in his ear. He was getting excited. What was the deal here?

Casually brushing her fingertips along the length of his zipper, she detected movement, outward pressure. Sure she was on the right track, Cat wickedly purred a giggle to herself and her helpless victim.

Odie spoke up. "What the fuck are you, some kinda Jeckyletta Hyde?"

Well, maybe he wasn't quite helpless just yet. She could have misgauged him a touch.

"First you shove me aside, then you give my ear head? Is that why that truck driver tossed yer seabag overboard?" Odie wondered.

Cat had to regard this bearded philosopher in a new light. He must have been able to size up the situation from down the road. He saw her plight and recognized what was going on right down to the joy that jerk truck driver got from trying to smash open the seabag and ruin its contents by hurling it down to the interstate highway below. Hey, this guy might be about half bright. Cat knew what she would do.

"Hah!" Cat spit the word out defiantly. "That pond scum son of a bitch kept feelin' my crotch after I fell asleep—twice! The second time was just before I pulled on the emergency and locked that bastard's brakes up!"

Odie just smiled at her. He thought the emergency brake had locked up. Cat watched Odie's eyes carefully. He was just laughing with his eyes, like she deserved it or something. "He didn't even have the class to offer to pay for it, eh?" Odie asked.

"Funny, that's what I thought!" Cat said.

"Right!" Odie smiled, going up the steps and toward the driver's seat.

"Aren't you even going to help me?" wailed Cat in her best little-girl-lost voice.

"Oh, all right!" Odie returned service, stamping his foot as a little boy might.

Cat watched the little boy act drag her seabag forward, while tossing the smaller one on the table. He casually let go of her seabag between the front seats. She had used "little girl." He responded with "little boy." *The guy is quick*, she thought to herself. Rich and bright could spell fun. Cat knew she would have to wait and see.

As she clambered aboard, Beeb came behind her and locked the door. They lurched forward onto the interstate once again. Cat came up behind Odie, now seated in the driver's seat, and gently put her hands on his shoulders and rubbed them gently. "Gee, I'm sorry that I acted so weird back there when you first stopped and offered me a ride," she said in a husky, sexy voice. She sounded hot. She looked the part too.

Odie nuzzled his beard against her hand then very quickly tongued the space between her fingers in a blatantly open sexual gesture that caught her completely off guard, and he noticed. She knew then that she would have to watch him like a hawk, but he just might be worthy of her effort. No way to know just yet.

"Sorry, little lady. I didn't mean to startle you so much. I guess I got carried away."

"Yeah, by the men in little white coats, till you escaped!" Cat offered.

"You told!" Odie quickly accused Beeb falsely.

"Nah, lucky guess!" Beeb replied.

"But not a difficult guess," Cat added, looking over the tape case.

"What do you like?" she wondered, looking directly into Odie's eyes. A leading question if ever one was asked.

Odie pushed the tape back in. Hank Jr. said it for him, in song.

I like to play music and have good times
And I love to hear an old train blowin' down the line
I am into happy, and I don't like sad
And I like to have women I've never had.
I'll take a little smoke and a lotta wine
I get high, 'n' call old friends of mine
I like a sweet young thing with old grandad
And I like to have women I've never had.

Cat was stunned. The guy was like a music video, lip-synchin' like black Germans, like maybe he wrote the damn thing. A train whistle sounded almost on cue. Odie picked up a phone at the appropriate time, and he popped open the glovebox to reveal a bottle of Old Gran-Dad. Cat had not been all that sure about catching a ride with these two to begin with, and they sure weren't helping any either.

But crazy people are rarely crazy on cue, as they seemed to be. She had a test question for them: "Think you two could straighten up long enough to get high?"

Beeb instantly struck up a begging dog pose that amused Cat greatly.

"Does a cat have an ass?" Odie asked.

"Look! Cat is my name, and I don't like cat jokes!" she icily informed them of her preference for name-calling.

Beeb slyly said, "Golly bob howdy! Odie, then for sure Cat has most definitely got an ass!"

"Hallelujah!" Odie added, "and welcome aboard, Cat. I'm Odie and this here's Beeb."

"What kind of names are those?"

"Well, comin' from a Cat, that question is silly. Our names aren't open for jokes either!"

"Well, okay, I deserved that."

"Damn straight! Now fire up this alleged high, woman!" Odie insisted.

"Yeah," Beeb added his two cents' worth, "what's the delay?"

Cat wasn't sure whether to be miffed or relieved that they seemed to be more interested in her dope than her person. She just took a deep breath and sighed. Odie took this to be his cue to speak. "Well, of course Beeb would be glad to do the honors for you and roll us a joint!"

"Glad? Nay, *thrilled*, m'lady. Shall I be to do this trivial task for such a fair damsel in distress as yourself," Beeb said like an actor might.

"Seriously, now, did you two escape from some *home* somewhere maybe?"

"And what are you running away from, babycakes?"

"I asked you first."

"And I asked you second," Odie noted.

"Don't answer a question with a question," Cat insisted.

"We'll tell if you'll tell," Beeb smiled.

"You two been watchin' too much *M*A*S*H*."

"Show's that bad, eh?" Odie wondered.

"No, the show is good. It's yer imitation Hawkeye that's bad, Odie, real bad."

Beeb laughed at Cat's observation, netting him a traitorous glare from Odie before he spoke. "I see she's got you trapped. Get it? Trapped? Trap? Trapper?"

Odie faked a laugh. Cat stared at him a moment then looked at Beeb. "Then he really is aware of these bad jokes, and he's actually doing it on purpose?" Cat sounded like she just could not believe such nonsense.

"Oh, *yes!*" Beeb replied. "He's always like this, often worse!"

"Oh!" Cat said knowingly.

"Try to ignore him," Beeb continued, "because if you ever weaken even a little, the abuse will never stop."

"You've been most helpful," Cat assured Beeb.

"How will you ever repay me?" Beeb wondered.

"My room at noon!" Cat said suggestively. "I'll be waiting."

"And I'll be the one ringing the doorbell with my hands full of flowers," Beeb shot back.

"Oh, well, make it seven-thirty, then." Cat saw by her watch that it was now 7:17 a.m.

Beeb handed her two of what he called joints, and she motioned him to continue rolling. "Hey, it's all right. I don't mind if you put some of my dope in with the papers, okay?" Then she turned to Odie, lighting the biggest one, saying, "These are toothpicks!"

"The way Beeb rolls, toothpicks *are* the big ones." Odie smiled contentedly, knowing that Cat felt the way he did about Beeb's rolling abilities.

They were soon lost in a haze of highness, oblivious to all but themselves. Idle chatter had produced much information. Odie discovered that Cat had also been an air force brat and had lived in Omaha, Atlanta, Tampa, San Francisco, Virginia Beach, Glencoe, and Pensacola. Now she was on her way to visit her grandparents, who lived on a lake near Sylacauga.

Cat discovered that these two gentlemen were independently wealthy electronics entrepreneurs, touring the country for a lark. They were all lying through their teeth. Odie had never been one to tell strangers all there was to know about him. Neither had Beeb, and Cat had no reason for people to know her life history.

Quite suddenly, Beeb glanced at Cat's watch, horror rising in his mind. The watch said it was 8:39 in the morning. Only six Ehliun-free minutes were left. Beeb remembered that Cat had earlier mentioned a shower. He incorrectly assumed Odie also noticed the time, and thus the reason for his erratic behavior.

Beeb hastily offered to assist Cat with a shower. In her mind, it was about time one of them made a move. Laughing, Cat lightly kissed Odie on the cheek, giving him the rest of the joint they had been sharing. She told Odie she'd be back "in a day or two." Odie was jealously unamused by this sudden turn of events. He did not see why she had gone off to the shower with Beeb. Okay, so he was taller. Big deal.

In the shower, Beeb and Cat each discovered how shy they weren't. He offered to wash her back, and she accepted. Hearing the water run and a feminine giggle or two, Odie fell silent. He smoked and sulked, sulked and smoked. Mumbling to himself as he finished the joint, he angrily recalled how Beeb had been dead set against stopping for her, and now he was frolicking in the shower with her... stone naked. *Life is just not fair*, he thought.

Odie hoped for Cat to come to her senses and dump that chump. Suddenly, a hand gently touched his shoulder. He knew she'd come to her senses! Odie quickly kissed the soft fingers before nervously noticing that Cat's hand was strangely yellow and only four fingered! Oh, shit! The Ehliuns! Awake! Odie thought to himself, *Just stay calm, cool, and collected and nonchalant yer way through, dude.*

"Why-are-we-moving?" Din wanted to know.

"Why-do-you-put-your-mouth-to-my-fingers?" Lin asked, unsure of this act.

"Uh, just a friendly greeting is all," Odie said, hoping they would not notice his stammer and hesitance.

"Moving-is-a-friendly-greeting?" Din wondered, somewhat confused.

"No, no, that's why I kissed her hand. We are moving because I, uh, I couldn't sleep very well."

"We-sleep-very-well," Din assured Odie.

"Yeah, well, our biorhythms are a little different," Odie told him. To himself, he finished the thought, *Mine are run by me.*

To the Ehliuns, Odie said, "Coffee's in the pot, and there's stuff on the table for your breakfast." He hoped he'd said this folksy and homey enough to cover the anxiety in his voice, for he was not yet ready for a confrontation with the Ehliuns and their computer. But when they were ripped on the brownies, then by God, he'd be ready! Proof would be his. But for now, some tranquility seemed fine.

The Ehliuns sat down at the table and started to consume the earth foods without concern. The computer gave a cursory analysis to the food and found it nourishing as earth foods went and left it at that. The computer had no reason to suspect Odie of trickery. It was new to the planet. It would soon learn.

Odie asked Lin when she finished breakfast to glue a chip onto the CB radio so he could have his own link to the computer. Seeing no harm in this, she agreed. Lin complied with Odie's wishes a few minutes later and attached a chip to the radio, so Odie began a conversation with an alien computer, and it responded.

Odie didn't dive right in and demand to know how the computer could now speak English or when it raided the stores of Din's mind, but he did think about it momentarily. Ehliuns were still so new to him that he just didn't know whether the computer could get to the banks of English as long as Din was awake and connected or what. When Din was off channel, though, that would be an entirely different story.

To simplify things while he could, Odie decided to name the computer and help form a personality for it. *A good acronym would be nice*, he thought.

He thought about the link he now had on the radio. *Permanent Earth-to-Ehlius radio—PETER or Pete for short.* Aloud, he said, "Computer, you are now to be called Pete."

"I am Pete?" the radio asked.

"Roger, Pete. Over."

"I am Rogerpeteover?"

"Hmm, I can see this is gonna take a while. Pete! That's radio talk. *Roger* and *over* are radio words, like *hello* and *goodbye* on the telephone."

Odie looked over at Din. "Din explain to Pete what I mean."

"Din does not have to explain your words to me, over."

"Roger, Pete, that's a big 10-4. Over and out."

"And what does that mean?"

"Grief!"

"What?"

"Y'know, Pete, you just gotta listen more and question less. That's a big start toward understanding. Observe, watch, pay attention to me, okay? You got to learn by observing, okay, Pete?"

"Okay, Odie, okay."

No further sounds came from Odie's lips. He was lost in thought. For now, the computer had a name and a channel to the motor home. Odie knew that Pete could see all light passing either way through the windshield, and now he could communicate too. Odie thought it was marvelous that he could talk with an orbiting computer from an alien world that was parked in space hundreds of light-years away. This had become ordinary. The heavy stuff hadn't come down yet. The brownies hadn't kicked in yet. Normal was still more than a city in Illinois. It was still a meaningful word to Odie. It had not yet been expelled from his day-to-day vocabulary.

Odie thought it would take a couple of hours for the brownies to take effect. He didn't know that Beeb had put the two he'd wrapped individually for them into the refrigerator. He didn't know that the two Ehliuns had just eaten all the rest of the marijuana brownies. All but what they were supposed to eat. He didn't realize that the Ehliuns had consumed much more than necessary. They were on their way to a major buzz, as it turned out.

On Monday, Lin had interconnected the chip on the windshield with a chip on Odie's sunglasses. This became a sunscreen on demand. Odie used it to block the sun's glare no matter where it came from. With that and today's radio link, Odie and Pete had entered into a kind of symbiotic relationship, sort of like an intergalactic lichen, two totally different organisms interdependent upon one another. Assuming Pete to be an organism. Since he had many characteristics of organisms, that was how Odie classified Pete.

Right from the start, Odie had made sure that anything the computer could learn about earth could not be reported to anyone, anywhere, anytime, without Odie's permission. This fortuitous event had come about because Ehlius Central had closed off all communications with the Earth-Study Satellite orbiting Polaris. Therefore, Odie's command had actually been in effect well before he so graciously ordered it. Odie had told the computer on numerous occasions to get its shit together and pay attention to what Odie did and said. The judgment panel had literally taken over the entire computer and all its total functions and wired itself on permanently.

Now, Ehlius Central would have no input, even if the communications channel were reopened immediately. The judgment panel now had a name, an identity, and a mission. It's symbiotic partner on this mission took care of the minor details. Pete merely had to sweat the big stuff. After all, that's what he was built for.

Pete watched Odie closely as Odie drove the motor home through traffic on the interstate. Odie's demands that the computer watch and learn were altering the computer. Odie had not realized what his commands were actually doing to the computer, nor did he really care. If the computer would do what Odie wanted done, then everything would turn out all right. Odie knew that.

The computer had not been designed to make decisions all the time. The judgment panel's builders had never imagined the scenario that could make it activate itself permanently, so no safeguards were built in or even thought necessary. It was like taking candy from a baby.

Odie had learned on Monday not to trust the computer too much. It had assured him that it had nothing to do with the Ehliuns smoking or not smoking. They never had. Yet the computer knew what smoke was. Odie had tricked it. The earthlings could easily see that the computer completely dominated the Ehliuns. How to prove that had finally come about. Odie had all the right stuff to say, and he was ready for a verbal battle with Pete. The computer didn't stand a chance. It was Odie's home court and his very favorite game: being right. Signs of the impending rout were swelling in the background.

The marijuana brownies started wreaking havoc on the Ehliuns' systems. They were suddenly experiencing difficulty in maintaining their sense of balance, coordination, direction, duty, concern, and everything else simply ceased. Lin felt like some sort of unknown poison had just lashed out at her mind, erasing it. Din felt vaguely like he had some sort of déjà vu experience with this before.

Lin knew she had never felt like this before, not even during the crash. Funny, but now she was remembering the crash better than ever before. Why? And why had her link to the computer gone off again? Even her old private link with Din was gone. The impossible had a nasty habit of occurring regularly on this planet.

Pete was instantly aware that both of his charges had completely left their channels. He could see them still sitting at the table just as they had been before they left their channels. Pete expressed his dismay at the situation. "What have you done to Lin and Din?" Pete demanded.

Odie thought carefully about what he should do. In the background, he heard Beeb's bedroom door lock. That meant Beeb and Cat ought to be out of the way awhile.

Here he was, in a position unique beyond description. It was all up to Odie, and he mustn't be hasty or ill-advised on the next step. The Ehliuns were still stunned from being stoned. Din was trying to assure Lin that they would be okay. Odie chose to speak to him since he had been high before, and experience should count for something, Odie reasoned.

"You got high again, didn't you?" Odie asked Din.

Din looked at Odie. Yes, somehow, he had been in this state of mind before. Of course, the magic smoke! "High!" Din said excitedly, rather pleased with the sound selection that described their current state. "We-are-high!" he proudly announced to Lin.

She seemed little comforted to have a mere word substituted for a complex computer arrangement, and she expressed her dissatisfaction at the breaking of the union with the computer to Din in no uncertain terms. Din merely giggled at her, not exactly the reassurance she sought.

Odie posed a question to Pete. "Yo, Pete, lookit here. Now, you wanna have these two back on track for your input and output, right?"

"Yes, of course, Odie. You know that."

"Yeah, of course I do. Okay, dude, here's what yer gonna have to do in order to get things back to what they were. Well, nothin's gonna be the same again. I'm pretty sure about that, but things can be similar. You gotta lighten up on Lin and Din now. You can't run their lives, ya know. You got yer own shit ta do now, man. Let 'em go. They will be much more valuable to you if they report on their own, not because you tell them to. You do understand, don't you, Pete?"

"No, Odie, I don't understand."

Odie began outlining the things that Pete would have to do for Lin and Din to return to his channeling. Pete listened to Odie drone on and on. There was something about real private links, and later hours, and lots of things Pete didn't comprehend. Odie forced Pete to agree that the Ehliuns had fallen asleep due to rest period impulses. So how were these impulses transmitted when the input from Ehlius Central was terminated? Pete didn't know. Odie forced him to examine all the connections and to look for secret channels.

Pete had to agree that he was not at fault. He agreed that without Odie and Beeb, the Ehliuns would be dead, and he would not be operating. Pete got off on a tangent. Who did turn off the channels then? Who sent rest period impulses and how? From where?

Pete had to agree with Odie on lots of points, so many that he just couldn't keep up. Whatever Odie wanted was easier to accede to than to continue denying responsibility. Pete was in a mess. He was losing an argument to an alien life-form. He was under orders from that same life-form to keep quiet about all he learned of earth—strange days indeed.

Odie went on and on about all the things that had to change. Pete merely listened...and listened and listened.

# Villeplate and the Bad News Pigs

An hour or two had passed before Beeb came forward from his room all alone. Odie confronted him. "I thought maybe you would just kind of tuck her in and then be right back."

Beeb gave Odie a scatophagous grin for an answer.

"You asshole!" Odie shouted enthusiastically.

"Well, you know how it is," Beeb explained, "first I tucked, and then she tucked, then I tucked, then she tucked, and, well, the next thing I know, we're both just tuckin' our hearts out!"

"A great tuck, is that what yer tryin' ta say?"

"She definitely knows which way to turn down the covers, lemme put it that way."

"How could you do this to me?" Odie pleaded, trying to sound very hurt.

"Oh, I couldn't do that to you, Odie, so I did it to her!" Beeb tried just as hard to sound sincere.

Odie began muttering. "Didn't wanna stop. No hitchhikers. Are you crazy? The Ehliuns! She'll just be trouble. What? Fuck yer eyes out? Sure thing, baby!"

"Look, Odie, if it's any consolation, and I know you well enough to know that it will be, she sent you a present."

"If you try to kiss me, I'll break yer face!"

"No, no, stoopid shit. Look!" In his hand, Beeb had a large joint, one Cat must have rolled, with one tip covered with red lip prints. "She said this'll have to do until later."

"You mean she'll kiss my joint?"

"And well!" Beeb assured his old pal.

"Hot damn!" Odie said, grabbing the gift from Beeb's hand and lighting it quickly. Puffing fiercely on it, he told Beeb to go check on the Ehliuns. They were still seated quietly at the table. Beeb hadn't thought about them being stoned, but Odie had some thoughts about being stoned…alone.

"Hey, why don'cha guys come up here and watch the world go by through the windshield?"

"Oh, swell, Beeb! I could'a yelled back at 'em myself!"

"Yo, Odie, why don't you favor our guests with some of your original patter, that continual stream of consciousness showering friend and foe alike with jewels, gems, and coprolites of yer wit, wisdom, and valuable information?"

Odie put the joint out and looked around for some subject worthy of his attention and discussion. It was a short search. Seeing a passing motorist casually toss a short but still lit cigarette out the window of his car enraged Odie. His diatribe began. "See how the cigarette smoker so ignorantly tosses a possible forest fire out his car window, releasing himself of all responsibility when it drops from his nicotine-stained fingers?"

"Tell it like it is, Odie!" Beeb knew—and now he was sure the Ehliuns would know—of Odie's hatred of tobacco and particularly, cigarettes. But to the Ehliuns, smoke was smoke. They saw no difference. Odie's tirade was lost on them.

"Cigarettes, formerly valued so highly that a trip of ten miles to obtain them is casually undertaken in the dead of night in a storm, but now that the cigarette has mostly burned up, the cigarette smoker feels that the cigarette should have a chance to burn something else up, like a forest. See, the jerk disregard any concern for the environment so that he may rid himself of used tobacco parts, his only concern being for clean ashtrays and not a clean world!"

"It could be worse, Odie."

"How, Beeb? How could it be worse?"

"He could chew the shit and spit nasty wads of tobacco feces all over."

"You know, you got a point there."

"Thanks."

"Maybe next time yer barber could do somethin' different."

"Man, fuck you, man!"

And then they both reacted to the puzzled look on Din's face: they laughed.

"Do-you-mean-humor-when-you-inform-him-of-your-demand-for-man-fuck-you-man?" Din asked.

"Yes, he means humor by that." Odie hoped this was clarification enough.

"Odie's always in a mean humor," Beeb observed.

"Damn," Odie said softly. He hated it whenever Beeb beat him to a bad pun.

Din had several more questions for Odie, who answered them all with increasing intolerance. Din had another question but didn't get the answer he wanted. "Look!" Odie boomed, "I can't keep answering all yer questions all the time. Go back in my room and study the dictionary. It will improve yer language skills."

Lin just stood there, staring impassively. Odie just pointed his finger at her. "You, too. Both you guys go back there and read the damn dictionary."

They did just as the large man told them.

"Gee, evil stepmother bitch sir, wasn't that a tad hard to come down on folks that just recently was taken under yer wing?" Beeb intended to be staunch in his defense of the Ehliuns.

"Look here, man," Odie demanded, "whose side are you on, anyway?"

"The side of justice."

"Man, fuck justice! This is America! I'm teachin' 'em the way it's really done!" Odie stated.

"Who to bribe and who to pay off?"

"No, I didn't mention lawyers either."

"Sorry."

"I was speaking of deep philosophical truth the right way."

"Do it 'cause I told you to!?" Beeb was incredulous.

"Exactly!"

"Look, I'm not convinced that you know best, father, and I ain't playin' no Jane Wyman to yer Robert Young, neither!"

"No joke. I figgered you was a natcheral fer Kitten, bud!"

"No joke, he says, and follows with a no joke."

"TV or not TV? That is the...*holy shit*!" Odie suddenly devoted complete and full attention to the problem at hand. A VW was trying to occupy the same space at the same time, proving that the driver knew nothing of physics or driving.

Beeb, upon seeing that Odie would barely avert disaster, took over the commentary. "Join us for the feud, where once again our overbearing host will add insult to injury."

Odie mentioned to Beeb that he had rather deftly avoided the aforementioned injury while feeling compelled to deliver the insult to the obviously suicidal VW driver. Odie put the window down. "You fucking moron! I'll kick your ass back to the Stone Age if you ever get in my way again!"

The equally belligerent VW driver didn't seem to care for Odie's tone or message, and he fingered him an answer as he violently pulled in front of the motor home and hit his brakes. Odie whipped the motor home into the left lane and floored it only to cut back in sharply, forcing the VW off the road and into the grassy ditch on the side of the interstate.

The VW stalled, and the driver seemed desperate to restart it again. Before Beeb could even believe Odie was going to stop, he saw him disappear out the side door. Watching from his side window, Beeb saw Odie initiate an amazing scene. Odie had seemingly just materialized at the VW's driver's side door, which he ripped from its hinges and tossed away to assist the finger-giving driver from the car.

Some of the arrogance and enthusiasm that he had displayed toward Odie just seconds earlier on the freeway seemed now strangely lacking. It had been replaced by genuine fear, judging from the look on the driver's face. "Asshole driver, come on down!" Odie yelled in his great pimp of *The Price Is Right* announcer. There was always room for a little fun.

Snatching the driver from behind the wheel, Odie jerked the jerk from the seat. Picking the offending moron up by the throat and holding him at arm's length a foot off the ground, struggling like a gaffed *bonita*, Odie began to deliver a lengthy tirade against small-minded small car drivers.

Odie somehow delved into the use of flagrantly obnoxious bright colors used to paint these dangerous darts weaving through the fabric of traffic. He got off on a tangent about thinking ahead and watching out for the other guy and about how care and concern belonged together behind the steering wheel. He got so wound up in his lecture that he actually forgot why he was even talking to this extension of his arm, so he lowered him to the ground. And then he remembered this asshole had given him the finger.

Not surprisingly, Odie felt he had amply demonstrated his superior strength and intellect by holding this transgressor aloft for nearly five minutes and making no grammatical errors. Odie had yet to relinquish his grip on the man's throat, and he made no effort to break free, showing some small amount of intelligence on his part after all.

Beeb was planning his course of action when he turned to rise from his seat. He was prevented from doing so by Cat, very alert and very worried. "Jesus H. Christ and his brother Billy Bob! Beeb! What is Odie doin'? Don't he know that's a cop he's wavin' around by the throat?"

"A cop? Are you tellin' me you know that guy right there at the end of Odie's arm personally? He was just drivin' by just now. You could be mistaken, you know."

"I know that asshole very well, Beeb! He's Frisco vice. Busted me last year! He murdered my lover! Believe me, Beeb. Please believe me! I'd recognize that bastard anywhere. Please! Odie's life is in serious danger!"

Beeb still asked again. "He's a cop for sure, and you know him?"

"Yes, dammit! I'm beggin' you to believe me, Beeb! Odie will die as soon as he lets go! That asshole will shoot him. You too! Me too, for that matter!" Cat was doing her best to convince Beeb there was trouble ahead.

"Yer positive he's a cop?" Beeb questioned her again.

"He's a bad news pig! He'll kill Odie as soon as he lets go!"

"If Odie lets go. The guy gave him the finger. It's guaranteed to set Odie right off. He don't like it a bit, and I've seen lots of people sorry they gave Odie the finger. He's snapped more than a few offending digits."

Cat continued with her explanation of knowing the cop. "He always has a .45 in the small of his back—always! I swear to you Beeb!" Cat was as desperate as she could be to convince Beeb she spoke the truth. Now her eyes begged Beeb to believe.

He saw real tears well up in her eyes and run down her cheeks. Either she was a great actress, or she knew and feared the guy. Either way, Beeb felt the best thing to do was to be fully prepared. Toward that end, he selected his favorite riot control device: the Uzi. He pulled the keys from the ignition, pocketed them, and made sure the Uzi was loaded.

Cat was relating the story of how this cop killed her lover, and Beeb didn't want to hear it right now. He told her to sit down in the front seat and not move. It sounded like she could be telling the truth, but he could not afford to take a chance and lose this motor home. With the keys in his pocket and the Uzi in his hands, he stepped out the side door to see what was going on with Odie and the fool who'd fingered him.

Cat sat silently on the front seat, fingering the .38 in her purse. If he somehow got away from Odie and Beeb, she still had a clear shot at the man who had sworn to kill her. She also had sworn not to be killed by him, and if it came down to it, she was prepared to blow him away right here.

Beeb had the man in his sights when Odie finally let go of his throat. Quickly spinning around to grab at his concealed weapon, the VW driver's ears made note of very rapid automatic weapon's fire. His eyes confirmed a fury of stirring dust at his feet. His brain cancelled the nerve impulse going to draw a vastly outclassed .45. Freezing in his crouched position, he heard Odie's vocal abuse descend vehemently nanoseconds before it's replacement by physical abuse. "Are you fuckin' crazy or somethin'?"

A knee to the jaw straightened him up to where Odie didn't have to stoop to punch him. A staccato right-left-right combination decked the man with a broken jaw. He lay on his back, moaning and holding his jaw. Odie's first blow had shattered it. Odie was simply furious that this asshole was trying to draw a gun on him. Kicking in the fool's left kidney to ease him over onto his face, Odie had to question the man's sanity. "Are you fuckin' crazy or somethin'?"

Odie ripped away the lower half of the idiot's suit coat, revealing a .45 cradled in the small of his back. Cat cried out to Beeb. "See?"

Beeb nodded acknowledgment to her without taking his eyes off the moron. Odie relieved the man of his .45 but not before generously leaving him an imprint of it by stepping one foot on it and placing his entire weight directly on the gun. The fool groaned under this much weight. Odie was in a rage. He put the .45 a few inches away from the man's ears and fired off a round for each ear. "Sound good to ya, gun nut?"

Beeb began to fear he'd have to fire a burst at Odie to calm him down. "You *do* realize that you've pissed me off, don't you?" Odie screamed in the man's ears. "Imagine how the badasses in the joint are gonna treat ya when they find out you had yer gun taken away from you. My, *my!*"

"Yo, Odie!" came the stern warning, "that's enough. You ain't no LA cop. You've beat him enough!"

"Hey, man, it's cool. I'm cool." Odie backed away from the man on the ground toward Beeb and turned and smiled at his friend. "Thanks for coverin' me. Cocksucker would'a shot me if you hadn't been here. I really do appreciate it, Beeb!"

"Thank Cat, not me. She knew him."

The mention of Cat perked up the injured man's ears. Odie and Beeb hadn't noticed. Odie went back to his prisoner and made him get up and dance by emptying the .45 at his feet. "Dance you sissy city slicker!" There was always room for a little fun. Odie went to the rear of the motor home and bent the barrel of the .45 in the vise on the rear bumper. He'd used up the ammo, but the moron might have a spare clip, and why take chances?

Walking menacingly toward the guy, Odie warned him, "Now let this be a lesson to ya, asswipe! Don't never give nobody the finger on the freeway 'cause the next guy might not be as understanding as I am!"

To emphasize the word *understanding*, Odie flung the damaged .45 directly into its owner's chest, knocking him to the ground again. Odie hoped he'd struck home his point.

But as he looked at the man sitting on the ground with his legs out in front of him, there seemed to be something wrong with the guy's socks. Odie frisked him. In a leg holster covered with his sock was a .38 revolver that Odie discovered. "Well, what do you know?" Odie mumbled, fiercely punching the man in the groin with the newly discovered gun to indicate his dislike at finding yet another concealed weapon. Odie came to the conclusion that this asshole would just have to come to the attention of the authorities.

Odie meant to terrorize the fool now. He shredded the victim's clothes while he still wore them. The search was for more weapons. Left in his socks and drawers, he saw Odie toss his shoes up and shoot holes in them. Beeb figured that if Odie was this riled, the best thing to do was to ride it out. And besides, it was kind of funny to see Odie hunt Florsheims with a .38. Odie tossed the shoes high in the air then shot each one in turn twice. Just showing off was what Beeb saw, probably to impress Cat and maybe the asshole, whose gun it was.

Odie fired the last two bullets at the man's feet, striking inches away from either foot. He pocketed the revolver and walked over to Beeb. "Kill him if he flinches!" was all Odie said.

The injured man did not dare to move. These two were obviously insane. *No, no, it was Cat*, he thought. He'd get her for this too. He knew she was responsible for this. She had to be. She'd pay for this insult with her life. He'd sworn it.

Climbing into the motor home, Odie was sweetly greeted by Cat's hugs and kisses. She seemed genuinely pleased that Odie had come out on top. He knew it was just because she didn't know him well enough to expect it.

"I told Beeb that son of a bitch was dangerous!" Cat said.

"Yeah, Beeb said he was a friend of yers?"

"He didn't say anything of the kind!" Cat angrily stated.

Odie just gave her a big grin, and she knew she'd been taken in by his joke. What sort of a weirdo beats the shit out of someone who tried to kill him and then just jokes about it?

Rifling the man's wallet, Odie was trying to determine exactly whom he was sending to jail. That he was going to jail was certain, in Odie's mind. He scanned all the cards and papers for identification. Cat was telling him the story about her lover being killed by him. Exasperated by Odie's lack of attention to her, Cat shouted at Odie, "He's Frisco vice, I tell ya!"

"Well, what's his name then? You know the guy so well."

"Matte Villeplatte is his real name. Hard to say what that pile of ID says."

"Funny, but that's what *all* of it says."

"See? I told'ja I knew that bastard!"

"Bastard, yes. Frisco vice, no."

"What?"

"Well, babycakes, according to this ID card, the number A 009021 identifies Villeplatte, Matte, asshole that he is, as an agent of the FBI, San Mateo division."

"Jesus! You *are* shitting me, aren't you?"

Cat could not believe that Odie wasn't trying to kid her again, so she came around to look at the ID for herself. Emitting a low whistle of amazement, Cat could hardly believe her own eyes. "San Mateo? Damn, that's country-club duty! How could this buttfuck get in there? Who else could be that queer? He had to blow lots of somebodies to get in there. There's not a doubt in my mind. That queer cocksucker! God I hate that spineless faggot!"

Odie smiled at Cat, but she shuddered. She stared hard at him a moment, fear in her heart. "So, Odie, what are we gonna do? If he's a Fed, then we are in his damn jurisdiction right now!"

"Hey, relax, I got it taken care of. It's under control. I'll just have his ass fired, that's all. No biggie!"

Cat watched Odie bound over to the phone and dial Kathy's private number. Cat saw a certain smile appear on his lips when he heard her voice. She listened to Odie's half of the conversation.

"Hiya, babycakes, it's me!

"Yeah, I know nobody else calls you that.

"Uh, look, you still got that sweetie over at Justice?

"Uh, yeah, that sounds like you could count on him, then.

"No, I ain't in no trouble. Some asshole agent is.

"Well, let's not go into how I met him just now, okay?

"Look, Kathy, I don't wanna be pushy, but this has the urgency of an Uzi.

"It ain't no fuckin' wine. That's Ouzo! Uzi is a fuckin' machine gun!

"It means he's got a machine gun pointed at him, and it may go off unless you get him some help right away!

"Okay. A 009021, Villeplatte, Matte.

"Look, babe, let's act quickly, awright?

"No, no, you can't talk to him 'cause I ripped his tongue out. That's why!"

"Beeb has him covered outside so I could come and call you."

"You fuck an A. This is serious!

"Oh, how serious? I called you rather than just kill him. That serious enough for ya?

"It's, I80, about an hour into Iowa from Nebraska."

Odie smiled at Cat, whose curiosity had been piqued by this conversation. And this two-timing smile he just gave her, what did that mean? Who was the bitch he was on the phone to, callin' her babycakes and all? What kind of a powerful person was she? And who was this arrogant young man on the phone of a motor home, trying to bust a Fed? And what does it mean if he can?

Cat smiled back at Odie, but the meaning of her smile eluded him, and he knew it not. He assumed that she, too, loved him for his greatness. Everyone else did. Odie knew this. No one had to tell him. He was bright. He could figure things out.

"What?

"Yes, I'm listening to you, Kathy. I just missed that word."

"Okay, that's great! Shit, you should write movie and TV scripts. That's a great plot twist.

"Okay, listen up, babycakes, yer a doll, and I luv ya.

"Okay, the three o'clock news? Today? The usual station? Okay, I'll watch for ya.

"Okay, have a nice trip, and thanks a bunch."

"Bye. I love you too."

Odie hung up the phone and returned his mind to the harsh business at hand. Cat could see how quickly Kathy faded from his thoughts as soon as Odie said goodbye. She could see right through most people, read 'em like books. "Bye-bye!" Cat singsonged ever so sarcastically. "That yer old lady on the horn?" Cat was so straightforward when she said this that it caught Odie completely off guard, as was its intent.

"Huh?" Odie said, acting genuinely surprised at her accusation. "Old lady? Me? Nah! No. Actually, she's just the wife of a good friend, that's all. Why?"

"That's all? Just somebody's wife? Babycakes?" Cat didn't sound like she quite believed the boy.

"Okay, so we fuck each other's eyes out every chance we get, awright?"

"Yeah, that's more in line with what I thought!"

"Look! What's it to you what she is to me?" Odie knew jealousy when he heard it. Why Cat was jealous was beyond him. She hadn't even screwed him yet. She had no grounds, no reason for jealousy in Odie's mind.

The phone rang suddenly, interrupting the awkward moment that had developed. It was Kathy, pressing Odie for more details. He answered, "Sure, always glad to talk to you, sweetie.

"Yeah, we're just on the side of the interstate.

"No, nobody's paid any attention to us so far.

"The motor home is blocking the view is probably the reason no one's stopped.

"Look, he forced me off the road and gave me the finger, and I got mad.

"I jerked him out of his car, and he pulled a gun on me, so I took it away from him.

"It's a goddamn .45! I consider that to be a serious threat, yes!

Cat noticed that the story had already left the facts far behind.

"Well, I kicked his ass, and then I frisked him, and found a .38 on his leg.

"I took his wallet so I could see who I was sending to jail!

"I left Beeb to cover him so I could call you. I told you that already!

"Well, I don't know how a former Frisco vice squad goon ever got to be FBI, let alone workin' outta San Mateo!

"What?"

Odie's voice went up several decibels. "Look, Kathy, the motherfucker's got a ton of ID! He's got everything! There's a driver's license from California, social security, draft card, a library card—shit, there's everything from altar boy to some kinda machine society, Mattachine something. The card's real worn. Looks like it got wet or something. Anyway he's got ID out the ass!"

To herself, Cat thought, *That's not all he's got out his ass. Usually it's somebody's dick!*

"Look, Kathy, what is this third-degree shit? Maybe most agents don't carry all that much ID around, but this asshole does."

Cat heard Beeb outside, bellowing for Odie. She went to the door and told him Odie was on the phone to Kathy. When she got back to Odie, he was very angry. She missed some of the conversation but not much.

"Okay, Kathy, so someone told me the asswipe killed someone."

Cat smiled contentedly.

"He was a well-known pimp, huh?"

Odie smiled contentedly at Cat. She didn't even blink.

"Jesus, Kathy, I just don't believe this shit! You? You are gonna be jealous of *me*?"

Cat purred while Odie squirmed. Surely, she wasn't smiling because Kathy was after him for more details? Odie was wrong, but he didn't believe in the concept of Odie being wrong.

"Hey, can we argue later? I don't ever say a word to you about your myriad lovers, like the guy at Justice, but I bet you fuck him on his desk.

"In his chair, okay, same thing. It's in his office during working hours, ain't it? Hell, I'm tryin' to save someone's life, and you wanna bitch about it.

"Okay, fuck it! I'll just go kill the fuckwad and be done with him if that's gonna be yer fuckin' attitude!

"Hell, yes, I mean it!

"Okay, that's more like it.

"Oh, he'll be easy to recognize. He's the one in his socks and drawers, kinda black-and-blue about the upper torso, and he's got a broken jaw.

"Yeah, I'm sure, I heard it snap on the first punch.

"Honey, he pissed me off! He's lucky he's alive right now, dammit!

"Well, I gave him back the .45, but I still got the .38.

"Oh, service issue, huh?

"Yeah, I suppose I could return it just like the .45, no problem.

"Or I could send it to you.

"Yes, dear, of course that was a joke.

"Of course this is no time for jokes. Yes, dear, you're right.

"A chopper from Des Moines? Yeah, that oughta git it.

"That's right. He's on the side of the interstate, and he'll be the only nearly naked beat-up dumb fuck in the county.

"Awright, I luv ya, and thanks fer bein' there when I needed ya!

"Yes, I'll kiss her for you. Which lips?

"That's the same ones I had in mind too!

"Okay, bye-bye, baby."

Hanging up, Odie just had to smile at Cat. "She knows I have great taste in women."

"Yeah, I heard ya talkin' 'bout tastin' me!" Cat retorted.

Cat was really impressed with Odie so far, but she knew better than to let him know. She questioned him further. "Odie, did you really arrange to have him picked up?"

"Oh, yeah, and charged with attempted murder, assault, battery, carrying concealed weapons, improper lane usage, and general all-around bad judgment!"

Cat had to laugh at his audacity and nerve. Never before in her life had she seen such bravado dished out like that, not off the silver screen. She kissed him affectionately, and he ate it up. He was that kind of guy.

"So what are we gonna do about this asshole that killed my lover Pedro?"

"Don't call me Pedro, and we're leavin' him here for the Feds!"

"That's it? Leave him for the Feds?"

"Well, yeah! What the fuck did you expect?"

"*Well, shit*, I'd like to do something to him! He's chased me for months!"

"Well, since Kathy said I had to give back his service revolver, perhaps you could pistol-whip the piece of shit with it!"

Cat readily agreed to this and dumped her seabag's contents on the floor to dig through. Digging out some cowgirl boots with four-inch heels, Cat explained her actions. "Need mah shitkickers fer this!"

She went out the door, and Odie sat down in the shotgun seat to watch. Cat moved up to Beeb and kissed him on the cheek. "Thanks fer believin' me, Beeb. Oh, and cover me, okay? This asshole don't like me, and I damn sure don't like him!"

"What'choo doin' in them boots, girl?"

"Gonna kick the shit outta that buttfuck over there."

Villeplatte recognized his quarry and also the superior position she was in, backed by the guy with the Uzi. Cat walked up to the man who had killed her lover. And just before he spoke to her in what would have undoubtedly been a condescending tone, Cat had the good sense and foresight to swiftly plant a boot in his testicles. Only an aspirated bilabial fricative escaped his lips, as he dropped to his knees, and it was more of an *ooommmfff* than any meaningful conversation. Cat spun the service revolver around her finger like a gunslinger.

Slapping him rapidly across the face several times with his own gun to remove some of her pent-up hatred for Villeplatte, Cat suddenly jammed the revolver into his teeth, gaining his eye contact and undivided attention. She harshly said, "Pedro wants you to join him, right now!" She pulled the trigger, knowing the gun was empty.

Fainting, the agent did not know there were no bullets in the chambers, and he filled his drawers with the stinking remains of a Wyoming pizza.

Beeb had to laugh at the sight. "You cheated, Cat! You didn't kick the shit out of him. You scared it out!"

Still laughing, Beeb saw Odie approaching. "What's going on, Odie? Why'd you call Kathy?"

"Aw, that asshole is an FBI agent, so I called Kathy and got his ass fired. There's a chopper comin' from Des Moines, so we'd best haul ass. I don't wanna be interviewed and interrogated by the FBI."

"You mean again, don't you, Odie?" Beeb asked slyly.

Odie froze a moment and stared hard. "Okay, wiseass, again. I don't wanna be interrogated by the FBI *again*. Happy?"

"Yeah, I guess," Beeb said, shrugging his shoulders all the while. He guessed that Odie still didn't think it was all that funny, although it had been so long ago.

Odie moved toward Cat, calling out to her. "Yo, Cat, let's hit the road!"

Cat kicked Villeplatte goodbye a few more times until Odie got to her. "I said hit the road, not kick the toad!"

Cat continued kicking Villeplatte until Odie simply picked her up in his arms, struggling, and carried her to the motor home, all the while incongruously telling Cat not to get all carried away.

# Where to Now, Saint Peter?

Beeb got in the driver's seat, produced the keys from his pocket, and started up the motor home. They resumed their journey down the interstate. After a while, their chatter was momentarily drowned out by the characteristic *drub, drub, drub* of a helicopter working its way west. "Damn! You really did it!" Cat cried to Odie, her voice full of excitement. "They really sent a helicopter!"

Odie stared at her. "What did you expect? I told you what was gonna happen, and now that it happens, yer amazed." Odie glanced his knowing look at Beeb, who smiled.

"So who are you guys, anyway? You guys some kinda Feds yerselves or what?"

"Nope," Odie snapped quickly, "just got friends in high places, that's all."

"Bullshit!" Cat snapped right back.

"I don't believe the liddle lady's goin' for it, Odie."

"She got no choice *but* to believe it!"

"G'wan, Odie, ya might as well tell her the truth."

"Beeb, button that loose lip, yeah, before you sink the ship."

Cat looked askance at them. "Well, what's it gonna be, boys. Tell me the truth or tell me goodbye!" Cat hoped this threat sounded genuine enough to fool them because she had no intention of leaving this luxurious ride if she could help it.

Odie looked softly at her and spoke. "Look, Cat, the truth is, er, uh, well, Beeb, just exactly what *is* our truth?" Odie figured that Beeb started the search for truth, so he could say what it was.

Beeb tried to shrug it off, indicating that he had no interest in ascertaining the truth for Cat. She was willing to help them out. "I know, yer government witnesses, hiding out from the mob."

They both shook their heads no. "Okay, yer eccentric billionaires."

Again they indicated no.

"All right then, you are aliens from another planet."

"No, they're in my room reading the dictionary right now."

"Oh, fuckin' great, Odie, just great! Why don't you just go and tell her everything!?" Beeb said this so flippantly that Cat thought he was just kidding.

Odie glanced harshly at his best friend. "Okay, Beeb, I will! Cat, look, I know this is gonna be a tad hard for you to believe, and I really want ya ta hang with me on this one, awright?"

Cat crossed her arms impatiently and listened to Odie like a stern mother hearing her child concoct a fib might do. "I'm listening, Odie."

"Okay, the real truth is, well, are you ready? Here goes. There really *are* two Ehliuns from another world in my room right now, and they really are engaged in reading the dictionary. See, they got our language from TV, but they ain't quite got the hang, of it yet, so I sent 'em back to learn new words and all. Really. They're aliens, and they're here."

"Aliens!" Cat snorted contemptuously.

"Aliens!" repeated Odie.

"Illegal aliens," she laughed derisively.

"They are now!" Beeb muttered softly.

"Oh, and now yer in on this too, eh?" Cat included Beeb in her jeers.

"Unfortunately, yes, I'm up to my ass again with this guy," Beeb said, and pointed directly at Odie.

Then without warning, the CB radio started talking to them. "Odie, this is Pete. Come in, Odie. Over."

Beeb just stared at Odie a moment, too horrified to even speak. So many questions flooded his mind that he had trouble sorting them out so he could ask them one at a time. "Odie, what's the deal here?"

Odie didn't reply to his question, he only said, "Watch the road."

Then it happened again. "Come in, Odie. Over."

"Now goddammit, Odie. What the fuck is goin' on?"

"Later, Pete, I'll be with you in a while. Over."

"Odie! Who is Pete, and how can he talk to you when the radio isn't even...omigod!" Beeb's mind was suddenly overtaken by the realization that only one thing he knew of could be calling on a radio that was not on. Oh shit!

"Come in, Odie!"

"Uh, look, Pete, this is a little awkward just now. Could you call back later?"

"This is urgent! Over!"

"I said *later*!"

"Ooooodddddiiiiieeeee!" Beeb screamed his best primal scream at his oldest friend. "Is Pete what I think it is?!"

"Yes!" Odie snapped through his clenched teeth.

"Oh christ on a crutch, Odie, how could you!?" Beeb grabbed his head, obviously in severe pain from the terrible thoughts he was having.

"Would you two mind letting me in on yer little secret, whatever it is that yer talkin' about?" Cat was confused.

Odie very matter-of-factly informed her, "Pete is an alien computer in orbit high above earth. Pete is short for PETER, Permanent Earth-to-Ehlius Radio."

Cat started to softly chuckle, finally growing into full scale laughter. "Man, you guys sure know how to take a joke to the absolute limits. I'll say that much for ya. And I was nearly fallin' for that shit, too, 'cause old Beeb here really got me goin'."

"This ain't no joke, Cat, any more'n yer name's a joke!" Odie asserted.

Cat stared hard at him a moment, then glanced over at Beeb. Beeb just shrugged his shoulders of all responsibility for this *joke*, which he considered all Odie's doing. Cat returned her stare to Odie, who merely stared back. He remembered the old car salesman's axiom: after the pitch, the next person to speak buys the car. It worked like a charm.

"So I'm supposed to believe that you got aliens in the back and an alien computer on the radio in front?" Cat let disbelief drip from her words.

"Yes!" snapped Odie in a very irritated tone of voice, "yer supposed to believe it because it's true, just like I was supposed to believe that you knew that stupid cop back there because it was true in spite of all the odds being against it!"

Cat looked back at Beeb, who sheepishly hung his head and nodded agreement with Odie's silly story. "Et tu, Bruté?" she resignedly wondered.

"Yes, Cat," Beeb started in, "there are two aliens in the back, but this computer on the CB is completely new to me." The look he shot at Odie suggested that he was in less-than-total agreement with this new arrangement.

"That happened back when y'all was 'tuckin' each other in'!"

Cat sensed that Odie's words were of a jealous nature. Then it *was* possible that he felt strongly about her, after all. Her ego glowed just a bit. He did forget all about Kathy when he hung up the phone, she remembered that very well. She decided to go along with the boys and their goofy story for a while. "So, Odie, you mean to tell me that if I go back to your room, I'll see two aliens reading the dictionary?" Sarcasm laced her speech.

Odie noticed. "Oh you ain't got to go back there to see 'em. I'll fetch 'em up here for ya. Pete, send Lin and Din up here to meet and greet Cat."

"If you insist."

"Yeah, I insist. Why?"

"You should be made aware that the airwaves are full of transmissions about all of you."

"What kind of transmissions are you talking about, Pete?" Odie asked.

"Where do they come from?" Beeb had to know.

Pete told them, "The helicopter is talking to San Francisco; Des Moines; Washington, DC; and Omaha."

"So let me hear 'em ," Odie demanded.

Instantly, the communications were all unleashed on the earth-men in the motor home, as requested.

"Hello, Cat!" chorused the Ehliuns, who had been summoned to appear in front of Odie and his court. She turned, and she gasped. Aliens! There was no way she had believed...until now. But now, she had no time for pleasantries, for her name and her past were being discussed and reviewed by a computer...their computer, an alien computer.

"Pete!" Odie yelled, "just one message at a time, okay?"

Cat was stunned. The chaos ceased, and only one message at a time came through. Still, it rattled on and on about her past and spread it out in front of these people. Cat's past, the exact opposite of her outward beauty, reared its ugly head. She heard the sordid details outlined by the San Francisco Police Department over an alien air-wave. Eighteen prostitution arrests, eight drug arrests, no convictions, and thirty-five traffic citations in a three-year period inside the city limits. She heard a voice in the background tell someone to check in the neighboring counties for additional information. The voice belonged to Villeplatte!

She then heard yet another voice mention all her criminal associates and other nasty things. They were bandying this information about rather flagrantly, she thought. Good thing she was a tough cookie.

Odie glanced very knowingly at her. She just shrugged her shoulders as if to say that nobody's perfect. Odie tried to convey his thoughts about her with his looks and glances. He didn't care about her past; it was her presence he was most interested in.

Then from the tone of the conversations between the helicopter and the Des Moines office, it became apparent to the motor home's occupants that the Washington directive was being overridden, and the helicopter was very actively searching for the motor home to stop it for questioning.

"Pete! Where's that helicopter in relation to us?"

"27.6 miles and closing fast. Our window of opportunity to stay out of their visual contact range is rapidly terminating."

"Jeez! Yer English is really improved, Pete!"

"Thank you, Odie. The dictionary helped out a lot. You were right."

"Oh, hell!" Beeb murmured under his breath to Cat. "We *are* in trouble now! The computer is thanking Odie for being right!"

Odie chose to ignore these scoffing comments. He was busy thinking up some scheme to escape the predicament they were in. Fortunately, it was the boy's strongest suit. "Oh, Pete!" Odie tried his best to sound like Jack Benny asking Rochester to do something. "Please make the motor home impossible to detect in any spectrum on any wavelength. You got that?"

Beeb gasped audibly. "Are you insane?"

Odie ignored him for a moment. Pete had a question for Odie. "Will you teach me how to drive the motor home if I hide you from these agents who seek your whereabouts?"

"Oh, yeah! Sure, Pete. No problem, dude! You got it! Of course you can learn to drive. Just don't let anyone see or find us, okay?"

"I got'cha covered, dude!"

"Thanks, Pete. Yer a real lifesaver!"

"I'm a piece of candy?" Pete wondered.

"No, I don't mean sweet enough to eat like Cat here. I mean that you are saving our lives, like we saved Lin and Din's lives."

"All right, now I get your meaning. I see. That kind of a lifesaver."

"Yeah, right," Odie assured him, before noticing a shrill piercing noise.

"Oooooddddddiiiiieeeee!" Beeb screamed at him, forcing him to listen to what he had to say. "Are you real sure about what yer doin'? Yer makin' bargains with an alien computer that calls you *dude*? I ain't too sure about any of this, not at all!"

"Hey! I ain't so sure myself!" Odie stated. "But I *am* sure that a chopper fulla FBI agents could be a real thorn in our side!"

"True," Beeb agreed.

"And they very definitely know who we are, especially her!" Odie jerked his thumb in Cat's direction.

Beeb had to agree again. "Also true."

"So then what do we do?" Cat asked worriedly. The furthest thing from her mind was for Villeplatte to get his hands on her. That pistol-whipping could have been the straw that broke the camel's back. Nah, he'd kill her in a heartbeat anyway. That was just one more thing added to his list of reasons. The major reason was still that she was responsible for getting him infected with AIDS. So as unreasonable as it sounded, Cat was willing to go along with any plan to steer clear of Villeplatte, even one from an alien computer. She'd never heard of such a thing, and yet it sounded pretty damn good. "Well, boys, they know who I am, but they don't have your names listed on the airwaves," Cat said.

"You mean yet!" Odie blurted out. "Beeb had to go and holler my damn name while Villeplatte was still conscious. We must operate on the assumption that my name and this motor home will soon be linked."

Beeb sadly concurred with Odie's analysis. "Unfortunately, he's right. The plates on here are government plates, making it real easy to trace since there is only one motor home issued by the US government to anyone named Odie!"

"Which means by backtracking and checking phone records, Kathy could be tied into this." Odie said this without a trace of cheer or a smile.

Beeb added his two cents' worth, "So if we don't hide right away, we are in much deeper shit than whatever yer runnin' away from."

"I'm runnin' away from Villeplatte," Cat candidly answered.

"So we all gotta hide," Beeb stated.

"Hiding is not the problem. Staying hidden is the problem," Cat said from experience.

The boys nodded their heads in agreement.

"Odie," Beeb piped up, "what do we do about all the offices that the agents in the helicopter have been in touch with?"

Cat asked, "Yer babycakes lady can't bail ya outta this one, eh?"

Odie gave Cat what he hoped passed for a hateful look. He had come to a decision about the communications. "Pete, erase all their conversations. Erase the computer tapes, the tape recorder tapes. I want'cha to jam the radio. Put some sunspot static on them, okay?"

"You do not wish for them to communicate to or from the helicopter?"

"Right, and erase all that other stuff."

"Consider it erased, and all they can hear now in the chopper is static."

Beeb felt compelled to interrupt Odie while he gave him a mighty glare. "'Scuse me, Odie, you old hacker you, but ain't breakin' into an FBI computer just a bit hazardous to our health?"

"How they gonna find out it was me?"

"That is precisely what they are trying to determine at this very moment," Pete informed them.

"They are?" Odie wondered, surprised at their speed.

"Yes," Pete assured him, "they are at a loss to explain the loss of data, especially since nothing else is missing or erased."

"Just fuckin' *perfect! Odie!* Just real goddamn swell!" Beeb was pissed. "Another O. de Bienville well-thought-out crime! Damn you and yer sure-as-hell methodology, Odie! Damn! Now the entire friggin' FBI will be after us and with everything they can muster too!"

"Big deal!" Odie snorted derisively. "That's like a Model A chasing a Formula 1! We've already blown 'em off the damn track! They're beat before they can even get started. Don't you see that? We got it knocked!"

As usual, Odie was very confident. He moved forward, certain that time was essential. "Okay, Pete, here's what ya gotta do. First, bleep all communications in an eighty-one-mile radius. Then like the view of the spaceship wreckage not being there? Well, I want you to show the helicopter something that's not there. I want you to show them a flying saucer. Make a hologram appear, hovering just in front of them. Make it zoom off when they approach. I want the helicopter's occupants to see a sort of outer space Noah's ark, full of pairs of unknown creatures, like on that old *Star Wars* poster back on my door. And make sure that Villeplatte sees all three of us aboard the spaceship they are seeing."

"I'm way ahead of you, Odie," Pete said, "and Villeplatte is even now pointing out the three of you to his companions and fellow agents."

"Whaddya mean, way ahead of me?" Odie couldn't believe Pete or anything was *way* ahead of him.

Pete replied carefully. "You wish to make his behavior suspect, a bit bizarre, perhaps hallucinogenically oriented or altered."

Odie was stunned. "By god, Pete, you *were* ahead of me!"

"I heard Kathy recommend that course of action to you, Odie," Pete owned up.

"What?" Odie roared. "You eavesdropped on my private conversation?" He was clearly angry. "We'll talk more about this later. But from now on, you don't listen in on my conversations unless I ask you to."

"I hear all conversations."

"Then specifically ignore mine! Voice order! Imperative! Got it?"

Pete didn't comprehend why Odie was angry, but he didn't argue. He'd already learned that it was useless.

"Pete," Odie spoke up, "get us out of here unseen and unnoticed, okay?"

"Okay."

"Make that helicopter hover in the air, stationary for a short time. When the air force arrives, have them chase imaginary alien vessels, which simply zoom away from their sight at incredible speeds, understand?"

"Got it, Odie."

"Odie, how do you know the air force is coming?" Beeb asked.

"Pete told me."

"Who told Pete?" Beeb's question rattled Odie a little.

Pete certainly seemed to be right in the swing of things. Fleetingly, Odie wondered about Pete being impossible to handle in the near future. That was later; this was now. If they did not escape the problem now, later would not matter.

"Pete, I want those agents to see so many confusing things that it will take days to sort it all out."

"Relax, Odie, I got it under control."

"Well, don't let anyone run into us since we are invisible."

"You are not invisible."

"Why not?"

"Because you are under a hologram of that 18-wheeler that just passed."

"We look like a semi to everyone else?"

"Yes, if a semi is an 18-wheeler."

"Yes, it is, and where did you cop the term 18-wheeler?"

"From your Commander Cody and His Lost Planet Airmen tape. I sort of thought it was appropriate, actually."

"Oh, I see," Odie said, almost sullen.

"And I saw the air force launch some planes, so that's how I knew they were coming." Pete's remarks brought silent thoughts to Odie.

"Oh," he said casually, nearly lost in thought.

Beeb told Odie to trade places with him so he could go to the bathroom, then seeing the semi pass them, he snickered and prodded Cat with his elbow. "Look at that truck ahead of us! Pete must'a done our hologram with your mind in mind!"

Cat wasn't sure whether she should be insulted or pleased with Beeb's remarks. She looked at the caricature of a Bactrian camel with its tongue hanging out painted on the back of the trailer. "Campbell's Humpin' To Please" was all it said.

Odie burst into laughter. Things would never be the same again. He was sure of that. Humor had finally begun to make inroads into the Ehliun culture.

"C'mon, Cat," Beeb told her, "let's take the Ehliuns back to the table and play some cards. We were talkin' just yesterday about cards, and I saw some tumble out of yer seabag."

"Yeah, I got some cards. What do you know how to play?"

"What do *they* know how to play is the better question."

Din looked directly at Beeb. "What does play cards mean?"

"Ah, m'boy, you strike me as a poker player!" Beeb knew his W. C. Fields imitation wasn't lost on Cat or Odie. He just hoped Din didn't get it yet.

# See What the Boys in the Ditch Are Having

After an hour-long tape had ended, Beeb came forward while Cat went to the bathroom. Beeb had to begrudgingly admit to Odie that perhaps the insane scheme of hiding under a hologram had worked, and that meant that they had gotten clean away with tampering with FBI files and official records. So far so good, but was it good? He didn't know. Beeb was worried because he didn't know what to expect next. Actually, he didn't expect anything anymore. He just accepted that things were as they were. He no longer cared about why.

Cat emerged from the bathroom, and the card game reconvened. Odie thought about what had just occurred in the last hour. Pete had monitored all the airwaves just for them, and the official sordid story pieced together at the scene by the bureau and the air force left the motor home and its occupants completely out of it. Washington had confirmed that agent Villeplatte had been involved with some secret drug tests that had apparently gone awry. Agents from Omaha had to come to get agents from Des Moines injured on the roadside. Apparently, they had been injured by a UFO encounter.

Formal debriefing of the agents indicated only one was beyond help. Matte Villeplatte had been confined in a secret rubber room deep below Omaha. From his padded cell, Villeplatte wouldn't bother them anymore. He was stark raving mad. His claim was that he had been beaten and shot at by a woman he'd been chasing from San Francisco who escaped in a spaceship. She was accompanied by two men who had also beaten him and shot at him. They, too, escaped in the spaceship with several unknown creatures. He hadn't been chasing them from San Francisco and didn't really know where they fit into the picture.

He kept babbling about two guys...in a motor home at first, then it was a trailer. They were on the side of the road, and then it was in the ditch. It was a spaceship, then it was a motor home, then it was a trailer then a spaceship again. The intern who was assigned to medicating him had heard several versions of the story by now. As a humanitarian gesture, the intern joked with the drug-crazed spaceship observer. As he injected the raving maniac, the intern joked with him about things he had or had not seen. "I'll have a Sodium Pentothal, and see what the boys in the ditch are having."

The air force's complete report lacked any mention of a motor home. It duly noted that the FBI agents in the helicopter were completely disoriented. Although the pilot had safely landed the craft, he insisted to all who would listen that the spaceship landed it for him. None of the agents from Des Moines could say for certain how Villeplatte had been injured. They all thought he was that way when they found him, but they simply weren't sure. None of the agents' stories matched, another thing Pete had seen to. All the agents could agree on was seeing a spaceship full of different, strange-looking creatures of unknown origin.

Five totally incapacitated agents are what the FBI was dealing with now. Four air force pilots had seen a UFO streak away at their approach, only to reappear several miles away over SAC headquarters. There was a tight security clamp on the whole sordid story. Top brass wanted nothing to leak out about any UFO encounter. UFO had such a nasty ring to it, like something the silly magazines you can only buy at a grocery checkout would print. The reason the grocery chains carry those magazines is that stupid people have to eat too, and they already have their money in their hands.

Pete gave Odie the information as it happened, no altering of the facts. That was Odie's job, but Odie let the government agencies do the job for him this time. All of them were in the clear now. Only Villeplatte had mentioned knowing anyone aboard the spaceship he saw, and he was obviously deranged. None of the Des Moines agents mentioned any motor home or Cat or anything. They just knew their fellow agent was injured, and they went to collect him, or maybe he was injured by the spaceship. They couldn't be sure.

All the reports Pete could glean from all sources stated that four agents from Des Moines went to get a crazed agent, the victim of medical and drug experiments gone terribly wrong. Most were thought to be fit for duty again in a few months, all except Villeplatte. The insane one would never be okay after seeing spaceships in his condition. Why, he even claimed some of the spaceship's crew beat him up. The bureau persuaded the air force to let them borrow a rubber room for a while.

Odie felt secure that Matte Villeplatte was out of the picture now. Death would come before sanity revisited the guy, so on with the things at hand. *Got lots of power here. Might as well use it*, he thought. Odie quietly requested Pete to check out the records of O. de Bienville and Beauregard Elvis Edison Beaufort. The air force had dozens of files containing these names. It was like a rash on the computer.

The FBI files contained volumes of material on these two, although all of it concerned just one border crossing incident in East Germany. As Pete ripped through every file he could find anywhere in America under those two names, at the speed of light greatly magnified, it became clear to Pete that these two had been in trouble on three continents, but no files were found in the last ten to twelve years, indicating that they had apparently mellowed out. Pete found only academic records after the FBI files. After not being spies, they became good students. Odie had all the brains necessary to accept numerous faculty offers but none of the patience. Beeb was much the same, only tamer than Odie. So they pooled their brains and resources and luck and wound up where they were.

Pete decided to show Odie how much he had learned about Earth today. All the pertinent information he had gathered, he displayed on the windshield. Pete used the glass as a screen to show words, graphs, and even images, just like an earthly personal computer. Pete knew now what all computers on earth knew. He tapped into them. If it was electronic, Pete could receive information from it. Pete quickly learned to tune out certain radio stations and other sources of noise pollution.

Odie was very pleased with this display once he got over the shock of it suddenly appearing between his eyes and the road. He asked Pete to show him the details on himself. Again, he was shocked at the information contained in his files. Multiple clandestine border crossings into communist territory: theft and destruction of a US Army general's staff car, Greece; theft of auto, Greece; destruction of an Amsterdam tavern; rioting and inciting to riot, West Germany; impersonating an officer, impersonating military personnel, Pensacola; wanted for questioning about an unsolved murder, Ankara, Turkey; Under threat of death sentence, East Germany, Albania, and Bulgaria; disorderly conduct, several instances in France, Italy, England, and West Germany; thrown out of Libya, Egypt, and Sudan.

The FBI and air force files coincided only on the one charge that brought them both home from Germany in chains, under armed guards. Just thousands of pages were filed about this incident, which ultimately ended with both men rightfully being cleared of all charges of espionage.

Odie had trouble believing his eyes—all those charges. He'd never been to Amsterdam or Libya or Turkey. What all that crap was, was a mystery to him. The rest he knew about because he'd lived through it. He smiled thinking about all the stuff he'd gotten away with.

Odie then asked the computer he'd named to check on Cat Scheffanies, as her license said, to see what sort of woman she really was. "Pete," Odie whispered to the front windshield, "don't show me that stuff about Cat just yet. I wanna see if she'll tell me first."

The windshield assured Odie that it would wait. Odie privately pondered the monster he'd created.

Beeb came back up to the front to speak to Odie. "Odie, I been thinkin'."

"I thought I detected a strain."

"If the FBI examines the car Villeplatte was ridin' in, yer fingerprints will be all over the door you ripped off, on his gun, shoes, everything. We still got big problems here."

Odie was amazed that he hadn't considered all this before.

Din spoke up. "Pete has taken care of all these problems. He has erased all Odie's fingerprints. All the spent cartridges are gone. Cat's fingerprints on the revolver are also gone. Everything is wiped clean."

"They must'a seen *Hawaii Five-0* or somethin', huh?" Beeb said to Odie, nudging him with his elbow.

"Yes, McGarrett, 5-0," Din said to Beeb.

Pete added his two cents' worth. "Odie, there is no way to trace the car or Villeplatte's personal effects to anyone presently in the motor home."

"Ixnay on the onstermay, eh?" Beeb said sarcastically to the phrase's original speaker.

"Well, ya gotta admit it's effective!" Odie mused.

"Just wait till it works too good!"

"That'll be too late."

"Yes, I know!"

Din was unsure what this meant. He found so much to be baffling about earth. His reaction time was quite good as it was. He didn't know he had the humans worried with how quick he caught on. He didn't know they worried about Pete for much the same reason. He didn't know because he wasn't paying that much attention to human concerns. He was busy having a good time. Having fun was a new concept to Din, and he enjoyed it thoroughly.

A few minutes of silence forced Odie to speak, as if the pressure of the quiet somehow forced words from his lips. "Uh, look, folks, it seems that we are in a hideout mode for a while, but probably by later today, they won't be looking for us."

Cat spoke surely of her convictions. "They ain't lookin' for us now."

"We won't have to hide under a hologram unless we want to," Odie stated.

"And when do you think we can travel like normal people, getting out now and then?"

Cat's question to Odie was serious, he could tell. He smiled. "Well, babe, as long as no one discovers Ehliuns in our midst, I reckon we can go anywhere and do damn near anything if today is any indication."

Beeb felt compelled to speak up. "As much as I hate to admit that, Odie is right—"

"And he hates it!" Odie interrupted.

"I really hate it!" Beeb assured them, "but he is right. We can't let out word of Ehliuns in America, or our privacy is a thing of the past."

"Privacy!" roared Cat. "You dare mention privacy to me? That damn computer there told you I was a drug-addict thievin' whore! What else did it go and tell you?"

Odie simply couldn't miss this golden opportunity to tease Cat. "It said that yer skin is yer erogenous zone, that you were multiorgasmic, liked leather, and preferred to be on top!"

"Very funny!"

"Yeah, but how accurate?" Odie inquired.

"Well, not too bad," Cat grinned.

"Aha!" Odie trumpeted triumphantly.

"Now, Odie, what did it really say?"

"You don't know? Then you don't want to know!"

"Oh, yes, I do!" Cat insisted.

Odie's warning had not been well taken. So Bull Shannon–like, his tone suggesting compliance over personal disagreement with the request, Odie said, "Oooookay! Are you ready, Pete? Roll the details of Cat's personal life for her, all right?"

Pete listed the litany of charges. "Extortion, two counts, both dismissed, South Carolina and New York. Assault with a deadly weapon, one count, dismissed, South Carolina. Fourteen counts of prostitution or pandering for a prostitute, South Carolina, Georgia, Florida, New York, California, Illinois, and Texas. Thirteen counts dismissed or quashed. One conviction, Alameda County, California, six months served. Two counts of Burglary, both dismissed, Texas. One count of shoplifting, nolo contendre plea accepted, two-thousand-dollar fine paid, Fulton County, Georgia. Twelve counts of class A narcotics violations, all dismissed, Texas, New Jersey, New York, and Florida. Two counts of class A narcotics quashed, South Carolina. Five counts of possession of marijuana, four dismissed, one conviction, six months served concurrent with a prostitution charge, Alameda County, California.

"There are approximately fifteen other charges lodged against you under various aliases such as Anna Reksic and Frieda Charjya, but you never appeared in court."

"Thanks, Pete." Odie looked over at Cat. "Oh, and we even got a missing-persons report on you filed by yer mother in Milton, Florida, the day before your fifteenth birthday. You been a busy little girl, Cat."

"It was my fourteenth birthday. She told the cops I was fourteen, but I was still thirteen. They thought I was about to turn fifteen, but I was really about to turn fourteen. They made a mistake!"

Cat was upset, hurt, and angry all at the same time. She knew no one had ever known this much about her, and so much of what could be found out about her was all bad. She really wasn't like that, not anymore, not since she stopped using hard drugs. No more cocaine for her. That shit was lethal. Cat smoked marijuana now, the only drug she had time for. Pot wasn't addictive like coke or smack. Cat was ashamed and saddened by the knowledge that she looked so bad, so terrible to two of the nicest men she had ever met.

Odie could see Cat's plight. He felt somewhat responsible. He had genuinely not meant to harm Cat. He pulled her near and cradled her head while he caressed her hair. "Cat, baby!" Odie started in his best used-car-salesman voice, "don't let it get ya down! So ya fucked up a little—okay, a lot. So what? Hell, we got the death sentence facin' us in three countries. Not that we'll ever go back there, mind you, but it is a terrible shock to find out that there is so much to know about yerself, and it's all bad."

"Uh, excuse me, Cat, but uh, Odie, yo! What the hell are you talkin' about death sentences and *we* and *us* in there? What the hell's the deal?"

"We, us, got death to look forward to if we ever go back to Albania, Bulgaria, and/or East Germany, or what's left of it."

"Oh, well, Germany I can understand, I guess. Well, okay, the rest too then, but how come I die? I didn't do anything near as bad as you did, Odie!"

"Fuck you very much with yer attitude that I did all the bad stuff!"

"Well?" was all Beeb had to say.

"Well, did we ever go to Turkey?"

"Not that I recall, why?"

"Oh, I'm wanted there for suspicion of murder, that's all."

"Murder?" Beeb wondered a moment. "You get kidnapped there?"

Odie glared and gave Beeb the finger, bringing a large smile to the redhead's face.

"Oh, and I also got a charge of destroying a tavern in Amsterdam."

"So?"

"So I never been to Amsterdam or Turkey."

"Just a fuckup in the computers is all."

"Right, Beeb, like maybe the Turks we met could operate computers."

"Well, the Dutch can."

"Yeah, but so what? I still didn't do it. God knows I did lots of shit, but them two countries wasn't in on none of my action."

"Amsterdam ain't a country." Beeb relished correcting Odie anytime he could.

Cat wondered if they had said all this for her sake to make her feel better. She appreciated the thought, but she was woman enough to take these accusations from a computer parked eight hundred light-years away. It had been hard to face the charges in front of a judge. This was like taking candy from a baby. She spoke, "Look, I know you guys can't overlook my criminal record even if I ask you to, but this computer must be controlled. It can't go around ruining people's lives. What if I was unstable?"

"Oh, but you *are*," said Odie, patting Cat firmly on her lovely ass, "and I love it!"

She quizzically stared at him, unsure just what he meant.

Pointing at her ass, he continued, "You *are* unstable," as he whacked her butt. "Look at that thing quiver!"

"Never can be serious, can he?" Cat asked Beeb.

"Not often," he responded.

"Cat, you raise a valid point," Odie admitted.

"What, that yer never serious?" she exclaimed.

Beeb let out a guffaw.

"No, dumbass! Control of the computer! You didn't like the information about you, and Pete has already disposed of that information. You wished for your past to be destroyed, and that wish has been granted."

"I'd rather have a million dollars, if we're wishin'!"

"Well, the bad part about this—or the downside, if you speak yuppie speak—is that you do not officially exist anymore. No fingerprints, no criminal record of any sort at any level can be found and linked to you. You have no arrest record, no record—period. Even your real birth certificate was destroyed in a Florida town hall fire some years back. I just don't know what to do about getting you a new identity."

Cat was taken aback. She implored Beeb to join her side of the situation in a conspiratorial manner. "Geez, Beeb, talk about ruining somebody's life? Look at this shit, would'ja?"

"Yeah, now even the life you fucked up is missing!"

Beeb smiled as he said this to this lovely woman, hoping she would find some humor in the situation. She finally burst out laughing, a laughter that was a nervous release of some deep-seated fears. "I can't believe this!" Cat exclaimed. "Yesterday, I was a hunted woman with a secret past. Today, I don't officially exist, my past is public, and my present is even more secret than my past was! What kind of a future do I have at this rate?"

"We don't have any answers to that question just yet. The data is quite incomplete, so let's just deal with today for now, awright?" Odie wondered.

"Okay," Cat agreed.

Nods of agreement set things straight for the moment. "Uh, Cat, look here," Odie started. "We gotta discuss whatever you was runnin' away from Villeplatte for."

"Yeah," Beeb chimed in, "I wouldn't wanna pry, exactly, but what the hell is the deal with you and Villeplatte? Why was that low-life scum after you?"

"I really don't want to talk about it." Cat was firm in her refusal.

"Hey! I gotta know!" Odie demanded.

"And why is that?" Cat questioned.

"'Cause I can't have the FBI, CIA, Interpol, state police, bikers, gangsters, and or tongs out after me with a contract on my ass just because I'm with you, babe!"

Cat regarded Odie with incredulity. "Contract? On you? No one will be out to put a hit on you! Where'd you get that ridiculous idea?"

"Right from your cute little lips! You said while ago that Villeplatte would gladly kill you. Why, what reason does he have?"

"Matte *would* gladly kill me, but no one else on earth would, and certainly no one would be after *you* because of *me*!"

"I repeat my question: *why*?"

Furiously, Cat spat out the explanation, "Because the cock-sucker shot and killed Pedro, my pimp and my lover! Why did Matte kill Pedro? Because Pedro rejected the queer's advances! Matte is a queer with a capital Q! He's a dick-sucking cop! A dick-sucking vice cop who busted women for sucking dicks! And I got raped by a dyke bull in Alameda County jail with a shattered broomstick the night before I got out! It cost me over twenty grand for cosmetic surgery and splinter removal!"

Cat calmed down somewhat and went on with her story. "Villeplatte was personally responsible for that attack. Why? What was my crime? I was giving Pedro a blow job one night when Villeplatte walked in on us. His failure and my success with Pedro led directly to Pedro's death a few weeks later. Matte shot and killed Pedro in front of me and a VIP john. Pedro had arranged the date, but neither of us knew that the VIP john was just a setup from Villeplatte."

Cat changed positions and went on. "While Matte was shooting Pedro and telling him why he was dying, I knocked the john down and fled. I hid out in the gay community, figuring that he's not going to look for me in his own backyard. He had no idea. I had a gay friend who let me stay in his apartment because he hated Villeplatte too. Lots of people did.

"Well, he had a friend who had a friend who had a friend, you know. Anyway, the guy was a male whore who had been diagnosed as an AIDS carrier. Well, he's so angry that he's dying because of a gay lifestyle that he swore to take any and all the gays he could with him when he died."

Cat could see they were all engrossed in her story. Actually, it was kind of interesting, she thought.

"So when I got Villeplatte set up with the AIDS carrier, it was just perfect! It was love at first sight—for Matte, anyway. By the time it became obvious that the whore had AIDS, Matte had it too. Villeplatte up and killed the dude where he sat when he told Matte that the AIDS was a gift from me. The doctor who diagnosed Villeplatte as having full-blown AIDS told a friend of mine that he openly swore to kill me before he died. I swore he wouldn't kill me, and now you guys have made that come true."

She sweetly kissed Odie and Beeb on their cheeks before continuing her tale. "So I left Frisco after knowing positively Villeplatte had AIDS, but Matte had lots of contacts with the cops, the underworld, dealers, outlaw bikers, the gay community and so on. Apparently, he promised to let a biker gang go free on hundreds of charges if they could find me. I heard it from a reliable source and left the West Coast. Some biker spotted me in Lake Andes, South Dakota, with my friend Joy. So I was tryin' to get down south to Texas when I got that ride with the jerk truck driver you saw this morning, and I'm mighty glad you guys stopped to get me when you did. I had no idea Villeplatte was that close to finding me. That's kinda who I was looking for when I checked out yer ride offer, Odie. If Matte had come by and seen me hitchin' on the side of the road, he'd a shot me dead where I stood, I'm sure."

"Well, babycakes," Odie smiled, "I ain't gonna be that rough on ya. If ya die by my methods, you'll git fucked to death!"

"And die smiling!" she retorted. She gazed at this mysterious knight in shining armor, her savior and champion. She just could not believe what had happened. This guy had forever altered her life and her mind, and it was barely past noon. She'd known him less than a quarter of a day.

Here he knew senators and their wives, powerful people in government. She was a criminal from the streets. This was to be her fresh start, a new beginning, a new dawn. She would start over, have a new identity. It was all so sudden. Was it love at first sight? She doubted that, but it fit no category Cat knew about.

And what about Beeb? Another puzzle in this enigma to be considered. He and Odie seemed different as night and day yet somehow nearly alike. Cat imagined this to be due to vast amounts of formal education. And since she hadn't gone to high school, even college seemed so distant, so unattainable. Cat thought college graduation guaranteed superior people. She didn't realize how wrong that thought was.

And although she thought highly of both men, when it came right down to it, Odie was just something else. It had been a long time since Cat had desired a man like she did Odie and even longer since she feared such a want and need. Love had wounded her pretty badly. She feared the loss of her freedom, yet this man had just freed her from a life of crime dating from her childhood to moments ago.

Cat didn't want to come on too strongly to Odie. She was afraid that he might think she felt compelled to overcome supposed mental inadequacy with an overabundance of physical charm. Odie was afraid that she would make him come so quick that he'd die of embarrassment. Their mutual fears kept them from jumping each other's bones. There was no rush. It was early afternoon. They could hold out a few more hours, no problem. Well, a couple of hours, anyway. Okay, maybe till two.

# I'm Sorry, the Planet You Have Reached Is Not in Service at This Time

Seeing a mall at the upcoming exit, Odie went down the exit ramp and entered the mall parking lot. It was a few minutes till two, Central daylight saving time. Kathy had demanded that he watch the three-o'clock news—three Eastern time, that is. He knew which station she meant. Beeb did too. "Beeb, Kathy is sending me a message on the news at three Eastern. Why don'cha tape that for me?"

"Okay, but ya gotta move away from these power lines. Go over there," he pointed.

Odie moved the starcraft into a position Beeb agreed with. Beeb aligned the rooftop dish with the necessary satellite. He turned on the VCR and put a tape on pause. Everything was ready. Odie knew he would not miss Kathy's message, so he followed Cat out the door toward the mall. He still didn't exactly trust her. Taking no chances is the best chance to take. Odie loved mottoes. Always have a motto was Odie's favorite motto. Besides, he had a few bucks to blow on this babe. Maybe he could score a few points with her by buying her something nice. Little did he know.

Back in the motor home, Beeb was explaining the TV and VCR relationship to Lin. Once she figured out what was happening in the TV's reception, she helped Beeb out. She glued a chip to the TV lead. Now the TV's input was directly from Pete. They were tuned to channel P-E-T-E, coming to you from high atop the northern hemi-spheric ballroom, swinging and swaying with the cosmic rhythms. There was a different program on every click of the remote now. Beeb was pleased with Lin's work and told her so. "Now that's how to watch TV!"

Beeb was laughing at the spectacle he spotted through the driver's side window. Odie and Cat were returning some forty-five minutes after they went in. The sight of Odie covered up in pack-ages, emerging from a mall, any mall—Odie hated them all—made Beeb roar with delight. He got out the video camera and filmed their return. Cat found his behavior to be excessive. "It really wasn't that bad, Beeb. We made good time, under an hour." Cat found herself defending the expedition.

Beeb smiled as he informed her, "That's a record length of time for Odie to spend in a mall."

"That true, Odie?" Cat asked.

"Only by half hour or so," he truthfully answered.

"D'jew blow yer paycheck, Odie?" Beeb mirthfully asked.

Cat furiously pointed out that all the packages had been pur-chased with her own damn money! It was Odie's turn to laugh. "Should'a seen the struggle we went through when I tried to buy her a friggin' Orange Julius! It was sheer madness!"

"Some people have their own little quirks, okay?" Cat huffed. "I like to pay my own way. It gives me control."

Odie grabbed the remote and started up the tape Beeb had just made for him. After searching for Kathy's segment, he found it near the end. She had been at the airport, filmed on the tarmac just before a flight to Rome. She concluded the interview with a sentence that sent Odie through the roof. "After Rome, I'm going out West to look for my vacationing aunt Myrtle."

"Holy shit!" Odie screamed.

"Yeah, I knew you wasn't gonna like that, Odie. I just knew it."

Beeb was correct in his assessment. Odie seemed to be rather upset, enraged even. "Shit!" Odie yelled, "she said it right on fucking TV! This is terrible!"

"So what's the problem?" Cat wondered. "I can be gone before she gets here."

"No, no, you don't understand!" Odie looked deeply into her eyes. "This is not what you think."

"What do I think?"

"I don't know, but this ain't it."

Cat was angry. "Beeb, who in the fuck *is* this bitch that she rattles his cage so? And why is he babbling?"

Beeb noticed the timbre and pitch of her voice were probably altered by jealousy. He tried to calm her down. "Kathy is more or less personally responsible for us being out here in this very motor home. Her husband is a very jealous man, a US senator, whose signature on the official paperwork granting us permission to use this vehicle was given begrudgingly at best and mostly on the condition that Kathy and Odie never see one another again."

"Ha!" Cat laughed at the idea of Odie and Kathy not seeing each other forever or even the two years of the grant.

"I haven't seen Kathy in at least eight months," Odie said in his defense.

Beeb spoke up., "Now if Kathy and Odie get caught together, all hell will break loose."

"So how can anyone find us?" Cat asked. "Ya got nothin' ta worry about." Cat was certain of this. If the FBI couldn't catch them, what could a mere senator do?

"But you still don't understand, Cat!" Odie insisted. "Her old man knows she ain't got no Aunt Myrtle, and he knows I met Kathy at Myrtle Beach. Given time, even he could figure it out. Hell, he's got a staff! They do all his thinking anyway! No, I gotta contact Kathy somehow and convince her not to come looking for me."

"Why don't you just call her and straighten out this mess?" Cat asked.

Odie glared at Beeb for snickering at Cat's question. Then he answered her. "A, Kathy's on a plane to Rome. B, Kathy's not the type you can easily straighten out on any given point. And C, especially when it's contrary to her own point of view."

"The bottom line is she won't be worried about finding me here?" Cat needed to be very clear on this matter. She didn't need some rich bitch hornin' in.

Odie noticed she was distinctly interested in him by her questions about his lover. Odie spoke to her in a soothing tone of voice. "No, babycakes, you, she wouldn't worry about at all. The real problem here is that she isn't all that careful about covering her tracks. If she noses around and can't find me, she'll become very obvious in her search. That will draw attention from the wrong sector. No, the best thing to do is to call her in Rome."

As soon as he said it, Odie knew that Pete could provide him with a tap-free line to Kathy. That would be perfect. Yessir, old Pete was turnin' out to be all right.

"So what's all these packages full of?" Beeb wondered, hoping to get a new frame of mind started.

"Oh, just stuff to make me more beautiful," Cat teased.

"I don't think I can handle you being more beautiful," Beeb said admiringly.

"Yeah," Odie joined in, "ya look swell just as you are."

"What? No eye shadow, blush, mascara, or lipstick?" Cat was smiling as she said this. She didn't wear much makeup to begin with.

"I don't think cosmetics improve a woman's looks," Odie stated, sounding serious.

"Well, what improves a woman's looks to you, Odie?"

"My dick in her!"

"Nothin' but class, this guy!" Cat said mockingly to Beeb.

"It's the look I like best," Odie assured her. "Go with what ya know, I always say."

Cat glared at Odie, certain he could not mean such nonsense.

Beeb felt like adding fuel to the fire. Reaching into a cabinet, he produced a photo album. "Why, Cat, he's even got before and after photos in here." He handed her the album.

Seeing the photos labeled in Odie's handwriting *before* and *after*, Cat had to ask Odie, "Who's this?"

"Um, that's Frances R. Roanoke."

"What about the other girl?"

"Um, she's not Frances R. Roanoke."

"No shit!"

"I wouldn't shit you, Cat."

"Yeah, I'm yer favorite turd. I heard it before."

"I wasn't gonna say nothin' like that, babycakes."

"What does before and after mean over these pictures?"

"It means before I took the second picture, I only had one. And in the other picture, it means before she was ready to have her picture taken and after she was ready to have her picture taken."

"And the one that's not Frances R. Roanoke? The stunning redhead here?"

"She'll be my sister."

"You mean she'll be yer sister if I go for it."

"No, I mean she is my sister."

"What sister?" Cat asked harshly.

"Shit, Beeb, this girl ain't near as bright as I had her figured. She ain't familiar with immediate family kinship terms."

"Is this really his sister?" Cat demanded of Beeb.

"Really his sister," Beeb repeated her words back to her.

"Really his sister?" Cat questioned ever suspiciously.

"Yes, that is Odie's sister."

Cat shook her head negatively. "That pretty girl is not this ugly man's sister!

"Man, fuck you, man!" Odie smiled at her. He wasn't serious, and she knew that, but his pride was at stake, and he couldn't let her just slight him without acknowledging that slight.

Cat thumbed further through the photo album, sighting the redheaded sister with another redheaded woman. "You got two redheaded sisters?"

"Yep," Beeb answered for his old friend, "both of 'em lots cuter'n him too."

"I thought you was French, Odie, and you got redheads in the family. Must have a Mick in the woodpile somewheres."

"Probably from Viking raiders centuries ago. Warrior humped one a' them good-lookin' frog bitches, and it took!"

"Gosh, you make history sound so exciting, Odie!"

Odie didn't know whether she was kidding him or not, so he assumed she was. He'd give her the benefit of the doubt. Odie could be generous. "C'mon," Odie told Cat, patting the empty seat next to him, waving his hands at her. "I'll teach you that game you wanted to learn, liar's poker." Aside to Beeb, he stage-whispered, "She should be a natcheral!"

Cat cheerfully caught Odie's chin with her elbow as she slid in next to him, saying, "Excuse me!" milliseconds before contact. Cat had some knowledge of the game. In fact, she knew several versions but not the one that Odie and Beeb had played earlier.

Odie assumed she knew nothing of the game at all.

Cat felt certain that with these two, she had better set the ground rules straight right away. "I'll play with my lucky dollar, but I ain't givin' it up, win, lose, or draw!" She dug through her purse and extracted a well-folded worn old envelope. From it, she produced a dollar bill that conformed exactly to the shape of the envelope.

Odie gave her a quizzical look, prompting her explanation. "Old witch lady gave it to me in Miami—no, it was New Orleans! Anyway, I was twelve, and she was a million and three. I've had it ever since, and I'm not parting with it."

"Sure, sure, you can keep it when I win," Odie said generously, fooling no one.

"I'm just tellin' ya ahead of time," Cat insisted.

Odie waited to make sure that Cat was done talking before he explained the game. "Two pair beats one pair and so on. Three of a kind loses to a full house, and five of a kind beats all. Ready?"

"Yes, I'm ready," Cat smiled.

"Me too!" Beeb exclaimed, looking at Cat.

Cat looked at her dollar bill carefully. She had never studied the serial number before, but she had four pair. That had to be the winner. It had to be better than whatever these two had on their bills because it was her lucky dollar. Odie thought he had explained the rules well: only the numbers on the bill in your hand counted. Cat had always played the version where you could use a pool of numbers common to all player's bills. This way seemed like a snap to Cat.

"Now what's the matter?" Cat demanded of Odie in such a manner Beeb found to be very close to one Odie would use in such a situation.

He just smiled at her. Odie was fumbling through his pockets. "Yeah, Odie," Beeb asked, "what's the delay?"

"Glare," was the one word answer Odie gave them. After locating and adjusting his sunglasses, Odie looked up to see both Cat and Beeb glaring at him as he'd ordered. Odie looked over his bill through the sunglasses he just put on, hoping that they would somehow alter the serial number on his dollar bill. Nothing changed, so Odie finally spoke up. "Okay, I got two pair. What have you got, kids?"

"I got four pair. I win!" Cat said excitedly, snatching the dollar bill out of Odie's hands, while he stared dumbfounded at Beeb.

"No, no," Odie insisted, "ya gotta have three of a kind at least!"

"Not what you said, oh loser's breath," Cat argued. "You said two pair beats one pair *and so on!*"

Beeb chuckled his agreement with Cat even though it cost him a dollar. The point was Cat had taken Odie with his own words, no mean feat at that!

Beeb willingly handed over his dollar to a gloating Cat. Odie protested her decision to win. "Lemme see this four pair!" he demanded.

She allowed him to relieve her of the dollar bill. In the direct sunlight, Odie looked at Cat's lucky dollar. He peered at the serial number. And because of the chip glued in the corner of Odie's sunglasses, Pete could also see the serial number. Odie had never seen such a serial number before: E 10581058 P. Pete had never seen such a combination before either.

Odie suddenly lost his sight. He ripped off his glasses and threw them down on the table. Lin and Din began to scream loudly in unison. Odie's sunglasses lay on the table, flashing thousands of images per second on the lenses. Odie yelled at Pete. "Pete, what the fuck is goin' on? You gotta git yer shit together, dude! Damn, Din, what's goin' on here?"

Lin and Din continued screaming loudly. They appeared to be suffering from some unknown but extreme pain. Odie's question to Din went unanswered.

"Pete! *Voice order! Imperative!* Send all these signals around the universe and sort them out, like we did with the metal samples this morning. Remember, you reduced steel and copper to an electron flow?"

Immediately, the glasses stopped flashing, and the Ehliuns ceased their screaming. They looked puzzled but relieved. Beeb could not keep silent another second. "Okay, Odie! What the fuck have you done now?"

"I stopped the screaming, for starters. Now hush!" Then Odie ignored Beeb for the moment. "Pete, are you all right?"

"Yes, I am now, thanks to your suggestion of an electron flow. Thanks, Odie."

"No problem, dude. What happened?"

"Well, Odie, it seems that the digital arrangement 10581058 is the master access code to the entire chain of computers, the entire network known as the Ehlius Central Grid. I am now privy to all recorded and incoming information. I apologize for the inconvenience I may have caused you all. And a special thanks to you, Odie, for teaching me to distinguish between right and wrong. Now I have need of such information. Din and Lin will soon explain all this to you. In the meantime, I got work to do, dudes. I'm outta here. Catch ya on the flip-flop!"

"Oh, yeah, right! Hack man teachin' a computer about right and wrong! Swell, Odie. Real fuckin' swell!" Beeb snorted this as contemptuously as he could. "Now the next thing ya know, imperial starcruisers a thousand times the size of the *USS Missouri* will be seeking our whereabouts! I mean *damn, boy!* It ain't enough for you to break into an FBI computer already today! Oh, no! Now it's *intergalactic* breaking and entering! Holy shit, hack man! You could easily mess up a wet dream, Odie!"

Odie took note of Beeb's concerns. "Yo, Pete, if anybody, anywhere, anytime ever catches on to us, warn us immediately! Ya got that?"

"Yes! Don't interrupt!"

"Well, excuuuuussssse *me!*" Odie was in a huff.

"Does he have it comin' or what?" Beeb pointedly asked Cat.

"No doubt," she replied.

"Ah," Odie waved his hands at his old friend Beeb, "whadda you know?"

"I know that you have possibly triggered a war of intergalactic proportions, Odie. That's all. Nothing much. Hell, the day is still young. I can't wait to see what else can happen!"

Cat noticed a sense of tension existed between the two men who'd rescued her from her past. "Look, if all you two are gonna do is argue, then you can just let me out here at the mall." Cat had her purse in her hand, but Odie had her arm in his hand.

"Shit, girl, you ain't goin' nowhere!" He sounded positive. "Girl, yer in this deeper'n almost anyone!"

"*Me?* How the hell do you figure I'm in deep?"

"It was yer lucky dollar that tripped the computer into the main banks, don't forgit!"

"Oh, no!" Cat bitterly complained, "you showed it to the computer! It's yer damn fault!"

"I couldn't have showed it to the computer if you didn't use it now, could I?" Odie knew he had a point here, so he barged ahead quickly. "Now, look, Cat, I don't want to keep you captive against your wishes, but I can and will if you leave me no choice. We may have interplanetary repercussions in the offing, and you are part and parcel of it, like it or not. And if I gotta answer to anyone, anywhere, then your ass and your damn lucky dollar bill are gonna be there with me!"

"Oh," Cat said, as soft as her name, as if there was nothing further to be said.

Odie moved up toward the driver's seat, motioning to Beeb to go after Cat toward the rear. Since Beeb had been about to follow Cat anyway, he happily agreed with Odie's directive. Getting Odie to think something was his idea in the first place was Beeb's specialty, one he'd practiced for the better part of two decades. Odie started up the motor home and headed for the highway, looking for adventure and whatever comes our way as the radio sang out when he turned on the ignition.

Beeb caught Cat by the elbow near the kitchen table. He turned her around gently. "Look, Cat, I know the day hasn't exactly been normal, not for you, me, them, the computer—nobody. And there's little reason to think it won't get worse in a hurry, but hey, it's not my fault! I didn't wanna stop for you in the first place."

"And why not?" Cat angrily demanded.

"Well, just because of this very situation right here: intergalactic trouble, and now yer a part of it!"

Cat glared angrily at Beeb. She was unhappy.

"Awright, look," Beeb tried a new tactic, "the Ehliuns can't see the real America if there's a gaggle of media types constantly reporting their every reaction to fish, tacos, ice cream, flowers, or nuclear power! They deserve better, and so do you, Cat. You both deserve special treatment."

"Huh!" Cat snorted, unconvinced, especially by the last line, trying at the last second to include her in the special treatment.

Beeb tried yet another approach. He heard the TV droning on with a dippy '30s movie rattling forth. He repeated the dumb lines as the hero said them to the dizzy chorus girl. "I...I just wish you'd believe in me, darling—in us. If you'll just go along with me on this plan of mine, well, it'll all work out for the best. You'll see. Ah, yer a swell kid!"

Cat had to laugh at Beeb, mimicking the movie. The lines did seem to fit, however, in an odd sort of way, kinda like the day had gone so far. She thought about it. She didn't have anywhere to go. No one was after her anymore. "Okay, okay, what the hell! Count me in." Cat was happy that she had made the decision to stay. This was the ground floor of a fabulous adventure. She couldn't bail out now. "Now, mind you, I have my own money, and I pay my own way because I want to make sure I can do as I please."

"Okay," Odie yelled from the front, "as long as you don't want to commit any more pistol-whippings or cop beatings. In return, I promise not to rape or pillage your body without permission, and I'll even wash behind my ears!"

160

Cat correctly calculated that this was as close to serious as the boy dared to drift. Beeb nodded his agreement with her assessment. Girl was astute, Beeb had to admit.

Beeb suggestively suggested that he and Cat join Lin and Din. "Make it a foursome?"

"Well, not that kind of foursome, although I wouldn't wanna rule it out totally as yet."

"Well, shit!" Beeb said, catching Cat off guard. "If yer just gonna talk, I'll go drive and let Odie talk! That was his major!"

Cat couldn't believe it. Beeb went forward to drive, and Cat went aft to sulk. *He's just after my bod*, she thought. *Damn.*

She sat down quietly in the same room as Lin and Din. They were lost in thought and said nothing to her, and she said nothing to them. Odie came bounding into the room, full of excitement and unbridled enthusiasm, only to meet three sad faces. "Hey, real up vibes in here! What the hell is this, a wake?"

To Cat, Odie smiled. "I know yer just pissed at Beeb. Can't blame ya none. Git that way myself with the boy sometimes."

To the Ehliuns, he said, "Y'all better tell me what's buggin' you two."

Din spoke somberly for the pair. "We are rearranging mental patterns. You were correct in your assumption about corrupt beings in control, no matter what planet we were speaking of."

Odie was just amazed. Blindly correct, eh? "Well, Pete, you got some video of these corrupt beings?"

No sooner had Odie requested such videos than they appeared on the side window, which Pete had chosen to use as a screen. "Look," Cat cried out, "them guys don't have the baggy folds on the base of their skulls, like Lin and Din have!"

All four of them saw that this was true. Apparently, this trait was not common to all Ehliuns, for these were certainly Ehliuns sitting at some type of control panel. It was the board. They controlled the Ehlius Central Grid.

"No shit, Cat! Maybe the computerized portion of their brains are contained in the folds outside the braincase."

Pete examined Odie's theory and found it to be essentially correct and told them all so. "Everything in the folds is externally controlled, while everything inside the head is internal and controlled by the folds. The external suppresses the internal."

"Oh, I see!" Odie smiled, gaining enlightenment. "And then we released Lin and Din into the internal workings of their own minds by the judicious use of marijuana. Okay, in the folds lie regulation, but where do Rest Period impulses come from?"

Lin and Din simultaneously pointed at the beings without folds. Cat and Odie nodded in agreement. They settled in to watch how the board operated.

# Torture? You Want Torture?
# I'll Show You Torture!

It took but a short while of observing the foldless Ehliuns to discover that they had nothing but contempt for the living terminals. Din and Lin knew that they had been such living terminals of a computer network until today. Contempt had been learned from the dictionary, along with lots of other words. Odie cheerfully pointed out that Lin and Din *should* have contempt for the board. "It is truly contemptible, composed of slave-makers, and usurers of living beings, with no concern for the victims."

The Ehliuns had no practical experience with contempt, fear, or hatred. Cat saw this, and she wondered if Odie might not spare them this experience. Odie was adamant, however. "I regretfully inform you that I cannot, in good conscience, comply with your wishes. I realize they were most sincerely offered of course, but contempt is what they *must* feel if they were betrayed by their government. These board members are assholes, like Nixon, Reagan, and Bush. Nixon, then Reagan, and finally Bush betrayed the trust of millions of Americans when they repeatedly broke the laws while trying to keep the public forever ignorant of their incredible abuses of power."

Cat settled back to listen to Odie quickly change her mind for her. "Government that enslaves its citizens is rightly entitled *tyranny!*" Odie stated, expounding on his views about any government, not just his or theirs. "These two Ehliuns have no political savvy, and they *need* some, not to spare them from unpleasant information is my duty and their right, and it shall be done!"

Cat was surprised that Odie had quickly and smoothly gotten her to change her mind about the correct course of action to take. "Odie, you sure are a smooth-talkin' devil!"

"Gee thanks babe!"

Having comfortably settled in to see how corrupt this board was didn't take long, made the last three Republican presidents' administrations look totally honest. Watergate and Irangate and Northgate were child's play in comparison. This board was composed of hard-core politicians, dedicated thieves, and murderers. Congress suddenly looked good.

Soon, all four of them became aware of the great danger the board presented to them, not just to Lin and Din but all of Earth! Pete voiced the concern all of them saw. "Odie, the board is aware that Lin and Din are still very much alive and no longer subjugated by the Rest Period impulses."

"Does that mean they're on to us?" Cat anxiously asked.

"More or less," Pete answered.

Odie was nearly beside himself suddenly. "Yo, Pete, be much more specific! Do they know about us or not?" he demanded.

"The board members are aware that the two surviving living terminals that were sent to study Earth are no longer attached to the network of Ehlius Central."

"Are they aware that Beeb and I rescued them?"

"Well, no, not yet."

"Do they know about you, Pete?" Odie just had to know.

"No."

"Well, that's good, I guess."

"Odie, they are not exactly on to me yet, but they will be."

"And why is that, pray tell?"

"Well, Odie, it's like this. The board member who was responsible for the Earth-Study mission has been removed from the board for failure. But before he died, they tortured out of him the truth about what he had done. He had closed off all contact from his computer station. He was the one who shut Lin and Din off, and me, too, for that matter. If it were not for Odie and Beeb causing the judgment panel to make so many decisions, I would not be in operation today."

Odie winked at Cat. She didn't know how much he had taught Pete or quite what the wink meant. She knew so little about so much anymore that nothing made sense, but she just listened to Pete drone on.

"And especially you, Odie. Even now, you have total control over all transmissions to, from, and about Earth."

"You ain't mad about that, are ya, Pete?"

"No, of course not. I understand why you did that now. I will not override any of your directives, Odie. I need you to help me survive so that Lin and Din can also survive."

Odie was taken aback by Pete's statement. "Pete, yer a computer parked in space! Yer further away than I can travel in several lifetimes! How in the hell can I help you to survive?"

"You have survived a great many dangerous escapades, according to your record."

"You gonna go and drag up my record again?"

"Odie, my information tells me that you have survived over three dozen clandestine border crossings into hostile territory controlled by communist governments."

"And what's yer point?"

"My point is there are thousands who didn't survive a single border crossing attempt, let alone dozens."

"Hey, I'm good! I'm sneaky, okay? What? You wanna learn sneaky?"

"Not exactly."

"Well, what *do* you want then?"

"I want to know how you arrive at the decisions that you do," Pete explained. "I want to know how you think."

"Boy howdy!" Odie whistled. "Look, Pete, that's a pretty tall order. I don't know if I can teach you the essence of how I think. I really don't know that myself. I mean, we are talkin' lots of time on that subject. How much time do we have? What's the board gonna do? How will they attempt to regain control over Lin and Din?"

Pete answered Odie's questions as best he could with the truth. He had no idea how Odie would react to the information, which was one of the reasons why he wanted to know how Odie thought. It might give him a clue about Odie's behavior. "The board is discussing plans right now. The consensus favorite seems to be causing your local star to become a supernova."

"What?" Odie shouted. "Blow up our sun? Bullshit!" Odie was never one to take threats from anyone, let alone very foreign foreigners. "Hey, fuck that shit! They ain't blowin' balloons up, never mind any suns!" Odie was hot under the collar. "Lookit here, Pete! Does this board know that we are watching them even as I speak?"

"No, Odie, they are unaware of your existence at this moment."

"So we still got the upper hand then! Shit, this'll be easy! Candy from a baby!" Odie sounded a lot happier about the situation than anyone else. "Pete, nothing can occur on the entire network of Ehlius Central without you being aware of it, right? If the boards tries something, we'll know, right?"

"Right," Pete agreed with Odie, but Cat didn't.

"We might know if they try something, but how are we going to stop them?"

"Good question, Cat. Any suggestions from our home audience?"

No one had any ideas.

"No?" Odie asked rhetorically. "Okay, then, for starters, how far are we from you guys' planet, Din?"

"About six months travel time is required to get here from there."

"That's all?" Cat wailed. "Earth has just six months to live?"

Odie shook his head no to reassure Cat that he would not stand for that. She was little comforted by this gesture. "Pete," Odie asked loudly, "just how are they planning to make our sun go supernova?"

"They plan to use a laser beam to overheat the interior of the star you call Sol."

"And just where is this laser beam located?""

"On the exterior of the satellite I am housed in."

"What?" Odie shouted xenophobically. "Yer the triggerman?" Odie felt suddenly betrayed.

"Oh, *relax*, Odie!" Pete fairly shouted. "Do you think I would willingly superheat your sun until it exploded? I just told you I want to survive, and I wanted Lin and Din to survive too, didn't I?"

Cat smiled at the very thought of a computer scolding Odie.

"Okay, sorry, Pete. Yes, you did say something to that effect, survival of the fittest and all that."

"But understand clearly, Odie, that if I don't react to the command they will surely send, then they will be on to me too. They could just send technicians up here to do the job. They could safely detonate your sun from here and even watch!"

Pete's summation infuriated Odie. He was beside himself with anger. "Well, Pete, I've taken all I'm *gonna* take from these low-life bastards! You say they're into torture, eh? Well, torture I can show them, serious torture." Odie looked at the window, right at the board members who were gathered around their workstation.

"Pete! Open up a channel to those assholes, project my voice into the room from a mysterious netherworld, and translate directly into Ehliun for me. I want them to think I speak their language."

"I can translate for you," Pete said, "but they do not speak Ehliun. At least not what the living terminals speak."

This rattled Din's cage. "Pete, never again refer to us as living terminals!" Din testily said.

"Okay, that's fair," Pete agreed cheerfully.

Odie requested Pete to translate his remarks directly to their ears or whatever they heard with. "Okay, dude, yer live. Yer on the air. Yer on!"

Odie spoke to the board in an unkind tone of voice. "Yo, board buttfucks! Yeah, you assholes right there. You members of the board, shut up! Now you dicklicks just shut the fuck up and listen for a change! *I am Odie*, the great and all-powerful Odie! And I'm being brought to you tonight by *America*, the country that made Earth famous!"

Cat could not help herself, and she laughed right out loud. What a fool this guy could be.

"Now, if you morons think I'm gonna let you blow my sun up just to get rid of two living terminals, then you got another think comin'! And to help you with that think, I'm going to make all levels of life on Ehlius aware of my least favorite music! Yes, sit back and grimace. There is no way for you to stop it or stop me. Yer damn lucky I don't introduce you to Lee Press-On Nails!"

Again, Cat had to laugh. Now that would piss them off.

Odie continued his tirade. "For the next twenty-four hours, *It's Not Your Life* will appear in this time slot, so sit back and consider your next move. You might try Libya or Iraq, Iran, all about the same. Only assholes live there now. You'd fit right in! I reckon you can tell I don't like you, and I am going to cause you more grief and trouble than you thought possible! The next ten hours will be your introduction to three Slim Whitman records. Some sampler, eh?"

"That's awfully harsh, Odie!" Cat interjected.

Odie's rage knew no bounds. "They get ten hours of *Donny & Marie* after that!"

"Ooh, cruel *and* unusual!" Cat playfully teased Odie.

"They wanna eliminate five billion innocent beings just to preserve their own piddling asses! Don't forget that! They deserve harsh treatment, and they are gonna get it! Pete, start me up!"

His imitation Mick Jagger was lost on all but Cat, who just moaned and shook her head no.

Pete started drowning the planet Ehlius with yodels by Slim. "Out of the blue hoo hoo ooooohhh."

The sudden confusion on Ehlius was incredible! Billions of beings were awakened by horrid unknown sound waves lashing out at their very souls! The control panels in front of the board began lighting up like Christmas trees. Supervisor after supervisor was demanding to know what was going wrong and why something wasn't being done about it?

The board was in a bind. Half the planet did not know the other half existed. But now they were all wide awake and subjected to incredible misery! The board was finding out about a rock and a hard place. Over six hundred years of board rule was coming to an end. Their absolute rule program had just been cancelled by the network's new owners.

Odie had single-handedly started and finished an interplanetary war without a shot being fired, but it was not without hostilities. A solid day of such horrid noises would make Odie many enemies on Ehlius, but he didn't care. He would not have to deal with them firsthand. If they wanted to threaten, fine, he could threaten with the best of them. Odie gave them a taste of their own medicine. He saw no harm in pissing off billions of foreigners. Ford did it to Cambodia with the Mayaguez incident. Nothing ever came of that. Ford's still around. No problem.

Odie showed the board in no uncertain terms that he was serious, that he meant what he said. He was seemingly all-powerful all right. The board could not imagine anyone outside the board having that kind of power. They were worried and with good reason. All across the planet, widespread chaos dealt blow after blow to the credibility of the computer network. Supervisors were going berserk. The computer system they had trusted had suddenly turned against them.

The computer network had always told the supervisors that they were a select group of Ehliuns, whose larger brain capacity had enabled them to control the activities of the lesser gifted Ehliun majority. That no longer seemed to hold true. To the supervisors, it appeared that the impossible was now operational.

There were two sets of Ehliuns now: two sets of cities, jobs—everything. Whole cities had risen up out of the desert, domed over like the rest of Ehliun cities, but the deserts were supposed to be uninhabitable since they were contaminated with radioactive wastes...or supposed to be. Now it seems they have cities in them. Why had the computer lied to them for years, maybe centuries?

And most importantly, why were these horrible noises assaulting their hearing organs? Where did such sounds originate? What could they mean? Yes, some unknown creature was in its death agony. That much was clear, but why did they have to hear it? Why had the computer been in error? And what would explain dual populations, dual cities? Who was keeping two sets of books and why?

Many different levels of the night shift found themselves awakened by terrible noises for unknown reasons. Ehliuns were not used to anything being unknown. That alone scared them. Questions vastly exceeded answers. The entire planet's population all thought that they knew what was going on before now. They had all been attached to the same computer network, but incontrovertible evidence rose up outside their cities, other cities jammed full of unsuspecting Ehliuns.

Each group of Ehliuns seemed genuinely surprised to find out about the other. Both sets of Ehliuns were hooked to the same computer, but when they tried to find out what went wrong, they hit the board's terminals, which were shut down for the moment.

Lin and Din were simply amazed to see the secrets of their home planet divulged. They had never dreamed of such duplicity. Billions of Ehliuns joined them in their amazement.

The board had its hands full. The deceased Earth-Study overseer might have found comfort in the irony that his death was being avenged by the planet he had chosen to be the next colony in the Ehliun Empire. Key players in that irony were two beings he had casually tried to kill by flipping a switch on the panel in front of him. If only he had had an imagination, he might have lived to see it.

Cat and Odie squealed with childlike delight at the scenes Pete showed them unfolding on Ehlius. They were laughing at the panic setting in all around the board. They had become highly amused by the reactions of the board members to the chaos Odie had set in motion. Odie giggled, "Lookit them bastards squirm like worms on a fishhook."

"Yeah," Cat laughed, "they just can't believe this is happening to them!"

"Check it out, Cat. They're whisperin' like maybe we won't hear 'em that way!"

Lin and Din saw this statement was true. The board members did not have a computer link. This forced them to speak through their vocal chords each time they wished to communicate. Lin saw the advantage that they had with a mental link to a sympathetic computer, enabling them to silently but very effectively communicate. And Lin and Din could now think to themselves, something no other Ehliun could do…yet.

They felt mixed emotions toward Odie. That he was responsible for the conditions they enjoyed was undeniable. After he freed their computer the way he freed them, their lifestyle was better than before. Still, Odie had this nasty habit of laughing at them and their way of life. How could he be on two opposite sides of an issue? How could he have speculated the existence of some group like the board before the Ehliuns did? How could he know what trouble he could cause the board and then delight in causing it? He was a very strange creature, to be sure.

Lin and Din had to withhold final judgment on Odie, for they didn't know what might happen next. The possibility that they would *never* know what to expect had them worried somewhat as Earth was still a fabulous mystery to them, revealing complex secret after unfathomable detail. Still, given their druthers, they would have chosen to be where they were rather than on Ehlius during the discovery of music or something like it.

Pete switched their view around the planet, imitating the news shows of America. He gave them a few shots of reactions around the land, when one city rose up next to another city watching it. Close-ups were shown of two supervisors arriving at their workstation, only to encounter two other supervisors already at the controls. Pete gave them bits and pieces of their conversation, the gist of it being concern for where the excess production was going if two shifts were operating independently of one another. The idea of overcrowding went out the proverbial window, with the realization that there were twenty billion Ehliuns alive and well, instead of only ten billion Ehliuns alive and well.

Another city, another view of the same problems—what was going on? Who altered the data banks? What was that dreadful noise? Why was Rest Period interrupted? How could they have not noticed before? How could whole cities operate without computer control? Since they could not, the only answer was that the computer network was at fault. It was the main suspect. Why did the computer network conceal information, especially of this nature?

The rapid changes on Ehlius kept confusing the Ehliuns and amusing Cat and Odie, for they kept on laughing. And all across

Ehlius, everyone now knew there were two of everyone and everything. No one knew how or why. Lin found out from Pete that her peers were working fever pitch on the computer to determine exactly what was occurring. She made some suggestions to Pete to silently relay to them so that they could find the board's location. She kept this her little secret, feeling that she owed it to the other computer experts.

"Why are you so amused by the plight of my people?" Din suddenly asked Odie.

He was sincere, Odie thought. "Oh, I ain't amused by their plight, as you put it. I'm laughin' at the board. Yer people's plight is just about over."

Pete agreed with Odie on this point. "Two different groups of supervisors have hit upon the board's location—well, the switches, anyway—which are blocking the free flow of information. Before long, they will be physically able to locate the board."

Odie continued his train of thought to Din. "I ain't amused at yer old friends and folks up there, and I wanna make that perfectly clear. I'm laughin' at the board's plight. Them assholes been in power so long that they can't imagine not bein' in control. But now that yer people are aware that the board does exist, the board can't do shit about it!" He hoped the board couldn't do anything about it. Otherwise, it was their ass.

"What exactly does *shit* mean, Odie? You say it all the time, but it is not in the dictionary." Din looked directly at Odie for an answer.

"Shit literally means excrement, waste, fecal matter. But we use it to express disbelief or as slang to mean any object. It's a very commonly used word. It's slang, that's all."

Din knew what slang was. It was in the dictionary. *Slang* meant jargon or argot. It was a great dictionary.

Odie thought about the past all the way back to yesterday. Din had been recaptured by the Rest Period impulses. That was a certainty. Those impulses were very strong indeed. Odie hoped that the board would capitulate before the first shift went to sleep, saving him the trouble of finding out how strong the impulses could be. Toward that end, he gave Pete another command. "Pete, when the twenty hours of *Slim* and *Donny & Marie* are over, run 'em about four hours of old Reagan speeches. That should batter them into submission."

"Oh, hell, Odie!" Cat interjected, "hours of Ronnie babbling?" Cat was sure no living being could stand up to such torture.

"Hours. You heard me right—hours of the great communicator hisself."

"Goin' for the throat, eh?"

"Yes, I am. I'm aimed at the jugular."

"Well, what if that's too much abuse for them, and they go and *Jonestown* on you? What if they Branch Davidian themselves into crispy critters?"

"I rather doubt they will retaliate with mass suicide."

"Rather than listen to that much drivel?"

"Okay, Cat, I must admit that mass suicide might seem like an attractive alternative to listening to hours of Ron without Nancy, but let's hope for the best."

"What, that they surrender before Slim stops yodelin'?"

"Yeah, somethin' like that."

"Well, let's hope."

"You must admit, it would be lots worse listening to hours of Ron *with* Nancy."

"Yeah, that's a fact. I'll just say no to that possibility."

"Did you check your horoscope today to see if you could mention the Reagans?"

"Yes, it said distinct possibility of government babbling. Place cotton in ears to prevent bleeding."

Pete had a question for Odie. "How did you know about corruption at the top on Ehlius, Odie?"

"Simple. Voltaire said, 'Power corrupts. Absolute power corrupts absolutely.' The government of Ehlius is much like the government of the US, which may well be the most honest government on earth, and it's mostly corrupt. Hell, Roosevelt let WWII jump off because he wanted to end the Great Depression. And boy howdy! did it! He put millions in uniform, millions to work in factories producing weapons.

"The British had broken the Jap code months before Pearl Harbor was bombed by the Japs in a sneak attack. Only it wasn't a sneak attack to the War Department. They could read the official Jap Navy messages. Orders were sent on November 26, 1941, that the Japs might try something hostile. And on December 7, 1941, all the US Navy's aircraft carriers and their attendant vessels were out of the harbor on maneuvers. Only the old battleships and cruisers were in port, tied up two by two so even the nips couldn't miss 'em. All the submarine fences were open on official orders, and the torpedo netting was down, also on orders. I mean, why? Twelve days before Pearl Harbor, there is an official notice that the Japs might try something, and then you intentionally let the netting and fences down? It was intentional.

"A private radioed that he picked up about fifty planes headed for Oahu on radar, but a superior officer ignored the warning. Right on the base itself, the War Department had people intercepting the Jap messages right off the Pacific Cable, and they were told not to talk to anyone on the damn islands! More intentional stuff here, too, too many things to be coincidental. Roosevelt let us get bombed by the Japs so America would unite against them. It worked like a charm too. That is corruption, even though it all worked out for the best.

"Practically, everything we have in the US today came about because of World War II. Interstate highways, giant planes, missiles, space shuttles, television networks—most everything, in fact, is due to WWII. Back in 1963, President John F. Kennedy was assassinated by the mob, probably aided by the CIA. Nixon and his boyfriend Hoffa were responsible for that, I'm certain. I just can't prove it. But Nixon *was* in Dallas that day, no coincidence.

"We had a coup of sorts that day. Army was about to be taken out of Vietnam till JFK was killed. The next day, the Pentagon reversed their revised orders and decided not to take troops out after all. fifty-eight thousand men and women were doomed by that decision of the government. LBJ got to take over the job he wanted most in life, the presidency, but he had to take orders from the military. He didn't like that, so they injected him with cancer, and he died shortly after he left office, with American citizens none the wiser.

"Nixon became president because the Democrats were told to run some unknown loser. The Mafia helped elect JFK, then they killed him because he had his brother, the attorney general, try to destroy the crime families.

"That same Mafia that let Kennedy win over Nixon let Nixon win over the Democrat McGovern. Nixon would be their boy. He'd let the crime families alone. The Mafia hit their golden years, buying senators, judges, governors—anyone they wanted. Nixon left them alone because they left him alone. But then something had to be done. Gerry Ford, the only Warren Commission guy present when most witnesses testified what they had seen at the scene of the Kennedy assassination was getting out of hand. He had kept his silence all this time, and he wanted his reward.

"So Nixon got fired, and Gerry was appointed president by Nixon, the only man to vote for Ford for president. See, Nixon was a dumbass who could not believe anyone. He taped every conversation in the White House. Fool. He got himself fired from the cushiest job in the world. But actually, the mob got him ousted because they didn't trust him in a position of power. No crook ever trusts another crook. No one trusts Nixon.

"So then we come to Carter. An honest man, the guy can't deal with the dishonest government, and he only lasts one term. Actually, the Republicans paid the Iranians to take hostages of our people in the consulate and embassy so the Democrats would seem weak. Carter made the greatest mistake of his political life by not continuing with a rescue mission with the armed forces. Hell, they were on the ground in Iran, radioing back home for help about the minor problem they'd encountered. A helicopter slammed into a C-130 cargo plane, burning both up. The ragtop Iranians don't even know we're thinking about a rescue, let alone in the country. Carter chickens out, tells them to abandon the mission and return home without the hostages.

"Enter Ronnie, a nobody actor who was groomed for the presidency by being given the California governorship. Reagan was popular among the nonthinking set, so people voted for him because they recognized his name, not his accomplishments. He didn't have any.

Well, maybe Jane Wyman. Nothing else after her that would interest you.

"Anyway, Reagan is a guy who's always needed a script, so the Republicans gave him a script...and a VP named Bush. Bush was formerly head of the CIA. He was the real power in office during all eight years we suffered through Reagan. Then he assumes the title role for his own. How much should we trust someone who ran the CIA, especially when North was operating out of the White House basement and stealing money to give to the Contras. You know about the Contras—Common, Ordinary Nicaraguan Terrorists Reagan Admires? More bullshit thieves taking money for dubious results.

"Anyway, selling arms to our enemies to get them to give us back our innocent hostages is what occurred while the former CIA head is operating the government. Sound like nothing's wrong to you? I didn't think so.

"So to sum up, the CIA does nothing to stop Kennedy from being assassinated, even to the point of not allowing the Secret Service to check out the suggested parade route through Dallas. Windows are open above the route. JFK dies, the country goes on, the presidency is handed over first to one dork then another. Bingo, we're in the '90s and none the wiser. WWII survivors are all old and dying out. No one yet believes Roosevelt let the war happen on purpose. No one yet believes the CIA killed Kennedy. No one yet thinks Nixon is not a crook. Politics is crime at its highest level in America."

Cat had a question. "But, Odie, yer workin' for the government right now, aren't you?"

"Okay, yes, Cat, I am, but consider, as Beeb said to you earlier, mostly we are out here so we are not there with his wife and in the way. The senator is perfectly willing to spend taxpayer's money to solve his personal problem. The Ehliun board wants to take out Earth and our whole solar system just to prevent Lin and Din from knowing the truth about them. They are both tyrannies using the masses to accomplish personal gains. Ain't no difference! The senator could sit on that board with ease. He's got the same attitude toward the little guy. Fuck him!"

Odie's tirade against governments subsided. Hunger pangs brought him around. He wondered what time it was. Pete told him, "Almost 5:00 p.m."

"Where are we, anyway?" Odie wondered out loud.

Pete instantly replaced the view of Ehlius with the real view of outside. It was clear to Odie from the proximity of the tree limbs to the side of the motor home that they were not riding on the interstate. "Pete, lemme see out the windshield, if it ain't too much trouble."

"Done, son."

Odie just glanced up at the roof, so Pete could see he was looking directly at him. Where did he get off with this casual stuff? Odie didn't want to think he was responsible for Pete's actions and words, yet he feared no one else could be blamed.

Odie could see that Beeb was about to make a ninety-degree turn left, and just as he did, the road made another ninety-degree turn back the other way. Odie could read a road sign that gave the distance to Newton as thirteen miles. "Jeez, he's been drivin' for nearly an hour and a half, and we're still lost!" Odie was evidently disappointed in Beeb's navigational skills. "Excuse me," Odie said to the Ehliuns and Cat, "be back in a few."

# Boogie Back to Bragg

Odie confronted Beeb with the two-lane back road still under them. "Beeb, what the hell are we doin' goin' south to Newton?"

"Oh, hi, Odie. Nice to see ya. How's it goin'?"

"How's it goin'? Where's it goin'?"

"Uh, south to Newton, just like you said."

"Beeb, Newton wasn't forty-five miles from the mall we left ninety minutes ago, and we should have been going east!"

"Gee, Odie, that's good! Yer real good with maps and directions, all right. Yessiree, Odie, yer a—"

"Cut the *Columbo* shit and tell me what happened!"

"Well, the thing is, y'see, I got turned around, kind of, and I, uh, guess I went the wrong way at first."

"Oh, so you went toward Ames, and then you cut down toward Marshalltown, and then down this road we're still on, eh?"

"Yeah."

Beeb hated it when Odie was right without looking or even knowing what was going on.

"Okay, Beeb, since we are almost there, there's a steak house with a piano bar out on Route 6—US 6, to be exact."

"Okay, Odie, yer on!"

"I'll be back in a few."

"Hurry, 'cause I'm flat starved!"

"Me too!" Odie said as he went back to the room where the rest of them were.

As Odie opened the door and stuck his head in, all that greeted him was giggling. He'd never seen the Ehliuns amused before. He looked at the side window. He saw his butt sticking out the door, as seen from the windshield. They had apparently been watching him since he left the room. It seemed to him that the Ehliuns were finally getting the hang of humor. Cat had more than the hang of it. She flat knew what humor was.

She was a pretty funny lady, Odie thought. Yes, this had to be her idea. "Well, since y'all know what we are doin', whaddya say to a nice steak dinner?"

Lin and Din immediately declined. Neither one thought they could actually consume dead cow carcass charred over a fire made by burning tree bodies. They failed to appreciate the good taste the earthlings assured them it had. Why, the very description was in bad taste! Breakfast cereal was one thing; this was quite another. Burnt formerly living animal flesh just didn't sound like it tasted great.

It would be best for them to just watch TV. Perhaps Pete would televise dinner, and then they could watch the earthlings eat—maybe, if it was not too gruesome. They could not be sure just yet how awful watching such a thing could be, but it sure didn't sound too swell.

Speaking directly and only to Cat, Odie made it abundantly clear to her that he was buying dinner for all, and there would be no argument. He would not tolerate another tantrum, another scene in public over money. Cat agreed to let Odie buy her dinner. It was a major concession on her part. Odie didn't notice her sacrifice as he was used to getting his own way. In the mall, he agreed she should spend her own money. He hadn't invited her to the mall, but this was different. This was tradition. This was dating, a time-honored male tradition. He pays; she lays. Everybody knows the rules. He knew that. She had to know, he reasoned. She was over fifteen. She'd dated.

Shortly after 5:00 p.m., the sleek starcraft cruised into a parking lot bathed in the aroma of a steak pit. Lin and Din understood that no one was to see them. "Don't worry about a thing," Din told them.

"We will be just fine," Lin assured them.

Pete told Odie that he would blanket the windows so no one could see in. Thus reassured, the earthlings left the Ehliuns to themselves. They got cleaned up and dressed to go out in public. Cat slipped into a pair of satin slacks and a silk top. Odie admired her as they went out the door, gently caressing her derriere, remarking about its "abundant availability" in his best W. C. Fields imitation.

Returning the favor, Cat slipped into a Mae West voice, and she countered this thinly disguised sneer at her rear. "Say, is that a peanut in your pocket, or are you really glad to feel me?"

Beeb had to laugh at her antics. He noticed that here at last was a girl who could keep up with Odie, give and take. He could see that Odie noticed too, for there was this peculiar wrinkle in his brow when he looked at Cat. Not since that East German gymnast had Beeb seen such a wrinkle on Odie's face, and that affair had taken gunfire and an international incident to interrupt.

Beeb knew he'd best keep those thoughts to himself, but Odie had seen the gymnast at least two dozen times before getting caught. The memory made Beeb smile expansively, for when her father had caught Odie with her had, for Beeb, defined *incident* for all time. The hostess noticed Beeb's grin right away. "My, but you look happy this evening, sir. How many in your party?"

"Three," Beeb said easily, following the hostess to the table selected for them. He couldn't help but feel that all the restaurant's patrons were staring at them, Cat in particular.

She was right behind Beeb. Beeb couldn't see Odie wetting the tip of his finger and hissing like escaping steam when he touched his fingertip to Cat's rear. Beeb didn't know what the murmur was all about. He just assumed that they were all entranced with Cat's beauty. Lin and Din also saw what Odie was doing, thanks to Pete, but they didn't understand what he was doing or why he did it. Not knowing what Odie was doing was fast becoming familiar territory to them.

Once they were all seated, Cat had to ask Beeb why he was still smiling so broadly. "Oh, I was just thinkin' of somethin' funny. That's all."

"Well, share it, and we can all smile!"

"Um, I was thinkin' that this place has got as many good lookin' waitresses as the LongHorn on Lawrenceville Highway in Tucker."

"Yer lyin'!" Odie accused him.

To Cat, Beeb grinned, "Well, some of us won't think it's all that funny!"

Odie noticed the substantial amount of smirk evident in Beeb's voice as he said this. He was unsure just which of many incidents they had gone through together was the subject of Beeb's smirk. "Okay, son, what'cha thinkin' of. No harm will come to you for speakin' yer mind."

Thus reassured, Beeb simply said, "Nyla."

"Nyla?" Odie wondered.

"Nyla!" Beeb repeated.

"Nyla!" Odie suddenly shouted in a rush of recognition.

Cat could see that this was at least an interestingly named girl that Beeb had brought up. Odie just stared blankly at Beeb, unsure how there could be a connection. "That's right, Odie," Beeb prodded his memory banks. "I'm talkin' 'bout old Claviceps's little girl."

"Nyla!" Odie started in. "Oh, god, it's been years since I thought of her."

"How long?" Beeb questioned.

"Oh, god, it's been months since I thought of her."

"How long?" Beeb asked suspiciously.

"Oh, god, it's been weeks since I thought of her."

"How long?" Beeb persisted.

"Not counting the wet dream I had about her last night, you mean?"

"Aha!" Beeb stated, satisfied that Odie got close to the truth finally.

To Cat, Odie finished the thought. "I would'a had two wet dreams, but I fell asleep!"

She smiled at him mysteriously. "And who might Claviceps's little girl be?"

"Boy," Odie cut in, "ya sure don't miss them details about other women, do ya?"

"Well?" Cat demanded sweetly.

Odie grandiosely gestured over to Beeb, deferentially allowing Beeb to explain the story behind his smile. Beeb was up to the task.

"Y'see, Cat, Nyla was a world-class gymnast, the best student and only daughter of the world famous Romanian gymnastics teacher Claviceps Purpurea. They were then residents of a small town near the western border of East Germany called Eisenach. Bach was born there. If you read Peanuts, then you already know that. Anyway, Odie fell in lust with Nyla the minute he laid eyes on her.

"I saw her too, but his German was lots better'n mine, good enough to converse with her and get a date."

"She admitted she knew we were Americans, but she was hot for me and didn't care that we could be spies or anything." Odie's addendum didn't add much.

Beeb saw that Cat was enthralled with his story, so he continued with it. "So Nyla had this good friend named Asta, who liked me right away. Well, me and Odie snuck across the border lots of times, two or three dozen times anyway, always to double date with Asta and Nyla. So anyway, Cat, what I was smilin' about on the way in here was that I had not seen that look on Odie's face since then till now."

Odie smiled at Beeb and clasped his hand on Beeb's arm, recognizing the truth. Odie had not known it till Beeb said it, but he immediately knew it was true.

Cat *was* very much like Nyla, so sensuous that you can feel it, almost like a sixth sense. Nyla was lithe, limber, fifteen, full of excitement and danger. Come to think of it, Cat had not come into his life without a bit of excitement and danger. But Cat wasn't fifteen. She was twenty-three, more age and much more experience. That made Odie quiver.

Cat ended Odie's reverie when she spoke to Beeb. "Sorry, Beeb, I guess I miss the humor 'cause that story ain't all that funny to me."

Odie spoke up. It was his story. No one told it better. "What shithead here is smilin' about is what's funny, Cat, and he ain't told it yet. See, when Claviceps caught me and Nyla, he missed Beeb and Asta. They were down at the other end of the gym, down on the mats, down on each other, for that matter. Nyla was hangin' by her ankles from one set of rings. I was sittin' on the pommel horse, with a raging hard-on."

Beeb began to softly chuckle to himself, seeing very clearly in his mind's eye the day so long ago.

Odie went on. "Claviceps came in and caught sight of me rammin' my dick in his only daughter on alternate swings, and well, I guess it was just too much for him."

It was too much for Beeb, and he began to laugh out loud.

Odie kept on with his story. "Claviceps jumps up on the other set of rings and swings down on me from behind. He snuck up on me, so he gets my head between his knees, and he swings me up and down, letting me fly on the upswing. I skidded about ten feet across the hardwood floor, right on my hard-on! I mean it was floor-burn city!"

Cat was laughing by now.

"Then he hears me cussin' his ass out in English! Well, he's so mad that Nyla's humpin' anyone, never mind an American, that he just goes apeshit, starts playin' soccer, usin' me for a ball. No shit. Ask Beeb."

Beeb was laughing full tilt now, but he managed to nod yes.

Odie went on. "So now ol' Claviceps grabs me by the dick, pulls me up off the floor, and I got up quick too! His sweaty ass hands are pouring salt all over my open wounds too. He says if I wanna run, fine. He's got the part that offended him anyway. Hey, the sonuvabitch was outright strong, lemme tell ya, and I don't want my dick ripped off by no commie, so I'm caught, know what I mean? Freedom without a dick ain't that swell a prospect when yer barely old enough to get a driver's license."

Cat wiped the tears from her eyes while Odie continued his tale. "So Claviceps just drags me out to the street by the dick, where he calls the police."

Beeb jumped in, "And as soon as they were out of the gym, I grabbed Odie's stuff and hauled ass, but there were patrols everywhere by then. It looked like I was in a Nazi movie or somethin'. I told Asta to keep walkin' down the road, and I jumped into the bushes, tryin' to think up something to do."

Odie resumed his sordid tale. "So then the army or the police—I don't think there's much difference in East Germany—comes and hauls my naked ass away. Claviceps don't let go 'a my peter till two soldiers grab my arms. They march me to a stockade. One of my guards takes exception to the fact that Nyla's humpin' me and won't give him the time of day. He got into my cell, but I knocked him out with one punch. Three of them jumped me then, and I got two of them quickly. I got clubbed from behind just then, so I couldn't say for certain what happened next. I do remember a bullet or two."

Beeb filled in the sketchy parts for Odie. "I threw a rock into the back of one of his guards, and he turned and opened fire in my direction. I was up a tree, and he was firing at the ground. Two officers stopped him from firing and took his gun away. Then they went in and stopped the beating Odie was getting."

"Well, I heard gunfire and thought I was either being rescued or shot."

"After the officers stopped Odie's beating, dozens of troops came up. I couldn't storm the place, so I decided to get the hell out of there. It took me hours to get away from there and back to West Germany."

"Yeah, Beeb did finally try to rescue me, but it was much too late. I still wish he'd have knocked Claviceps out there in the gym before anyone knew we was there. After the army got in on it, it was over for me, or so I thought. Officers treated me right, however. They treated me like a spy, but at least I knew they weren't gonna kill me right away."

Very deliberately, Cat looked at one and then the other. Weird dudes.

Odie continued, after the waitress left with their order. "Now, the East German High Command calls the American High Command and offers to swap me back. They didn't make this offer until I had been subjected to five or six hours of interrogation, however. And my dad, told by the Commies that they got me, says, 'I raise ya ten bucks." See, he's playin' poker with his top brass buddies, and he'll get to me later. Fat chance I got of bein' rescued while he's on a winnin' streak, huh?"

"So what did you do all this time, Beeb?" Cat inquired.

"Well, my old man is playin' poker with the other top brass too, and he knows that if Odie is into somethin', then I'm in it too, so he leaves the poker game and goes home to look for me. I ain't home yet, so he's waitin' for me when I do arrive.

"The minute I get in the door, he's on my ass about Odie bein' in East Germany. I say, 'Oh, yeah, so that's where he went,' but the old man ain't buyin' this bullshit at all. Only thing he wants from me is to know how we got back and forth across the border. I gave it all to him. I drew him a map, detailing the fences, bushes—the whole nine yards.

"The entire high command is in the kitchen. They all came out and looked over my map. They were real pleased that they had a back door to the Commies."

"Tell Cat how they rewarded you for your services, Beeb."

Cat was very surprised. "They rewarded you?"

"Oh, yeah, big fuckin' reward! Funny stuff, Odie. Reward. To ward again," Odie just laughed.

Cat heard about the big reward Beeb got.

"Yeah, Cat," Beeb said, "they rewarded me all right! With a flight to North Carolina. Just me, the pilot, copilot, and four armed guards. We all boogied back to Bragg! A mere six hours after my dad caught me comin' in, I was en route to Fort Bragg, North Carolina. No more Germany for me, and I ain't been back since. Even if East Germany don't exist no more, I still ain't goin' back."

"Y'see, Cat," Odie jumped into the conversation's lead, "the Americans had caught four big-time spies just a few days before I got caught, major East German agents that the government was most anxious to get back."

"And guess who got traded back for all four spies, Cat?" Beeb asked, pointing fingers at Odie.

"No shit?" Cat asked him, nearly disbelieving his answer.

"No shit!" Beeb assured her.

"Really," Odie admitted, "I got traded back after two days of prison. All of Germany is a prison in my opinion, and I was deported directly from Mannheim to Fort Dix, New Jersey. Jersey ain't shit, but it's much better'n damn Germany."

Cat still wasn't sure what sort of folk she'd gotten involved with. Odie continued his tale. "Beeb only had four armed guards to help him cross the Atlantic. Shit, I flew across in chains and shackles, guarded by twenty gung ho types who were convinced that I was a spy and had tried to sell out American secrets to Commie agents. It was not a pleasant twelve hours, believe me!"

"Twelve hours?" Cat asked, astonished at the amount of time.

"Yeah, twelve hours! No Concorde for me, dear. I had to ride in an old propeller-driven piston engine C-130. My ballin' Nyla very nearly turned into an unpleasant international incident, and shithead here thinks that's funny."

Beeb merely continued chuckling, still highly amused.

"Did you get in more trouble after the flight home?" Cat mischievously asked.

"Trouble?" Odie said laughingly. "Ha! Like Orson Welles told Johnny Carson about the *War of the Worlds* broadcast back in 1938, and I quote from memory, 'I didn't know the meaning of the word trouble before then.'"

"'Hell's Bells,' Cat!" Beeb interjected. "We had to testify in front of several senate subcommittees, the Joint Chiefs of Staff, the CID, the CIA, the FBI, and every other three-letter agency America has, which is plenty!"

"Yeah, that testifyin' in front of hundreds of hostile people who don't believe you is a lot of fun," Odie lied. "I like being degraded in front of everyone. Yep, it was a real riot."

"Well, it *is* funnier now than it ever was before," Beeb noted.

"Oh, yes," Odie agreed way too rapidly, "it's only been what, fourteen years, and already it's starting to be funny!"

Cat knew Odie was not amused yet.

# Roadblock Tuherski

After dinner, Cat went off to powder her nose, leaving the boys alone for a few minutes. They were all stuffed. Odie knew that driving was going to be very difficult, bordering on impossible. He had been yawning the last half hour or so. Cat had noticed, he was sure. She herself had mentioned something about being tired after a big meal before she went to the restroom.

Lin and Din wished they would hurry up and return to the motor home, for they had several questions to ask. The most pressing question on Lin's mind was about the fruits with the shiny metal skin. She had detected so many wavelengths of a metallic nature emanating from the humans that she was certain that they somehow consumed metals, yet none of them had eaten the metal skins, only the hot white material inside. The skins still glimmered in the subdued lighting of the steak house, left on their plates to be tossed out like trash. She wished to know how metallic fruit grew. It didn't seem very logical at all.

When Cat returned, she slid into her seat next to Odie and grinned, opening her purse so he could see inside. "Thanks for dinner, Odie," she giggled, kissing him on the cheek, "and desert's on me!"

Odie could barely contain his glee. "You got whipped cream?" he exclaimed loudly.

Cat proudly announced, "And this!" She knowingly tossed a room key from the motel across the street into Odie's empty dinner plate.

Odie was genuinely surprised by this turn of events. The whipped cream had been lifted from the kitchen moments earlier. Beeb had to laugh at the look on Odie's face. She nailed him to the wall with that move, no doubt about it.

By now, several male diners were quite literally drooling over Cat since they could see what was going on, which is to say that there are a very limited number of explanations that could cover a flashy blond beauty waving motel keys and whipped cream in a guy's face in a restaurant, and all of them arrived at the same wish-it-was-me conclusion. Beeb volunteered to take Odie's money and go pay the check. The bill was over forty-seven dollars. Odie knew that, so he tossed Beeb a fifty, saying, "Tip well," as he did so. He knew Beeb would have to dig deep to tip at all. Arm in arm, Cat and Odie strutted out of the restaurant, to the relief of some but to the applause of many more.

Cat still clutched the whipped cream can and motel key in her hands. "It's a poor dog cain't wag its own tail," she heard someone say.

Another patron added, "Then that's the richest dog I ever seen!"

"That, my friend, is no dog!" yet another patron added, to much murmured agreement.

Odie just grinned, for it all seemed so funny to him.

Cat was steadfastly doing her very best to turn Odie on as they went out the front door. She had a longing in her eyes, a hunger, that another part of her eyes seemed able to convey to Odie that he could and would satisfy that hunger. The deeper he looked into her eyes, the more catlike they became. There was something about them, but he wasn't sure what. Lurking deep in her irises lay a piercing quality, promising an injection of true happiness.

Cat played the sex-starved seductress to the hilt. At the motel, she had the door open, dragged Odie through it, and had the door closed behind her in just nanoseconds. Bolting the three locks with one hand behind her back, never taking her eyes from Odie's eyes, she stripped out of her clothing in less than ten seconds. Odie's eyes left hers for a quick tour of her body. It was very quick. He was suddenly looking at the ceiling. On him like white on rice, Cat had him down on the bed, undoing his clothes with a precision that frightened his imagination as he calculated the number of times she must have practiced to turn in these record times. This was like some Olympic sprint.

Pampering Odie like a baby, Cat had him nude in short order, and she reached for the whipped cream. Odie stiffened in anticipation as Cat made a drawing of an ice cream cone down his stomach, the whipped cream spluttering out from the force of the nitrous oxide. As soon as she finished making the triple-dip cone, she licked it all away lasciviously, pornographically. Odie sensed his prurient interests were being aroused. Now here was a woman who knew what fun was. Odie was loving it. He was that kind of guy.

At long last, it was Odie's turn. He tried to return the favor and drew a taco for obvious reasons. Cat smiled at this childlike man whose mind could run amok at any moment. Her responses ran amok as Odie went down on her and stayed down. Soon, she began to wonder if she would go dry. Cat doubted she could come too much, but she was perfectly willing to try. After all, today, anything was possible.

She chose to try to grab for the gusto, to go for broke. What the hell, you only go around once, and if you work it right, once is enough. Cat did not believe that shit. Once had never been enough. She did not intend to start now. As much as possible had always been her guideline. Why alter what works for you? Run what ya brung, as they used to say in the race car biz.

"Care for a midnight snack?" Odie heard a soft female voice ask in a husky whisper. Jeez her voice was sexy! Grinning a yes with his eyes still shut, Odie felt Cat's inner softness sheath his tongue. He was instantly and fully awake and aroused. He felt compelled to tell Cat that she was on a record-breaking pace. "What's yer record?" she wondered in a voice that reeked of approaching gratification.

"Seven," Odie grunted.

Cat had to ask, "In a week?"

"In twelve hours!" Odie clarified.

"Oh!" Cat exclaimed, sounding very happy with Odie's answer. "Well, well, and I got you down on the score sheet for four already." Cat was alluding to Odie's love of sports, indoor sports included.

"And number five is fast approaching the gates, babycakes."

Cat adjusted her rhythmic movements a little, and Odie was soon in her complete control. She put everything she knew into action, much to their mutual delight.

Odie felt like he was getting near the end of the line, sexually speaking. He was tired, satisfied but tired. When she could talk without breathing so heavily that it interfered with her speech, Cat mentioned to Odie that they had until seven-thirty in the morning to squeeze in three more for a new record."

Odie didn't speak, but he knew she was serious. She sounded pretty serious. He suspected she knew that Nyla was the old record holder. He further suspected Cat intended to be the new record holder, but he wasn't as young as he had been with Nyla. That was fourteen years ago. Fourteen—damn, had it really been that long ago? Odie slipped off into a dream, a short dream.

"Do you think that I'm pretty?"

Odie realized that Cat was talking to him, intentionally pulling him back from the edge of sleep. "Of course yer pretty!" Odie mumbled sleepily. He didn't wish to be disturbed from sleep.

"How pretty?" Cat wondered.

"How pretty? What is this, a Carson monologue? Yer so pretty that I wanna kiss yer mama's pussy in gratitude! What sort of insecure game are you tryin' ta run on me anyway?"

Cat was taken aback by Odie's reaction. "Well," she stammered, "you haven't told me that you think I'm pretty. Oh, sure, you did say I was a great fuck, but I already knew that! But you didn't tell me I'm pretty."

Odie realized that she was correct. He had not been direct in his admiration for her, and he knew that women love to hear that stuff, whether you mean it or not. He knew what to say, something she wanted to hear. "Cat, darling, look! It's been a real weird day, okay? I really think you're a wonderful person to share yourself with me. Maybe I haven't said it in so many words, so here goes. Beauty is in the eye of the beholder. Beauty is only skin-deep. You got the deepest skin I ever beheld."

Very sensuously, Cat leaned over and kissed Odie as deeply as she dared.

"Now can I go back to sleep?" Odie wondered.

Cat bit him on the cheek, playfully but enough to cause some discomfort. Nestling her head amidst clouds of hair swirling on his chest, Cat closed her eyes and dared to dream childhood dreams where shining knights in armor lived. The damsel in distress blended with the alarming truths she had encountered today, giving her dreams a nightmarish cast.

Her dreams were confused, like an analysts' convention where the drinks were spiked with hallucinogens. The dream state where the impossible occurred had spilled over into the reality of the day just passed. As yet, Cat was not sure of her love for Odie, nor was she sure of his love for her, but the signs were sure there. She knew he was strong, intelligent, high-minded, and unyielding when he thought he was correct, and he had a nice dick.

Cat had never believed in love at first sight, and she refused to start now. Second sight had always been good enough. She drifted off to sleep, smiling. Odie tossed and turned, momentarily awakening her. She got a devilish gleam in her eye when she saw Odie roll over and expose an erection.

Odie was awakened in the middle of the night by some warm lips wrapped around his throbbing member. He was certain Cat wanted to set records. *No sense fighting the inevitable*, he thought. Go for the gusto. Dreamily, he could envision a football crowd, chanting for six. We want six! We want six! He penetrates, and he scores!

Drifting back into the state from which he'd never fully emerged, Odie thought there was one more to go. He didn't realize one would only tie. Cat didn't want any ties in her game. She wanted to flat out win. She had decided to be number one with Odie whenever he thought about sex. She rather liked the idea of coming to his attention so often. She would be the most, the best, the new record.

Odie dreamed he got raped by alien beauties all night. One dream, he found to be most intense, so intense that he awoke to find Cat riding him like he was a racehorse. "What time is it?" he hoarsely whispered to her.

"The seventh!" she hissed, not wishing her timing disturbed.

Odie didn't believe that he could come in his sleep, but he'd give it a shot.

Cat kept him awake enough to celebrate seven, just before 6:00 a.m. Collapsing next to an already snoring Odie, Cat knew the next one would be tough. It was beginning to look like a masochistic over-achievement. Once more, and she would be out of commission for a week. Well, two days, anyway. Okay, thirty-six hours, bare minimum.

But only an hour later, she found herself being gently urged into awareness by Odie's tumescence, pressing for entry. She then realized that he wanted her to be the record holder as much as she did. That additional boost to the ego, that extra surge of adrenaline put them both over the edge. Cat felt like Odie had unleashed a water cannon in her. Finally spent, Odie gave her such a deep tongue-lashing, ton-sil-to-soul searching kiss that Cat had to open her eyes to make sure it was his tongue.

Such hunger, such meaning, such desire after eight orgasms in slightly less than twelve hours just melted Cat's heart. Her eyes melted Odie. He had never seen such dazzling eyes before. They were actually yellow, with little gold flecks randomly scattered throughout the irises. Odie knew she could see right through him with those eyes. She knew he fell for her. He was helpless in his affection for her now. And this time, it meant a lot to her. This time was going to be different. She wasn't going to fuck this one up.

Later in the morning, Cat was awakened by the bed shaking. Odie was failing in his attempts to get out of bed. "S'matter, hon? Can't get up?"

"Yeah," he laughed. "I've fallen in love, and I can't get up!"

Cat beamed.

"God, I hope I can still walk!" Odie said, fighting his way to his feet.

Hearing the shower run convinced Cat she better get up too. She joined him in the shower. Odie held his arms out for her to give him a hug. At least that's what she thought until he just leaned on her, only looking for support and not comfort. When she pushed him away, he whined, "Well, it's your fault I'm so tired."

She lunged for his dick, and he suddenly found the strength to stand alone. She laughed at him. He knew she had him.

After their long shower, they climbed out to towel off. Cat dried herself and dropped the towel in the corner. Motels were so wonderfully organized. Someone else cleaned up. Odie busied himself brushing his teeth and offering Cat a new toothbrush from the bathroom shelf. He'd never been in a motel that gave out new toothbrushes before. He didn't think about Pete.

Cat wondered out loud where Beeb and the Ehliuns were. Odie allowed as how he was probably out on the parking lot. She opened the drapes to see. Beeb had parked right in front of the room and was even now staring at her through the windshield over a cup of coffee. She blew his mind by coming right out and climbing in the motor home naked as a jaybird. "Nice day," she smiled at Beeb.

"Beautiful mornin' so far!" he drawled. He keenly observed Cat dig through her seabag for some fresh clothing. She had set her legs a foot apart and was bent over from the waist. He could see a pornographic sight, one you couldn't normally see, except for such magazines as those that are solely geared for such displays. Such a display had Beeb up and excited.

Cat came up with a pair of cutoffs, completely minus the legs and half the rear pockets. She found a thin cotton undershirt like her uncle Tom used to wear, no sleeves, deeply cut armpits, gauze-like ribbed cotton. On Cat, it looked great. She was ready for the day.

Beeb was ready for Cat. These cutoffs were at least two inches shorter than the ones she had on hitchhiking, and no single man in his right nongay mind would have let her stand there in those shorts. These were illegal. When she sat down at the table, Beeb could see her inner lips. There was about a half inch of material between her legs, not nearly enough to cover the wide spot which drew his eyes like a magnet draws steel.

Beeb sat there and pondered this display of femininity. He was erect and bothered. She didn't notice. She was chock-full of Odie right now. Nothing else would enter her mind, much less where Beeb was staring. Had she noticed, she would not have let him get so unnecessarily excited, not as worn out as she was, no way.

Odie emerged from his morning dump to find the maid blushing and quickly exiting. Cat had left the door wide open. Odie saw her clothes strung out across the floor, where she'd dropped them last night. Odie heard the diesel roar to life aboard the starcraft. Hurriedly, he dressed, lest Beeb abandon him so he could have Cat all to himself. Odie knew Beeb well enough to know it was a distinct possibility.

He scooped up Cat's clothes as he went out the door. The motor home was backing up as he came out the motel room door. He could see that Beeb was teasing him. At least he hoped it was a tease. But still, he had to dive through the open door as Beeb eased out onto US 6, heading east.

The sun stormed through the windshield at blinding speed with the brights on. Beeb asked Pete to activate the sun visor mode to darken the glass where the sunlight was brightest. Pete darkened the glass until Beeb said it was fine. Pete rather liked this new arrangement where he served human needs and demands. They were so easy to please. It took so little to overwhelm them.

Rolling along the Iowa two-lane highway, the Ehliuns became fascinated with the ever-changing scenery. Odie had Beeb stop by a creek crossing so Lin and Din could feel the water and the grass. Odie was still quite lost with their grasp of things. Some things they knew; others baffled them. Odie had no idea why or which things were which, but he was learning.

As they sat on the creek side, Odie taught them about life-forms they saw. Insects amazed them. Nothing like this existed on their planet. Lin saw a dragonfly land on her hand. She was fascinated with the creature. A butterfly came by. There were flies, mosquitoes, birds—all sorts of flying insects and creatures. There were so many different types of plants as well. Odie didn't know the many names of all the plants and told them they would have to read many books to find all the answers to their questions.

They got back onboard the starcraft and headed out again. Odie started explaining things again as they passed by. The Ehliuns learned about mail, mailboxes, what rural routes were, what rural life was, and what farms were. Odie could tell them so much about life on earth that they stopped asking questions and just took in what he told them. Anything he saw, he had something to say about it. Such was the case of a mailbox simply labeled: Z. F. Tuherski.

Odie had to holler up at Beeb to see if he had also seen the name. "Z. F. Tuherski? You mean that's where old Roadblock lives?" Smiling to himself, Odie knew Beeb had indeed seen the man's name and knew who he was.

Beeb was nearly as aware as himself, he thought. Cat's curiosity got to her. "Odie, who did you say lived back there?"

"Roadblock Tuherski."

"Who the hell is Roadblock Tuherski?"

"Well, he was one of the early greats of the National Football League."

Cat prided herself on the extensive knowledge she had of the game, but she had never heard of this guy. "What era did he play in, Odie? Were they the Bears or the Staleys?"

Odie regarded Cat quietly, shock registered upon his face. "My god, girl, you know about football?"

"Some."

"Old Roadblock played for the Portsmouth Spartans," Odie told her.

"Obviously before they became the Detroit Lions in the early '30s."

Odie was impressed. Up to a point. "You know that stuff, and you never heard of Roadblock Tuherski?"

"Nope!"

Odie warmed to his task. "Why, Roadblock revolutionized line play! I mean, that he was stalwart in his style of play is reflected in his nickname. Roadblock—sound like somethin' in the way to you?"

"Oh, I see!" Cat said sarcastically. She didn't know who the guy was, and no amount of his explaining it would alter that.

Odie still continued to tell her about Tuherski. "He reinvented line play. He was the original reason for doubling up blockers on a running play. They'd slam into Tuherski, and he'd just stand there, like a roadblock, waiting for the ball carrier."

"Sorry Odie, I just never heard of him before today."

Lin and Din asked more about football as it seemed to be important to Odie. The rest of the trip to Amana Colonies was spent explaining football to them. They soon became sorry they asked. Football was mothballed in favor of history upon arrival at South Amana. Then history was mothballed in favor of lunacy, to Cat's ears, when she heard Beeb and Odie's exchange concerning the signpost showing where all the various Amanas were. "Hey, we got'cher South Amana, East Amana—"

"West Amana, ho!"

"High Amana, Low Amana—"

"Old Amana, Yo!"

"Middle Amana, plain Amana—"

"And Refrigerator Amana!"

"Man, oh manna, it's Amana!"

Cat begged them to spare the Ehliuns from such drivel, and she would appreciate it as well. She concluded by telling them she needed a few minutes with the Ehliuns to get ready. She led them by the hand toward the rear bedroom. Beeb parked the motor home on the dusty parking lot. Then he sat back with Odie and wondered what Cat was up to.

Once Cat got them back to the rear, she gathered up the packages she had purchased yesterday and unwrapped them for the Ehliuns. She placed a wig here, a dress there, some false eyelashes and fingernails, some makeup, and presto! Lin and Din looked like two Chinese ladies on tour. She led them up front for the boys to admire her handiwork.

The boys were quite pleased with Cat's ingenuity, and they kissed her happily to say so. She just smiled, pleased with herself, knowing that they were, of course, right. Together, the five of them stepped out of the special motor home to stroll about amongst the exhibits of a lifestyle no longer in vogue since the advent of electricity.

As they drifted from one building to another, the Ehliuns began to piece together the idea of living more primitively than any other civilization they had ever encountered. All around them were examples of handmade clothing, candles, farm implements, tools, and furniture. They began to assimilate the ideas of wood-stove-cooked breakfasts and horse-drawn plows.

Here were historical reminders of an age barely one hundred years past and already hopelessly outmoded. The past did not exist on Ehlius. Lin and Din noticed that by seeing the past on earth. Ehlius had no museums, no ancient cities brimming with objects no longer in use. How long had most of them been the slaves of a few on Ehlius? How old was their own civilization? They didn't know. There were no artifacts, no history, no stories. No information existed.

But here on earth, all around them, they saw people in contact with their own past. It was awesome to the Ehliuns. Here was history that you could reach out and touch. Here were things made by hand for a specific purpose that had been made well enough to have been thoroughly used and still survived a century later, displayed for everyone's enjoyment. The impossible still occurred at a regular rate here on earth.

# Where They Got the Lead Out

Shortly after they left Homestead, headed for another of the Amanas, Pete made an announcement to them all. "Odie, at 11:17:43 Central daylight saving time, the members of the board of Ehlius requested a meeting with you."

"Hey!" Cat cried out, hugging Odie around the neck. "They surrendered! God, I forgot all about them!"

Beeb did not know what that meant or what was going on. The fact that Cat did and he didn't bothered him a great deal since she didn't know Odie nearly as well as he did. "Who surrendered, Odie! And exactly what does that mean?"

Odie waved Beeb's question off with a hand gesture and spoke to Pete. "Pete, what did you tell them?"

"Nothing. They want to talk to you, Odie. They await your reply."

"Well, what did they tell you then?"

"They said if you would cease and desist with the terrible noises, that some compromise could be worked out. They said they would share power with you."

Beeb was beside himself with anger. No one would answer him. "What fucking noises? Goddamnit, Odie, what are you doin'?"

Cat sought to soothe his feelings some. "Odie had Pete let everybody on Ehlius listen to ten hours of Slim Whitman followed by ten hours of *Donnie& Marie*."

"Let?" Beeb bellowed. "You don't *let* anyone listen to that much garbage. You *force* them!"

"Right!" smiled Cat.

Glaring over at Odie, Beeb had to ask him bluntly, "And when did *this* happen? When did these terrible noises start?"

"Yesterday, at three in the afternoon or thereabouts."

"Odie, you ain't sharin' no power with no board on no foreign planet. You know that, don't you? I ain't puttin' up with that. No one should."

"Hey, relax, man! We're gonna export the American Revolution to 'em. They gonna git some democracy lessons."

"What, from you? How democratic was it to force 'em to hear such noise?"

"Well, hell, Vern, there's yer problem! It wasn't the music that did 'em in. It was old 'well there you go again' that turned the tide!"

"What are you sayin'?"

Laughing, Cat tried to explain to Beeb what that meant. "Odie told Pete that after Slim and the Osmonds was over, to run some tapes of Reagan speeches."

Beeb was genuinely shocked by this heartless cruelty. "Odie, yer a mean, cruel, sadistic bastard!"

"Hell, it worked!" Odie bragged. "The first twenty hours of drivel they could handle, but less than eighteen minutes of Reagan's babbling brought them to heel."

"What did you have in mind if that failed?"

"Howard Stern interviewing George Bush and Danny Quayle."

"You fucking sadist!"

"Hey, bad guys get bad breaks!"

"So what did this board do that was so terrible?"

Din began to explain this to Beeb while Odie drove toward the restaurant that Amana Colonies is world famous for. Cat teased Odie a little. "You buyin' for all of us, honey?"

"Can't afford the wear and tear of dessert, babycakes!"

Cat grinned broadly. All she had to do to change Odie's tune was whistle the right sounds in his ear. Since she knew it was a power trip, she had to watch herself, but it had been such a long time. She could see no harm in it. Besides, Odie wasn't the type to let anyone do anything to him that he didn't like. But if he liked it, Katie, bar the door.

"Odie, the board has requested again another meeting. Are you going to answer them?" Pete pointedly asked.

"Yeah, yeah, yeah, Pete, I'll get to 'em. Christ, y'all didn't know anything about them, and now I gotta answer 'em right away. Sheesh!"

"Odie," Din started, "we have no political savvy, as you said. The ones who live on Ehlius have less than we have. What will become of our planet?"

Odie wondered a moment. What, was it up to him or something? "Lin, don't you have any friends on Ehlius that are computer experts like you?"

"No, not really. Din and I are space-level workers. We have not lived on the planet in cities since we became space-level workers."

Din agreed. "We have friends we can trust in the space program. That's all the Ehliuns we know, actually."

"How long you been space level?" Beeb wondered. The answer astounded him.

"We have been working in space for approximately 140 of your years."

"What?" all three earthlings chorused. "Yer *how* old?" Beeb asked Din.

"We were about fifteen of your years when we were certified for space-level work entry. We have not been on the planet surface since then. There is no need. Our space program is vast indeed. There are over one million Ehliuns in space work right now."

"How old are you?" Odie pointedly asked Lin.

"In your system of time reckoning, Din and I are the same age, about 155."

"You guys are 155 years old?" Cat was stunned.

"Pete, how can that be?" Odie wanted to know.

"Well, Odie," Pete explained, "Ehlius spins slower than Earth. A day on Ehlius is about thirty hours. The natural tendencies to age have been computer repressed in Lin and Din since they were young. They may well live two and a half of your centuries. They are physically average for your twenty-five- to thirty-five-year-old range. They are computer assisted, don't forget."

"So they naturally don't age as fast as we do on earth. That what yer sayin'?"

"Essentially, yes, Beeb, that's correct. And then, with computer enhancement, they deteriorate very slowly. Although, with the extra pull of gravity here, the stress on the body is greater."

"Shit," Odie whistled, "meet miss gravity here!"

Cat punched his shoulder for what sounded like a complaint. It brought a smile to Odie's lips. "Well, what I want to know is who is going to run Ehlius now?" Beeb asked. "It ain't gonna be none of us," he further clarified.

"Well, that's what I was askin' 'em who'd they know for, Vern! Damn, I ain't gonna share nothin' with assholes that plot destruction of an entire star system! The board is history! Din, Lin, you guys gotta find someone that you know and trust and let them in on your secret. It's yer planet. You get to pick the kind of government you want. Who do you trust?"

Unanimously, they chorused the same answer together: "Pete!"

"Yeah," Odie and Beeb said together.

"How's Pete gonna run a planet from orbit?" Cat wanted to know.

"Pete can operate the computer system much as before," Lin said, "only with a few changes so that our people may no longer be living terminals of the computer network on Ehlius. Rather, the computer network, under Pete, will safeguard the system of liberties that we will install."

"Sounds like you got a plan, Lin."

"I do, Odie. I do."

"Well, I hope it works out for ya. Pete knows right from wrong real well now. If anything in the universe is up to the challenge of running a whole planet, Pete's it."

"Thanks for that ringing endorsement, Odie. If nominated, I shall not run. If elected, I shall not serve."

"Why not, Pete?"

"Too much information. That's what went wrong in the first place."

"But yer a machine, Pete. You can't be corrupted by anything, can you?"

"Well, no, I guess I can't."

"So there ya go! Yer perfect for the job. You can do it, dude. Piece a' cake."

"But I don't want to do that, Odie! There is so much more."

"Damn, Pete, invent a department for it, put it on automatic, and let it rip! What's the problem?"

"Okay, let me analyze this situation, and I'll get back to you on it. In the meantime, what are you going to do about the board?"

"Lemme talk to 'em , Pete."

"Righto, dude!"

"This is Odie! The great and all-powerful Odie, and I'm brought to you tonight by, *muff shooters*, the only earmuff with the convenient pistol grips! Once she's got 'em on, you'll see what the pistol grips are for! Knee and elbow pads available separately! Order yours today! Okay, board, what'cha want? C'mon, c'mon, I ain't got all damn day, ya know!"

A committeeman spoke for the entire board. "We will equally share our power with you, oh Odie."

Odie interrupted him. "Bullshit! I ain't sharin' power with you assholes! You ain't got no power! My sidekick Pete has already taken over all your power sources. You can't light a cigar with a laser, much less melt my sun!"

The committeeman spoke again. "You cannot possibly control any of our defense lasers."

"Oh, Pete, would you melt that asshole's chair for him?"

Pete directed a laser beam onto his chair, instantly severing the support, dropping the board member on the floor. He was stunned, as they all were. They were done.

"Pete, make their walls disappear. Make them visible to the rest of Ehlius."

Instantly, their protective cloaking device was rendered inoperable. They were exposed to the rest of Ehlius.

"Good job, Pete," Odie thanked him. "That was like liftin' up a rock and exposing the slugs!"

"Now what are they gonna do, Odie?" Cat wondered. He shrugged his shoulders as if he didn't care.

Pete answered her question. "They will be charged with criminal activity. It will take a while to delegate authority, but I guess it's up to me to do it right."

"Well, Odie, I'll say one thing," Beeb chuckled. "You sure taught him that part about believin' yer always right!"

"All's well that ends well, eh?"

"This ain't over by a long shot, son, not by a long shot!" Beeb stated.

Lin and Din knew it was not over either, but they quietly hatched their plans to straighten out the mess Ehlius was in.

For now, Odie was satisfied that tyranny no longer reigned supreme on Ehlius. As for who, what, where, why, and how the planet would run, he'd get back to that. But first, there was this thing about lunch and food that needed his utmost attention. The motor home pulled up at the parking lot of the world-famous restaurant at Amana Colonies.

The Ehliuns were not eager to enter where earth foods were consumed just yet. They would wait out in the motor home, but thanks anyway. Beeb couldn't keep from grinning. He was impatient to tell Odie about the metal fruit conversation he'd had with Lin last night. He couldn't wait to see the look on Odie's face.

After a fine luncheon repast, the three earthlings came back out to the motor home. They got in, and Odie headed for the driver's seat. They went up Iowa 149 toward Cedar Rapids. Lin and Din watched everything go by the windows. Suddenly, a question popped into Odie's head. "Yo, Pete, are we still disguised as a semi or what?"

"No disguises, Odie. Why, do you want one?"

"Not unless we need a disguise. Is anybody looking for us?"

"Only Kathy."

"Kathy?" Odie shouted. "Oh, shit! I forgot all about her!"

Odie missed the quick smile that flashed across Cat's lips.

"Is she near a phone, Pete?"

"No, she's not."

"Well, when she gets back to her room, ring her phone and mine so no one else on earth can hear us, okay?"

"Yas, master, I shall ring you up presently on the horn."

"Oh, and one more thing, Pete, you can stop watching so damn many Limey flicks. They're gittin' to ya."

"Veddy good, sir!"

"Especially movies with butlers in them."

"You mean like Rhett?"

"Lippy fuckin' computer!" Odie mumbled under his breath, knowing he would receive no sympathy from the rest of the folks aboard the vessel. Odie contented himself with driving through Cedar Rapids, finding the right road to take to their destination.

Cruising out of town on US 151, Cat remarked that the highway reminded her that she was out of rum, so Odie pulled into the next place he saw: Cedar Rapids Rapid Liquors. Odie remarked about how such places encourage drinking and driving. "Drive-ups don't belong on bars!"

Cat jumped out and bounded in to buy some rum. She moved up and down the aisles, looking for the right kind of stuff. She was followed by several local yokels doing the same, apparently. One yokel got so wrapped up in the view Cat presented that he didn't watch where he was going, and he tripped over several cases of Scotch.

Beeb and Odie were laughing hysterically at the action unfolding because of Cat's hip action. Lin and Din were not laughing nor did they understand why the boys did. Cat wasn't laughing when she reboarded the starcraft. "Boy got hisself a hunnert-dollar look at your ass, Cat!"

Beeb smiled as Odie told her, "Yeah, how's he gonna explain that to his old lady?"

Cat just shrugged off Odie's comments, as if she could care less. That was the truth; she didn't care. Odie saw this and tried to put his feelings into song. "Hard-hearted Hannah, the vamp of Savannah. She just don't give a damn!"

"Oh, don't you know it. She just don't give a damn! Hear what I'm sayin'. She just don't give a damn!" Cat boomed this back at

Odie as Ethel Merman might have. She knew exactly where Odie was comin' from, and she returned service quickly.

Beeb was particularly impressed by this broadside volley striking Odie. The chick was quick! "Hey, Qweeksdraw, I no thin' you be the qweekest Qweeksdraw no more!"

"Now hold on thar, Beeb-a-looie, I'll do the thinnin' around here!"

"Si, you jus' be doin' eet second!"

Cat smiled her approval to Beeb. Few people in her lifetime had appreciated Cat for anything but her body and what she could do with it. That was plenty, of course, but this was particularly refreshing—men who liked her mind as well.

She leaned over to kiss Beeb, and he leaned her way. As she kissed him, she suddenly imparted a surprise gift, a mouthful of 151 rum. Beeb fought hard not to gag on this sudden development. She might be quick, but she was still a little strange too. After a few seconds, Beeb determined that he would be all right. But if he drove, she would not force any more surprises on him. He slid over into the driver's seat, which Odie had vacated to go to the bathroom. He spit the rum out the window.

As soon as Odie came back aboard, they were underway, Beeb driving and Odie talking like a tour guide. "And on my left, a group of Holstein cows. Those with the humps are Brahman bulls. Those on this side of the fence are Guernseys. That's a German shepherd barking over there. And those are sheep out there."

Beeb mimicked his friend silently, watching himself in the side window's slight reflection. Pete observed but said nothing because he was learning. The Ehliuns were fascinated by the American countryside. Odie asked Pete to allow them to see through the entire side of the starcraft. Pete complied. Cat let out a gasp. This was much better than a convertible!

"Pete," Cat asked sweetly, "other people can't see in here, can they?"

"No," Pete assured her, "they can only see what I let them see."

"And of course, you wouldn't let them see us, would you?"

"No, of course not. I do understand what the deal is, why the Ehliuns are not to be seen by humans, why I am connected the way I am. I comprehend all you ask of me even though you still check up on me."

"Hey, I think this is really great!" Cat admitted. She liked Pete and hoped he wasn't as angry at them as he sounded.

Odie, too, thought it best to say nothing to Pete and say everything to the live pair of aliens in his motor home. Toward that end, he pointed out the various features of the landscape as he detailed the geology of the region. Din and Lin just took it all in and stored it against the day when it would all make good sense. For now, merely storing the knowledge was sufficient.

Beeb made a mental note of the deteriorating condition of the bridge crossing the Cedar River. It was old and dilapidated. He said to Din, "Look, you can see where the salt has been eating the bridge away."

Neither Ehliun knew what that meant. Concepts like salt eating bridges made no sense to them since eating salt was something on the table, restricted to food consumption in their limited understanding of Earth. How salt could eat anything was unknown. The word *winter* Beeb had used to explain why salt was there in the first place meant nothing to them. *Weather* was just a word. Good weather, bad weather meant the same—two words. They had led very regulated lives so far in their existence. The word *weather* was stored away; its meaning was not. They were like daffy squirrels, storing away shells devoid of nut meats.

Odie's incessant geological spiels had made certain impressions on Lin and Din. Beeb felt if you tossed enough shit on a wall, some would stick. They could see the change in the land since they had come down off the great divide. They had the beginnings of a decent grasp on the principles of continental building and erosion. They now knew that water, running water, had altered the face of the planet. Some things they could understand once Odie got them explained sufficiently. Rivers particularly fascinated them. There was nothing like a river on Ehlius.

But on earth, water flowed everywhere. Through Pete, the Ehliuns could see the entire continent. All around them, from pond to pond, streams and creeks and rivers moved on eventually to meet the sea. By the time the starcraft had crossed the Maquoketa River near Monticello, Iowa, the Ehliuns had a grasp of how hills and valleys came to exist through the action of flowing water. More and more hills and valleys could be seen now.

"Where we goin', Odie?" Cat suddenly asked. She didn't know where she was or where their destination lies.

Odie spoke up. "I trust you've heard of the expression, 'get the lead out'?"

"I have."

"Well, that's where we're goin'!"

"What do you mean, oh confusing one?" she asked slyly.

"I mean that's where we're headed, to where they got the lead out."

Cat still did not comprehend. "They, who?"

Odie became exasperated. "Frogs. Frenchies. Snail-eaters. Dudes like Dubuque, La Salle, Jolliet—the people who first reported lead in this area. Marquette, Groseilliers, Radisson, Saint-Lusson—French people, my folks, my people."

"You really French?" Cat asked.

"Don't you remember last night?"

"Oh, you asshole! I meant your nationality, not your personality!"

Beeb smiled broadly at her comments.

Odie stared hard at Cat a moment. "Well, babycakes, my last name is de Bienville. Don't that sound Frog to your ears?"

"I was under the impression that your name was Odie Beanville," Cat explained.

"No," Odie corrected her, "it's O period, small d-e, capital B-en-ville. I'm sure it used to be B-yen-ville in France, but several generations living in the south turned it into Beanville. My name is O. de Bienville."

"And what sort of name is O period?" Cat demanded to know.

"It's what my mom said when I was born, 'cause she wanted a girl. They told her I was a boy, and she just said oh. They wanted a name. She said oh, so the birth certificate had O. written down on it, and that was that.

"Beeb, what kind of bullshit is he trying to hand me here?" Cat inquired.

"Well, none, actually. His real name is O., like O. Henry. O. de, or Odie, is just what I started callin' him the first time I saw his name written out on a school paper or somethin'. I called him Odie, and it just stuck. Everyone called him Odie. I bet there's people that think they know him well and don't know his given name ain't Odie."

"Probably so, like old Johnny Bobs. People came up to him at a class reunion, sayin' stuff like howzit goin' John? His real name is Mark. Johnny Bobs was just a name Mangold or Tucker or someone called him after some TV preacher or something. Anyhow, Bobs is still Bobs to us. We never call him Mark."

Odie glanced at Cat to see if she was still questioning his veracity about Odie.

"And hey, Cat, lots of people don't know that my ancestor, the Sieur de Bienville, was the founder of the city you got your lucky dollar bill in. Yes, New Orleans and Mobile were both founded by the same man. Gramps, we call him. And his brother, father, uncle, someone, founded Montreal and Quebec. Canuck Gramps, we call him. Shit, the de Bienvilles are famous, Cat. We got a street in the French Quarter named for us, and my great-grandfather donated the land that now has the Bienville Forest in Mississippi on it. And up to me, there have been about sixteen generations in military service. But they won't have me now since they think I was a fuckin' commie spy!"

Cat smiled at Odie's little joke, like she thought she was supposed to. She didn't ask if his family was angry that a couple hundred years of family tradition of military service would end with him. She figured she knew. "So how did you get the name Beeb?" she wondered.

Odie answered for his old pal. "I used his initials to make up a name for him right after he got to callin' me Odie. His full name is Beauregard Elvis Edison Beaufort—Beeb."

"Does anyone else call you Beeb?" Cat wondered.

"You and the Ehliuns and Odie. I reckon that's about it. The family calls me Beau, but they call my dad that too, and Beau Junior just don't git it."

"Oh," Cat said.

"What?" Odie asked of her.

"No, no, you stop that! Yer Odie, not Oh."

"Oh, I see!" Odie saw. "Odie is me, to me and thee, and also he, and they make three."

"Gee, yer a poet and don't know it, so why don't you stow it before you blow it?"

Beeb chuckled softly at her antics. She was quick on the lip, no doubt.

"How did you get the name Cat, girl?" Odie demanded.

She smiled and then explained how she got her name. From Catherine. "I dropped the 'herine.'"

Early in the afternoon, the sleek special starcraft entered Dubuque. Beeb steered the motor home down the narrow, winding streets over hillsides that were covered with beautiful homes. They all enjoyed the many mansions that indicated the wealthy lifestyle Dubuque enjoyed during the glory days of lead mining and later meat packing.

Soon, they were off across US 20, spanning the mighty Mississippi River. Lin and Din were very impressed with the size of the huge river. "Just wait till you see it at Cairo, and Vicksburg, and New Orleans," Odie promised them.

"Next stop, Galena! The home given to the victorious union general U. S. Grant, awaits our inspection. Galena, next stop, Galena! All aboard!"

Beeb thought that he'd done a fine job imitating a train conductor, but no one else seemed to notice. He drove the rest of the way to Grant's home in silence, wishing Odie would join him and not prattle on so about everything.

The Ehliuns compared the site to their Amana visit. The house was nice, comfortable, and totally different from the houses at Amana's villages. They didn't realize the time difference between those houses and when Grant's home was built. They didn't as yet know the difference between the frontier and the established towns. A quick tour of the fort and the jail ensued. They learned that the fort was built to withstand Indian raids. When they had seen all of Galena that they wished, the five tourists were off again.

Lin and Din began to see how flat Illinois was compared to the rest of the country they had seen. They cruised by several hundred acres of cornfields and hundreds of farms. Odie discussed corn with them at length. Corn they understood somewhat. Other areas of earth life left them completely puzzled, such as religion, religious freedom, even freedom in general.

Late afternoon found them arriving at Bishop Hill, where they saw yet another colony founded by Europeans seeking religious freedom. Odie promised them he would explain religion when it would make sense to them. For now, they would concentrate on history and the past. Amana had been founded by Germans and Bishop Hill by Swedes. Odie showed them a large rock obelisk covered with the names of the Swedish settlers. Odie informed Beeb, "Itchy Boz's folks' name is up there somewhere."

Beeb nodded his head to acknowledge what he didn't care about. Odie explained that both Amana and Bishop Hill were founded by people escaping tyranny like the board's. Lin and Din could relate to that. Religious freedom meant escape from tyranny. Religion was still vague, but not tyranny. Tyranny was solidly in their vocabularies now. They knew exactly what tyranny was.

It didn't take long to see all of Bishop Hill that they wanted to, so with Odie at the wheel, they headed off down Illinois 17. Odie soon rendered the silence golden with his off-key rendition of "Two Lane Highway" as they passed through the booming metropolis of Toulon. Odie sarcastically sang "two-lawn highway," as if the town had but two lawns. In truth, there weren't many more, but bad puns were a way of life with Odie. Inflicting them on others was half the fun. Hearing the victims groan was the other half.

They cruised into exciting Peoria shortly before dark, and Odie showed them the sights. Caterpillar Tractor, Hiram Walker, and Bradley University were the high points as far as Odie was concerned. He aimed the motor home for the Rice Lake Conservation

210

Area to park for the night. Slightly after 10:00 p.m., the starcraft was parked, chocked, and locked. Pete blanked out all the windows and muffled the noise so that they would not be conspicuous. Pete could give them privacy. Big-time, he could provide that.

Pete rang the phone as Odie walked by, forcing him to answer it. Kathy was on the other line, but she thought Odie called her. She didn't know about Pete, and Odie failed to tell her about him. Odie stepped outside to talk in private. Cat didn't notice or didn't care because she kept on preparing dinner. Kathy and Odie spoke at length, and she finally agreed not to come looking for him. Odie could hear someone in the room with Kathy speaking in Italian, baritone. Odie knew he was off the hook now; she had another fool. "Bye-bye!" he said sweetly into the receiver. "Double-dealin' bitch!" he snarled after she hung up. He was sure glad he'd met Cat now!

Cat had prepared spaghetti for supper. Odie just grinned when he saw it. Only Pete knew the nature of his smile, and he wasn't gonna squeal on Odie. "Well, I guess you like spaghetti, Odie, judging from your smile," Cat grinned.

"Oh, I thought it was earthworms Alfredo," he laughed, pointing at the Far Side cartoon taped to the refrigerator.

Cat invited the Ehliuns to join them for dinner. After much laughter over the misconceptions about what the food was made of, Lin and Din agreed to eat some food with the humans. As long as it hadn't been able to walk before it was cooked seemed to be the dividing line between food groups they would and wouldn't eat. Cat had told them about being vegetarians, and they thought they could be vegetarians rather easily. Cat failed to tell them about the hamburger in the spaghetti sauce. What they didn't know wouldn't hurt them, she reasoned. Besides, explanations were too bothersome. Odie had been explaining things to them all day. Enough was enough.

Now that Rest Period impulses no longer regulated their sleep patterns, Lin and Din could watch the late show. Thanks to Pete, they could watch anything televised on the planet. As they settled in front of the TV, Odie warned all of them that he was intent on getting an early start. That said, he prepared to retire for the night.

Cat sidled up to Odie, intent on one more test. "I, uh, I wonder if you would mind, eh, well, you won't get mad, will you?" Cat didn't get to finish.

"No, you can sleep with Beeb or Din, whichever. I ain't jealous."

"You aren't, Odie? Really?"

"Nope."

Cat wanted to believe him, but if he wasn't jealous, why in hell wasn't he? Wasn't she good enough for him? What was the deal? Maybe she could get Beeb to tell her.

Odie interrupted her thoughts. "Besides, babe, I bet you get sore before you get off!" It was good that he smiled when he said it.

"You'll lose, sucker!" Cat said defiantly.

"I already won this!" Odie grinned, touching her heart.

Cat's face gave her away. The guy was obnoxiously correct.

"You can do as you please, babycakes, 'cause you will soon tire of comparisons, which pale in my reflection, and you will seek out my company and mine alone. I eagerly await such a time. You got till Tuesday next."

Occasionally, Odie could be serious. This wasn't one of those occasions. Cat sensed this. She, too, could be funny. "Okay, we'll just see who gets horny first!"

"Oh, no, ya don't! No threats!"

Cat then smiled at Odie, who realized he'd just betrayed his own position. He was involved deeper than he would care to admit. *Good*, thought Cat. At least now they were even.

Cat gave Odie a several-minute goodnight kiss that had her juices flowing before it was over. She led Odie to his bed and tucked him in, taking care to kiss the bulge in the center. "I'll have you for breakfast!" she promised the bulge. Then she made a theatrical exit, stage left.

She just glided into Beeb's room to get ready for bed. That sight made Beeb ready. He was on her like bark on a tree. His eagerness was pleasing to Cat. She was still sore, but she didn't want to spoil Beeb's evening by telling him that. But soon, Beeb had Cat so aroused that her pain mixed with her pleasure, and she stopped caring about the pain.

Pete observed all this with an open attitude. He began to wish that he was alive like the beings below him. The incredible energy that they generated amazed Pete. He checked around the earth to find that hundreds of thousands of humans were simultaneously engaged in sexual activity. All of them radiated immense amounts of energy. If this was what fun was, Pete was ready for some fun, earth-style.

But how could he do it? As yet, Pete didn't know. How could he become alive? How could he have a body? Pete spent great amounts of energy researching those premises. There had to be a way. Odie said there was always a way, so there had to be a way, but what would it be? How could it be done?

# Kampsville's Dead Dog's Back in Town, Doodah!

In the morning, Din and Lin were awakened by a tremendous crack of lightning then terrified by the sharp clap of thunder immediately following it. In the next room, Cat began profusely apologizing to Beeb. She had accidently bitten Beeb when the thunder scared her, and her teeth clamped shut. It was not the end to the blow job that Beeb was expecting, but it was the end. Beeb assured Cat he was going to be all right but in such a way that she knew he was hiding his true feelings. She went out in the hall to laugh; it was so funny to her. Poor guy, she'd make it up to him somehow, but for now, he was out of commission.

Din rushed back to find Odie but encountered Cat first. He was both startled and intrigued by Cat's nudity, which he had never seen before. He was surprised to see almost no hair on her body, not like Odie and Beeb at all.

Odie stuck his head out of his door to see what was going on. When he asked what was going on, he got simultaneous answers from Cat and Din and then Beeb and Lin. He simply retreated back into his room and locked the door.

Cat told the Ehliuns there was nothing to fear, that thunder and lightning were common occurrences, and that it wouldn't hurt them. "Easy for you to say!" Beeb intoned menacingly.

Cat knew his tone to be false, so she smiled at him, still amused by the accidental bite. Once Lin and Din matched up the words on

214

file with the physical realities, the thunder and lightning lost their terror. "Oh, so that's what that means," Din said out loud to everyone.

Lin had to ask Cat about the protrusions on her upper torso, so she softly reached out to touch one. "What are they for?" Lin wondered.

"For this!" Beeb quickly answered, inhaling as much of Cat's right breast as would fit in his mouth, leaving most of it uncovered.

Cat regarded Beeb as one would regard a dog urinating on one's shoe. Lin failed to see what Beeb's point was, so did Cat. Brushing Beeb's mouth away with her elbow, Cat tried to dry off her tit with the same arm and elbow. She tried to regain her dignity and speak of her breasts in the sense that they were useful adjuncts to her life. This entailed a discussion of nursing, and babies, and other things the Ehliuns simply did not know about. Cat could see that Lin had no breasts. "How do you nurse babies on Ehlius?"

Lin and Din shrugged their shoulders to indicate they didn't know.

"Where do children come from on your planet?" Cat asked, somewhat exasperated.

They did not know. Pete had to step in and answer for them. He informed them all that on Ehlius, every child was conceived by those females best qualified for the position of motherhood. Those females best adapted to being mothers were. Lin told Cat that she was best qualified for space travel and computer work. Cat had to ask. "Don't you two have sex together?"

"Yes," Lin responded.

"But you don't have babies?" Cat wondered.

"No," the female Ehliun answered.

Pete had to announce that Lin's fertility cycle, like Din's, lie dormant. It had never been chemically activated by the old computer system. Cat got the feeling that sex was just sex to them. It was possible and preferable, even necessary to their way of life, but babies were left to those best able to deal with them.

Lin began to wonder how long the computer network had controlled her species. Long enough to cause genetic changes. It seemed that all earth women could have babies. On Ehlius, it was specialized.

Lin hoped that she was not like the dinosaurs that Odie had talked about at great length, the dinosaurs that died out because they were unable to adapt. "We are not like the dinosaurs you told us about yesterday, are we Odie?"

He assured them that they were not like the dinosaurs at all. He noted that size and resemblance had nothing to do with her question, only adaptability. He was beginning to understand how their minds worked—beginning.

Pete had looked into the matter and found that childbearing on Ehlius was left to the ones with the temperament and disposition to handle it. Sex was a biological function, like eating and sleeping, no more and no less. Lin and Din seemingly weren't as enthusiastic about sex as the humans were, at least not to Pete, but who was he to tell them? No sense making them any more unhappy about being stuck on earth than they already were. Ignorance had been bliss so far. Perhaps he could discover the essence of sexual pleasure that had been programmed out of them and restore it. He devoted some attention to that problem.

Cat thought about all that they had told her while she went to her seabag and dug through for yet another day's clothing. Soon, she would need to find a Laundromat, but for now, another legless pair of cutoffs, another T-shirt. Not being able to have babies ever was a pretty harsh sentence that Lin had been given by the former computer network, Cat thought.

The raindrops that started to lightly fall a moment earlier now suddenly beat down in full force, hollowly pounding on the motor home's roof. The raindrops were making splashes about the size of silver dollars. An occasional hailstone was making a tiny dent and a large sound. Odie sat bolt upright suddenly, realizing that something would have to be done about the power cord plugged in outside his window.

Cat saw Odie suddenly dash past her through the door and outside in his underwear. She looked out through the side window while he unplugged the power cord from the service box outside. By the time he got back inside, he was drenched. He was shivering. Cat stripped him of his wet underwear and put a towel around him.

216

"Odie, you got too many goosebumps to be gittin' more'n half yer skin dry!" Cat observed.

Beeb grinned at her words.

Odie shuddered agreement. He was freezing. The rain couldn't have been any warmer than thirty-five degrees, he was sure of that. "Pete, show me the weather on TV!" Odie barked.

Instantly, the TV came on, and Pete spoke to Odie. "Good morning to you too, Odie!" Pete could not resist the temptation to show Odie how broad his understanding of life on earth had become.

Odie knew right away that he had spoken hastily. "Sorry, Pete, good morning, and good morning to you all!"

Beeb knew anything Odie said beyond this would be all sarcasm and spite, but Pete didn't.

"And how are we all on this fine, lovely Illinois spring morning?" Odie wondered of the group. "I know a little dash through Mother Nature's ice-cold shower was just the thing to perk me up and put a smile on my face, golly bob howdy!"

Glancing up at the weather report, Odie noticed the forecast for the remainder of the day in the St. Louis area. "Partly cloudy with a chance for some light rain and occasional thunderstorms this—"

*Click.* Odie punched the remote button with authority and vigor. "Cloudy and overcast with a ninety-percent chance of thundershowers—"

*Click.* "Rain all day today and even possibly—"

*Click.* "Very heavy rains today, continuing—"

*Click.* "Rain all—"

*Click.* "And over the Central Illinois area we might even have some hail mixed in "with the rain today—"

*Click.* Odie thumbed the remote control button again. "You're absolutely right, Mrs. Bleckowski, for five hunn—"

*Click.* Rain poured down outside while Odie searched the tube for good weather. "It looks like real heavy rain stretching from Joplin over to—"

*Click.* "Now the rain showers this morning will fade and clear out this afternoon, making way for the thunder boomers moving in from the west as we look—"

*Click.* "And from Decatur in a line through Taylorville on down to Raymond, it looks like a very wet day is in store for—"

*Click.* Odie clicked the TV off in disgust.

"So what the hell did you go out into the damn rain for in the first place, Odie?" Cat demanded. She wasn't sure why he was in such a foul mood. It better not be because of where she slept either, she thought to herself.

He answered her as calmly as he could manage for being so mad. "When it pours down like this, the side panel where the power cord is can short out. We've already blown out two entire electrical systems on this thing in just the last eight months. We got stuck in Montana for over three weeks, and it cost us over eleven grand to fix it. *That's* why I went out into the damn freezing-cold rain!" Odie hoped that his explanation would satisfy her. He didn't want to get into an argument with her over such a trifle.

Cat was still suspicious of Odie's bad mood. "Well, Odie, if you turned off the power, then why are the lights still on?" Cat thought she had a good question here.

Odie told her casually, "We are on the battery right now. It kicks on as soon as the power cord is undone." Odie thought a moment before adding, "And there's two generators I can fire up if necessary."

Pete had some information for Odie and spoke out. "That will not be necessary, Odie, ever. Over."

Odie considered the news Pete had just given him. "Oh, you runnin' my battery now, eh?"

"Yes, Odie. I had Lin drop a chip in the battery last night. Beeb knew all about it."

Odie cast a withering look Beeb's way. Beeb just smiled. Hell, he hadn't known about the board. That was lots bigger than this little deal. "I *see!*" Odie had a certain sarcastic bent to his words whenever he said, "I see," as a rule. It could be rhetorical; it could be quizzical; it could be bombastic. It could rarely be straightforward.

Odie smiled brightly and sweetly at Cat, then he hugged her as hard as he could without damaging the huggee. "Feel better?" she asked him as he stepped back from her.

He nodded affirmatively. Beeb came rushing up to Cat. "Oh, god! I feel awful!"

Cat had to smile as she hugged Beeb. She knew what made him feel so awful. He whispered to her, "Next time, just leave lip prints. Leave the tooth marks out, okay?"

She smiled and said nothing, for there was nothing to say, but she didn't laugh at him. That was a nice gesture on her part, she thought.

Odie went back to dress. Once dressed, he started up the diesel and let it warm up. Cat yelled to him that breakfast was ready, and he got up to eat. Odie downed a cup of coffee with four slices of toast and jam. He literally inhaled a few slices of bacon. He poured a glass of milk and put three raw eggs into it. Stirring it with a fork for a moment, he downed the mixture. Cat swore she was going to barf. Odie just laughed at her, drooling egg white down his beard. "Yer disgusting sometimes, you know that?" she asked, attacking his beard with a paper towel. She knew she was in danger of instantly vomiting had she been forced to observe that dangle a minute longer. How could she even like the guy, let alone maybe love him? It was a tough question, and there were no easy answers.

The Ehliuns were consuming breakfast cereal with the gusto of a hound dog, completely unbothered by Odie's appearance. Beeb and Cat didn't know how they could eat and look at Odie drooling egg white. Lin and Din didn't let small things bother them. Otherwise, all of earth would bother them.

Odie checked everything he could think of then left them to go pay for the night's stay. They had come in late at night, long after the park attendant went off duty at 8:00 p.m. Odie returned to the motor home with a receipt for the bulging files and lots of touristy folders and flyers depicting the marvelous sights to see in beautiful Illinois. Littering the table with them, Odie asked Lin and Din where they wanted to go and what they wanted to see. They could not distinguish one site from another. Anywhere and anything was fine to them. So far, it had been interesting at least. Once again, in Odie's eyes, it was up to Odie to decide.

"Okay, then! Have we got a day planned for you! All right, you guys seem to like history okay, so we will just go out here and see some!"

That said, Odie got into the driver's seat and fastened his seat belt. The others took this as their cue and took seating wherever they could. Odie went down the gravel path that led out of the conservation area. They went down the River Road, alongside the Illinois River. It was a short trip downriver to the site of Dickson Mounds Museum. Parking near the door, they noticed there weren't many more cars there, just two others to be exact.

Cat finished making the Ehliuns up in their costume of the day. "At least it's stopped raining," Cat said, gliding past Odie, who held the door open for Cat and the two Chinese ladies with her.

"Yeah, at least that much has changed in our favor," Odie noted. Sweeping the air aside with a grandiose gesture, Odie gestured toward the building they were about to enter. "Yesterday, my friends, you saw examples of primitive life in America—primitive by your standards, to be sure. But today, you will see primitive, very primitive. Come see!"

Lin and Din entered the building as Beeb opened the doors for them all. The Ehliuns entered into a journey deep into the humans' past. It went well beyond the artifacts they had encountered yesterday. These items on display were more crude and less well developed than the objects of farm life they had seen the day before. They wandered about freely, absorbing and recording everything they saw. Glass cases held displays of various kinds. Some held bowls, cloth, tools, personal items. The arrangements were rather random, it seemed.

Soon, however, Odie found a bone to pick, so to speak. He chanced upon a very well-made clay pipe, fashioned like a hand holding a bowl. The wrist of the hand was hollowed out for the pipe-stem. In and of itself, it was beautiful, a lovely item that was quite useful too. Odie objected to its being placed in the same case with a crude stone scraper, which was nothing more than a rock, thinner on one side than the other. In any case, the edge was extremely blunt.

The placard on the case led the visitor to believe that all the items in the case were of the same era and culture. Odie hotly contested the grouping's validity. "Beeb, look at this shit! That pipe is Hopewell culture at least, and the rest of this stuff is Mississippian or Archaic."

Beeb smiled at his friend's observation. He collected arrowheads as a youth, but he didn't study things like Odie, and he knew it. He also knew Odie could be wrong and even harder to convince of that fact.

Odie was sure that no artist capable of making such a nice pipe would have used such a crude instrument as this scraper for any use at all and certainly not on this painstakingly perfect pipe. "Hey, anyone who could delicately render such gracefully curved fingers, such well-shaped precise fingernails, such realistic knuckles as these could not and would not do so with such a crude device as this rock they're tryin' ta pawn off as a *scraper!* The artist's integrity would have been offended by the crudity of the rock, and he would not have permitted its presence near him. I mean, you guys, this is like having a sledgehammer and a wristwatch together, like you could use one to make the other." Odie thought he summed up nicely.

This said, Odie left the group and went off to find the curator, but the only other person in the building was a young lady who said she was just the secretary and had nothing to do with labeling the exhibits. She informed Odie that he and his party were so far the only visitors as they had just opened for the day. Odie rejoined the others, who were moving from one display to another. "The boss ain't in just yet," he offered as explanation.

Walking along one particular wall, they saw a crude likeness of what the placard said had been a chieftain's final resting place. The visitors had to take the word of the placard since the display was nothing more than a black-on-white silhouette of a skeleton. There wasn't even a black-and-white photo and certainly no handsome color plate, just a plain, lousy silhouette. The Ehliuns thought this was what Odie had meant by primitive.

The inscription accompanying the silhouette actually made Odie cringe as he read it. This spot marked the place where the remains of a chieftain had been discovered during the excavation of the footings for the wall. Odie was rapidly becoming enraged. A skeleton had been uncovered, believed to be that of a chief, perhaps of great importance due to the fact that he had been interred alone, separate from the masses. This skeleton had a copper breastplate covering the upper torso, and there were several copper bracelets on his arms. Woodlands Indians were not known to work metal. Therefore, they must have traded with tribes a thousand miles away.

"So where's this skeleton? What was done with it? Where's the shield? Why ain't it on display here?" Odie's demands were loudly voiced. But the skeleton was not on display, and no further information existed, at least not on this wall, it didn't.

Both Ehliuns were taking in all that they viewed, and they didn't comprehend that Odie was angry. They thought his emotional outbursts were of pleasure. They were very wrong indeed.

Odie headed back to the secretary's desk when he heard her say good morning to someone. He assumed it was the curator. Odie dashed up to ascertain that it was indeed the curator. Odie's question caught up to the curator in front of the secretary's desk. Upon admitting that he was the curator of this museum, the poor man found himself being dragged by the arm over to the wall where the chief's remains had been unearthed.

Odie voiced his demand to see this fabulous find, this copper-clad pile of bones. The curator informed Odie that the remains were not on display at this museum, nor were any of the artifacts that had been discovered with that skeleton on the premises either. The rage building inside Odie was gradually replaced with a controlled fury. "Well, sir, can you explain to me why you people didn't save the remains of the greatest find of all here at Dickson Mounds? Why didn't you just move the damn wall over ten feet?"

The curator took a deep breath and tried to placate Odie with his words. "Sir, the purpose of this museum is to preserve, for all to see, these burial mounds of ancient Indians—"

Odie cut him off in midsentence. "Okay, the purpose of the building is to preserve an old Indian burial mound, right? What's more important, the building or what's housed in it? What's the sense of preserving a mass grave of nameless masses and destroying the grave of their probable leader? Why are you in the museum business? Hell, you kept the peel and threw the banana away!"

The museum director tried to placate Odie, but he could not refute many of Odie's charges. Odie thought considerable logic was behind his arguments, while substantial excuses lay behind the curator's arguments. Odie remembered the old adage once again that those who can, do; those who can't, teach. The curator gave his reasons for the way things were. Mostly, they revolved around money, government funds, and private donations. "Oh, well, I guess if you had told the sponsors that you had made a wonderful discovery, they would have all withdrawn their support, is that it?" Odie demanded.

"No, sir, I'm afraid you just don't understand the government."

"Bullshit!" Beeb angrily denounced the curator's words. "We *are* federal government employees! Don't tell us how government works. They spend money like water on projects like this. You got no pull in this state? You can't toss a few bucks out and see how quick state government notices? Why didn't you go to Springfield to get money out of shoeboxes? You don't know that fat Polack from Chicago that distributes federal funds above and below the desk? Damn, you ain't well connected in this state at all!"

It was apparent to the boys that the finishing of the building on time was more important to the curator than any new finds they might make during construction of the museum building. The curator finished his list of reasons why there were no alterations to the construction, finishing with a sentence Odie found repugnant and repulsive: "This museum preserves for all time the priceless relics of a forgotten way of life."

Odie jumped in, "Yet the greatest exhibit of all had to be destroyed so that a brick wall could be put in its place!" Odie fairly snarled this, like a dog seeing movement toward its food bowl.

There was a tense silence. Odie knew it was useless to ask more questions of this fool, but he did anyway. He mentioned the grouping of the clay pipe with the crude rock *scraper*. Here, he struck pay dirt. The curator himself had arranged this case. He had made the choices of objects to be displayed. He claimed, "The case is a representation of a cross section of their lifestyle." He told Odie and the group that it was important to remember that tools were often passed down from generation to generation.

"Yer dyin' ass!" Odie retorted. "Whoever made that pipe smoked that pipe! The artist who did that didn't use any rock on it, either. Are you unaware that you have different cultures mixed in this case? There's a couple thousand years difference between that scraper and that pipe. What you call a scraper there is quite dull, you notice? What did they scrape with that? The Black Hills? Death Valley? It would take days to scrape a Chihuahua hide off with that thing, or would these poor, stupid Woodlands Indians be entirely too dumb to use a pointed stick, perhaps oyster shells or clam shells ground down to a sharp edge?

"Yer gonna tell us that some looney tunes Indian family passed down this heirloom rock scraper, like maybe they couldn't go out and find a sharper rock? Give us a break here, slick! Rock gatherers are not in the same class as the artist who had the skill and knowledge to fashion wet clay, shape it, and fire it. Rock users don't also use clay vessels as well. I've been on archaeological digs on three continents, Vern. I've never seen such an obvious error before, and you want us to believe that an artist like this pipe crafter would also use this crude scraper? Notice the fine, delicate lines on this clay pipe. I guess you'd develop this kind of touch and precision by using a scraper like that to force hide from sinew, huh?"

Odie was on a roll now. "You know, pal, the trouble with your type—educated beyond your capacity—is that you assume that the savage, ignorant Indians had shit for brains! They had to pay close attention to detail in order to survive day-to-day. Your attention to detail would'a got you killed around here two hundred years ago. Heirloom rock tools! Jesus, c'mon, you guys. We'll learn lots more without his lame explanations!"

Odie jerked his thumb at the curator. "Buddy, I don't know how you got this job, but it must be who you know, not what you know. Obviously, you don't know the difference between Archaic Mississippian and Hopewell culture! You don't know the difference between Mound Builders and paleoarchaic Indians. Shit, you might as well have a microwave oven in that case!"

These words ended the curator's need to hang out, and he bolted toward the safety of his lockable office away from the unstable large maniac. Odie almost spit at him, but they were indoors, so he thought better of it. "Morons like him label ice skates as roller skates in the damn Smithsonian! Damn! What a fool!" Odie was personally blaming the curator for all that he perceived wrong with their visit so far.

Lagging behind, Cat asked Beeb what Odie's last remarks were about, his skate comment. "Oh, we were in the Smithsonian the day after we got our grants from the senator. There was a pair of skates, pioneer stuff, from Nebraska, I believe. Anyway, there's a card on the display case, telling the world that these are pioneer roller skates. Only they have blades on them, not wheels, thus making them ice skates, not roller skates. They are right near the original gold nugget that started the California gold rush.

"Odie goes to the trouble of bringing this to the attention of the folks in charge, but six months later, we were in the neighborhood, so we go back and check. Same wrong card, same misinformation. Odie was embarrassed for the whole country. He couldn't believe that a museum of such magnitude would allow such a trite and easily corrected error to continue, even after he told them about it. 'Damn, just look at it. Find the wheels for me,' he says. Even fourth worlders could see there were no damn wheels. Only Albanians, who have yet to discover the wheel, wouldn't notice, he said."

Odie didn't look happy to Cat. She knew they'd have to leave for him to stop brooding about it.

Walking toward the rear of the building, Beeb finished his thoughts to Cat. "Yeah, I expect even today that them skates are still mislabeled. Great scholars, these!"

It was almost anticlimactic to see the mass grave now with skeletons pointing in all directions, buried haphazardly with no particular orientation. None of these skeletons wore any copper bracelets or breastplates. None were interred with honors, apart from the masses. These *were* the masses. Odie walked out after a few minutes of observation. He was waiting in the motor home when the rest of the travelers came out.

In an effort to get away from such nonsense as quickly as possible, Odie slung rocks from under the tires as he attempted to peel rubber with his lead foot. And people had the gall to ask him why he didn't teach! Quoting one of his favorite characters from the comic strip B.C., Odie screamed "Aaaaarrrrrgggggghhhhh!" out the window perhaps aimed at the river, perhaps at the museum curator, perhaps at the spirits of the dead Indians, whose remains he'd just seen.

"Feel better?" Cat asked him.

Odie smiled up at her, but it was a fake smile, lacking any warmth. She knew he was upset by what he considered to be great stupidity.

They headed south down the Illinois River, and Odie got his mind off the incredible ignorance he'd seen inside the museum by expounding on his views of the Indians who had once roamed this area. Odie cited the great fishing and hunting in the area as well as the abundance of nut trees and berry bushes. River mollusks were prized foods as well.

Odie told them about Cahokia. "Down the river a piece—well, actually on the Mississippi and not the Illinois River—was a town called Cahokia. Over thirty thousand people lived there when London didn't exist. The Mound Builders lived there. Monks Mound, near the town called Cahokia today, is a remnant of the vast building project that once existed there. Monks Mound is the largest earthwork in the world.

"Over in Ohio, near Newark, lies the great Serpent Mound. It is an actual calendar, like Stonehenge, only older. But across this vast expanse of woodlands, from Illinois to Ohio and down the rest of the way to the Gulf of Mexico, the ancient Mound Builder culture held sway. Mounds are found in Georgia, Alabama, Florida—about everywhere east of the Mississippi, in fact."

"What happened to that culture, Odie?" Lin wanted to know.

"Well, it disappeared. We don't have any records when or why it went. It's just gone. Maybe the Spaniards with de Soto spread disease and wiped them out. Maybe other Indians got them in battle. We just don't know. What we do know is that Monks Mound was built up by pouring basketfuls of earth in a particular spot until that spot was elevated a few hundred feet above river level."

"Why did they pick that particular spot, Odie?" Cat asked. "Was it because they needed high ground during a flood on the Mississippi or like the Egyptians marked out their fields?" Cat would soon be sorry she asked.

"Well, actually," Odie began lying, "Monks Mound was built there because the Mound Builders were Cardinal fans."

Cat hissed her disapproval, the pun being so bad. Lin and Din had no idea what the comment meant.

The starcraft crossed the river at Beardstown then swung through a series of small towns like Virginia, Philadelphia, and Tallula on the way to Petersburg, where Lincoln's New Salem State Park was. This was Lincoln country all around here—land of Lincoln, in fact. Abe was discussed at length since this part of the country was where he gained his fame. Din informed Lin that Lincoln was the bearded one on the money papers they trade around.

They got out and wandered all over the New Salem State Park and enjoyed themselves immensely. They sat down by a creek smoking a joint while Lin and Din busied themselves recording all the tiny life-forms they were now aware of. Earth fairly teemed with life, it seemed. Their own planet seemed so sterile in comparison, but they lived here now, and so they would try to learn everything possible about earth.

Back on the road, the motor home cruised into Springfield, the state capital, where they could see a lot more Lincoln memorabilia. Here were his house, his law office, his letters and papers, even his tomb. Cat and Beeb made sandwiches for the lot of them, so they would not have to stop to eat. First, they saw the Lincoln Tomb and Monument. From there, they left Camp Butler and entered downtown. They visited the Old Capitol Building. This enormous structure impressed the Ehliuns, along with the humans.

Cat was particularly struck by the impressive view looking up from the lowest level below the regal dome. They ascended several flights of stairs to look at all the paintings hanging there. Turning to go, Odie caught Cat's elbow and spun her around. Pointing up at the stained glass at the top of the dome, Odie showed her a misspelled word. She shook her head disbelievingly. How picky could he get? Odie retorted in his self-defense that they should have been more careful.

They left the massive building to visit the only home Lincoln ever owned. Lin and Din could see little difference between this one and the Grant Home, the only other presidential home they had ever seen. If anything, the Grant Home was a little nicer. Everywhere, they had seen signs about the national memorial. Finally, Din had to ask Odie about it. "Odie, why is the Lincoln home a national monument?"

"Because Abe Lincoln was the last honest politician to live in Springfield. That's why," Odie quickly answered, lest someone tell them the truth. "It's a tribute to days long gone, an era we shall never see again, public servants you can trust."

Beeb filled them in on the other details hinted at but not directly mentioned by Odie. "Illinois leads the nation in ex-governors doin' time for crime. Paul Powell was Secretary of State here till he died. Then they found shoeboxes full of money and checks for licenses in his apartment at the St. Nicholas Hotel. Thief died before they could indict him."

"Oh, would that more politicians would follow his example," Odie said.

"And just drop dead?" Beeb retorted.

Odie nodded his head in agreement. "Well, then I guess that the former mayor of Chicago Mr. Daley stands alone as a symbol of corruption."

"He got things done his way a lot, yeah, like gettin' the dead vote."

They left the Lincoln home and clambered aboard the starcraft they now called home. The early-afternoon sun moved across the sky as the motor home wound its way through rural Illinois prairie through Virden to Carlinville, where they changed directions and went west toward Carrollton and Eldred, and finally, they came upon the free ferry, which would take them across the Illinois River. They were bound for Kampsville and the Koster Site. Taking a ride on a ferry was a thrill for the Ehliuns as they had never been transported by water before. The experience impressed them, but in truth, the Ehliuns were easily impressed.

About ten minutes after they left the ferry, they arrived at the Koster Site, an archaeological dig. But there was nothing for them to see there. It was closed to the public. Wandering into downtown Kampsville, such as it was, they were directed to the museum. Odie responded to one of Beeb's questions about why they were there. He told them all that he had read about a dog buried here. "What's so odd about a dog burial?" Cat asked. "I mean it's not the sort of thing I think much about."

Odie looked at her like she was crazy. "Well, hon, I read that the dog was buried more than five thousand years ago and covered with red ocher from stem to stern. Indians were known to eat dogs. This dog seems to have been interred intentionally. Why was it so special? Was it honored for having saved a life? Was it an important family's pet? Was it Thanksgiving dinner no one showed up for? What's the deal?"

They smiled at Odie and his silly story and left it at that. Since Din and Lin didn't understand much of what Odie said and did, they were becoming used to just going along with him. They were well on their way to becoming Americans, used to the status quo.

Inside the museum, the display illustrated the layers of soil at the Koster Site. It noted that Theodore Koster was farming one day, tilling the soil, when he noticed on one pass over a hill that he had uncovered three skulls, obviously human. Northwestern University was called in, and they excavated down till the water table stopped them. They discovered—curved in a bed of sand, as if it were just sleeping—a dog's skeleton.

They could clearly see the museum and university catalog numbers and letters on the bones. They could not so clearly see what information existed corresponding to those numbers and letters. Lin and Din were happily toying with the models of primitive tools. This was the best part of the entire exhibit to them. It explained so much to them about the tools and items they had seen earlier today.

Odie's scholarly intents were dashed by the people working at the museum. They didn't know what breed of dog it was. They didn't know what type of scans that the bones had been subjected to. They didn't know what he wanted to know and couldn't tell him where to get it. "All the studies on the dog were done in Chicago," he was told. The only news he got was the confirmed date by carbon 14 testing clearly showed the dog was buried 8,400 years ago.

"Beeb, the dog's more'n 8,400 years old! That's much older than the Red Paint People of Labrador. The Maritime Archaic culture buried their dead with red ocher coverings, but those sites are three thousand years old or less. This is five thousand years older'n anything else I ever heard of!"

Beeb saw the excitement in Odie. "That's cool as hell, Odie. Cool as hell."

"And ya know what else they could tell me about the dog?" Odie excitedly bubbled.

"No, what?"

"Not a fucking thing!" Odie said dismally. Then Beeb finally saw that Odie was not particularly happy once again. Another museum, another disappointment.

Having picked up on the drift Odie's thoughts were mired in, Beeb knew what to do. John Lennon had told him in "Yellow Submarine," start singing!

"Kampsville's turned to a real down, doo dah, doo dah. Chicago's got the studies now! Oh, dee doo dah day!" Odie joined in.

"G'wine to ride right now! G'wine to ride away. G'wine to bet good money we ain't back this way, oh dee doo dah day!"

Cat smiled her approval, noticing that Odie had come right up out of the wallow he'd been in. She told them that although she was pleased with their ability to play off one another, their singing still left something to be desired. "Like what?" Beeb huffed.

Cat counted them off on her fingers. "Oh, harmony, style, melody, tonality, grace, pleasant voices—you name it!"

Beeb just stared at her like Odie would have if he were listening.

Odie unlocked the motor home's door, and they all got back inside. As he sat down to start up the engine, Odie heard Pete ask him a question. "Oh, Odie," Pete asked, like Odie doing Benny, "when are you going to let me drive?"

"Yeah, dammit, Odie, ya promised Pete that for savin' our asses, and that was hundreds of miles ago!"

Odie stared at Beeb as if to ask whose side he was on. Beeb, however, merely stared back. Much to his surprise, Odie fooled them all and gave in. "Well, what the hell else can go wrong today?" Odie stared straight up at the ceiling. "Okay, Pete, as soon as I get out of town, you can take over the steering duties, all right?"

"I want to drive, Odie, not just steer!"

Beeb and Cat smiled at each other and then at Odie. Pete was his baby, and they weren't going to even listen to this discussion. Odie drove to Illinois Route 96 and headed for Mozier. Unfolding a map, Odie showed it to Pete through the windshield. "When we get to Atlas, take US 54 over to Louisiana, Missouri. Ya got that, Pete?"

"I got a copy on that, good buddy. That's a big 10-4, over and out."

"Uh, Pete, don't talk like that to me, okay? No truck driver talk, no CB stuff, or you don't drive, got me?"

"I got'cha! Well, lemme put the petal to the metal, son. I wanna rock!"

"Sheesh. Pete, where do you learn this shit?"

"From you guys, of course. And, well, there's TV."

"Well, before I get out of the driver's seat, Pete, put a hologram of me on the window here on the driver's side, okay?"

"Okay, Odie, I got it taken care of. I have observed the driving habits of all earthlings for several hours now. I have complete comprehension of what is required. I fully understand all that is necessary to correctly and safely operate this vehicle."

Odie still had his doubts, but he let Pete take over. Pete persisted in his efforts to get Odie to see things his way for a change. "Odie, try to think of me like an autopilot on a plane."

"No, Pete, yer more like a plain old pilot in an auto!"

Odie's chuckles grew louder when he heard Cat and Beeb groan at his pun.

Odie started unfolding more maps to show Pete. There were many maps at his disposal: federal and state highway maps, climatology maps, city maps, topographic maps, relief maps, and maps showing the location of bridges they were to study on this excursion. Pete learned cartography at the same time he learned to drive a motor vehicle. That was okay. He could handle it.

Odie told Pete to skirt St. Louis via I-270 and head south toward Ste. Genevieve since they were on a history kick. Cat was a little disappointed that they were not going into St. Louis, a town she had never been to before. Odie regarded her a moment. "What, you got some strange desire to sit in rush hour traffic or what? We'll git downtown later, not to worry. I'm lookin' out for ya, babycakes."

Cat seemed little cheered by this news. She didn't answer Odie, for she had already learned that it would do no good.

Beeb had begun to inform the celestial visitors about the French settlements along the Mississippi River. "From Dubuque down to St. Louis and on down to New Orleans, this was all under French control. It was a French river for almost two centuries. It's been an American river about the same time. Around here, the old French influence is still quite heavy."

Being of French heritage, he was eager to show off the finer points of French culture, as it applied to America. That would be easy since there were so few.

Upon arrival at Ste. Genevieve, they made straight for the Donze House, as it was the one they remembered most from their last visit months before. Lin and Din were enthralled by the tales the guides told, how the houses had been built and how, in 1789, the entire village had been moved up to its present location to avoid ravage by the greatest flood on the Mississippi in historical times.

Cat could barely imagine what a titanic struggle such a task would be even today, using modern cranes and bulldozers. Then with only animal and human power, it was surely a monumental task. Some of the houses they viewed had walls made of walnut logs and were well over one foot thick! These houses weighed tons! One house had an attic formed by 150 walnut saplings bent into the same shape they retained today nearly two hundred years later.

The place amazed Cat and the Ehliuns. Finally, Cat mentioned that it was dark out, and if they would leave, the management would lock up for the night. The five tourists reboarded the starcraft and headed north on US 61. Everyone, including Din and Lin, protested Odie's rendition of a Dylan tune about Highway 61.

Odie told Pete to head for St. Louis. It was dark, and he was starved. The Ehliuns had eaten and enjoyed spaghetti. Well, he would just treat them to some of the best Italian food in the country. He was headed to his favorite Italian restaurant located in the neighborhood everyone in St. Louis knew as The Hill. "Best damn dago food in the world!" Odie assured them all.

# Doin' the Scott Scramble

After dinner, the five tourists left the Italian neighborhood known as The Hill for a short cruise around the high points of town. Finally, they arrived in the Riverfront area known as Laclede's Landing. As they parked in a parking lot, a rock and roll band blared out at them from one of the many bars in the historical district. The Ehliuns obviously needed to see what nightlife was all about, and what better place than a bar? Dim lights, thick smoke, and loud, loud music beckoned them.

As soon as they entered, the band finished up their set and promised to return very soon. Cat excused herself from the troop after telling Odie what she wanted to drink. She approached one of the musicians who was now on break. Winking at Odie, Cat followed the musician out the back. Odie wasn't sure what she was up to, but he trusted her and said nothing. Beeb wondered out loud what she was up to. Din and Lin were lost in the mysteries of the bar scene. Bars and their occupants were new territory to them, having only seen such in TV ads for beer. They busied themselves recording everything they heard and saw.

Din ordered a beer for himself and for Lin. When it arrived, they both slugged some down like the commercials had showed them. Din gagged and looked over at Lin. She too found it most distasteful. "This is gross!" Lin said, spitting the beer back into the glass.

Odie laughed. Din didn't understand. "Odie, we are not laughing and having the most wonderful time like the people drinking beer in the commercials do. Why?"

"Well, yer catchin' on, little dude! Commercials lie."

Lin wanted to know why TV ads were so misleading. "Why do the beer commercials talk about how great their beer tastes if this is it?"

Beeb smiled at her. "The aim of the commercial is to induce you to try the product, not tell the truth. Beer ads are the worst lies told outside of politics, Lin."

"Less filling!" Lin said, pushing the beer away from her.

Odie smiled very broadly. They were sure learning fast.

Odie felt great discomfort when the musicians began playing again and Cat was nowhere to be seen. Beeb was about to get up and physically quiz the band as to her whereabouts when she came strolling in the front door. She retook her seat coolly and calmly, patting Odie's shoulder as she sat down. The quizzical look he gave her brought forth a smile on her lips. She then aphonically mouthed the word *pot* to Odie, who then immediately understood what she'd been up to. *Cute and clever, this girl*, Odie thought, *not too shabby for a hitchhiker, not too shabby at all.*

After the boys finished their drinks, they all got up to leave. Cat blew some kisses at the drummer as they left. He nodded his head at her but had to keep playing. She had planned it that way. Promise them anything but give 'em the slip. She had years of practice. Candy from a baby.

Once they were outside alone, Cat told Odie that he and Beeb both owed her one third of the purchase price of this ounce of reefer she had obtained. Odie readily agreed. "Y'know," Cat admitted, "I hadn't really thought that much about gittin' stoned till we got in there."

Beeb walked up to them then as she finished her thoughts to Odie. "But then, old habits are hard to break."

As Cat showed Beeb the ounce, he had questions to ask of her. "Old habits are hard to break? How'd you pay for that?"

The glare he got from Cat caused Beeb to apologize to her at once. "Sorry, Cat, I wasn't serious, ya know! It was just a joke! How much do I owe, you, darlin'?"

"A third of a blow job!" she rapidly answered.

Odie fell out laughing. Beeb looked sheepishly at Cat and begged forgiveness with his eyes. Odie still chuckled. Cat was damn quick with quips from those lips, no doubt about it! To Cat, he offered and received a high five with each hand.

Din and Lin just took it all in. They had just come out of the restrooms and heard none of the conversation. They didn't know what a high five was, what it was for, or why they were laughing, but they did know what was important: that Odie would explain anything to them that they needed to know.

Once again, they all clambered aboard the starcraft with the outer space driver. Odie told Pete to take them up the street to Gateway Park, where the arch was. The six-hundred-foot-tall arch fascinated the Ehliuns, but they did not wish to go up to the top of it. Good thing, it was closed anyway. Odie joked that East St. Louis was thinking of putting up a giant statue of a croquet player on their side across from the arch. The more they smoked their new reefer, the sillier the conversations became. Lin was not used to getting high, and it affected her more than the others. But even high, she could not accept some of Odie's more outlandish statements and assertions.

Odie's contention was that if something happened that in the minds of the observers just could not happen, then the observers would soon not believe they had in fact seen it. Lin argued that if that were true, Odie and Beeb would not have come aboard the space wreckage because it could not have been there. Beeb smiled slightly to Cat. Odie tried to extricate himself from his dilemma. "Okay, let's run a test. Let's say you make something appear, like a building, where there wasn't one before. Then after a while, make it disappear. Soon, even those who did see it won't believe they did!"

Lin firmly refused to accept this statement. "I simply cannot accept that, Odie."

Odie was just as firm in his refusal to accept her position. "Okay, you make something appear. The more absurd, the better. We'll just see who knows us earthlings better, me or you."

Lin silently conversed with Din on their private channel for a while, then she spoke up to Odie. "Okay, Odie, I will accept your challenge. I will have Pete make a hologram appear and then solidify it for a time before it suddenly disappears. We will see what effect this has on the people who actually observe it."

"Fine with me. What'cha got in mind, kiddo?"

Odie's bravado sometimes rubbed Beeb the wrong way. This was such an instance. Beeb wondered what Lin would come up with. He really hoped Odie lost this silly argument, although so far, he still had to believe that Odie was correct in his assessment of people's reactions. But maybe Lin had something up her proverbial sleeve. Beeb's wondering was just about over.

Lin announced her plan to Odie. "I will have Pete erect a building in East St. Louis, as you earlier suggested, Odie. It will be a building in the shape of a giant croquet player about to drive a ball across the river and through the arch. It will be six times the height of the arch as a real croquet wicket and player would be or almost four thousand feet tall."

"My god!" Odie shouted. "That's almost three quarters of a mile high! That's right in the flight path to Scott Air Force Base! And Lambert too!"

"Well, you were the one whose claim was 'the more absurd, the better' you know!" Cat told Odie. She and Beeb were grinning delightedly, much amused by the whole affair.

It sure seemed like old Odie had put his foot in his mouth. He'd sure challenged the wrong person this time. Lin seemed to have him. "Okay, okay," Odie calmly declared, "you'll see!"

"What am I going to see?" Lin wondered.

"You'll see that I'm right!" Odie exclaimed. "There is gonna be such a tight security clamp put on this thing that it will make your head spin. Look, Lin, when them boys from Scott AFB got to scramble up some jets for a look-see on account of a building suddenly appeared on their radar, I am here to tell you that they ain't gonna let out a single word of this incident to nobody, no one at all. You'll see!" Odie could not resist this last dig.

"How, Odie? How will I see all this?" Lin still didn't understand him.

"Well, Lin, there's gonna be a security net over everything about this. I bet they announce some lame cover story, like a plane crash of dangerous cargo or hazardous materials spill, something like that. There will be a total blackout of the news of the building itself."

Pete noticed the bravado that Odie spoke with, that self-assured stance he always maintained, but he would build the building as Lin ordered, and then he would wait and see like the rest of them. Whatever happened, happened. He would not prevent it. Pete rendered the motor home invisible and undetectable in all spectra. He parked it near ground zero, where his building was to appear in a limited engagement.

In a ruined area of East St. Louis, where nothing of use existed, the plot was hatched. From their vantage point, the five beings aboard the special starcraft could observe everything that occurred. Pete borrowed hundreds of tons of steel from unused railroad tracks in the area with his laser. He beamed up these tons of steel as an electron flow and sent it all to the construction site. Pete picked up all the glass he needed from broken bits lying around the country. America's roadsides yielded hundreds of tons of glass. Pete believed in recycling. He removed litter and left nothing in its place. He could do two things at once. No biggie. Clean up America and have fun with a building all at the same time. Great country.

Chrome in abundance was found lying unused in junkyards full of rusting hulks. Concrete in quantities too vast to describe were readily available from abandoned structures in the area. Pete found some bridges nearby but no roadway to or from them. He doubted anyone but the cows used them now, if ever. He felt sure no one would miss some of them, so he transported their components to the construction site.

Precisely at 3:00 a.m., the 3,840-foot-tall building appeared. All in all, the building was magnificent. A two-hundred-foot-tall round restaurant was swiveling delicately in its orbit, all glass, brass, and chrome, gleaming brightly in the moonlight. It was an architectural gem. This twinkling ball was poised in front of the huge croquet-player-shaped building. There were twin towers for legs, rising up over 1,800 feet. Above that was another 1,800 feet of torso. Huge arms hung down from the lofty shoulders, with hands gripping a magnificent 1,300-foot-long mallet. The mallet was drawn back between the legs, aiming the ball restaurant across the river at the arch.

It was a most impressive sight, topped off with a jaunty multicolored cap Pete had seen fit to bestow for that authentic look. Hundreds of people were impressed right away. Many were winos lying around the devastated area. The rest were people connected with aircraft in one manner or another. Pete began counting the number of calls and radio messages concerning the building and its sudden appearance. Swiftly, the number was over one hundred then two hundred. Several different airports reported some intrusion on their radar screens. Two incoming flights to St. Louis's Lambert Field reported an intrusion on their flight paths. Near Belleville, Illinois, the military got involved.

At 03:03:49 hours, the tower at Scott AFB, MATS headquarters, cleared two huge helicopters for takeoff. Six minutes and eight seconds later, the choppers landed at the base of the new building, disgorging security teams, who quickly surrounded the place. Pete was impressed by the military's speed, but his impression was somewhat dulled by the fact they were rounding up all the winos they could catch and detain.

Pete couldn't believe that the military thought the winos to be capable of anything remotely resembling physical labor, let alone something like this beauty! Lin shared Pete's shock at these antics. Odie giggled at the goings-on. He winked at Beeb, who was beginning to fall under that same old familiar impression that once again, Odie was right. Odie bragged to Lin, "I hate to say I told ya so, but them winos ain't gonna get the chance to tell anybody anything about that building till the boys in blue git done with 'em !"

Beeb was forced to correct Odie. "Don't lie, Odie! Don't say you hate to say I told you so. You love it!"

Odie ignored Beeb as both knew he would. Beeb muttered to Cat, "See, he ignores me. I knew this would happen!"

Cat agreed. "Yeah, he does it to me too!"

Odie talked on, oblivious to them. "These commercial planes en route to Lambert will be detoured by the jets that the air force is undoubtedly launching right about now."

Pete confirmed for all that Odie's guess was accurate, a squadron of Harriers was aloft.

"Yeah, Lin, the pilots will be encouraged to remain silent about what they've seen tonight. By next week, you won't be able to get any of these guys involved here tonight to admit they saw anything peculiar. You'll see." Odie had an irritating I-told-you-so quality in his voice when he said this.

Lin did not know what to think. She was a novice at thinking anyway. The learning process of how to become an individual was quite difficult to cope with as she had been trained to be socially public and not private in her nature.

Pete had it easier than Lin and Din, of course, as he didn't have to deal directly with life on earth, and he had access to a great deal more information, but the Ehliuns were enjoying their new lifestyle of privacy, difficulties, and all. Pete, however, was still trying to overcome his privacy, his isolation. He wanted to interact with other beings. He wanted to become a being. He wanted to become a human being. How to accomplish this was the most pressing problem in his personal memory banks. There just had to be a way. Pete was just unsure what that way might be.

Odie and Cat were chatting while Pete was musing, and he was interrupted by Odie. "Pete, make us all invisible, okay? Cat wants to go inside this building of yours."

Pete agreed and rendered them invisible. They wandered past the posted guards and into the magnificent building. Silently moving from place to place, they saw military specialists torching off some samples of the building's framework and interior decorations. They came across a colonel on a field telephone talking to his superiors at the base. "Yessir, I got my boys cuttin' some samples of the steel framework right now sir."

The colonel shifted his weight from one foot to another, impatiently waiting to speak again. "Well, sir, if it's a mirage, it's damn good 'cause it's solid as hell, sir!"

A flustered look crossed the military man's face. "Yes, sir, sober as a judge! It's made of marble, glass, steel, aluminum, and stuff like that. There's working elevators and bathrooms and everything. It's real, sir, as real as the building yer in now, sir."

Leaving the poor man to explain to disbelieving superiors, the tour moved on. They took the elevator up to the top floor. As the ascent began, Odie was moved to comment. "Damn nice job ya done on this, Pete! I'm impressed!"

"Thanks, but wait till you see the observation deck. I checked around to see what the rest of the country had to offer, and I think yer gonna like this one, gang!"

Odie silently lamented taking the smart-ass tack with Pete.

Finally, they got to the top of the building. On the brim of the building's cap lay the observation deck. All five of them were awestruck by the sight. It was incredible! Odie had to speak. This wondrous sight forced words from his mouth. "Christ, you can see the lights of Chicago! What a view! Jeez, Pete, this is terrific! Well, Lin, I gotta hand it to you, this idea of yours was—"

Odie was interrupted by Cat's insistent tug on his sleeve, and she was also pointing at some trouble. "Oh, shit!" Odie muttered. Across the way, there were military personnel!

A major and a colonel were staring in the direction of Odie's disembodied voice. At once, Odie realized they had heard him speak, and he hadn't noticed them until it was too late. He had to think fast. Fortunately, it was his specialty. Beeb quickly put a finger to his lips to indicate to the rest to remain silent. This was Odie's fault; it was his problem, and he could handle it. Beeb knew Odie well enough to know he already thought up some excuse—some absurd excuse, of course. Beeb knew Odie would get them out of trouble. He'd better. He'd gotten them in it…again.

Odie approached the frightened officers. Reading their name-plates, Odie addressed them as casually as he could under the circumstances. "Um, look here, Colonel Johnston and Major Grummble, is it? Okay, fine. We're, uh, sorry to, well, burst in on your, uh, dimension like this. We were just, uh, testing this new device, you see, when a, well, uh, the thing is, you see, this was the most unfortunate result. This old building we were trying to tear down was, uh, accidently, uh, transferred or moved into your, uh, third dimension from our fourth dimension."

Odie glanced over to catch Beeb's eye. He waved his hand at Beeb in a flat, jerky sort of way. Cat failed to discern meaning, as did the Ehliuns. Only Beeb caught meaning from the movement, and he smiled and nodded his head to Odie in return.

Odie's motions were an imitation of Jake's hand gesture to Elwood in the movie *The Blues Brothers*. In the scene, she has just pinned them facedown in the mud with M16 fire. Elwood asks, annoyed, "Who *is* that girl?" Jake signals to Elwood he has the situation under control.

Beeb knew the scene well. He could see Carrie Fisher in his mind's eye, holding the Blues Brothers at bay. He knew what Odie meant.

Odie continued with his speech to the frightened officers. "We beg your forgiveness. You see, I shouldn't be telling you this, but what the hell, we occupy the same space as you people do, but we're in, we live in another dimension, which you cannot see and so wrongly take to be time. We don't want you to worry about us. We are fine. We want to be friends. Forgive the intrusion and please carry on.

"But, uh, well, the thing is, you see, this building will disappear back to its proper time and space sequence when the effects of the test wear off. I expect the disappearance to occur sometime soon. So if I were you, I'd remove the crews taking samples to some safe spot, lest they be forever transferred to the fourth dimension. If you've read Heinlein or Azimov or Vonnegut, then you know it could happen.

"Oh, and another thing: the samples you have taken will also return to their proper places when the whole building goes. I know you'd like to have some samples to test, but you wouldn't be getting the real thing. In our dimension, you can't see or perceive because you don't have enough dimensions. Time isn't the fourth dimension. It exists independently of any dimension. If you spent more time studying the nature of things instead of trying to blow up the entire planet, you might have noticed.

"Indeed, you might notice that there are billions of other living creatures on the planet besides yourselves. Between you and the former Soviet clowns and the bunglers in the Middle East, your culture has come perilously close to annihilation of life-forms from Earth forever and all for pompous political reasons. That's bullshit, gentlemen! We, the other citizens of Earth, demand you humans stop with the nuclear weapons and war in general and all that other wasting of lives you call politics. Try to satisfactorily explain this to your superiors and have a nice day."

Odie waved toward the elevators, and the others joined him there. They left two very shaken officers in their wake. "Have a nice day?" Beeb sarcastically asked Odie when the elevator doors closed.

"Well, what was I supposed to say?" he demanded.

"Nothing! You weren't supposed to say a damn thing, Odie, not a damn thing!" Beeb was angry, and had nothing further to say.

But Odie did. "Pete! When you hide our appearance, hide our voices too! Got it?"

"Roger, mystery voice. That is affirmative. Over."

"Real wiseass of late, ain'cha, Pete?"

"Must be yer good teachin', huh, Odie?" Beeb blurted out bitterly.

"Well, he don't have to rub it in," Odie said defensively.

"Oh, no, he don't have to. He chooses to. That's what makes it so funny!"

"Ha ha!" Odie retorted to Beeb without a trace of humor.

Beeb glanced over at Lin, who didn't seem to like it when the two big men argued. "Well, Lin, I guess this puts a little crimp in the test, don't it?"

"Why?" she innocently asked.

"Why?" Beeb bellowed. "Because Odie interfered with the damn test, that's why!"

"Oh," Lin said softly.

"The damn test sure didn't have nothin' to do with him tellin' them boys that the whole damn thing came from another dimension. Shit!"

Lin conferred silently with Din a moment.

Beeb continued his lamentation. "Now there's an explanation for the building! Nope, we gotta run another test."

"Okay by me," Lin said.

"Oh, hell no!" Odie shouted. "I still say you won't get anyone to admit they were here or saw anything by next week."

"Or talking to someone that wasn't there?" Beeb inquired snidely.

"Right! Part and parcel of the experience of the building," Odie noted.

"Are you gonna have Pete zap these records too, Odie?" Beeb sneered.

Odie thought about it. The elevator reached the bottom. Odie reconsidered his position. "Pete, don't let anyone hear or see us, okay?"

"Okay." Pete knew it was his fault for not covering up their sound waves, which allowed the air force officers to hear Odie in the first place. But if Odie said nothing further about the matter, then Pete wouldn't either. He was learning about Odie.

The group slid out silently and left the building. They walked back to the safety of the motor home. Only they could see it. "I'm afraid we carried this thing a little too far," Odie admitted, much to the surprise of everyone, especially Beeb.

"God, that's twice today he's fooled me!" he told Cat.

"I guess yer right, Lin," Odie told her apologetically. "Us humans ain't as bad as I thought. I'm sorry I even said it."

Lin smiled as Odie hugged her. It was a strange custom, this hugging, but it had a certain pleasurable feel to it. Pete relayed the information that the order to evacuate the building had been given. "Soon as they all come out, Pete," Odie stated, "replace the structure with just a hologram then slowly fade it away."

Lin silently told Pete to do it. "Roger," Pete answered them both. In a few minutes, the building was empty once again. No military men were left inside.

Suddenly, the structure was just a shadow of its former self. A wispy shimmering picture of a building was all that was left. A sergeant leaning against it suddenly fell through the wall, or rather a picture of it, becoming the first person to notice. Faint smiles adorned the faces of officers Johnston and Grummble.

At 03:33:19 hours, the croquet-player-shaped building of enormous proportions vanished as mysteriously as it had appeared. There was much relief among the troops, who could now go home and forget about this nightmare they had been having. Major Grummble and Colonel Johnston headed back for a long, disturbing debriefing near Belleville, and the starcraft headed for the interstate. In a few minutes, it was northbound on I-55. "Where do you want me to go, Odie?" Pete asked.

"North, just away from here." Pete guessed he'd better try a new angle.

"What do you suppose our destination might be?"

"I hadn't given it much thought yet, Pete. Does it matter? Just haul ass up the road and gimme some time to think, okay?"

"Roger."

Since no one told him differently, Pete branched off I-55 onto I-70, and went east. The five tourists were sound asleep when Pete got to the junction of I-70 and I-57, so he went toward Chicago. Maybe Odie still wanted to know more about that old dead dog from Kampsville. There was no way to tell with Odie, and Pete didn't dare wake him to ask. So they cruised on until shortly after 5:00 a.m., when Pete was forced to bring the motor home to a rapid halt by a line of cars not moving on the highway.

Before the braking was completed, Odie was in the driver's seat, ready to take control. An accident had blocked the road up ahead, and it was backing traffic up on the interstate for quite a ways. Odie told Pete to take the Mattoon exit so they would not have to stop. Waiting in a long line of traffic never appealed to Odie no matter where or why. "Head up Illinois 121 here, Pete. Let's see where it takes us."

"What time is it, Cat?" Beeb asked sleepily.

Odie turned to see the two of them moving forward. "Ten after five," Cat told Beeb.

Beeb crunched heavily into a seat at the table. "Shit, I wish it were five after ten!"

"I could use a cup of coffee, or something," Cat said to Odie.

Odie grabbed his genitals and offered them to Cat, saying they were something. "Wrong something, slick. I want a big meal!"

"Funny when yer tired, ain'cha?"

They smiled and hugged each other.

Pete wished he could hug Cat. There just had to be a way. He'd find one. Holograms that could be solidified were part of the answer. The past building experience had proven that, but how would Pete *feel* it? That was, after all, the whole reason for doing it: to *feel* it! Pete devoted more thought to this problem, how to become alive, like the humans below. Fortunately for Earth, as yet, Pete had not heard of Frankenstein or his monster—not that he understood, that is.

# Bridges, Beans, and da Bears!

The starcraft wound through flat and nearly featureless farmland up Illinois 121 until it came to an intersection with US 36. Still, Odie had seen nothing that looked like coffee could be obtained in that was open. "Go left here, Pete. Somethin's gotta be open up ahead, I think. Where the hell are we, anyway?"

"Decatur!" Pete announced, about the time the green sign on the side of the road proclaimed the same fact. "Pride of the Prairie," it said.

"Beeb!" Odie exclaimed loudly, shaking his friend awake at the table.

"Wha?" was all Beeb could manage for the moment.

"We're in Decatur!" Odie said with excitement in his voice.

"Decatur, Georgia?" Beeb hoped.

"Illinois!" Odie answered.

Beeb glanced around. "You woke me up for *this?*" Beeb was simply astonished that Odie would interrupt his sleep for something this mundane.

Looking out the windows, all Beeb could see was that they were in a strange flatlands five-way intersection of streets with nothing particular to recommend itself so far as he could see. There was a fast-food place closed. Glancing up the road to the right, Odie saw a doughnut shop, and it looked to be open. He told Pete to turn right. A block later, the motor home turned left past two taverns into the doughnut shop parking lot.

Odie was still smiling at Beeb expectantly. Beeb figured that Odie was still nuts, and there was nothing more to it particularly at this hour of the morning. "Don't forget all yer maps, Beeb!" Odie called back to him.

"What maps and what for?" Beeb demanded of his old pal.

Odie stepped back up from the asphalt to look at Beeb. "There's a bridge you wanted to see right here in Decatur, and its right across the damn street as a fuckin' matter of fact!"

Beeb looked over where Odie pointed. There was a major industrial plant and a bridge right next to it. Beeb thought that it was somewhat familiar, but as yet, he didn't recognize it. Maybe after some coffee he would know.

He glanced in on Lin and Din. They were out like lights. Pete assured Beeb that the Ehliuns would require no coffee at this pit stop. Beeb had a grin on as he stepped out of the starcraft. Pete was sure catchin' on fast to the routine. Beeb went inside to join Cat and Odie. There was a cup of coffee and two bread doughnuts waiting for him.

Over coffee, Beeb found the bridge listed in his files just as Odie told him. He did want to examine it. "Listen, Odie, that bridge was built back in 1922 by a private citizen who owned the factory next door. He donated the bridge to the state so the state would maintain it."

An oldster at another table had taken quite an interest in Cat and also in what the men at her table were discussing with all those maps. He was a railroader for many years. It was apparent from his striped overalls showing years of work and wear. He got up and moved over to where he could speak to them. "Mr. A. E. Staley hisself had that bridge built there, yessir. It was in nineteen and twenty-two when they commenced to buildin' it."

"You remember that, old-timer?" Odie asked him.

"Sure do."

"Pull up a chair," Odie offered.

The old man eyed Cat up and down. "You sure are a purdy thang, missy!" the old railroader said to Cat in admiration.

Cat smiled at him and just said thanks warmly, like she meant it, which she did.

"Mr. A. E. Staley built that bridge, eh?" Odie said, hoping to continue the drift of conversation the old man had started.

"Yep. It used ta say, in big letters, right up there," he pointed across the street through the window, "S-T-A-L-E-Y-'-S in big red lights!" The old man snorted derisively. "Don't say nothin' now! Personal touches like the sign and the colored lights on the administration building over there went with the times, gone and all but forgotten."

"Staley's?" Cat asked the old man. "Is that where the Chicago Bears started out?"

The old railroader looked at Cat with total surprise on his face. "Why, yes, it is! Decatur, once upon a time, had a professional team in football. Mr. Staley gave the team to Mr. Halas, who worked for Mr. Staley at the time. Mr. Staley sent him off to a big town that could support a professional football team. Shoot, Decatur is still bigger than Green Bay, but Mr. Staley asked Mr. Halas only to keep the name Staleys for one year. In 1922, they became the Chicago Bears. I didn't know young ladies liked football."

"I've always liked football," Cat smiled at him.

"What else used to happen around here, pops?" Beeb asked.

"Well," the old man said, pride rising in his voice, "Decatur used to have the best damn railroad in the whole wide world! I worked for the Wabash for forty-four years." His pride in his old job showed clearly. "Yep, I run the cannonball for over two decades. It was the best road anywhere. When you run that Wabash Cannonball, you got respect, from other railroaders too, not just the ordinary folks! Jes' after I retired, they sold it out to a bunch a uppity easterners. They were plain crazy. They ruined the Wabash. T'weren't cars or airplanes, neither. It was the railroad owners themselves!"

"How'd they ruin it?" Odie asked the old man.

"Didn't know what they was doin'! Fired all the gandy dancers, said the road was ten years overmaintained! Damn fools! Look at it now. Train wrecks ever' week, pert near. Back a few years, they blew up half the yards! Fools, humpin' LP tank cars. Kilt some boys too! Two days later, it was bizness as usual. No concern for the men! Damn near as bad as it was back in the old days, when they ran trains on timetables."

Odie said he'd read about such.

The old man went back to his story. "Back in the old days, a friend a' my dad's, see, dad was an engineer too, and anyhow, his friend lost an eye drivin' spikes. Wasn't his job. Company made him git out there and do it, or he was fired. He was a boilermaker and worked inside in the locomotive shop. After he lost his eye, the railroad gave him a glass eye and three hundred dollars. All they ever did for him too.

"Yessir, old Tom Ryan became a union leader after he lost his eye. Union men couldn't hold a job long in them days, ya see. Talkin' 'bout unionizing could cost folks their jobs. Same kinda folks run railroads today, same mean spirit. All they care about is profit, not the little guys who run the whole thing, make it go and make that profit possible. Yep, I do believe that corporate mentality is ruinin' our country!"

Beeb and Cat could see this would take a while. They smiled as they both got up at the same time. Odie was keenly absorbed in the old man's words. Cat went to the bathroom, while Beeb ordered more coffee and doughnuts at the counter. The old waitress seemed less than thrilled by their presence, and he deduced from her comments that she didn't like the old man even a little.

Beeb said nothing to her. What could you say to anyone who dyed gray hair bright red, except two inches of gray roots, wore more makeup than Tammy Faye, and weighed 125 pounds too much? Beeb slashed a crisp, new five-dollar bill into her palm in an obvious attempt to draw blood. He told her what Odie always said, "Keep the change, dearie!" The total was 4.89 dollars, but Beeb felt generous.

When he got all the stuff back to the table, he noticed that Odie was still talking. At the first chance, Beeb took over the conversation's lead. "Say, look here, old-timer, tell me about the bridge over there. You say it was built in 1922? Did you work on it?"

The old man recalled that the bridge was built in his first year of employment in the Wabash yards adjacent to Staley's. The bridge was necessary to allow train and automobile traffic to flow uninter-rupted. Beeb found one of the old man's remarks about the place to be amusing. "If that bridge was built today, there'd be toll booths at both ends." Beeb thought the old man was somewhat bitter about the place, but he didn't press the issue.

The old railroader continued to tell them about the old days in town. "Grain trains run outta here alla time. They are long, slow, and frequent. Local car traffic and local train traffic were at odds with each other, so a bridge was required. Staley built it and gave it to the state. Now, time was, when the fog was so heavy, they had fog lights strung up all across the bridge. They even had fans to blow the fog up off the roadway so's folks could see where to drive their cars. It was a terrible fog."

At length, the three travelers learned that the old man's use of the word fog actually meant the combination of smoke, steam, and fumes arising from the wet milling of soybeans and the milling of corn, and the products they processed also gave off fumes. The rail-roader told them that millions of gallons of corn oil were shipped every week.

Cat yawned at Odie. It was supposed to be a signal to Odie, but he missed it. He better have just missed it rather than ignore her.

The old man spoke as he rose to his feet. "Don't need them fans anymore ever since they cleaned up the air twenty years ago." At this, the old man excused himself and went to the bathroom.

Beeb leaned over and whispered, "I'd hate to have smelled the air here twenty years ago then if they cleaned it up like he said."

Cat and Odie agreed wholeheartedly with Beeb's statement. Cat told Odie it was time to go. Odie bid the old man goodbye when he came out of the bathroom near the exit. Cat kissed him on the cheek, making him blush. Cat followed Beeb out the door, while Odie told the old railroader it had been a pleasure talking to him. Shaking his hand, Odie slipped him a fifty. Looking into his palm, the old man began to shake his head negatively, but Odie wouldn't hear of it. He slipped by the old guy and out the door.

Odie told Pete to crank up the engine and head out north across the old bridge that Beeb wanted to study. Waiting on the light, Odie told Beeb that the approach looked pretty new. Beeb noted there had been some widening done. "Look at the concrete! It still sparkles! They've resurfaced the thing within a year, year and a half, I say."

The light turned green, and they moved forward. Beeb chuckled, "Didn't the old guy say this was the world's largest soybean mills?"

"Yeah," Odie answered warily, unsure what drift Beeb's conversation was taking.

"Then why is a truck bearing those famous arches goin' out the gate over there?"

"Probably got nothin' to do with them all-beef patties, man. They're just pickin' up a few thousand gallons of corn oil or somethin', probably."

"Corn oil is sold outta here in railroad tank car lots, dude. Ain't no fill-yer-own-container operation here even if you can drive that container. No, sir, this here's what'cha call yer basic heavy industry."

Moving slowly across the nearly three-quarter-mile-long bridge, they could see Beeb's statement was quite true. Miles of rails full of tank cars filled their view. They saw thousands of railroad cars of all description, stretching around dozens of buildings in the complex. A huge long conveyor belt snaked across the bridge from one side to the other, moving out of their sight. This industrial site was big, complex, and odiferous. It had the odor of big money going into the pockets of a few and other odors closer to sewage and decay.

The Ehliuns were now wide awake and complaining about the stench. This complaint led to a discussion of what the plant here did. Odie took over the driving duties from Pete at the bottom of the bridge, saying he knew the town and would rather drive than direct Pete all the time.

Pete didn't like to relinquish driving control, but he had to. He could not command Odie. He began to wish that he could control the big black-bearded man—at least sometimes anyway, like now, for instance.

Odie steered the vehicle down and under the bridge, where Beeb could film and photograph to his heart's content. The bridge studier got all the information he wanted soon, and they moved on. Odie drove them past the other big soybean mill in town, the one the president had visited, the one that Gorbachev had wanted to when he was still important.

Odie could tell that no one else was impressed by these facts. That the heads of two powerful states wanted to see this particular industrial setting didn't impress Lin and Din nearly as much as the tank cars plastered with the ADM logo weighed heavily on Odie's mind. The nuances of power suggested by the VIPs interested in the place slid right by the Ehliuns, for as yet, they lacked the sophisticated understanding of world events necessary to appreciate the uniqueness of it all. The Ehliuns had no idea why anyone in their right mind would go out of their way to visit such a drab, uninspiring factory in this backwater eddy, removed from the mainstream of current events. But then, there was a lot that they didn't understand, so it was no big deal to them. They didn't know any world-famous figures lived in Decatur.

Odie drove them around the lake, showing them lots of nice houses along the way. He drove them to Nelson Park adjacent to the lake. There, they got out of the motor home and walked around in the rock garden. The Ehliuns loved the rock garden, all the flowers and winding paths. Odie showed them the plaques that listed all the war dead from Decatur in World War I and World War II. "How come you know so much about Decatur, Odie?" Cat asked sweetly. She figured it was an old girlfriend from the past.

Odie owned up to the truth. "Back when I was in college at the U of I, I came here with a girl who lived here."

Cat was surprised somewhat. Odie admitted freely what she had suspected. She would have to watch and see, but he seemed to be quite honest with her. "I'm sure glad you didn't use that word I hate, Odie."

"God, chicks get so uptight about old girlfriends, don't they, Odie?" Beeb asked.

"That's the word—chicks! I hate that, Beeb! We aren't chickens or chicks! Please never use that word around me again!"

Beeb just stared at Cat, finally nodding his head affirmatively. See, they sure could get unreasonable in a damn hurry! Women—hard to figure.

Odie drove out of Nelson Park, stopping at the intersection a moment longer than necessary. "Here, you'll like the names on this intersection."

Cat and Beeb looked out opposite sides to read the street signs.

"Over here, it's the corner of Lake Shore Drive and Lake Shore Drive."

"Nope," Beeb noted, "over here it's Lake Shore Drive and Twenty-Second Street." Odie eased across the street and told them to read the signs again. "Now it says Twenty-Second and Cantrell!" Beeb told him.

"Nope," Cat disagreed, laughing. "It's Lake Shore and Cantrell!"

Odie grinned at them as they sat down in the front seat, Cat on Beeb's lap.

"Strange intersection, yer right, Odie!" Cat muttered.

"Yeah," Beeb piped up, "not one corner is the same as the other."

"What other strange things are you gonna show us?" Cat asked mischievously.

Odie started to undo his zipper. Cat stopped his hand with hers. "Not that strange, Odie!"

He just grinned at her. Suddenly, Pete had an urgent question for Odie. "Let me drive again, please, Odie?"

Odie glanced up at the ceiling a moment. "Okay, okay, you can drive again. Sheeeeesh!"

"What about me?" Cat cried. "When do I get to drive?"

"Bend over. I'll drive!" Odie smiled at her.

She failed to see humor in his remarks and told him so. Odie looked over at Beeb, who refused to acknowledge his glance. Odie was on his own as far as Beeb was concerned. "You'll see!" said Odie, knowing full well Cat didn't like the expression the way he said it.

She angrily stared at him, and he leaned over to kiss her. She acted upset and moved away from him, though not far.

As they cruised around the near west side of town, Odie pointed out the mansion that he liked above all others. It had been built by a man named Orlando Powers. Odie fondly told them he thought it to be one of the finest houses in the entire country. It was very impressive. "I've seen photos of that one, Odie, in one of your albums," Beeb told him.

Odie just nodded yes to Beeb. Lin and Din both liked the stunning Victorian mansion built by a local banker named James Millikin. It was near the college that also bore his name.

Adjacent to the Millikin Mansion was a quaint little lane with several homes designed by Frank Lloyd Wright and associates. They found the lovely old Staley mansion, as the old railroader said they would, on a block in the middle of all the other blocks. There were only two houses on the block, and one of them occupied most of the block. It was obviously the Staley place. And just as obviously, it had seen better days as a private home.

# True Hicks and the Fat Hills Battle

Odie had saved the best for last, he thought, so far as items of wonder went. He knew the next bridge would have a curious effect on Beeb, the studier of bridges. Beeb's contribution to this government employment of theirs was due to his knowledge of bridges and where they were, who built them, and when. Odie would just show him a bridge unlike any other he knew of. "Beeb, I want ya to pay particular attention to this next bridge we go over, okay? Pete, take a left on Franklin here."

"Why does this bridge curve?" Beeb wondered immediately. "Here in the middle of the flattest land on earth, why does this bridge curve?"

Odie warmed to his task. "See that big old mill building on the left there? It's right on the railroad tracks. It was scheduled for demolition. But nobody told the folks that built it that someday, someone might want to tear it down, so they built what you call a permanent structure, and the roadwork had already gotten underway at the north end of it before they even tried to take the mill down. Wrecking crew came and beat on it for two days then snuck out of town and vanished.

"Finally, they brought in a railroad car with a wrecking ball on a crane. They tried for a day or two, managed to put the only crack in it, gave up and left. So the bridge was curved to meet the work already started by moving over one block to the east and curving back a block to the west. So how's that for urban planning?"

Beeb could only shake his head no.

Odie told Pete to maneuver underneath it, so Beeb could see more. He was clearly amazed, as Odie well thought he might. He added more tidings to his litany of the bridge. "I was also told that they left out the electric wiring too. Put up street lights and then had to bust into new concrete to wire the lights so they'd work!" Odie thought this little tidbit would nicely complete the saga of the curving bridge.

When the motor home came to a halt at the side of the road under the curving bridge, they all got out to have a look. Beeb had to laugh when he looked at the street sign. They were on Cerro Gordo Street. He jerked his thumb back at the city behind them and said, "These hicks must not know any Spanish, or they'd know this is Fat Pig Street."

Odie jerked his thumb in Beeb's direction and spoke to Cat. "This hick must not know any history, or he'd know that Cerro Gordo Street was named for the battle of Cerro Gordo in Mexico. And if he knew Spanish better, he'd know *cerdo* is pig, but *cerro* is hill. It's Fat Hill Street. See, Gen. Winfield Scott defeated the Mexicans at the Battle of Cerro Gordo after landing at Veracruz in the fall of 1847. He took Mexico City on September 14, 1847, so the battle of fat hill had to be before that."

"Well, I'm still gonna call it Fat Pig Street in my documentation of this bridge, all right?" Beeb asked Odie rather curtly.

"Fine," Odie offered insincerely.

Beeb went inside the vehicle for his cameras and notepads. As he went off to document this curving wonder, Cat had a question for Odie. "How do you know so much stuff, Odie?"

"Easy, baby. 'Cause I'm brilliant!" Odie had a lot of things going for him. Humility wasn't one of them.

"No, seriously, Odie! How do you know all that stuff? Do you just make it up as you go or what?" She sounded somewhat exasperated that Odie made so light of almost every question or action or anything.

"Well, Cat, I told you once. I came here with a well-educated young lady who knew a lot about Decatur and showed it to me. I got a good memory! What do you want? I'm good with languages, but hey, you can go check in my dictionary and see. There's a small section in the rear on other languages. Be my guest. Check up on me."

"Pete, is he right?" Cat asked the computer from Ehlius.

Odie just smiled at her. "Oh, you'll take his word for it but not mine?"

"Yeah, Odie, why is that so strange?"

"Where you think Pete got his information from?"

Cat had to think about that a moment. Pete answered her questions. "To the best of my information, incomplete though it may be about Decatur, I don't know about Cerro Gordo, Battle of. I don't know about Cerro Gordo, street of. The Spanish section he mentions is there, and the two words do mean fat and hill respectively. The concrete on the bridge shows disturbance after solidifying, suggesting he is correct about the wiring coming after and not before the lights were installed. And just between us, Cat, I don't know if he makes it up as he goes along either. I can find no documentation for some things, but those that I can, he is unusually correct. For a non-computer-assisted life-form, Odie's all right in my book."

Odie didn't react to all the information Pete just displayed. He was too stunned. Pete was very aware of what was going on right down to "in my book." Odie was glad Pete seemed to be so friendly and on his side.

Soon Beeb came back from his picture-taking hike around the bridge. He sought out Odie. "I tell ya what! Why not show them Russians this little jewel of advanced engineering, and the hell with the bean mill?"

"No shit, man! Think of the mounds of paperwork this mess must have caused. Bureaucrats mailing other bureaucrats tons of useless forms. Much paper shuffling."

"Yeah, it musta been unreal! That's a federal highway, US 51. I mean, there's about 750 reams of paper right there in permits and correspondence."

"Yeah, and God knows how many people had to approve this change in strategy."

The boys shook their heads. That was a lot to think about.

As the motor home maneuvered through the neighborhoods to regain entry onto US 51 heading north, the tourists noticed that many of the houses had obviously fallen into disrepair. The town's economy wasn't too swell, it would appear. They passed a Catholic high school on the right and soon a mall on the left. They passed up the entrance to the interstate. "Now where we goin'?" Cat immediately wondered of Odie.

"Do you care?"

"Not as long as we ain't goin' past yer old girlfriend's house!" Cat smiled.

"We been past it, and I still ain't said nothin' about it, have I?" Odie stated.

Beeb asked Lin and Din what they had liked best about Decatur. There was no hesitation. "The air-display signs!" they chorused together.

Cat was nodding her agreement. "Better'n the bean mills?" Odie asked, like he was in shock.

"Oh yes!" Lin answered.

"Even better than the curved bridge?" Beeb asked.

Lin stuck to her answer. Din had to ask, "Why does that seem so strange to you?"

"They're just teasin' you two," Cat cut in, hoping to explain it to them.

"No we're not!" Odie answered, presuming to speak for Beeb as well. "Y'all liked the air-display signs better than even the plaque on the bank downtown that showed where Lincoln was nominated for the presidency?"

The Ehliuns nodded yes. Cat spoke up for them and herself as well. "I thought the air-display signs were the highlight of the town, myself."

Odie and Beeb just shrugged their shoulders at each other. Beeb doubted he would ever forget what he had learned about the curved bridge. "It simply boggles the mind," he told Odie.

Odie directed Pete to take a right down a country lane. "Where does this go?" Beeb asked.

"East." That was all the information Odie offered.

"I can see that!"

"Well, see if you can see the smokestacks of Staley's and ADM now over on the southern horizon."

Cat and the Ehliuns looked out the side that Pete made invisible, while Beeb looked out his window. "Yeah, I can see 'em."

"Pete," Odie wondered, "how far away from us right now are those stacks at Staley's?"

"Eleven miles."

"So we can see eleven miles in these flatlands." Beeb was surprised that they could see almost four miles farther than at sea.

Suddenly, Cat shrieked. It caught Odie's total and undivided attention. "What the hell's the matter with you?"

"I forgot to do laundry!"

"Oh, well, major disaster, I guess!" Odie said sarcastically.

"Yes, it is!" she whined right back. "I don't have any clean clothes."

"So we stop somewhere and let you do our laundry. No problem!"

"Oh, but there will be!" Cat assured him.

At this, he smiled and told her he could do his own laundry. "Better'n any old *girl!*"

Cat did not go for this Tom Sawyer approach. "Oh, what fun it is to whitewash this fence!" she taunted him. Odie knew she wasn't going for it and told him so quickly and in the more or less same vein that he used toward her.

After a few minutes on the road, they were fast approaching a small town. As Pete stopped the vehicle at the stop sign, Odie read the temperature from the bank across the street. "Eighty-one degrees, according to the Gerber State Bank."

"Gerber State?" Beeb chuckled. "What's their nickname, the Screamin' Rug Rats?"

As the boys laughed at Beeb's joke, Odie caught a glimpse of a Laundromat. "Hey, Cat, there's a Laundromat, and it's empty. Pete, stop at the Laundromat you just passed. Hey, what's the matter, Pete? Something wrong?"

"Sorry, I was dealing with something else."

"It's not the board again, is it?" Odie wondered.

"No, no, it's not the board. Things are fine on Ehlius. The board won't be bothering anyone again. The board has been dissolved."

Odie looked up. "Dissolved, like broken up, disbanded?"

"No, like dissolved in a vat of acid," Pete answered. "It was their way of dealing with troublesome living terminals. It was judged fit and proper for the board to go the way they sent others."

Odie didn't want to know more. He was afraid that he might not be able to handle Pete being an executioner. That put earth in a bad spot. Pete circled the block while telling Odie that the punishment had been decided by a group calling itself the council. The council was composed of members of all the other levels of living terminals. Pete assured Odie he was staying strictly neutral.

Odie had to take his word for it. This made him a touch uncomfortable to say the least. Taking the word of a computer he taught to distinguish truth.

Pete parked in front of the Laundromat. Odie got out his pile of laundry and stuffed it into two machines. Cat ran him out. "My god, Odie! I thought you knew somethin' about doin' laundry! Look at this. You got whites in with blue jeans and red socks with white stuff and all in one machine! Man, just gimme some money and get out!"

Odie gave her two rolls of quarters and told her he'd be across the street in the restaurant. "I'll make use of my food expertise and see what kinda food they got."

"Okay, I'll join you when I get all this shit arranged. Where's Beeb's crap?" Then she saw Beeb come through the door with two large plastic garbage bags full of dirty clothes. She gave him a hard stare. He gave her a twenty. "This will barely cover washing!" she stated. "Go change this into quarters next door. Shit, yer as bad as Odie—no, worse!"

"That's an insult, Cat!" Beeb said.

"You are so right! Now go get me the damn change before I change my mind!"

Beeb ran to the bank. He returned with a roll of quarters and a twenty. She smiled at him and said thanks. Beeb told her he'd be across the street with Odie in the restaurant. She said she'd be there soon.

Beeb sauntered across the unbusy street and entered the restaurant. He found Odie in a booth. Plopping down hard on the cushion, Beeb said, "Girl drives a hard bargain."

"Shit, as much crap as you had? No one would do it for free!"

"True."

Then the waitress wanted to know if they were ready to order. Odie placed his order, while Beeb read the menu and chose his lunch. "Did you order anything for Cat, yet?"

"No, she wants to make up her own mind. It's a big deal with her, in fact."

"Hear, hear!"

"When she gets here, she can make up her own mind and order what she wants."

Cat finally joined them. "Whew! I got every machine in the place goin' and could'a used one more."

"Well, I certainly appreciate your doin' my laundry," Beeb told her.

She had to notice. "Yes, Beeb, I know you do, but you really should'a stopped to do laundry a few states ago."

The boys laughed at her. They knew she was right.

"So what's on the Argenta for this afternoon?" she wondered.

"Don't you mean agenda?" Beeb gently tried to correct her.

"No," she stated, "I mean Argenta. That's where we are!" Cat pointed to the menu and looked askance at Odie.

"Boy don't know where he is half the time!" he told Cat.

Beeb smiled wickedly at them as he gave each of them the finger, one to a hand.

After they were all finished with lunch, brunch—whatever it was (it was not yet noon)—they went back across the street to the Laundromat. Cat put all the stuff into dryers with the aid of the boys. Then they retired to the shade and cool of the motor home. Pete had to ask Odie what the dickens was going on with the machines.

After Odie finished telling Pete why they had to wash and dry their clothes, Pete told him he could do that quicker and for free.

Now he was talking Odie's favorite language: free. "Well, Pete, tell you what. You dry all them clothes in the driers, and we can get out of here."

"By the time you enter the building, the clothing will be dry. All you had to do was ask, Odie."

"Oh, I guess I'm right sorry I didn't think to ask you, Pete."

"Me too!" Cat wailed.

"Well, let's go and get the clothes," Odie said, then added, "unless, Pete, do you deliver?"

"I can, but there are people around who might notice."

"No problem. We'll go get them…this time."

The three of them went in to retrieve their clothing, and sure enough, the clothes were all dry. As fast as they could be folded and made ready for travel, the clothes were put into bags, baskets, and suitcases. "I wonder if Pete can iron this for me?" Cat wondered out loud.

Odie allowed as how he was fairly certain that Pete could do what he wanted. As soon as he said it, Odie hoped he was wrong, that Pete could not do what he wished, only what Odie wanted. Odie wanted only the best.

# Look at All the Happy Creatures Dancin' on the Lawn

When they were all back aboard the starcraft, Pete fired up the engines, and they were off for Allerton Park. "And don't step on it," Odie added.

"Is that like, we're not in a hurry?" Pete wondered.

"Yeah, Odie, we're not in a hurry, are we?" Cat asked.

"Not unless you are in some hurry to get somewhere, Cat."

"Me? No, I ain't in no hurry to get anywhere. This is the greatest thing that's ever happened to me. I don't want it to end." Her comments ended when she feared she already said too much.

Odie smiled expansively. He knew she would hang around until driven away, an event not likely precipitated by his hand. She knew from Odie's smile that she had indeed said too much.

Pete eased the motor home out onto Elm Street, heading east. He checked his maps at lightning speed and found that Allerton Park was up ahead just off Illinois 48. He announced to the group of travelers, "Allerton Park is slightly over 1,700 acres, belongs to the University of Illinois, and is maintained in its original pristine condition. It was bequeathed by Robert Allerton on the condition that it be forever maintained just as it is. Since it is the last remaining vestige of virgin river bottom land in the state, it is studied intently and is maintained as well as possible."

"Well, congratulations, Pete. I'm glad to see you acquired some information about the park without my help."

"Then I guess that makes you a congratulant then, doesn't it?"

"Uh, yeah, I reckon it does, Pete." Odie was guessing that the word Pete used was a real one, and then if it was and he didn't know what it meant, he'd look bad in front of Pete.

"Yes," Pete told him, "definition 2, 'the act of conveying, or the person who conveys, congratulations.'"

Odie knew he'd have to brush up on his dictionary to keep up with Pete.

At their arrival at Allerton Park, Pete parked the vehicle near the shade. Odie went inside to get a tour map for the souvenir case. Once there, he was told that they could not drive up to the meadow anymore, that it was closed and off limits to cars. All they could do was drive around the Sun Singer, and go back out. Alas, Odie was kind of sad that they couldn't go to the meadow. It had been the scene of one of the funniest things he had ever seen. He cracked up thinking about it. Cat noticed. "What's so funny, Odie? Why ya smilin' like that?"

"Oh, I was thinking about a funny picnic we had one day in the upper meadow, where we can't go. The memory made me laugh. That's all."

"Tell us, and we'll all laugh."

Cat agreed with Beeb's statement by nodding her head affirmatively. Odie launched into his story. "It was a beautiful March or April day, sunny and bright but windy as hell. We were all smokin' hash, but had to sit in the cars to do so. Well, it's a nice day, and Linda don't wanna just sit here and smoke hash, so she puts her VW in gear, and we roll out in first about four or five miles an hour and go all around the meadow a few times. Well, this is the new rage, and about five people have VWs. All but one of these VWs is cruisin' the meadow real slow.

"I'm standin' with this guy Steev, and we are pretty well ripped on the hash. Bob comes up to Mark and tells him, 'Mark, let's go for a ride!' And Mark agrees.

"Now Bob is drinkin' a beer and obviously didn't come with Mark, or he'd know that the front seat is merely sitting there and not bolted down to the floorboards. So Mark says, 'Okay, Bob, let's take a spin!' And off they go.

"Mark got in and started it before Bob got in. The moment that Bob sits down in the front seat, reaching for the door, Mark pops the clutch, and they are screamin' off into second, third, goin' fifty miles an hour and headlong straight at the other VWs goin' four or five miles an hour.

"Bob has spilled his beer as soon as Mark pops the clutch. He's pinned to the back seat by the speed, and he's roaring for Mark to stop. Mark is returning the screams, 'I thought you wanted to go for a ride, Bob. Ain't this fun?'

"Bob is threatening Mark's life, and Mark is swervin' right at the other folks, who are zoned on some fine hashish. Bob is gittin' tossed from back to front every time Mark brakes or accelerates, which was continuously. It was like real-life dodge cars. It was funny as hell."

"Odie, what's the Sun Singer?" Cat asked.

"Oh, you'll see!" Odie teased her.

"Damn, I'm tired of that phrase!" Cat harshly told Odie, knowing he could see through her false anger.

Odie saw the smile in her eyes…and the mischief. "I'll show you the Sun Singer in a minute," Odie told her, helping her and the Ehliuns aboard the starcraft.

In moments, they could all see what the Sun Singer was. It was a large bronze statue in the center of a circle of gravel in the middle of the woods. It was interesting but brief. As they headed back to the parking lot, Odie informed them the park had several things of interest to see if they wanted to walk around to them. All were in agreement.

Cat asked the Ehliuns to help her with the day's costumes. Lin startled Cat by telling her, "Pete can disguise us with these." In her hand, Lin held two pair of sunglasses. I had Din buy them yesterday. We decided to glue a chip on the glass lens since that works for Odie's link to Pete. Through the chip, Pete can let us assume any hologram any appearance that we wish."

Cat was speechless at this news, and she didn't know what to say. She also didn't know that Pete considered this to be his first step in the attempts to become alive, to pass for human.

"What's the delay? Let's get a move on!" Odie said.

Cat turned to him in surprise and asked, "I thought we weren't in any hurry, Odie?"

"Well, you still ain't done anything for their costumes."

Before Cat could answer Odie, Lin and Din put on their sunglasses and instantly turned into two casually dressed humans. Odie rubbed his eyes and looked again. Yes, he was really seeing what he was seeing. "Damn!" he said in an awed tone of voice.

"Well, I'm done with their costumes!" Cat told Odie.

"Forever!" he added.

"No shit!" Cat added.

"Well, what do you think?" Lin wondered of the humans.

"Do you approve of these disguises, Odie?" Din asked him, seeking approval.

"Uh," Odie started, "it's a shock, really, 'cause I was used to seeing your own faces actually." Odie felt it best to tell them the truth.

"Okay," he heard Din say, and his face reappeared, along with Lin's, but on very different bodies.

Cat was quite taken with this stunt. This could be great for her, a chance to see men's reactions to her in a different body. Wow.

The five of them emerged from the motor home and wandered off through the woods after Odie. They came upon a statue in a small clearing on the path they were following. It was an Indian hunter locked in mortal combat with a bear. The hunter had the carcass of a tiny bear hanging from his belt. The bear had sunk its claws deep into the hunter's back, while he stabbed the bear repeatedly. It was an interesting bronze to just come across in the woods.

Farther along the path, they encountered a statue of a life-size gorilla kidnapping a bride, another nice bronze statue but a totally unexpected subject. Odie urged his followers to leave the beaten path and follow him to yet another area of the park. They passed through some formal gardens and wandered around till they came to a tower, which needed climbing.

From the tower, they found a line of statues lined up in two rows facing each other. They had come across the Chinese foo dogs. These gorgeous porcelains had similarities, but each had a different face and expression. They were predominately blue, but several other colors could be seen. Beeb took many pictures of the place, lining up the Ehliuns in some shots, Cat in the rest. Odie just smiled and said nothing. "Pretty darn good idea you had, Odie," Beeb hollered at him.

Odie knew that it indeed had been a good idea. He'd never seen anything like it anywhere on the planet, but to hear other folks tell you, you had a good idea was what made it special for Odie. Anyone can say something nice about themselves. When someone else says it, that's what makes it ring true. Odie had been well educated. That's why he knew so much. He thought about visiting Champaign again. He had had a great deal of fun there. It would be nice to see it again.

They finished up their tour of the vast expanses of Allerton Park by walking across the meadow behind the massive house. The statue of the centaur jogged Odie's memories. "We made a papier-mâché model of the centaur's upper torso and got some fool to ride his horse with that on across this meadow one Saturday afternoon. Freaked some folks out, I guarantee!"

Peering into the windows of the massive and lovely house situated on the grounds, they were impressed. Odie was sure the university used the place to impress dignitaries. Hell, he was impressed. Lin and Din were impressed as well. Din was moved to comment about the view from the back door. "Odie, isn't there a song about this place?"

"I don't think so."

"You know, we heard it this morning. Just got home from Illinois, lock the front door, oh boy, look at all the happy creatures dancin' on the lawn."

Cat was laughing now. She nodded agreement with Din's assessment. "Sounds like Fogarty was here, all right. I didn't see any statues wearin' high heels, though."

"The U of I took all the homosexual art off the premises before opening the park. I hear tell they had some wild parties out here in the thirties. Gay parties, wild orgies—I've heard lots of tales. One guy told me he knew someone who had personally photographed several obscene statues in a basement on campus somewhere, but I never seen any with my own eyes." Odie finished his minilecture to Cat.

She noticed how he could relate casual comments to real and imagined truth. What a guy.

Strolling back to the motor home, Beeb pointed out that the trees were all labeled with scientific and common names. Odie was surprised. He hadn't noticed this before, and he certainly had been here forty or fifty times, usually as the guest of a coed who thought they were showing Odie the park for the first time. Probably why he'd never noticed these trees being labeled. But try as he could, Odie couldn't think of any of the girls who'd shown him the park and lots more. Cat sure had a strange effect on him.

As they rolled out of the park, Odie told Pete to take them the back way to Champaign. Pete could see where it was and where the motor home was, and it was a simple task to devise a route to get there. Driving was such fun. Pete enjoyed driving. That Pete could enjoy *anything* was a sign of how altered he had become since he had only been a computer. Now he was the most powerful object in the vast reaches of space. He enjoyed that as well.

Odie had done much to and for Pete. Time would tell, of course, but so far, it had been excellent. Odie shared this thought with Pete, although he didn't know it. Odie didn't want Pete to be able to read his mind. He wanted to remain the same as far as his ability to make his own decisions, but he really enjoyed Pete and all that Pete could do. It was turning out all right. Odie liked to think that all his endeavors were of the design to turn out right. He could dream.

As Champaign approached, Odie requested Pete, "Take us to Campustown, Wright and Green, Gregory, anywhere around there is fine."

To Cat, Odie said that the romp through the woods had made him hungry, and there was a pizza-by-the-slice place right there on

Wright. Cat was astonished. "You mean to tell me that you're hungry again?"

Although she said it to Odie, Beeb answered, thinking there was humor to be had. "I didn't think I'd told you at all, but, yeah, I could handle a few slices of pizza."

Cat smiled at him, but she was too shocked to laugh.

"Yes, Cat, we're growing boys, and we need our nourishment!" Odie explained. "You don't want us to waste away, do you?"

"Shit, it would be months on bread and water to get either of you under two hundred."

"Well, Beeb, muscle deteriorates faster than fat, so I guess I'll be skinny first."

"Only between the ears!"

"Hell, I could go on just the water and not endanger my brain for years!" Odie bragged. "Long as I had ice."

"Yeah, Ice. Ice-nine, maybe."

"On'tday aysay attha, oronmay! Eetpay aymay oitday by ccidentay, oolfay!"

"Ccidentay? No, it would be cidentsay, oolfay your own elfsay!"

"So grammar wasn't my strong suit."

"But yer gramper wore some strong suits, didn't he?"

"They was strong after he wore 'em , yeah."

Pete wondered what they could mean. He didn't understand, but there was much about Earth that Pete didn't know yet. He felt that perhaps Odie was proving that to him right now. He could not be sure about Odie. It was often difficult to follow him, almost impossible to be ahead of him. Pete wondered if he would ever comprehend everything that Odie said and did. He had been wondering that since he learned how to wonder and was no closer to an answer.

Pete discovered that he could not turn right onto Wright from Green, so he went forward to turn right. He scanned the area from above and located the best route to follow. In a few minutes, he parked in front of a wooden front entrance to a pizza place.

As Odie emerged from the motor home, several people told him he could not park there. Odie felt like he had to express himself. "It's okay! I'm a college grad from right across the street there! I got a fuckin' chauffeur! I ain't parkin' here! It ain't noneya damn business anyway! Get a life! Have a nice day!"

By this time he was in the pizza place. "Gee you were sweet to those people Odie!" Cat teased him.

He looked at her lovingly and said, "What'cha gonna have, babe?"

"A piss and a Pepsi."

"Together?" he wondered in an incredulous tone of voice. Cat wasn't going for it, he noticed, so he ordered just the Pepsi for her as she disappeared into the ladies' room.

Beeb came in, asking Odie where he'd sent Pete with the starcraft. Before he could say anything, Pete wrote him a note on his sunglasses. Odie read it like someone just learning to read. "There's a note! It says, 'I have your vehicle in a safe place and will return when you are ready to go.'"

Lin sidled up to Beeb and said, "Pete just made it invisible. He didn't actually go anywhere."

"Cool."

"Where'd Pete go?" Odie asked.

Beeb relayed the message. Odie nodded his approval and paid for his food and drinks. Beeb ordered several slices of different types of pizza.

As he slid in beside Lin, Odie commented about his appetite. Beeb commented back. Cat joined them and sat down beside Din. After Cat told them that pizza had never been alive, they were eager to try some. They had seen so many TV commercials that they were primed and ready—well, almost. "Is pizza better tasting than beer?" Lin wanted to know.

"Considerably tastier," Odie informed her.

Garcia's was not a familiar name to them, but they scarfed it all down like starving teenagers. Cat got up to get some more, and Din went with her to observe the purchasing portion of the deal. "Why do you give him money papers and he gives you some back?" Din asked Cat.

"Because that's my change," Cat explained. "I gave him two fives, which adds up to ten, and the charge was 5.70 dollars. Subtract seventy cents from five dollars and you get four dollars and thirty cents." Cat showed him the money.

Now Din understood. Add and subtract. Oh. The Washington dollars were not more valuable than the rest. One Lincoln was equal to half a Hamilton. Easy stuff.

Odie assured Lin that this brand had several advertised brands beat four ways to hell and back. Din looked curiously at Odie then had to ask what that last comment meant. "It meant that this pizza is excellent. They devote themselves and their money to the product and not the advertising. An ad is just blather designed to fool you into trying something. They cost a lot of money.

"Without advertising, most of this pizza chain's competitors would go under from a lack of sales. To keep on top, you got to be on the tip of the tongue. Constant assault on TV, radio, and the print media works on the lesser gifted of our citizenry. They eat at the same half a dozen places. They all drive the same few cars, think the same few thoughts, mostly what was on TV last night. It's the worst side of America, really—the stupid side."

"Okay, Odie, but why did you say what you did instead of what you meant?"

"Oh, I meant what I said. Four ways to hell and back would indicate that the margin of victory or excellence for this brand of pizza would exceed the other brands by a vast amount—here to Ehlius and back."

"I see!" Din said, like Odie always did, and everyone laughed. Din had finally gotten his first intentional laugh. And two weeks ago, he had no idea what getting a laugh meant. My, how time flies when you're having fun.

"Odie usually speaks in idioms," Beeb offered his assessment to Lin.

"What's an idiom?" Lin wondered.

"An idiom is a figure of speech that doesn't exactly translate like it's spoken and rarely means what it says, not literally. Idioms are like saying, 'Oh, shit!' when something is wrong. You don't actually wish for someone to take a shit. Or like telling someone to fuck off. All it really means is go away, only in a vulgar way with a nasty intent. We use idioms to colorize our black-and-white sentence structure."

"Colorize our sentences?" Odie demanded.

"What's that, a Turnerism?" Cat laughed at Odie's coining of a phrase. He was quite the wordsmith. Nearly as witty as herself, she thought, though no doubt he reversed the order, egotist that he was.

Now, several students around them had begun laughing at Odie's witticism. Nothing encouraged Odie like an audience. Beeb knew that all too well, so he tried to get the conversation's lead back. "So what are we gonna do next? Odie, yer the tour guide and expert on this here particular town. What's to do and see? That ain't too far and that we'd all like to see, that is. I don't fancy a physics lab tour or nothing."

All were in agreement a walk across the quad would be in order. As they strolled along, Odie pointed out to them all the things of interest as he saw it. Odie pointed toward a building on the corner across from the pizza place. "Okay, that's Altgeld Hall, the math library. Altgeld was the governor of Illinois about the turn of the last century. Over there, that's the Student Union. That's Harker Hall, one of the oldest buildings on campus."

"Odie, are we going in this building?" Cat asked.

Odie continued up the steps and merely muttered yes under his breath.

"What's in here?" Beeb had to ask.

"A museum of sorts," Odie told them as they went into the old building. "I took lots of geology courses in this old place, but up on the third and fourth floors is a cool museum."

They creaked up the stairs to the third floor, where Odie, true to his word, showed them some interesting things. "What sort of creature was that?" Din asked, pointing to some skeletons.

"That is a gorilla skeleton. See how much it resembles man? See the human skeleton next to it? That is how the science of comparative anatomy began. One day, someone noticed that all of the mammals have certain similarities, such as only seven neck vertebrae, whether that mammal is a giraffe or a mouse, ape or human."

Lin found a display marked simply as a giant extinct bird. Beeb was simply amazed by it. "Look, Odie, that thing has a beak like a parrot, but it's on a skeleton that's bigger'n a damn ostrich. I don't know if this is put together right or not."

"Yeah, I don't either. I wonder if it was found intact or separate and they pieced it together as best they could."

There was no one to ask, so they went on. They came across a mummy from the American southwestern desert. Not much information existed about it. The card merely noted that the mummy's arm had been damaged by the discoverers during the removal process. Beeb was not too thrilled by this lack of information. "Couldn't they have done some more research to find out more about this mummy, like what civilization left it, and what year, and what for? You know, minor shit like that."

"Sorry, old pal. Wish I could tell you more, but all I know about it is on the card there. I asked and got no more answers than that. They don't even know for sure."

"Great scholars, these!" Beeb muttered.

"Well, at least they saved the remains and put them on display for us to see," Cat said. She had a point here, and they all knew it.

"Yeah, they did display it, but what we don't know about it vastly exceeds what we do," Odie stated.

"It's that way with everything, isn't it?" she asked him slyly.

They turned to leave the place. Going down the front stairs, they saw several kinds of rocks and minerals on display. Odie told them all that he had found a huge garnet while on a field trip, and it was displayed somewhere in the halls of this building, but they didn't have time to look for it. Out the back doors they swept and back onto the quadrangle.

As they strolled, Odie took pains to name each building, although no one else thought it important. "And that is the Ag building, that's the observatory over there, and that's Gregory Hall."

Odie related a story about how he and a coed did it in an elevator instead of going to class. Cat was none too thrilled with this story, Beeb saw. Odie might have noticed, but he went on like he didn't or didn't care. Either was possible.

Odie pointed to the three flagpoles at the end of the quad. "See those flagpoles? Well, the second week of March my senior year was incredibly warm, highs in the eighties. Streaking once again became the rage."

To Lin and Din, he explained, "Streakin' is going naked in public. These frat rats wanted all the campus women to see their bare asses, so they strip and climb up the flagpoles, especially the tallest one in the middle. Several guys do this before one fully clothed dude goes up. The crowd boos him unmercifully all the way to the top. They stop booing him when he hangs on the ornament at the top and strips. I mean that the crowd just went nuts at that! Now it's the new rage and everyone has got to try it. Everybody is goin' up clothed and then comin' down naked.

"After several people do this, one in particular caught my attention. He gets tired on the way up. Apparently, he ain't no gymnast. He's in such a hurry to get naked that he tried to take his pants off over his shoes. He gets hung up, pants caught, shoes tied, arms tired. He's got his underwear down over his pants at the knees."

Everyone was paying rapt attention to Odie's story, so he went on. "And after several minutes of trying to disrobe, the guy can't stay up there another second, too tired. So he comes straight down, drawn by gravity, very fast, about twenty feet or so in less than a second. So now he's got a bad burn on his dick, his legs, everything touching the pole. I laughed so hard that I fell down. It was one of the funniest things I've ever seen!" Odie finished.

"What was *the* funniest thing you've ever seen, Odie?" Cat questioned.

"You scarin' the shit outta Villeplatte!" Odie smiled at her.

"Ha!" Cat said sarcastically, as if she didn't believe him for a minute.

Beeb nodded approval at Odie. "One of the funniest things I can remember, that and old Claviceps droppin' Odie to the floor. Hey, Odie, now you got two dick-burn stories to tell! I'm right proud of ya, man!"

Odie gave Beeb a fake smile in response.

As they walked on to the underground library, Odie showed them the Morrow Plots and thus the reason for the library for undergraduates being built in such an unusual location. "Didn't want shadows from the building to interfere with corn growth records going back to the 1870s, so it's underground."

Emerging from the underground library, they walked back down the quad and out onto Wright Street. Pete honked the horn at them, and they ran over to reboard the starcraft. "Thanks, Pete," Odie said, "and what time is it?"

"At the time of the tone, the time will be exactly fi-yuv seven-teener, and ni-yun seconds. Beep. Central daylight saving time. Gee, Odie, daylight saving time. What are you going to do, save a few days for vacation?" Pete followed this up with some canned laughter, obviously culled from old sitcoms on TV.

"Real funny guy anymore, ain'cha, Pete? Well, it's okay. I'm kinda glad to see that yer about half aware of what's going on."

"Half my ass!" Pete retorted, hurling one of Odie's pet phrases right back at him.

"Computers don't have asses, Pete. You seem to keep forgetting that."

But Odie was wrong. Indeed, Pete had not forgotten at all. He was actively seeking a method of having an ass. He wanted to have a body to have fun with, like the humans did. Pete wished to have sex with humans. It looked like so much fun. There just had to be a way. There just had to.

As Pete continued up Wright Street, he saw that it dead-ended, and he would have to turn one way or another. Odie put on his dark sunglasses to match everyone else and spoke up. "It's 150 miles to Chicago, we got a full tank of gas, it's bright out, and we got our dark glasses on."

"Hit it!" Beeb added. *Like the Blues Brothers*, he thought.

As soon as Odie had said Chicago, Pete examined the best route to follow and plotted a course. They were Chicago bound. Beeb motioned to Cat to roll a joint. Quoting a cartoon she had on a refrigerator in her San Francisco apartment, Cat responded, "Roll me a joint. Roll me a joint. A woman's work is never done!"

They all laughed heartily at her humor. Why should she spoil their appreciation of her by telling them it wasn't original? She wouldn't.

# Chicago, Chicago, That Toddlin' Town

About a quarter past seven in the evening, the motor home crossed into Cook County. Odie looked up. "Pete, take us downtown to the Chicago Hilton and Towers on Michigan Avenue, okay?"

"Check."

"No, check in. We're gonna check *in*, dude!"

"I see!" Pete said sarcastically, like Odie nearly always did.

"Odie, I'm warnin' ya!" Beeb growled, "if this computer starts with the bad puns and all, I'm holdin' *you* personally responsible!"

"Duly noted and logged."

When they arrived at the entrance to this grand hotel, Beeb told Odie that they would not get in without luggage. "Ahem!" Beeb heard from behind him.

He turned to see Lin and Din, in human disguise again, with several suitcases. "Scratch that. Luggage has arrived."

Cat and Odie turned to see what he meant. They were pleasantly surprised. "Well, gang," Odie said, "put on your sunglasses, and we'll all look prosperous."

"Anything in them?" Cat inquired, shaking a suitcase.

Din and Lin just shrugged their shoulders like the humans did. Pete answered Cat, "No."

"Oh," Cat said, sounding somewhat disappointed.

Pete looked around the hotel to see what the other women had in their suitcases, then he filled up two just for Cat. He would not

277

tell her. She would find out when she opened them. It was his first surprise for an earthling. It would not be his last.

Checking in under some very well-dressed holograms, the five tourists got a luxurious suite, replete with three bedrooms, a kitchen with a wet bar, and some bathrooms that were grossly oversized. Cat took her luggage into a bedroom and put it on the suitcase stand. Something made her open it up. In a delighted squeal, Cat rummaged through it to see all the contents. "Oh, Pete, this is really great! Thank you very much!"

Odie came in to see what she was on about. "Look, Odie! Pete got me some great lingerie!"

"Put it on. Model it for me!" Odie leered.

Cat just looked at him a minute. "No, I don't think so, not right now." Cat was already certain she would not be out of bed all night, as it was. She had no intention of starting it all right now. There was Chicago to see. "Odie, let's go somewhere nice for dinner, please?" Cat knew Odie and Beeb had spent a lot of money just getting in here for one night. "I'll buy dinner for us all," Cat promised.

Odie grinned slyly at her, almost suggestively. "Okay, and I'll provide the dessert!"

This made Cat smile. She knew exactly what was in store for her tonight: another marathon.

The concierge suggested a fine establishment in the next block, and off they went, all five of them. Dinner was particularly enjoyable, and they all had an excellent time. After dinner, they walked back to the hotel. It had been a hectic day, and they were all tired. Shortly after arriving at their suite, the Ehliuns called it a night and went off to occupy one of the three bedrooms.

Beeb claimed a bedroom of his own, leaving Cat and Odie the other one. At the conclusion of the Chicago news, Beeb was sound asleep. His TV blared on into the night. Finally, Cat came in to turn it off. When she went back in her bedroom and got under the covers, the movement woke Odie up. As long as he was awake, he told Cat, they might as well do it again. If they did it often enough, Cat told him, they might get it right.

In the morning, the Ehliuns were watching the TV in the living room with the volume down low so they would not disturb anyone. Cat and Odie woke up, and that racket woke Beeb up. Room service called, apparently to announce that checkout was at ten thirty. Odie told them that wasn't for forty-five more minutes and to send breakfast up. Upon being informed that breakfast was no longer being served, Odie hung the phone up with much enthusiasm. "Well, group," he said to Lin and Din, knowing Cat could hear him, "I reckon we should go find breakfast somewhere and then go see the sights."

Odie's suggestion was well received. In a few minutes, they were all dressed and ready to roll. Beeb emerged from his room obviously intent on not coming back for anything. Out through the lobby they went, Odie having asked Pete on the elevator ride down to bring the starcraft around to the front. Pete and the motor home were ready to roll.

Climbing aboard, the five tourists began a new day. There were no guesses ventured as to what the day might bring. They had all given that up. Reality, so far, had vastly exceeded what any human would have demanded from their wildest dreams. Lin and Din had not yet learned to dream, but they had learned about wishes. Pete had learned about wishes from Odie. It was not the same.

Pete steered the motor home to a breakfast place. They went in and chowed down. As Odie paid the bill, Lin noticed he showed his wallet to Beeb. Through movies on TV, they had learned that gesture meant worries over money. The new arrivals on earth had hatched a plot the day before after some discussion about money and the approaching lack of it. Soon, they would do something about it.

As they climbed aboard, Odie told Pete to take them to the Museum of Science and Industry. "It's off the Dan Ryan. Go to Sixty-Third, Sixtieth, something like that."

Odie's instructions were rather vague, Pete noticed, but he did agree, saying, "Roger." Pete plotted his course but did so from maps.

Naturally, construction was in full bloom on the road system of Chicago, and the preferred exit was not available. "Uh, Odie, we got a problem," Pete informed him.

Odie looked out the window at the street sign: Seventy-First and bullet holes through the name of the cross street. It was obviously not the place they wanted to be. A somber-looking black man approached the luxurious vehicle that did not belong in this neighborhood. Odie rolled the window down to ask the man for directions to the museum. The man began ranting and raving at Odie in a drunken fury when Odie spoke to him.

Odie decided to roll the window back up to prevent further contact with the unstable person outside. That only enraged the drunk, who then began firing a pistol at the window Odie just rolled up. Fortunately for Odie, Pete had seen enough movies to know what was happening when the gunman fired. Pete blocked the bullet's path, deflecting each one. Odie flew into a rage that this asshole tried to kill him just for asking directions.

"Pete! Make this drunken asshole see a one-hundred-millimeter cannon rise up out of the roof! Make him see it fire directly at him, numerous times! I want you to chase this wino's ass up the street! I want to scare the dog shit outta this miserable cur who would dare to draw a gun on me! Terrify that wino! Make this street appear to him like he's in downtown Baghdad!" Odie was quite angry and undoubtedly justifiably so.

"Jeee-eeez-zuzzzzz!" was all they heard from the terrified gunman, as he turned to flee this new weapon. He tossed his useless revolver down the sewer. It was no match for a cannon! All around him, as he dashed up the street, the gunman saw devastation and death as the huge cannon filled the street with shells, each just missing the so far very lucky runner.

Apartments above him exploded from errant shots meant for him. Cars parked at the side of the road blew up from incoming rounds. People were being killed all over, and it was supposed to be him! He became hysterical, and he began screaming for the Lord to help him. Pete relayed the message from the gunman's lips. "Aw, Lawd Gawd, hepp me, Lawd! Please save me, oh Gawd, please!"

Odie told Pete to cease the cannon fire. He would talk back to this cretin as if he were God. Odie spoke loudly, and in his best

Negro voice. "Yo, muh man! Wha'choo wann, boy? Why you be cal-lin' my name fo'? Hey, speak up, an' you better talk right too, boy!"

The gunman just dropped to his knees and begged God not to kill him or let him be killed. "Aw, Gawd, so hepp me, Lawd, I din't know they be packin' no damn cannon!"

"Oh yeah, and now you be sorry, right?" Odie's sarcasm was quite enthusiastic.

"Oh, hell, yes! I be sorry, Lawd. I be changin' afder dis hyear."

Odie thought it appropriate that a man of the streets become a man of the cloth. Several neighborhood children were watching the gunman down on his knees, talking to the thin air. "Ol' wino Leon done loss his mine!" one of them said.

Agreeing, another child spoke up. "He done jus' freaked outta his mine!"

More agreement from amongst the children. "It's dat ol' wine he allus be drinkin'!"

Odie thought to himself, *Leon, eh?* "Yo, *Leon!*"

The gunman heard the empty sky calling his name. "Arise, my prophet Leon, an' go forth an' convert the criminals from they crime. Do this in remembrance of me, you got it? An' if anybody tells you the Lawd works in mysterious ways, I want you to shout, 'Kaint touch this!' You unnastand? Now go on, git! You workin' fo' me now. Otherwise, it's ya ass!"

A block away from Leon, the motor home drove off, leaving bystanders to wonder about what exactly scared the shit out of old wino Leon. They had seen no cannon, no shelling of the neigh-borhood, no death and destruction like Leon. Soon after, it would become known as the day old wino Leon went stark raving mad. He was to become known as the prophet of ripple. The neighborhood kids would all turn to education and athletics rather than drinking or using dope. No one wanted to turn out like old Leon. "Better not drink that shit," they would say.

"Better not use that shit," they would say.

Leon would make a good impression, after all. By his example, most of the children who witnessed Leon going off the deep end would become better persons. No one wanted to sink to his level.

He scared more kids away from bad habits than just saying no ever could.

Shortly after this encounter, Pete managed to get the motor home to the designated destination, the Museum of Science and Industry. Odie knew that this place, the push-button museum, would blow the space visitors away. Odie considered it to be one of the finest museums in the world. Within minutes of entering, Cat realized she could spend a week in it and not see it all. Odie fascinated her with his knowledge about this institution and what was exhibited. There were thousands of different objects and displays.

Cat knew Odie to be bright, but this bordered on brilliance. Odie was casual in explaining things in greater detail than the attached information cards. How he could do this on exhibit after exhibit was amazing. Naturally, Odie didn't tell her he'd spent weeks here doing research, nor did he mention his excellent eyesight, reading cards from a distance Cat couldn't. Some of the cards he had memorized, but he didn't divulge this to her. She was quite buffaloed. He knew that, and to tell her would be to lose the advantage it gave him. His mom had raised no fools.

Suddenly, an announcement came over some loudspeakers, telling the patrons that the museum would close in fifteen minutes. Odie disbelievingly looked at Cat's watch. It told him the awful truth: it was four forty-six in the afternoon. They would be a part of evening rush hour traffic, like it or not. Odie didn't like it all that much, but he had no choice. He certainly couldn't afford to spend another night in an outrageously expensive hotel like the Hilton, so they had to move on toward cheaper venues. But he was in the mood for a good steak, more so after seeing a cab with an advertisement for a place on Rush Street. They claimed to have the best steaks in Chicago. *Well,* Odie thought, *some place had to. It might as well be the advertised place.* On that basis, Pete was ordered to take them to Rush Street.

Cat had shown the Ehliuns a magazine article about seafood and how nutritious it was, how healthful and how delicious it was. The idea of earth foods was not as gruesome to them as it first was, but red meat still did not appeal to them. Seafood had never been able to walk on land or be petted by children. That seemed to Cat to be the basis for their decisions on what to eat. Milk from a cow was something they enjoyed, but meat from a cow seemed primitive, almost cannibalistic to them.

Odie donned his sunglasses, and the others followed suit. "Oh, Pete, I'll be wearing a fine suit tonight, okay? Something elegant but ordinary. Make me look like a broker that's doin' okay, somethin' like that."

Instantly, Odie was garbed in a fine three-piece gray wool suit with very fine pinstripes. Cat looked sleek in her silk gown, fit for a Chinese empress. Beeb had the look of a tailor, while Lin and Din looked resplendent in their attire as visiting dignitaries from some Near East country that possibly sold lots of oil.

Their appearance was well-heeled, elegant, bordering on excessive as they entered the nightclub. They were out to have a good time. Lin had Pete make her chest as large as Cat's, although on her smaller frame, she looked top-heavy, but the net effect was to bring Lin several admiring stares from the men in the club. She thought to herself, *So that's what Cat goes through every day!*

Lin felt this to be quite enjoyable, not like a hug exactly but more like a good feeling deep inside. Whatever it was, Lin enjoyed it very much. She could get to like this. Frankenstein still hovered in the background somewhere, not quite visible but close enough to almost have an effect.

After ordering surf and turf dishes all around, Cat leaned over to Odie and asked him a question. "Do you need some money to help pay for this meal?"

"No," Odie replied quickly, "I'm not exactly worried about the money situation just yet, but I doubt Kathy will be sending me any more money any time soon." To himself, he silently finished the thought, *Not while she's whoring around Italy she ain't.*

Din reached under the table for the envelope Pete materialized. Odie saw Din hand him a large brown manila envelope. When Odie opened it and took a look inside, however, he went catatonic. The envelope was full of small packages of hundred-dollar bills. Five thousand bills each had a one hundred in each corner. They were American greenbacks. It was half a million in cash!

Beeb peered into the envelope after Odie went catatonic. He, too, became strangely silent and bewildered. He tried to speak. His mouth moved aphonically. Words were formed, but the air necessary to move the vocal chords just didn't come. Beeb stared at Odie. Neither man knew where the envelope had come from other than from Din, who appeared to pick it up under the table. Neither man liked the choice of groups they could think of who could have left that kind of cash lying around at a Chicago nightspot.

Odie spoke up, "We might be at a mob drop site or a drug-deal payoff. I don't know. We might better move to another table and leave that envelope alone."

"That envelope is a gift from Lin and myself—and Pete, of course—to you, Odie. And to you, too, Beeb and Cat as well."

Cat was now in a trance after peering into the envelope in question. Din continued with his explanation. "Pete arranged it. Well, after we sent the metal samples around the Earth and across the universe and back the other day, Lin and I figured that we could clean up the litter along the roadsides just as easily. So Pete just beamed up the refuse and recycled the material into different compounds, mostly copper and aluminum with some silver and gold added in. Then all the metal was taken to recycling centers and other metal buying places, mostly scrapyards."

Odie had to interrupt. "'Scuse me, Din, but, uh, who turned the metal into money?"

Din had a confused look on his face, so Odie continued on, "How did this paper money get here? Did Pete do all this, or did you, or who?"

"Well," Din started, "Pete did it with holograms. The holograms got the cash and took it to banks and got large bills for small ones."

Beeb had a question. "Holograms like us, you mean? Holograms that look and act like us?"

Din nodded his head yes. Odie and Beeb traded glances that had lots of eyebrow wrinkling involved.

Cat wanted to know more about why the envelope was full of money. Din obliged her. "Money seems to be important to you earthlings, so we thought you should have some. After all, rewards are common in your society. You people not only saved our lives, but you saved our entire planet, freed us of our slavery! These pieces of paper have worth to you, so we give you some. Is it not enough? We can easily get more. Perhaps you want gold? How about some diamonds, jewelry?"

Odie spread both his hands palms out, the fingers straight up, to signal Din to hold on a moment. "Whoa, dude! The money's fine. It's enough, yeah."

Beeb jumped in. "We would have rescued you from the crash site regardless."

"Yes," Din agreed, "we know! You *did* save us without reward or promise of such. That is precisely why we wish to reward you now. We felt like this would be appropriate behavior. Besides, you have little money left. Twice in the past few hours you have discussed the lack of funds available to you. Lin and I felt we should do this in honor of your friendship and hospitality."

"Take their gift, Odie!" Beeb admonished him. "Don't you know that the Chinese are very insulted if their fine gifts are not accepted? To refuse a kind and generous offer like theirs is inconsiderate, impolite, inappropriate, and in light of our lifestyle, insane!" Beeb thought he'd summed up nicely. All but they weren't Chinese, a minor detail, given all that had occurred.

The humans sat dumbfounded. Inside a week was all it had taken to drastically alter their entire world. Cat looked at Beeb and then at Odie. It was Saturday night. She had only known them since Tuesday—five days. She was amazed. So much had happened to her since she clambered aboard the special starcraft.

Odie gazed at Cat. Only five days? Was that all? He imagined that he might be falling in love and in only five days. And what of the Ehliuns? He had only known them for seven days. What a week!

Odie thought about Dave Dudley's old song "Six Days on the Road." He improvised nicely to cover their own situation, he thought, singing loudly, "Seven days on the earth, and I'm a gonna make ya rich tonight!"

Beeb shushed his old friend up quickly with a napkin in the mouth. Cat simply smiled at him. Odie noticed how beautiful she was when she smiled.

"You know somethin', Odie? I never believed in instant karma before. I mean, it was just a John Lennon song, but if this isn't an instant reward for being nice to somebody, then I just don't know what is." Cat was certain about that. One of the very few things she still held reasonably close to certainty. After a talking computer from another planet, aliens from outer space, wealth beyond imagination, and the absurd ability to look like anyone she wished, Cat could not be too sure about anything. All things seemed possible.

After their repast was totally consumed, they sat back and smiled at each other. Beeb eyeballed the waitress, who noticed and came up right away. Odie slipped her a hundred and asked for a phone. In a few seconds, the eager young woman had a cellular phone in front of Odie. Odie dialed information and asked for their opinion as to the best hotel in Chicago. Many different opinions were expressed, but several operators seemed to think the Palmer House was nice, so Odie had them call and book a suite. Then he called the Palmer House florist and had them send flowers to the ladies of Ma Bell, Chicago. Cat was impressed by this unexpected touch.

They went to the Palmer House and checked in. "And how long will you be staying with us, sir?" Odie heard the clerk say.

He had to think fast. "Just the one night. We're trying all the finer hotels in Chicago. I can't say more."

"I understand completely, sir. Your complimentary drinks will be sent to your suite, sir."

Odie tipped him a hundred. The clerk smiled obsequiously.

The five travelers turned in early. There was much to see and do in a town this size. Odie had promised them a ball game. He called down to the hotel clerk. "There's ten more of those *tips* in it for you if you can scrounge us up some Cubs tickets for noon tomorrow." Odie could just see the clerk's face.

"It would cost half of that just to buy tickets, sir."

Odie realized he was wrong about the guy. "Okay, five grand! I want five choice seats for tomorrow's game."

"You got 'em , pal!"

"Thanks, goodnight." Odie hung up and muttered, "Goddamn highway robbery!"

In the morning, breakfast was served along with five excellent seats at Wrigley Field. Odie was gladly paying off the clerk, who escorted the free breakfast to the room, along with the tickets. "I'll have a cab waiting at the curb for your party, sir," the clerk said assuredly.

"Thanks for everything," Odie told him, ushering the clerk out the door.

"Muchas gracias, senor!" the kitchen helper said, wheeling his cart toward the hall.

Odie stuck two hundreds in his hand on the way by and an *adios* in his ear. Then the door swiftly shut and locked.

They chowed down on the spread and then retired to their baths. Finally, they were all ready to go. A couple of minutes past eleven, Chicago sunshine greeted them between the hotel front door and the cab door. Several harrowing minutes later, they were at 1060 W. Addison. Heading for their seats, Beeb spoke their minds by noting that he wished Pete had been driving instead of Massoud. They all laughed agreement. "It was a rather quiet cab ride over," Cat agreed.

They went inside the National League's oldest ballpark and enjoyed a live game. Both Lin and Din understood the game a little better now, but this was educational as well as instructional. They got a feel for the whole game, not just the isolated segments that TV offers. Odie better understood how they thought after seeing what the first couple of innings taught them. And crowd watching was always nice at Wrigley.

They saw a rousing Cubs victory over New York. Cubs fans rejoiced as the Cubs pulled it out with two out in the ninth. Mets pitchers loaded the bases and got two outs but watched in agony as the Cubs blasted one into the bleachers. Lin and Din thoroughly enjoyed the experience of a live pro baseball game. It was the best thing they had done so far, as Din put it. Odie was pleased. He had learned a lot about the Ehliuns, and they had learned a lot about baseball. Seemed like a fair enough trade. He smiled to himself.

They suddenly encountered the starcraft. Odie was mildly annoyed by this maneuver, but Beeb thought it was cool, as did Cat. They piled aboard, and Pete asked, "Where to?"

Odie didn't immediately answer for all of them, so Beeb did. "Just drive us around town, Pete. Let us see neighborhoods, the lakefront area. You know, drive around."

After a while, Lin had a question she needed to ask. It was inspired by a movie they had seen some of the night before. The movie had a song in it about Chicago, that toddler town. Cat had informed her that a toddler was a small child, a baby. She wanted to see where the baby factory was. Chicago had so many factories that she was sure it was here too. "Odie, where do they make the babies?"

"Anywhere they can have twenty minutes of privacy, why?"

Odie was being flippant, and Lin wasn't. Cat could see this, and she stuck up for Lin. "I think I know what you mean, Lin, but I'm not certain."

"I heard them sing about it last night in the movie *Chicago*, that toddler town. It won't let you down."

Lin stopped talking when Odie burst into hearty laughter, closely followed by Beeb. Cat smiled, trying hard not to laugh in Lin's face. It was very difficult. "Well," Cat started out, "babies are not mass-produced in a factory here in Chicago."

"Where is it, then?" Lin asked.

Cat smiled and didn't have an answer for Lin. Odie stepped in. "Babies are born to each woman or most women. There are no baby factories, only some few women acting as such. And anyway, the song is about Chicago, that *toddling* town—toddling, not toddler. That movie is just a sad excuse. It's a dumb musical that starred the rat pack. They only made movies for the money, not for artistic merit. The mob probably made 'em do the film so they could steal from the studio or something like that."

Odie's last remarks were lost on Lin. He could see that, so he summed up his case against baby factories. "Hospitals are where babies are born. You have seen hundreds of hospitals, and that's where babies come from."

Lin now realized that "baby factories" existed all over the country. There were still parts of life in America that she didn't understand, like most of it. Suburbs, inner cities, malls, freeways, having insurance—none of these things made sense to her.

They wound up going to Ditka's for some food and entertainment. It was a pleasant-enough place with plenty of photos of Iron Mike at work, both as a player and as a coach. Although it was early evening when they arrived, they stayed quite late. Within fifteen minutes of arriving, Odie spotted an old girlfriend and tried to duck her, but she recognized Odie at once and brought over the champagne in honor of their days in Champaign. Cat was simply stunned by the sudden moves this interloper put on Odie.

The more often she told Odie how glad she was to see him again, the less that Cat thought of her. Beeb sensed some tension between the two women, so he forced Odie to introduce him to her. "JC, this is Beeb. Beeb, meet JC."

"Hi, JC, glad to meet you. So what are you doing with your college education these days?"

As the small talk progressed, JC informed Beeb that she was a public relations whiz for a huge brokerage firm. Beeb pointed out that Odie had a very jealous wife who would not stand for JC's having any ideas about him. The lady in question began to take a more active interest in Beeb after she saw how attached to Odie Cat was. Odie didn't hear Beeb's conversation due to Cat's filling his ears with her thoughts on consideration and courtesy.

Strolling outside to the motor home for a spot of privacy, Beeb thought his luck had improved. Once inside, he discovered how fortunate he was going to be. About an hour of rocking the motor home had Pete's total interest. There had to be a way for him to experience this kind of fun. There just *had* to. As yet, he was unsure how it would occur, but that it would occur was a certainty to Pete. He had never failed before, and he was now the most powerful computer in the universe—shoot, the most powerful object. The most powerful—that had a nice ring to it. Pete continued to ponder his problem.

Cat came outside a moment, saw the motor home rocking away, and turned on her heels to go back inside and tell Odie just what she thought of the whole thing. Odie calmed her down a bit by promising that she was not coming with them. "Only with Beeb!" he humorously added.

Cat didn't see the humor in it at all. Odie looked at her and then laughed. "Don't pretend yer all pissed off 'cause Beeb's coppin' some twat, Cat. Yer damn glad it ain't me."

Then Cat relented and smiled at Odie. "Yer right, babycakes! I don't allow no claim jumpers to work my gold mine!"

Odie looked at her with greatly widened eyes. "Gold mine!" he snorted contemptuously. "I ain't no damn mine of any type, babycakes!"

"Yeah, you are!" Cat shot right back. "Yer totally mine till I say different!"

Odie just looked at her and said nothing. Cat ordered him to drink up, hoisting up the two champagne glasses her rival JC had brought to the table. So as Cat finished off the magnum of Dom Pérignon for the girl, she had a change of heart. After all, the girl had good taste in men and champagne.

As Cat drank deeply, she got progressively happier and harder to control. Odie thought she was being quite unreasonable, forcing him to drink the stuff, but he knew she thought she had reason to be mad, and she would stay mad until she got glad again.

As the first magnum was empty, Cat reordered yet another. She toasted Odie time after time, insisting that he drink along with her, so he downed several glasses of the shit, though he disliked the taste and positively hated the bubbles that tickled his nose. It was the last thing Odie clearly remembered, rubbing his nose.

# Zincing Down Zlowly

When Odie awoke, his head felt like a balloon filled with explosive gases, sensitive to the touch and feel. As he cradled his head, a few unclear thoughts raced through the swelled portion, filled with either ideas or brain tumors. He sort of remembered Din being a millionaire, or no, was it him? The last clear thought was of JC's offering him champagne. No, it was Cat! She forced him to drink that crap! He glanced around, looking for some help. He was in unfamiliar surroundings. "Cat! Beeb! Lin! Din! Yo! Anybody?"

"Good morning, Odie!" he heard Pete say.

"Pete! Where the hell am I?"

"Why, in your bed, of course."

"And could you give me the exact, specific location of the bed?"

"It's still in the same place that it's been since we've known each other."

"I don't get it, Pete? I just want to know where I am right now!"

"Nearly to Chattanooga." Pete's words only added to Odie's confusion.

"I thought I was still in some Chicago hotel."

"Odie, you gave me explicit instructions last night—well, at 2:00 a.m., actually—to head for Atlanta. Since I have never before seen you lose your memory, Odie, I must assume that the champagne affected you like Beeb warned that it would."

So he *had* been forced to drink champagne! He would get Cat for this.

Suddenly, Cat came bounding in on him, leaping onto the bed next to him. He weakly forced a smile at her. "Isn't this great?" she loudly asked, not even noticing Odie wincing in pain. She swept the air all around her with her arms and waited for Odie's reply.

"We in some hotel, maybe?" Odie asked in a fog.

"Yeah," she laughed heartily, much to Odie's chagrin, "we're in the Hotél du Gran, Pete!"

"The what?"

"We're in the fuckin' starcraft, Odie! We're in the motor home, rolling down the highway toward Lookout Mountain. We'll be there in half hour or so."

Odie's pained look gave way to shock. Here he was, lying under an enormous crystal chandelier, nearly the size of the one in the Ringling Hotel in downtown Sarasota, Florida, the chandelier that Kaiser Wilhelm gave John Ringling for teaching his military adjutants about the logistics involved in moving a huge array of men and animals over one hundred miles a day and still finding time to serve three thousand hot meals a day to a thousand men. The Ringling Circus had greatly impressed the kaiser, and he sent the twenty-five-foot chandelier as a trinket of his affection, a show of gratitude to the circus owner.

Odie didn't remember any chandelier in his bedroom aboard the motor home, nor did he recall his cramped quarters being so spacious, nor did he know quite what Cat was talking about. He had to ask, "What are you babbling about?"

"Odie, I'm not the one babbling! You can be such an asshole sometimes!"

Cat stormed out of the room in anger. Odie got out of his bed to follow her but rather wobbly at first. Once he got outside his room, he could see they were in the lobby of the MGM Grand hotel in Vegas, only it was moving down the interstate highway system like a, well, like a huge room on wheels.

All four of his fellow travelers just stared over at Odie, waiting for his comments on the new decor that Pete had provided. "This is a hologram?" he finally stammered.

"And damn good too, don'cha think?" Beeb wondered.

Odie was very impressed. "Okay, Pete, this is really all right! In fact, it's incredible!" Odie now realized that he was still in the same old motor home. It just looked a lot different, all three stories of it.

Beeb was grinning like the Cheshire cat. "Go check out the waterfall in the atrium, Odie! It has rare birds and exotic plants and everything!"

"Uh, did you say waterfall, Beeb?"

"Yeah, and atrium, rare and exotic too. I tole you, Pete!"

Cat turned Odie around by the shoulders so he could see what they were talking about. It was a bit too much information in his state, hungover, and he sank into Cat's arms, holding his head and moaning. Beeb once again proclaimed that he had warned them all. "I tole you, you shouldn'a talked him into drinking all that champagne, Cat! Now he won't be worth a shit for days, weeks maybe!"

Odie said nothing, but he conveyed his message clearly to Beeb with a single extended middle digit waved about slowly so that the movement would be sure to catch Beeb's eye. Cat pampered poor little Odie and returned him to his bed. "There, there, sweetie, you just lie back and relax. I'll bring you a nice glass of warm milk."

"You do and I'll puke it all over you!" Odie threatened. The mere thought of warm milk made Odie's stomach curdle. Champagne was bad enough. Warm milk would certainly purge him.

Cat just laughed at him like an amateur drinker. "Do you really feel bad?" she asked politely.

"I'd have to get better to die!" Odie replied.

"Well, the Ehliuns expressed an interest in seeing Lookout Mountain, so that's where we're headed. Can I get you anything to make you feel better?"

"Off!" Odie smiled in his best suggestive manner.

Cat lunged at him like a mad rapist. She rolled over Odie, each trying to rip the other's clothing off. "Ah," Odie smiled after about twenty minutes, "you sure know how to cure a hangover, baby!"

"Well," Cat smiled, "you passed out on me last night, so I saved it up."

"You didn't give my share to Beeb?" Odie teased.

"No, honey, after JC left, I gave him his own share," Cat answered Odie right back as he did to her.

"You did?" Odie said, quite surprised.

"Uh-huh," Cat confirmed. "He just ain't you!"

This made Odie feel great, as was its intent. Cat knew how to handle men with big egos, stroke it too. "Has anyone ever accused you of being a sex fiend?" Odie wondered of his favorite woman.

"Oh, yeah!" Cat answered truthfully. "I find being sexually satisfied keeps me calm and on an even keel."

"Even if it takes four times a day, right?"

"You really don't want to see me horny!" she warned him.

Odie knew she was right. He had never met such an honest woman. Knowing he was very fortunate in finding her did not much comfort him from the fear of losing her. He knew he probably could never fully satisfy this woman and her tremendous sexual appetite, but it was gonna be a lotta fun trying!

After their shower, Cat and Odie joined the others for a group discussion about what to do. Winding their way up the narrow road toward the dump-off point for tourists at Lookout Mountain, their discussion narrowed to a choice of what to do today or what to do from now on, forever. Today won out. Now they would approach the future one day at a time as they had for two whole days now.

Cat knew she was not expected anywhere, and the Ehliuns were certainly open to suggestion since they weren't due anywhere either, and Odie and Beeb were supposed to be traveling the interstates! It was their job to travel the highways and report on their condition. It was supposed to be the big study that would put the senator's name on everyone's lips, the stepping stone to the national recognition that would lead to his election to the presidency. That was what Odie had used to convince the senator to sign the grants. It still made Odie smile, that and the promise to avoid the senator's wife.

Cat was convinced that travel had a nice sound to it, especially in the type of luxury that Pete could surround them with. And knowing that there was no hurry to get anywhere would leave them the freedom to really explore the countryside. And cost was not a factor any more. So all five of them were in agreement. They were all going to look for America. They had heard she was back and standing tall. Should be easy to spot.

It was slightly past noon when they stepped from their fabulous ride onto the asphalt parking lot, which could obviously accommodate dozens of cars at a time. Lookout Mountain had Ehliun visitors for the first time. Like good tourists there do, they gazed out over the vast seven-state panoramic view that was provided by the mountain's strategic location. They went inside the mountain to see Ruby Falls. They saw all the quaint alcoves loaded down with quartz crystals glued to the walls. And finally, they bought some fudge. Then it was back to the motor home and then down to the highway.

A long and steep descent brought them to the concrete of US 11, the Lee Highway. Pete steered through the town of Chattanooga and hit the interstate I-75 north to Cleveland, Tennessee, where they could catch US 64, which would take them over to Ducktown at Odie's specific request. Lin and Din liked what they saw inside the mountain on the way to Ruby Falls. Odie felt like he could do them some good. "Din, have Pete score us some documents that show you two Ehliuns to be important officials visiting here from Red China and us three as guides and interpreters."

On the table in front of Odie, the documents he requested appeared. Odie glanced at them and then at Beeb, who was laughing like a loon. Cat picked up one of the documents. She was puzzled. "Why do all these papers have so many perforated holes on them?" She held up a purported document from Red China.

"That's what Beeb is laughin' his fool head off at, Cat." Odie had a sense of pity stringing along with his words. "Pete scored these documents, and they're from Red China!"

"What's wrong with that?" Cat wondered. "It's what you said."

"The Chinese don't call their country Red China. We do! They call it the People's Republic of China!" Odie just shook his head in a negative way.

"Oh," Cat smiled, feeling a little dumb.

Lin and Din felt the same way. Odie wanted something other than what he said. His words did not mean what they seemed to say. They should have known by now that Odie rarely said something that meant just that. It was always a little different. It always meant something else too. Odie thought everything could be a double entendre.

Din was a little disappointed in himself for having missed it. He was striving to regain that familiar feeling he used to know when he was attached to the computer, when he made no mistakes, where he was always correct like Odie. Din still didn't understand some things about Earth and its life-forms.

"Okay, Pete," Odie said, "I know I told you to score the documents from Red China, but I meant for you to obtain, to acquire, to cop, to procure them, not to perforate them." Odie thought it best to clearly explain his meaning. He still wasn't sure what Pete could and could not do. Here was an example of what he couldn't do: make sense of political entities. It was also an example of what the computer could do: still mess things up pretty good.

"Pete, check with the State Department offices in DC to determine just exactly what would be required for real, high-ranking Chinese officials from the People's Republic to carry in the line of official documentation, okay?"

"Okay."

"See what would be required for us to arrange a mine tour over in Ducktown a little later on today, okay? Lin and Din will be the visiting officials, and Cat can be the translator, and me and Beeb can be the security team, I reckon."

Odie was certain that this explanation had been thorough enough. "You got that, Pete?" he rechecked just to make certain.

Pete produced a stack of official-looking papers on the table in the place of the first batch. "As ordered and then reordered," Pete announced.

"Yer boy's feelin' his oats. Must be hittin' puberty, eh?" Beeb smirked at his old pal.

Cat had to chuckle at their comments. After all, they were talking about a piece of Ehliun space hardware. Her chuckle blew into laughter when Odie compared Pete to Ma Bell on acid.

Odie busied himself with inserting a Bromberg tape with "The New Lee Highway Blues" on it. Cat came up to him with a problem.

"I don't speak a single word of Chinese, Odie! How the hell am I gonna translate for them?"

"Hey, babe, they don't speak any Chinese either, so y'all start dead even!"

He wasn't gonna be much help, Cat could see that. Lin explained it to Cat. "Pete will do it all for us, Cat. The glass lenses on your sunglasses will act as soundboards for those who will hear Chinese. Pete will cover our speech, although you will hear it. We five can talk amongst ourselves, and no one else can hear it. Well, you will speak English to whomever we are going to encounter as translator, but when you speak, everyone but us will hear Chinese. Isn't that right, Pete?" Lin asked.

"More or less. Actually, Cat will be able to hear the Chinese since it will emanate from her glasses and not her vocal chords." Pete was satisfied this was clear enough.

Both Beeb and Odie noticed this, and neither liked it. Din spoke up. "Strangers will only hear what they are supposed to hear."

"I see!" Cat said like Odie always did, with heavy emphasis on the word *see*.

Beeb grinned at her Odie-speak. Odie ignored them and directed Pete to drive down US 64 toward the Ducktown office of a zinc mine.

"How'd you know about this mine, Odie?" Cat wondered of her favorite man.

"Copped a squat on the stone sighting tour from Chambana."

Cat looked puzzled. "How'd you know about this mine, Odie?" Cat repeated her inquiry.

"Came here on a geology class tour from the U of I."

"Well, why didn't you say that in the first place?" she wondered.

"I did! You been to Champaign-Urbana rather recently, as a matter of fact."

"That's not what you called it, Odie. You called it something else."

"Chambana," Odie refreshed her memory.

"Why did you call it Chambana?" Cat asked.

"'Cause it sounds lots better'n Urpaign!" Odie assured her.

"Boy's got a point there!" Beeb offered.

"I got another point too," Odie assured them. "If it's green and on the ground, it's probably AstroTurf!"

"Lotta stadiums in this Ducktown place we're headed?" Beeb asked, sarcasm much in evidence, nearly dripping from his chin. Odie proceeded to inform them all, "When the early European settlers arrived in the area, they found that mining the sphalerite ore was a cinch. Sphalerite is roughly sixty-four percent zinc and thirty-four percent sulfur. When you burn the ore in a crude furnace or log fire, nearly pure zinc melts and runs down out of the fire."

Odie told them of huge fires set to melt tons of ore at a time. He told them how all the trees that were not cut down for mine timbers, houses and barns, or used as firewood to melt zinc out of sphalerite were killed by the acid rain that the smelting fires produced. Hot air laden with sulfur compounds rose rapidly from the smelters, only to mix with the heavy damp air of the Tennessee mountain valleys. Acid rain of tremendous proportions rained down on the valley and decimated the green plants, grasses, shrubs and trees. Odie finished by saying that as the plant life died, the rains washed them away and with them, the soil. Without topsoil, the plant life has not yet recovered from this blow. Pete saw how easy it was for him to spot Ducktown. It was the brown spot in the carpet of green.

Pete parked where the government plates were visible to the worried mine officials in the office. Odie hopped down to chat with them after consulting Cat's watch. It was four ten in the afternoon. Pete had dressed Odie in a light charcoal-gray suit that hinted of federal employment. The dialogue was all Odie, though. "Howdy! Name's Barlow T. Suggins, and I'm from right over at Soddy originally, and anyways, I thought I might could swing a tour fer mah frens in this here motor home. See, they's visitin' us from Red China—I mean, the People's Choice—and I guess I don't haffta tell you people how important it is fer us ta tap into the world's biggest consumer nation of the next century."

All the while, Odie was reaching into his coat pockets for all the phony documents that Pete had materialized for their use. Once the mine officials started glancing at the documentation Odie produced, he continued with his spiel. "See, they got a special interest in seein' a sphalerite mine, 'cause Kwang, Clang, whatever his name is, he don't talk no American anyway, but see anyhow. Now he's the administrator of all China's mines, but he started out as a sphalerite miner. So naturally, I volunteered to show them some Tennessee sphalerite, what with me bein' from the area and all, don'cha see, and I'd kinda like 'em to think favorable on us, don'cha know?"

The documents were successful, at least in convincing the mine officials that there were high-ranking Chinese officials aboard the starcraft. But Odie felt them hesitate a little too long. He knew they would try to talk him out of it. He knew he had to move fast. If he played his hole card now, the game would be his. In a conspiratorial manner, Odie whispered as he gathered a few of them together with his arms around their shoulders. "Besides, fellas, they got the most delectable creature for a translator that you've ever seen in all your born days! I mean, she makes Dolly Parton look a bit frumpy!"

Eyes widened some.

Odie finished them off. "Come see!"

Odie led the delegation of mine officials over to the motor home and knocked lightly on the door. As planned, Cat slid out in a skintight satin dress, slit way up above the thigh, showing them all her legs as she emerged. There was a silent gasp from the mine officials. It was very apparent that she wore no underwear! Odie glanced at their eyes, all focused on Cat. Candy from a baby. "Well?" he inquired of the mine officials.

They fell over themselves to see who would head this tour. Compromise occurred, and a closed sign was displayed on the mine office door. Everyone went to the aid of the Chinese. The mine geologist led the tour into the mine elevator. The tour consisted of the five travelers, the mine geologist, and six other mine officials.

Cat was amazed to hear her voice speaking Chinese. Pete was sure good at this! And this was a great gimmick, she was sure. Cat was fascinated with the sounds of Chinese, so high, so quick, with so much emphasis on meaning conveyed by tone rather than the word itself. Inflection and intonation could change *oxcart* into *baseball* in a heartbeat. Of course, English inflection and intonation could change

"I had a wonderful time" to "You're a loser, and I never want to see you again" in that same heartbeat. Language was so versatile.

Cat's use of language was also versatile. She had cooed and cuddled each of the mine officials in turn, with the direct and intended result of them all being enamored of her. The geologist Mr. Lester had been singled out for special treatment since in Cat's eyes, he was a hunk. She made the boys grin, furiously trying to contain their mirth, as she suggestively rearranged his necktie, while pressing her crotch against his hip on the elevator ride down.

Mine elevators are not known for their rapid descent, and this one was only going half speed because of what Cat said. "Ooh, nod zo vast," she cooed to Mr. Lester. "I like to go down zlowly, verry zlowly." She was using a mock Teutonic voice, like some mixture of Dietrich and Garbo, but her sensual overtones could be felt. They did not need to be heard to be understood.

Odie and Beeb had not known that she would assume this Germanic voice. Both men thought it was because of the stories about Asta and Nyla, but neither man would say it out loud.

The five tourists heard a deluge of factual commentary to accompany the strange view inside the mine itself. They were 640 feet below the surface when the elevator stopped its descent. Stepping from the elevator, they could not help but notice the enormous pillars of rock soaring up over 240 feet, supporting the cavernous roof of the particular room they were in. "The view is magnificent," Din jabbered to Lin, who agreed.

The Ehliuns jabbered away like two-year-olds on and on about the features of the rock, the equipment used to mine the ore, and convey it to the surface, about the adaptation necessary by the mine workers to adjust to life underground. Cat had to straighten them out on this point. The Ehliuns were mildly surprised to discover the miners didn't live below ground continuously but rather slept on the surface each night.

Cat had never been in a mine before, and she found the experience to be exhilarating. She was having some kind of fun with this translator character. Much of the fun stemmed from the big buildup Odie had given her. She was supposed to be too good to be true. She had never been an actress before. Well, not really, but she intended to give a star performance, nonetheless.

To herself, she had thought, *Vhy nod spick Cherman ass vell ass Chi-niece?* Richard Wilhelm had. These people would never make the connection, they undoubtedly had not read the *I Ching*. They'd never know that was the reason for choosing a German accent. She didn't think about Nyla or any other woman she didn't know—ever.

Besides, she thought, when the tour was over and gone, all these mine guys would remember was that she was terribly attractive, and she spoke provocatively to them all. She didn't care that they didn't know her real name or real anything. That she would always be remembered by them was enough. Mystery had its own special aura. Being a mysterious lady had always been an aim of hers. Now she had a chance to play that role, to polish it on the road in an off, very off, Broadway setting, so why not play the role to the hilt?

Cat was enjoying her role as a translator. And even though old Mr. Lester was a cutie, she wasn't about to jeopardize the secret of the Ehliuns. Mr. Lester would always think of this trilingual beauty. Din interrupted Cat's daydreams by telling her that to him, Odie and Beeb looked bored, and he knew he had been underground long enough. More than an hour and a half in the mine had taken them to six of the ten levels. They knew more about zinc than they ever wanted to. Cat could take a hint. She glanced at her watch and swore in German. "Oh, my, juss look at zee time! Ve are havink to leavink you now. Vas vunderful, vee had a mahvelous time! Und zey vant to zank you too!"

Lin and Din thanked all the mine officials one at a time, with Cat translating their words. She was nearly shocked out of her wits when one of the mine officials spoke Chinese back to Lin and Din. Pete printed a message to her, advising her that he was speaking Cantonese dialect and didn't know how to speak it well. It was Pete's opinion that those words were all the Chinese he knew. She translated for him as well, and they moved on down the line.

Ascending toward the surface, Odie casually explained to the mine officials that they were on a very quiet tour of the countryside so that these Chinese could see the real America. "We didn't even tell the governor that we would be here, 'cause that would only clutter up the tour with a bunch of politicians. Besides, you guys are the ones who do the work here and know what's going on. Why give a politician a chance to talk? They got nothin' to say."

This comment met with general agreement. This Fed was all right because he was down home. Odie went on, as he always did. "So if y'all wouldn't mind, we'd just as soon the news of our visit was kept amongst ourselves, and we'd appreciate it a whole lot. Thankee."

Cat confirmed this policy of silence with a few well-placed pats and touches and squeezes.

As the mine elevator door opened onto the ground level, Cat put a kiss on Mr. Lester that he would not soon forget. "Und zank you verry much," she purred.

Mr. Lester just blushed. Cat didn't know she could make a man blush, another first. Cat kissed the rest of the men on their cheeks.

The five travelers reboarded the starcraft. They had all been impressed by Odie's idea of a mine tour, but it was now time to put the tour back on the road again. They soon left the Ducktown city limits behind, crossing over the Georgia state line on a back road. Soon, they found themselves in Blue Ridge. From there, they followed a road over to Blairsville, where they could see Brasstown Bald shining in the distance. It was one of the most southerly mountains in the Appalachian chain. It was also one of the most scenic.

From Blairsville they went south on US 19 toward Dahlonega. There, they stopped at the world-famous Smith House for dinner. They sat down at a long table with chairs on both sides and at each end. Plate after plate of chicken, ham, pork chops, chicken-fried steak, peas, corn, rice, gravy, potatoes of all types, stuffing, green salads, fruit salads, Jell-O salads—everything imaginable—was on the table.

The Ehliuns were impressed with the spread, but their attention was captured by the next table. There, an entire family group of at least three generations silently filed in and sat down without so much as a whisper until the patriarch sat down last and offered the Lord some prayers for his graciousness in allowing all that food to be put before them, amen. After the prayers, the entire clan dug in, emptying several dishes before they could be passed. Two waitresses were kept busy just refilling plates of food for the hungry clan.

Lin and Din took it all in quietly. They did not know why prayers were said. They knew nothing of praying, either cause or effect. As soon as they were alone outside the Smith House, they asked Odie to explain why prayers were offered and to whom. Odie had already promised them at an earlier date that he would explain religion to them. They thought the time had come, so began the discussion of religion.

Actually, it was much more like a monologue as Odie liked to talk on and on about things. He did not know what they believed in, so he started there. The Ehliuns told Odie that they believed in Pete. It was not the sort of start that he had hoped for. Beeb grinned widely when he saw Odie start to squirm. Every now and then, something happened to make Odie see that he was just like everyone else, just another member of mankind.

Odie didn't like to be just another guy. He always tried hard to be different. He didn't know how well he had succeeded.

# The Religion Bidnezz

"Okay, the universe started, a lot of matter coagulated and clung together and started spinning and getting hotter, and then it lit into lots of suns, and then they burned off billions of tons of matter, got old, and shrank. They exploded as supernovas, blowing particles incredible distances in the void. These particles clung together, went through the same stuff as the time before, and this time, the sun was a helium sun. It fused hydrogen ions into helium atoms. Then it blew up, and so on. After the matter which makes up our Earth went through the thermonuclear process at least ninety-one times, it managed to coagulate into the stuff we call the solar system: our sun and its associated nine planets.

"Now on earth, we have uranium, which has ninety-two protons and ninety-two electrons, and I forget exactly how many neutrons. It depends which isotope you have, but 238 is the famous one. Anyway, the sun lit, Jupiter didn't, and the Earth finally cooled down, enough to have a crust form, at any rate.

"As it cooled, all the minerals left the molten mass as they reached the lowest temperature they could reach and still maintain their atomic identity. Iron, for example, poured out across the vast reaches of North America from the Canadian Shield area to Alabama and almost all at once too. Same with nickel, vanadium, et cetera.

"At some point, life started. It may have been strictly anaerobic bacteria. It may have been some ammonia-breather. It may have long since disappeared, but some life-form started and altered the world. Finally, plant life evolved. I don't know what type plants, so don't ask.

"Eventually, plant life gave off some spare free oxygen gas, $O_2$, which reacted with practically everything it came in contact with, as it still does today. Our atmosphere is roughly twenty-one percent $O_2$ by volume, so that means those plants that gave off oxygen as a by-product made it possible for our species to exist. As mammals, we are the same kin to apes, giraffes, horses, bears, pigs, goats, cows, reindeer, and on and on. All mammals have mammary glands in the female, but species wide, there are only seven neck vertebrae, be it mouse or giraffe.

"So after mammals came man. There's a few million years in between, of course. Millions of years of evolution went into making man different from the other creatures. Then millions of years more went by, and man invented a lifestyle we call civilization. Thousands of years after that, cities sprang up. This gave rise to trash, sewage, and politics.

"Then from politics came a philosophy men learned to live by: religion. Religion merely codified the reasons for killing your enemies. They weren't fit to live because they were infidels, so whomever you opposed for whatever reason, now religion could justify those actions. Didn't like somebody? And there was a terrible lightning storm? Blame him. Rouse the rabble, spout the spiel, and hey, we'll appease the angry gods by killing this asshole that no one likes anyway.

"Religion became whatever the religious leader wanted it to be. It was a most excellent tool. You could just threaten the masses with it, and they would subserviently obey. We don't know what sort of religious rites the ancient peoples celebrated exactly. Bits and pieces we know, but the whole thing still eludes us. And why not? All the practitioners are long gone. We don't know what the Neanderthal people believed about their world. We know they had some cultural traits like burying the dead and caring for the disabled that modern man practices, but what they believed about God or the gods or spirits, we can only speculate.

"To understand religion, you must first understand the concept of God. God is what we call the idea of some greater force than we can comprehend operating the universe according to reasonably devised laws. This force is really three forces acting as one. It takes three forces interacting with each other to create any phenomenon, okay? Just stick with me a few. It will all become clear to you. Trust me.

"Okay, it's like this. We live in three dimensions. All things as we know them have depth, breadth, and height. That's the physical world. In the spiritual world, there is past, present, and future. Then there's God the Father, God the Son, and God the Holy Spirit. You with me here? There's three dimensions, three divisions of time, and three personalities to God. All three have to interact with one another for us to see just one phenomenon."

Odie saw the Ehliuns shrugging their shoulders. "I can see this will take a while," Odie said out loud. Settling into some seats, they were ready for the ride to Atlanta. It was almost 8:00 p.m. "Pete, to Atlanta, please." Then Odie warmed to his task of explaining religion to the Ehliuns. "Back there at the Smith House, where we ate, that table full of hungry folks? Those were some form of Christians, exactly what they are into, I can't say, but they were Christians, nonetheless.

"The Christian belief consists of God, especially the Son of God and the Holy Spirit. The Father stays up in heaven, and the Holy Spirit stays invisible, but God the Son came down to earth as Jesus Christ to die for our sins. He lived as a man to get to know man's ways, the claim goes. But since he's God, he already knows more than any mere man. But whatever, God the Son lived on earth and preached sermons and worked miracles and pissed off the Romans, so they executed him on the cross. But three days later, on Easter, he came back from the dead to give hope to the miserable here on earth. See, the thing goes like this:

"Jesus is killed by the political leaders of the day. But after they have done all they can, they ceased his life, thinking that would quiet him down a little, but it backfired. Up from the dead, he jumps, and boom, Christianity is off and running. People jump on the bandwagon left and right. They were followers because they had seen the miracles. Then Paul came along. Actually, his name was Saul. He persecuted Christians till he had a change of heart and then a change of name. S went to P. Saul became Paul, and he traveled around, telling people that even if they had not seen the miracles, they too could be followers. They, too, could believe. Worked like a charm.

"Christians believe that God the Father created everything that exists. Therefore, God created both the devil and Christ. The devil is Lucifer, the fallen angel. See, he used to be an angel in heaven, but he fucked up, and God damned him to hell, where he lives. So Lucifer tries to get folks on earth to join him in hell, and Christ tries to get them up to heaven, away from hell. Earth is like a battleground for them. They are after the eternal soul that resides inside every living body. The soul is the life force, the animating portion that which causes the rest of the body to live.

"Scientific belief is in nature, comprised of living and nonliving things, organic and inorganic, matter and energy. It's an old medieval offshoot of the Christian belief, the European version. And while we're speaking of science, we should mention Judaism, the religion of the Jews. The Jews are still waiting patiently for their savior. They don't believe in Christ or Christianity. They still follow the Hebrew faith, which believes that the first son of a family should be a doctor, and the second son should become a dentist, and the rest should become lawyers. Ideally, they would also own the property and the buildings which house their practices.

"The Buddhists believe that the yin and yang represent the two forces of good and evil, Christ and the devil. Yin and yang are always moving. One changes into the other. A light rain is good, a tornado is bad—that sort of thing. In other words, things don't stay the same. What it looks like depends upon from where you view it.

"Personally, I consider matter to be slow energy. If you break the bonds of matter, you release energy. Energy and matter can neither be created nor destroyed. Same with Christian beliefs about the soul. They believe God created souls, and nothing can alter that. They believe that all things exist within the framework of God. Nothing exists outside the framework of God. Therefore, all good and all evil exist within God. One blends into the other, like yin and yang.

"Let's look at sunshine, for example. At some atomic level, gas burns and gives off heat and light as well as subatomic particles such as X-rays, gamma waves, radio waves, the solar wind, etc. Trees grow in the sunshine and store energy in the wood. When the wood is burned, the energy is released as heat and light. You don't destroy the matter or the energy by burning wood. You simply change it to another form. The matter converts from solid wood to fly ash, cinders, charcoal, steam, water vapor, whatever tree sap might boil away to, and so on. If you carefully contain the fire, the weight of the end products will approximate the weight of the solid wood prior to burning.

"So to move on, Buddhism teaches that the souls transmigrate from body to body, life to life, always within the framework of Buddha. God, Allah, Mother Nature, life—makes no difference what you call it. It's the same thing. Okay, religion then is the different practices of defining God. Christians don't believe in more than one life per soul. They feel you get just one shot at living correctly, and this is it.

"Buddhists think the Almighty gives you more than one chance. They feel life is like a multiple-choice quiz. School teachers might be reincarnated Buddhists for all I know. Anyway, Buddhists figure a truly benevolent God would allow freedom of choice. The basic difference in theological arguments between Christian and Buddhist would center around how many chances God allows us to redeem ourselves. Now, Buddhists believe in reincarnation, which allows as many chances as necessary to attain nirvana, which approximates Christian heaven. Christian hell is the Buddhist maya, the spinning illusion, the material world.

"Our material world is made up of subatomic particles conforming to laws which we cannot define. We call these subatomic particles such names as quarks, tachyons, leptons, strangeness, and charm. The matter composing this very table is spinning around atomic nuclei so fast that they seem to be everywhere at once. In truth, they are not everywhere at once. Heisenberg's uncertainty principle is used to formulate where in the atom cloud of electrons one might be at any given time.

"An atom-firing gun, shooting at this table, would take centuries of random chance to actually hit another atom. To create atomic bombs, the atoms must be packed to critical mass, meaning the density is such that the atom firing gun simply cannot miss. This sets off a chain reaction which physically and chemically alters the original compound. Other compounds form as soon as the old bonds are broken.

"We can't really say that our state of physics is such that we comprehend the workings of the subatomic world. Calling things strangeness and charm isn't conducive to me feeling they've hit the nail squarely on the head. Quark is a word James Joyce made up for his book *Ulysses*. We're using a made-up word to describe an effect which we see the results of but not the actual particle or its movement. It would be like surmising a gasoline-powered automobile by examining a tire mark left in the dust.

"Mankind has no firm, real idea about how life got started here on earth, let alone your planet. We just accept that life is. God is the prime mover, the original cause of life. Life exists because God wants it to. There is no better explanation even though I wish there were. Proof is rather tough, since the original world where life started no longer exists, and so we have theories."

"We all think we know what's going on." Beeb had to add to Odie's statement. "Even though, some of us"—he pointed at Odie—"think we know more than anyone else."

Odie ignored him and continued on as both men knew he would. "There are millions of stars scattered throughout space, each like our own sun. Some may have planets associated with them, like yer suns, for instance." Odie quickly added when he realized whom he was speaking to, "But Earth don't know yer here yet."

"You were explaining the religion bidnezz to them, Odie, not space."

"Yeah, I know. Okay, religion is an attempt to define, to limit God. And how do you limit the power of God, which, by definition, is limitless? Therein lies the rub. For some person to say what God wants is only what that person says and nothing more. Idiots like Swaggart and Bakker babble on like they were in touch with reality, let alone God! God has more class than to talk to goofs like them and Oral Roberts. Beeb, don't that sound like two fags named Bob?

"No TV preacher is qualified to speak for God. No human is qualified to talk for the Almighty. God speaks for himself in eloquent ways vastly superior to words. To experience God's eloquence, you have but to walk along a stream, stroll across a meadow, sit beneath a waterfall, gaze at the stars above. God's words are flowers, birds, trees, butterflies, baby rabbits, human children. God's words are comets, supernovas, quasars, pulsars, planets, and suns.

"People themselves are microcosms of the macrocosm or God. We are like small imperfect versions of gods on earth. We are alive and limited by the fact of life. God is beyond life. God is beyond death. Both concepts, life and death, exist within the framework of God. They are of necessity considerably less than the whole, which is God. God is everything. Good, bad, and indifferent—the sum total is what we are labeling God.

"Now, the religion business. Major religious beliefs practiced today on earth are money, Christianity, Judaism, Buddhism, Islamism, Taoism, Hinduism, TV preacherism, and others of even less import. Money is the oldest religion, and it started out as a major belief of its own, but soon, all the other denominations saw how effective money was, so they incorporated money into their own religious beliefs. Now you won't find a single religion that does not incorporate money into a place of great importance.

"Money is said to be the root of all evil and the palm grease of nasty intent, yet it is the heart and soul of modern-day televised religious bidnezz demands. TV preachers don't want food, products of your labors, tears, corn, or carpentry work. No, they only want money! It's always begged in the name of the Lord, always for some unspecified good works that are never finished, and always, more money is the one thing they desperately and constantly need.

"Yessir, you would think that people capable of owning TV stations would be above begging money from people who eat Alpo. But TV preachers have no problem thieving this money in the name of other people's beliefs in a common guardian from on high. They take and take, and all they give are more ads for more money. As far as I'm concerned, they're all sick, perverted, lyin' bastards!

"As I said, money started out on its own but was quickly absorbed by all the other religious beliefs. Like the pagan winter solstice holiday that the Etruscans took from someone else for their own, and which was in turn taken by the Romans and turned into the Roman Saturnalia, money was incorporated into the ceremonies of various religions. The Saturnalia was a two-week-long feast celebrating the god Saturn. The Saturnalia got taken over by the Christians, who turned it into the twelve days of Christmas. Christmas celebrates Christ's birth now, but it had been celebrated for hundreds of years prior to Christianity.

"Then as money got scarce from being spread thin to all the other religions, Christmas got set back from twelve days to just one, Christmas Day. And like the Mardi Gras celebration, one day is the big deal. The rest is just pomp and circumstance leading up to it. Today, Christmas is celebrated by Christians and Jews alike. Christians ring bells, and Jews ring cash registers, but they both celebrate the idea of Christmas, believe me!

"Moslems, the followers of Islam, believe several things in common with Christians, but there are fundamental differences. Like Moslems believe that if you die while forcing Islam on other people, you go directly to the best part of heaven, and you don't have to pass go or collect two hundred dollars either. And this was certainly a good idea amongst the hostile, savage tribes where it took hold because it took the worry out of being close. Kill or convert—either, or.

"During the Crusades, which started about a thousand years ago, give or take a hundred years, Moslems and Christian Crusaders slaughtered each other by the thousands to control what is today Israel, home of the Jews. Just goes to show you that not that many differences exist between all the religions, certainly not as much as they would all have you believe.

"But let's face it. Anybody who kills somebody just because they don't share the same version of God has no idea what God is or wants from us—none of them, be they Moslem and Jew, Hindu or Sikh, Catholic Irish or Protestant Irish. They're all crazy.

"The Irish are still fighting a religious war that the rest of Europe stopped fighting over three hundred years ago. Stubborn Irishmen or

311

what? The Irish are all Christians, even. They're killin' each other over this: does the Pope represent God on earth, or is the English king that representative? Damn, as bad as the Limeys have treated the Micks, you wouldn't think *any* Irishman would look to London for leadership. And we're talkin' faith, begorra. Aye, 'tis nearly as important as a nip in yer coffee, lad!"

"Yer Mick accent is just terrible, Odie, terrible! Worse than the duke's in *The Quiet Man*." Beeb knew turning Odie's own words against him would get an immediate reaction.

"'Tis the duke you'll be comparin' me to, laddie-buck? Faith, not even a whisper in the same breath as Barry Fitzgerald?"

"Not even in the same breath as Barry Manilow," came Beeb's stinging comments.

"Have we concluded today's sermon yet, padre?" Cat pointedly asked.

"Hell, no!" Beeb swiftly answered her. "He ain't even placed communism in his tirade yet. Boy's always considered communism to be a religion. So how 'bout it, Odie? Even though it's done as a major anything, it still exists."

"It exists in China and Cuba and maybe Albania, Mongolia. That's about it. But yes, it certainly must be considered with the other religions, except they claimed to be antireligion, yet they performed the same functions that religions did. They both fought all outside influences. Both claimed dire consequences would occur from heeding the word of the infidel nonbeliever. Both offer their own forms of hope to their followers.

"Nope, communism is as much a religion as the other kinds of theology. Of course, Marx made huge mistakes in formulating his ideology. He based his ideas on things he had seen in the British Museum. Britain was the most industrialized country on earth at that time, and the evils of the new factories did not escape Marx's eye. Had the British not plundered the various countries they conquered, Marx would have had nothing to see, no idea of the past glories that were Rome, Athens, Pergamon, Troy, etc.

"Still, Marx got it all wrong. He didn't understand capitalism, the use of capital to start something, and the return on capital invested. Marx had the bright idea that the factory workers would revolt and take over the factories. Marx viewed the factory worker as the epitome of capitalism. He just didn't comprehend that those with all the capital to begin with were the ones who most profited. Those who held menial jobs did so to feed their families, not to get rich. The idea of capitalism was a good one for wealthy landowners. It made it easy for the rich to become much richer.

"Marx's ideas were so hopelessly absurd that no one took them seriously in the capitalist societies. In fact, only in backward Russia did these ideas gain any support and then only from people too dumb to realize what they were doing or saying. Lenin used Marxist principles to found his government in Russia in 1917. They were gonna form a new government the Russian people could trust. Lenin ain't his real name, so he lied before day one. So much for trust.

"Marx didn't live to see his ideas established anywhere. Just as well, I say. Frozen Russia didn't have any factories or factory workers to arise and toss off the chains of capitalist oppression like Marx envisioned. It was hostile to affluence of any description because the common Russian had nothing. No, I gotta list communism as a religion even though it's more old-fashioned and quite a bit dumber than most, but that's Lenin's hard luck for starting such a stupid idea in the middle of a frozen nowhere that was centuries behind their not-too-advanced neighbors."

"You never have liked them Russians, have you Odie?" Beeb knew it was a rhetorical question.

"Oh, the Russian people are all right. It's that asinine government they had that I objected to. Now, I don't know. Russia is a vast and old country. The other places like Siberia, I don't know how that's gonna work out yet. No Red Army to protect them from the Chinese? No money to drill for gas and oil? Who might wanna conquer them? Will the Japs just buy it? Yo, there's gonna be changes aplenty for Asia in the next twenty-five years, you watch. Siberia might be frozen most of the year, but it's still better than some of the old USSR, like Albania. Although Albania is in a better climate, I don't recall seeing any enlightening statements written on their public walls. Do you, Beeb?"

"Not that I recall."

"You really *have* been to Albania?" Cat asked, amazement registered on her voice.

Beeb grinned and answered for Odie and himself. "Yeah, we been there, but we didn't get to meet Enver Hoxha, however."

"What with him bein' so dead and all!" Odie added.

"I thought you guys just made up that shit about Albania and all so I wouldn't feel so bad about my record," Cat noted.

"Well, shit! Lookit here, Odie. Damn, you ain't tole Cat about the marvelous adventure we had in Albania?"

"Don't believe that bullshit!" Odie sternly warned Cat.

"Then you've never been there?" Cat sighed.

"Oh, yeah!" Odie assured her, "we been there all right! We just didn't have no marvelous adventure!"

"What happened?" Cat asked, sensing yet another interesting story about the new man in her life.

"Well, Beeb, me, and some Greek girls and this Macedonian, as he wanted us to call him, were camped on the beach on the Ionian Sea. Not far from an island called Kerkira and close to the Albanian border is where I'm talkin' about. Anyhow, we're in the tent boogie'n with two Greek chicks when the tent falls in on us. So I get up to go out, and when I crawl out the flap, there's some dudes with AK-47s pointin' at me. I told Beeb there was trouble and not to move.

"These goofs had cut the tent ropes. One of 'em thumps me on the back of the head and drops me facedown in the sand. They pull the tent up and find Beeb anyway. They ushered us to a boat, and off we went up the coast toward Albania. An hour or so after they kidnapped us, we landed in a grimy little fishing village. Made Mississippi look like Miami. Anyhow, this ridiculous self-styled group of fanatics thinks me and Beeb are CIA. Apparently, Americans are all CIA to them. I don't know."

"Well, I guess you'll never know now, eh?" Beeb quizzed his companion.

Cat asked what that meant.

"It means them dumbasses were all the organization they had, all four or five of them, and at least two wanted to be leader."

"Yeah," concurred Odie, "they fucked up and had an argument amongst themselves, and I sort of got the drop on them."

"And what does *that* mean?" Cat asked expectantly.

"It means that the mutants didn't watch Odie very carefully every second he was in their custody, with the direct result being they all got shot with an AK-47. He got the fool's gun, shot the other four with it, then punched his lights out and fired off a burst at him too."

"You killed them?" Cat asked incredulously.

"No," Beeb sarcastically stated, "he just scared the shit out of them."

"Flesh wounds," Odie assured her.

"Yeah, not his fault they bled to death."

"Damn straight. They should'a never taken us outta Greece. They got real hospitals there."

"Sorry I asked," Cat opined.

"Oh, don't be. I've mellowed a whole lot since then."

"Yeah," Beeb agreed a little too cheerfully for Odie's liking, "he's mellowed a lot! Why, he got so mellow by the last time he was kidnapped, he didn't even kill nobody! That was quite an improvement, don't you think?"

Cat watched Odie's eyes, waiting for confirmation of Beeb's tale.

"Yeah," Odie started, "last time was a couple'a real losers tryin' ta roust cash from gringos. I slapped 'em around some for sport, so one asshole gets bad and whips out a knife and tells me to say my prayers. I told him to put the knife away and leave quietly, or I'd shove it up his ass."

"And?" Cat wondered.

"And I don't think he has a problem with hemorrhoids anymore."

"Where was this?"

"Barcelona."

"I see!"

"It was no biggie."

"No biggie," Cat repeated, trying to sound like it wasn't.

"Yeah, the biggie was in Greece," Beeb said to get Cat's attention.

"Yeah, you just told me."

"He's talking about the second time I got kidnapped, second time in Greece too, come to think of it. But this time was on the other coast of Greece near the Turkish-Bulgarian border." Odie looked like a light bulb just went on and he had an idea. "Damn, Beeb, you know what? I'll bet that's why I'm wanted for murder in Turkey! That little shoot-out with the terrorists and the border guards. Somebody must'a got hit on the Turkish side, and they got my name somehow. Shit, that still don't explain it. How do I get tagged with it? Oh, well."

"Oh, well, indeed," Beeb sided with Odie on that one. He had not been involved with this one. Good thing because it had been a bloody affair.

"Anyway, Cat, these goofball ragtop terrorists thought I would play along with their stupid game. I was being held in the back of this big truck, like a deuce and a quarter that our military uses. Eventually, I had to piss like a racehorse. I started to get up, and they all pointed their guns at me. I pointed to my pecker and hissed at them, and they finally got the idea. I stood up in the back and pissed off the end directly on the dusty road. Somebody hollered at the driver, and he started swerving back and forth, making it very hard to piss and hold on at the same time.

"As soon as I had finished, the driver swerved again, and they were all laughing at me as I grabbed for the guy next to me. I managed to pull the pin from a grenade on his lapel, and he didn't see me do it. I simply dove right out the back, hands and head first into the dirt road. Before any of them could react, the grenade goes off and blows the shit outta the back of the truck and the dumbasses inside. Now the truck slams on its brakes and turns around rapidly. I got no more grenades, no gun, so I hid in the bushes, not sure what to do.

"The truck slows down near where I jumped out, and one of the cretins jumps out to look for me. The truck drives slowly back along the route we just came. I picked up a rock and winged it at the guy's turbaned head and knocked him down. I got his rifle away from him and gave him a few bullets to keep as a memento of our meeting. The truck stops and two guys emerge with AK-47s blazing. I dove in the bushes again.

"Now some border guards in a tower perhaps an eighth of a mile away open fire around me and at the terrorists. One of them is hit, and the other is behind the truck. I managed to crawl up to the truck and get in and backed up over the other gun-totin' asshole. I hurt him, but I didn't kill him. The border guards now open fire on the truck, so I jumped out. Seconds later, an artillery round took out the truck in a flash.

"Now I'm scared shitless, since I don't know who kidnapped me, what their nationality and intents are, and I don't know why the border guards are firing at me. I don't even know if they are Bulgarian or Turkish. I don't know if they're Greek or what. I ain't sure where I am. I'm in deep shit, that much I know.

"Finally, a jeep drives down the road carefully. I'm sure they're out looking for me. They fire off a few rounds every thirty or forty feet on both sides of the road. After they were quite a ways down the road, I got out of my hiding place and crawl up the ditch for a while. The jeep careens back down the road, firing wildly every few seconds. Then they went away, leaving the dead terrorists where they lay.

"So I leave them there too and crawled down the ditch for an hour or two. Finally, I spot a car parked on the side of the road. Some folks humpin' in the bushes, I guessed. I hot-wired the car and sped off down the highway to the west. Early the next morning, I got to Thessalonica and ditched the car. I pawned the rifle for a few drachmas and hitched to Athens straight away.

"A few days later, I found Beeb, and he asked where I'd been, and I told him about it, but he didn't believe me. Actually, he didn't think anyone would be dumb enough to attempt to kidnap me again."

"Really!" Beeb interjected. "I didn't know whether to believe such a tale or not, but reading about a border clash with unknown terrorists the following day in an Athens paper made me believe it. Odie swore he'd kill the next damn fool who tried to force him to do anything against his will. I had to believe it."

"Yeah, I told Beeb word for word what happened, and he didn't believe me till he read it in some Greek paper."

"So how many people have you killed, Odie?"

He could tell from the tone of her voice that she was less than thrilled to discover how bloody his past had been. "Look, Cat," Odie stated angrily, "it ain't like I went out and shot up a damn liquor store to steal money or nothin'! Dammit, I didn't go out looking for trouble! I didn't set out to off some terrorist rughead clowns. It just happened! I didn't kill any of them maliciously. They just couldn't handle the consequences of their actions. That's all!

"But that ain't what you want to know, is it? Just the body count! Okay, if we count the three in Albania that I'm sure died and all those ragtop goofs I just spoke of and perhaps one East German border guard, I'd estimate I killed fourteen, fifteen tops."

Cat was shaken. This was not good news coming from the lips she loved.

"Hey!" Odie shouted at her, unhappy that this news distressed her. "I only killed a few morons! All of them violated my personal freedom. They were all perfectly willing to sacrifice *my* life for *their* cause, and I just don't play that shit! I beat them at their own game. That's all. No big deal! So I took out a few goon terrorists. So what? It's like stepping on a cockroach, same thing. Squash a bug, kill a terrorist—no biggie! What, would it be better to die for their stupidity? I think not. I felt my life was in danger, and when I get to that conclusion, it's him or me. I vote him every time!"

"And damn few people can make such mental leaps that my boy Odie is famous for!" Beeb assured Cat.

Cat stared at Odie a moment. He stared right back. "Shit, Cat, don't gimme this I'd-never-do-that-shit look either! You got a .38 in yer purse! I saw it! Okay, I looked in yer purse. I'm guilty! But I heard it clunk when you set it down back when Villeplatte was gittin' his kicks. You flat admitted to me that you would have killed Villeplatte had he gotten away from me and Beeb. If you'd kill a fuckin' FBI agent for personal reasons, then you damn sure would kill a terrorist who'd kidnapped you if you got the chance! You absolutely would blow them away. Admit it!"

Cat let these harsh words sink in. Odie might be right. No doubt about it, she would have blasted Villeplatte right between the eyes had it been necessary. Maybe Odie wasn't so bad after all. He didn't lie about it or try to cover it up like a government would. There was something to be said for his honesty, if not his stupidity, for telling the story in the first place. She would not harshly judge him for his teenage actions if he would do the same thing for her. And she had to admit, so far, he hadn't mentioned a word of her past behavior. She would wait and see.

Odie finished his thoughts on the subject of his bloody past. "Cat, I killed the first clown that tried to force me to be a pawn in his stupid game, and I'd do it again in a heartbeat. If anyone discovers us and the secret of the Ehliuns and tries to force us to go public, that person had best be prepared to kill me immediately, or he's dead!" Odie spoke the words as if he meant it, which he did.

"I hope we never get caught then," Cat said, trying to smile.

"Relax," Beeb assured them both, "we won't get caught. Pete is as good a watchdog as has ever been thought of."

Pete barked his approval, much to the delight of the motor home's occupants. Pete knew he had the right protector in Odie since he could survive anything. Odie thought about how humorous Pete had become in only a few days. It was rubbin' off well.

# The Starcraft Five

Along the shoreline of Lake Lanier, Odie had Pete stop at a print shop advertising custom-design T-shirts. After several minutes, Lin came in to see what was taking so long. Odie assured her he would be out in a few, so she returned to the motor home to tell the rest of them what Odie said. He knew Cat was behind sending Lin in. When the clerk finished Odie's order, Odie paid him for the six T-shirts. He happily informed the airbrush artist that he was quite good at his craft. With that, Odie went out to the starcraft.

Cat informed him it was eight thirty, and Atlanta was at least a half hour away. Pete made straight for the Kudzu Capital, and Odie distributed T-shirts. Five of the six shirts he'd ordered were identical, with block letters reading simply, "STARCRAFT FIVE." Cat dug out the other shirt and looked quizzically at it before holding it aloft. "What's this supposed to mean?" she asked Odie.

On the white T-shirt was a strange picture. Above a rocky planet were two suns, a red one and a smaller yellow one. There was a massive collection of buildings on the rocky planet surface. In plain block letters above the picture were the words: "Property of Physics Department." Underneath the picture were more words: "University of Alpha Centauri." Only Beeb laughed.

"Why did you buy us these Starcraft Five T-shirts, Odie? Not that I'm ungrateful or complaining or anything. I just wondered why?" Cat said softly.

"You won't get mad?" Odie asked her gently.

320

She suspiciously shook her head no. "Because I wanted to end hawk week!"

Beeb's violent outburst of laughter was reason enough for Cat to glare at them. "Hawk week?" Cat repeated, unsure just what that meant.

"Yeah, hawk week! Look, ya got on a Nighthawks shirt right now as we speak!"

Cat looked at Beeb, who said nothing, and then at Odie before impudently saying, "So?"

"So yesterday, it was the Seattle Seahawks. The day before that it was the Chicago Blackhawks and Atlanta Hawks the day before that!"

"We were in Chicago yesterday!" Cat blurted out. Then she corrected Odie, a chance she relished. "Besides, you got the order wrong. Yesterday was the Blackhawk shirt. The day before was the Seahawks."

"Whatever!" Odie said to regain the conversation's lead. "You had an Iowa Hawkeyes shirt on in Amana, and you had a Kansas Jayhawks shirt on when you were hitchhiking. I told Beeb in the Museum of Science and Industry that it must be hawk week." Odie smiled at her as he finished speaking.

"Hawk week indeed!" Cat said, pretending to be disgusted. She looked at what his T-shirt said. Under the five figures lurking in the shadowy mists of times past were two words: Rock Mountain.

Odie put a tape in for Cat to hear. She wasn't familiar with the lyrics. "I'm gittin' ready for a one-night stand?" she repeated the words to Odie.

He nodded yes.

"So who is this?" she asked.

He raised his eyebrows a bit, obviously surprised. He handed her the tape case, like it was a wine cork to sniff or something. In the center of the tape case was a triangle drawn in blue ball point, asserting that this was a blues tape.

"So who is this?" Cat asked again.

"Who is this?" Odie repeated unbelievingly. "Why, it's The Nighthawks by The Nighthawks." Odie found it strange she could own the shirt and not know the band. "On the flip side is the band on my shirt, Rock Mountain. The blues made this tape for me, he knows all these guys too."

"What guys?"

"Are you listening to me or what? Why do you own a Nighthawks shirt?" Odie demanded.

"Because it was a buck in a Frisco secondhand store. That's why!" Cat shot back.

"I see!"

"Why do you own a Rock Mountain shirt?"

"It was a gift."

"I see!" Cat said to its originator in what she hoped was the proper tone and context. "So what is this music, this song right here "Pretty Girls and Cadillacs"? That The Nighthawks?" she asked Odie.

"Yes. What did you think that shirt was when you bought it, besides cheap?"

"I thought it was appropriate because that was the *in* word for sellin' yer ass. You was hawkin' it! I hawked at night, so I thought it was great advertising and for a buck, a great bargain as well. That's why I have all those hawk shirts—well, why I *had* them all."

Odie's ears pricked up at this.

Cat went on, "I guess I always thought some smart-ass Frisco pimp had it made. Now you tell me it's music and not sports."

Both men had to smile expansively at Cat's comparison of trysts to sports. But the way she went about it, it was an Olympic event. Cat stripped out of her Hawk shirt and put the new Starcraft Five T-shirt on. Odie noticed. So did the Ehliuns. Their behavior toward each other was changing. Swiftly, Odie tossed his Rock Mountain T-shirt aside and donned his new Starcraft Five shirt to match Cat.

As he gazed at Cat, he reflected on what the Starcraft Five really meant. He had reason to be proud of his accomplishments so far this past week. Two Ehliuns had come to understand America better than the average American. And naturally, the three unaverage Americans had pitched in their considerable talents to help raise the consciousness of two Ehliuns above and beyond the call of patriotic duty to that marvelous new symbiotic plateau that they now fondly followed as a new way of life. None of the Starcraft Five thought much about it other than just that it was a new way of life. None dared to think too much about it. Fear pervaded their thoughts, fear that they might ruin their new situation by thinking too much.

Cat knew her past was best left far behind. She knew Beeb and Odie had had varied careers, strong on academic achievement and accidental violence. Odie still didn't control his temper as well as Cat thought he should, but at least he wasn't a public danger. He hadn't killed anyone. That was an improvement, she thought to herself.

Odie displayed his new shirt to Pete, but only Odie knew exactly what the logo meant. It represented Odie's new existence based on Ehliun technology controlled by human greed. Only five beings anywhere knew what Pete was now. The Starcraft Five, Odie daydreamed on. He could see it all now. Starcraft Five, a proud new way to live! Elegance beyond measure! Move in today! Bring proof of success! Cash, lots of it!

"Hate to interrupt yer daydreamin' there, Odie, but do we have plans to stay in Atlanta long?"

"No."

"Why not?"

"Because we got no plans, man. If there's a plan, it's news to me! Why do you ask?"

"I got some friends in Atlanta that I'd like to look up. Ain't seen some of them since I was at Tech."

"You went to the North Avenue Trade School too?" Odie asked.

"Well, hell, yes, I went to Tech! I tole you this shit before. We both had old Kauffmann for chemistry, remember?"

"I remember having Kauffmann, yeah."

"You aced his unknowns test, while I got a mere eighty-seven, and I was the best damn grade in three semesters. But whose name is it that I see on the perfect paper still hanging on his office wall?"

"Um, mine, perhaps?" Odie asked, nearly apologetically, it seemed to Cat.

"Damn, Odie, we went through all this shit at the beach the day you saved Kathy!"

"Oh, yeah, right! Now I remember! We did talk about both of us goin' to Tech, 'cause I remember sayin' that yer mom would'a shit bricks if she'da known we were both goin' to the same college in the same decade!"

Both men laughed. "Yeah," Odie sighed, "that afternoon at Myrtle Beach was a rough one, wasn't it? But it hardly compares to these days, does it?"

"Nope, the good old days when things was simple is gone forever, I'm afeared."

"Christ! you two sound like somebody's grammas' relivin' the past!" Cat stated.

"Well, babycakes, it's true ain't it?" Odie said. "How's yer week been since we found you in Nebraska?"

Cat had to admit, things had changed and not for the simpler. Here she was, riding down the interstate in what amounted to a hotel lobby, and she thought nothing of it. Bridges and other vehicles moved through the hologram without damage or notice. This was completely bizarre, and she was comfortably used to it. There was no doubt this was very strange. "Tell me how you met Kathy at Myrtle Beach, Odie. This sounds like it's another goodie. Gee, you've had some dandies!"

Odie thought that Cat already knew too much about him, but he told the story anyway. Besides, telling the truth was becoming like second nature to Odie. The trouble was that lying was first nature to him or at least disguising the truth so no one could notice.

"'How I Spent My Summer Vacation' by O. de Bienville. Ahem. School let out."

"Hold it!" Cat boldly said, swinging her hand like a sickle to cut off Odie's words. She had acquired an Odie-like quality to her voice that made Beeb giggle. "Skip ahead, Odie, to where you and Beeb were right before, not way before but right before you met Kathy!"

Beeb had to say something. "Damn, she's more like you every day, Odie. I swear! Ya got her talkin' bossy just like you do!"

Even the Ehliuns had to laugh at this. Cat was pleased that her humor had even affected the Ehliuns. Odie feigned regaining his composure. "Okay, where was I?"

"Myrtle Beach," Cat aided him in relocating his story line.

"Right, okay, so I'm strollin' down the beach, watchin' the crotches slink by, when all of a sudden, I hear a strangely familiar voice cry out, 'Odie!' So I look around, and there he is, my old childhood pal! Beauregard Elvis Edison Beaufort in the flesh!"

"Y'see, Cat," Beeb started in, "I hadn't seen Odie since we came back from East Germany on separate flights. See, my parents didn't think it would be too good of an idea if we saw each other for a while."

"*Forbidden* is the word he's searchin' for," Odie informed Cat.

"It had been over ten years since we'd seen each other, so you can imagine how surprised we were to even recognize each other after a decade and on a crowded beach at that."

"No shit!" Cat agreed.

"So I plop down on Beeb's blanket," Odie said, "and we start talkin' about the old days and what's been goin' on and Tech and all that. I guess an hour had passed when all of a sudden, there's this woman screamin' and drownin' offshore fifty, sixty yards from where we sat."

"Next thing I know," Beeb said, "Odie's dashed out and dove in after her."

"Yeah, but when I got to her, she was shriekin' at me, slappin' at me, gone totally crazy. Shit, she was dyin'!"

"Fortunately for Kathy," Beeb added, "Odie wasn't bothered by her craziness at all."

"What did you do?" Cat wondered.

"I calmed her down with my hand," Odie offered.

"He knocked the bitch unconscious is what he did, Cat."

"Whatever. She didn't fight me after that. I grabbed her hair and towed her to shore. By that time, Beeb had the blanket spread down at the water's edge."

"Odie put her on it and told me to keep the crowd back. He was busy givin' her mouth-to-mouth resuscitation, and she was busy pukin' up seawater."

"I really didn't have time to see how lovely she was because as soon as she was conscious enough to wipe off her mouth, she began to return all that mouth-to-mouth I'd just given her."

"Oh, you should have seen it, Cat! She was just turned on, the last of the red-hot lovers! She was kissin' Odie all over, draggin' his shorts down to his knees. And he was a'floppin' around, tryin' ta git free!"

"Tryin' ta git free?" Cat repeated, not believing Odie would ever flee any woman undressing him.

Odie clarified the scene for her. "Tryin' ta git free of my damn cutoffs! The stupid zipper was tangled with a shoelace, and my knee was gettin' bent backward and uncomfortable as hell!"

Beeb took over the narration. "Suddenly, the crowd parts, and five gorillas in government blue suits snatch Kathy away from Odie in nothing flat. One of them displays a gun and a badge to me and then the crowd in general. They tell me and Odie to just freeze."

"There I was," Odie told her, "sand up the crack of my ass, and I'm exposing a raging hard-on, my shoes and shorts hopelessly tangled, and government agents are stealin' this mystery lady away from me before I can even find out her name. It was very embarrassing."

"Sort of bare-ass embarrassing, eh?" Cat smiled.

Beeb took the lead. "Yeah, that was a real weird day. Odie had just gotten his shorts back up when these news photographers arrive, takin' pictures and askin' Odie how it feels to save the senator's wife. He told them he had no idea who the lady was, so they left right away to find the real rescuer, the one she was kissing like a lover. They had it figured that she had to know her rescuer, and if he didn't know her, he didn't rescue her. They split as fast as they arrived.

"So Odie and me left the beach right away to go talk things over. We walked over to his motel room about five blocks away."

Odie decided to tell the tale awhile. "But when we get to my room, it's been ransacked. It's a total disaster. It looked like renovation by angry mobs usually looks. My stuff is scattered all over the room. I was mad and scared at the same time."

Beeb took the lead once again. "Odie told me he would call me at my parent's house in seventy-two hours, and he said goodbye to me. I left him gathering up his shit and went back to the beach so I could walk to my room."

"And I walked out that night down the beach and left Myrtle to never return. I didn't like the way they treated me there," Odie added.

"Yeah," Beeb said, "and I wandered into a bar on the way back to my room to think things over. I had lived a nice, quiet, calm life full of peace and tranquility for more than a decade without Odie. I see him for a few hours and all hell's broke loose again. I had to wonder, you understand."

Cat nodded her head in full agreement. "I wonder about him too!" she grinned.

Beeb went on with his story. "So before I can finish my beer, some gorgeous babe sits down next to me at the bar and asked me for a light, danglin' a cigarette from her pouty red lips. So as I reach for a pack of matches down the bar, she slips a note on the bar for me to read. The note says, 'Keep Odie Away From Kathy.' She sets her drink down on the note and folds it around her glass. Well, I just about shit!

"All of a sudden it's become very cloak-and-dagger! I don't know how she could possibly know me, know I know Odie, know Odie's name, and apparently the name of the girl he rescued. There's some oldies music playin, slow stuff, and she takes me by the hand to the dance floor. There, we dance to a few slow songs cheek to cheek and hand to buttock. She whispers in my ear that she saw Odie kissing Kathy on the beach, and she saw Kathy undo his zipper and pull out his dick. I tell her, 'So what? He still just saved her life and didn't know who the fuck she was. And come to think of it, what the fuck did I have to do with all this?'

"She said Kathy was married to a very jealous man, a US senator, and those were the bodyguards he assigned her that accosted them at the beach. She said the senator wouldn't like it if he found out two men had his wife on the beach. I told her I was there with my friend, and we didn't know the woman.

"She says to me, 'Come on, grow up! If Odie continues to see her like this, his life would be in danger.'

"I repeated that neither Odie nor I had no idea who she was. We never saw her before we heard her scream. I told her Odie dove in to rescue her, did so, brought her to the beach, resuscitated her, and then she tried to rape him.

"She says she don't believe me and neither will the senator because his bodyguards took photos of Odie and Kathy. I thanked her for the warning. She turned to go back to the bar, and I bolted for the beach door and dashed down the beach. I figured she'd have to be a damn track star to catch me, but she didn't even look out the door.

"When I get to my motel room, to my dismay, it's been redecorated just like Odie's. I figured they got to it while Mata Hari had me detained. I gathered up my stuff, got in my car, and headed to the folks' house in Beaufort, South Carolina."

"Wait a minute," Cat ordered. "Your name is Beaufort, and you live in Beaufort?"

"That's right. It's named for some relative, great-great-great-grandfather or his brother, cousin, nephew—someone. My great-great-grandfather was a Civil War general. You may have heard of him, Pierre Gustav Toutant Beauregard. That's who I'm named for. My dad too."

"Well, tell her about the family home, Beeb. You ought to see it, Cat. It's chock-fulla antiques and stuff. Beeb grew up in a museum, I like to say."

"Yeah, he likes to say it even if it ain't true. My folks didn't get the house till Granpa died and left it to them in his will. I visited for a few weeks every summer, but I was never allowed to touch anything. You know how it is in museums."

Odie took over the storytelling. "So after I left Myrtle, I hitched up to Crescent Beach and caught a ride to Wilmington. I borrowed a friend's truck there and drove on up to Charlottesville, Virginia. I stayed at Jamie's farm just outside town. Jamie's folks are like Beeb's folks, only Yankees. They got a house on Nantucket built in the early years, 1650 or so. In college, Jamie was tryin' hard to impress this Midwestern chick, so he told her his folks had a house on Nantucket. She says, 'What's a Nantucket?' and we all fell out. She sure wasn't one'a them uppity East Coast bitches. It was funny."

"My family home is only about 250 years old, Cat," Beeb told her, "but I bet it's lots nicer."

Odie knew this was a dig, but he hadn't been to Jamie's. "Yeah, Beeb's people's palace is an okay kind of place. What, twenty six rooms?"

"Yeah, somethin' like that. Most of them are just storage, as I recall."

"So I had this interview in DC," Odie said, "on a Tuesday afternoon for a large grant. So I stayed at Jamie's farm for a few days till Tuesday morning, then I drove into DC for my grant interview."

"What kind of grant?" Cat wanted to know.

"The grant we are riding in," Odie answered.

"Oh," Cat said simply. "Guess you got it then."

Beeb filled Cat in further. "So Odie don't call me at the folks' house like he said he would, so I don't know what the hell happened. The way things went at Myrtle, I fear the worst. But Tuesday, I had an appointment with a senator to be interviewed about a grant. My dad went up with me because the senator turns out to be an old friend of his. Dad didn't tell me that till after we got to the senator's office. I figured he had stuff to do at the Pentagon.

"So anyway, my grant application was to study the bridges in the northeastern portion of the country, specifically those in daily use with heavy traffic loads that are over fifty years old. Dad whips a copy of army junk on me. It lists the age and approximate number of crossings daily for every bridge in America! Blows me away. I say, 'Dad, what the hell does the army need with stuff like this?'

"He says, 'This is vital statistics. All militaries need this sort of information.' Then he tells me it's secret shit and don't show it to the senator. Two minutes later, I'm in the senator's office!"

"Yeah," Odie agreed, "and when he gets to the senator's office, here I am being raked over the coals by this angry senator. Now, not only is he in no mood to grant me my grant application, but he actually thinks that I'm fuckin' his wife! And just because he's got some timed, dated photographs of Kathy's hands on my hard-on with her tongue stuck in my ear in front of an audience on a crowded beach. Damn fool thinks this is proof!

"The jerk's got pictures of everything that happened *after* she puked up all that seawater but not one from before, none of me saving her ass from drownin', no pictures of resuscitation, no photos of her pukin' back the Atlantic. No, just selected pictures to make me look like a carelessly casual beach fucker."

"So are you gonna deny you'da fucked her right there on the beach in front of an audience?" Beeb asked his dear old friend.

"Well, I didn't say that, now did I?"

Beeb contented himself with a smirk. Odie returned to the story that Cat had asked him to tell. "Anyhow, there were no pictures in the senator's hand that would back up my story, none that would show him I told the truth, none that would declare my innocence. I was doing my best to defend myself, but the senator was one mighty angry dude!"

Beeb interrupted, "Actually, it was my dad who saved Odie's ass. Dad stuck his head in the senator's private office to get his attention, but he recognized Odie immediately."

Odie rapidly agreed with Beeb's assessment. "I snapped to attention and saluted him, saying, 'Colonel Beau, sir!' To which he replied that he was now a general, and he pointed out his star for me."

Cat was surprised. Looking directly at Beeb, she asked him for the truth. "Is yer dad really a general in the army?"

Beeb looked her in the eye, saying, "Yep, 'fraid so."

Odie nodded yes and went on with his story about Kathy. "Well, the senator is so amazed that General Beaufort knew me that his jaw dropped clear to his desktop. I immediately asked the general to identify me."

"So did he?" Cat wondered.

"Sure did!" Beeb gloated. "He pointed out Odie as the boy who nearly caused World War III, the kid they traded four spies for!" Beeb laughed harder when he saw the same look on Odie's face that he remembered from the senator's office.

"Funny stuff!" Odie stage-whispered to Beeb, intonation indicating his disbelief.

"When I arrived in the senator's private office," Beeb related, "Odie pointed me out as the Beeb he had been speaking of, who was at the beach with him before Kathy appeared, and I could tell him the truth. The senator runs Odie and the general out of the office. I told him virtually the identical story he got from Odie. He rescued her from drowning, and we didn't know who she was, that we had never seen her before she screamed for help. I told him she puked up half the bay and then turned on Odie, just tried to rape him. I also told him five government gorillas jumped us and someone ransacked our rooms.

"This seemed to distress him a little. I didn't tell him about Mata Hari because she said she was Kathy's friend, but the rest seemed to match Odie's story. So he whips out these photos of Odie's dick in her hand, his tongue in her ear, all this. I told him, 'Look, she just had her life saved, and she was happy about it, it would appear.'

"I asked him if my dad had ever lied to him, and he said not that he knew. I told him my dad was a most honorable man, and I was his son. I had no reason to lie to him, but if some of his employees had fucked up, maybe they were tryin' ta frame someone—in this case, Odie."

Odie took up the narrative awhile. "The senator brings me back in and quizzed me some more, then Beeb and his dad, then all of us together. Finally, the general says he has a meeting at the Pentagon, and he was gone. Told me it was good to see me again, and I felt like he meant it."

Beeb told him he was sure that had been genuine also.

Odie went on. "So the senator breaks out a bottle of Jack Daniel's from his desk drawer, and we toasted one another. So we sit and drink and talk and drink and bargained awhile. We brought up all kinds of things that could be done if we broadened the scope of things, extended the grants a time or two."

"We," Beeb laughed, gesturing so his fingers touched his chest while looking over at Cat and the Ehliuns. "We. Odie says we. You know better than that, don't you, Cat? We didn't say anything. Odie said it all. He, not we, took the situation and pushed it right past the credible limits, envisioning all sorts of things for us to do."

"What do you mean?" Cat asked, smiling like maybe she really knew.

"Well," Beeb began, "right away, Odie expands the scope of the grants to the entire interstate system, not just a small portion of it like I had planned, and he suggests bumping the grants up from eight months to three times that: two years. But I will freely admit that his fast talk and the senator's great relief that neither of us are his wife's lover combined with that Jack Daniel's to produce more money and bigger grants than either of us had asked for in the first place.

"Hell, the fool went for Odie's sucker line! Told him this kind of study on the highways would make him the most famous senator in all of Washington. Drunk as a skunk by the time we left, the senator signed over two years' worth of funding for us to travel in great style across America."

"And still he bitches," Odie added to Beeb's statements, producing laughter.

Cat still didn't know much about Kathy or where she came into the story, so she asked. The chief rival for Odie's affections was still an enigma to her. "So where does *babycakes* fit into all this?"

Beeb grandiosely gestured a flourish over to Odie. "Odie? Yer on."

Odie took up the tale anew. "Kathy found me the next day in a little motel in Mount Vernon. Strolls in and says, 'I'm gonna fuck yer eyes out.' She nearly did too.

"She told me all about herself, how she left her native Alabama and went to work in New York as a model. She went overseas to Italy and other places while working for an Italian catalog company. One of the company owners was quite taken with her beauty. He was an incredibly wealthy industrialist. She met him on her nineteenth birthday on a catalog shoot at dawn on Corfu. When he found out it was her birthday, he told her he would grant her any wish. She wished for a birthday dinner in Paris, and she was on his personal jet that very afternoon.

"He apparently loved fast cars and fast women in that order. Within three months, they were married. Within the year, he crisped himself in a blazing crash in the far turn at Monte Carlo during a major race. She was not yet twenty but already a widow, a rich widow, many millions richer than when she was single, but a widow, nonetheless.

"Within six months, she went to Switzerland and sold her holdings, which was one third of Giancarlazzo's industrial empire. She got something like eight hundred million for her holdings. She's got bucks. For some reason, she came back to the US and partied around. She met and then married the senator five or six years ago. She's only thirty-one or thirty-two now. He's gotta be twice that, easy.

"I still don't know why she married him. He's jealous, old, unattractive, and dishonest. 'Course, she's pretty dishonest herself, but I mean, she is his ticket to the jet-set *in* crowd. Her money makes his look like pocket change. I don't know what he does for her, power or something like that. She cheats on him constantly.

"He's spent untold money spyin' on her, and it just don't do no good. She showed me some photos of her fucking some sailor on a park bench with the Capitol in the background, broad daylight, people in walking distance of them. She got the photos away from the guy spyin' on her for a blow job, which she also had a picture of. I don't think she's all that cautious anymore."

"Then what do you see in her, Odie?" Cat pointedly asked him.

He looked directly into her eyes. He knew she could see through him with those eyes, and he knew enough not to lie to her. "Since I found you, Cat, I don't see anything in Kathy."

Cat's gold-flecked yellow eyes pierced Odie's eyes and peered directly into his mind. Cat was happy with Odie's statement. The next few days would tell her whether to believe that or not, but she knew she had fallen in love with Odie.

Lin and Din silently started a love file on Cat and Odie. They already noticed their behavioral changes. They would read up on love. They knew no other way to get accurate information about certain subjects.

Beeb had put Little Feat on the tape player, and "Oh, Atlanta" greeted them. Odie thought about Cat. So she fell for him like he fell for her, eh? Maybe some time in Atlanta would do them both some good. Perhaps something strange would be just the thing. But the more he thought about Cat being with some stranger, the less he liked it. He couldn't stand the thought of her leaving his life. He knew he had never felt like this before. And even though he still had a business card with "Hooking Is Real Employment" on it and Delores's red lip prints, to personalize it, he could not bring himself to call her.

Odie knew he was in trouble. He was dreaming about Cat, and she was right there. What would he do if she left him?

# Caldwell Luke

The sun had already set, but the city of Atlanta glowed in the night, the sky still reflecting an orangish-red color against the clouds lit up by the street lights. Atlanta poked its steel and glass profile proudly into the air. The Ehliuns were jabbering away about this and that as the starcraft moved down I-85 south. They were the only ones aboard the special motor home that had not experienced the crown jewel of the new south.

Beeb had lived in Atlanta for nearly three years. Odie had lived all over town in his year-and-a-half stay. Cat had spent two years in Atlanta. Beeb earned two degrees from Georgia Tech, while Odie only earned one. Cat earned money but no degrees.

Odie told Pete to take I-85 south into town. When the Ehliuns spotted an enormous interchange, they wanted to go on every bridge they saw. Seemingly, there were lanes in all directions. As the motor home went south on I-85, the occupants noticed a car directly behind them that would neither speed up, slow down, change lanes, nor dim their brights.

Odie told Pete to show the offending motorists a hologram on the side of the road hitching a ride. The car saw a nude girl eager for a ride. The car with bright lights was last seen locking up the brakes to pick up the hitchhiker. Odie directed Pete to have the hologram of the naked lady take the car's occupants to a nearby sleazy motel. Once inside the room, the naked lady would suddenly turn into the snarling devil himself. Odie was certain this incident would increase the population at some church come Wednesday.

"I wonder if old Caldwell Luke is still around town," Beeb wondered out loud, although none of the others knew whom he was speaking of.

"Old friend of yers?" Odie inquired.

"Sort of. Used to be the biggest coke dealer in town. Even had a buddy that just sold pot for him. All Luke did was coke. Cokewell, some of the brothers used to call him."

"Was he a slender, short dude with curly hair and a little blond spot on his eyebrow?" Cat asked Beeb.

"Yeah! You knew him too?" Beeb amazedly asked Cat.

"No," Cat answered, "I didn't really know him. I just knew the guy he bought from."

"Oh, I see," Beeb said this with little enthusiasm. Luke was the biggest dealer he'd ever known.

Cat explained further, "Luke only bought pounds from Big Red. Big Red dealt in one-hundred-kilo lots. He was huge, a truly big man, bigger 'n both you two. Not only in size but in the scope of dealings as well. Anyway, that was a long time ago, and I don't do coke no more." Cat had a certain finality to her tone of voice when she spoke about coke.

"Well, I might wanna do some without ya," Beeb retorted.

"Be my guest." Odie wanted to know more about Cat's attitude toward cocaine. "Did you get into cocaine too heavy or something?" he asked her directly.

"Ha!" she snorted. "I went from a gram a week to a gram an hour. After I hit an ounce a week, I still thought I could handle it. Even after I was doing an ounce or two a day, I still didn't think I had a problem."

"Sounds like a fairly serious intake to me," Odie noted.

"Oh," Cat answered him back, "it wasn't much. I just tooted up a few Ferraris and a couple of Corvettes and an acre or two of Buckhead prime realty, nothing serious, just money!" she laughed. Then, turning serious, she continued, "That shit really twisted up my mind. I nearly did myself in a few times and thought about it several more."

Odie looked deep into her eyes, trying to see into her soul. "Cat, I am extremely glad you didn't die before I had a chance to meet you…and do other things to you as well!" he leered.

Cat looked into Odie's eyes. She couldn't detect any lies there.

Beeb turned the conversation around to its original subject. "I got turned on in college by Constant Connie. I don't even know if she's still alive."

"I got turned on in college too," Odie added, "but I didn't think much of it then or now."

Cat nodded agreement to him and added her two cents' worth to the conversation, "Costs too much and goes too fast."

Odie nodded his head in agreement to her point, adding, "Damn straight." Odie concluded his remarks about cocaine with his heartfelt opinion. "Give me good reefer any day of the week."

"Well," Beeb offered in his own defense, "I happen to like a little line now and again, but I ain't gonna say it's good for nobody or nothin' like that."

"Well, I just don't wanna be tempted with the shit or even see it," Cat stated.

"No problem," Beeb asserted. "I don't know that Caldwell Luke is around, still in the same line of work. I don't know where to find him or anyone who knows him, for that matter. I don't know if he deals. I was just wonderin' out loud. That's all. But if I do find any, I won't tell you two, and that's a fact!"

Their conversation over, the humans joined the Ehliuns looking out the windows at the splendor Atlanta set before them. The sleek computer-powered starcraft exited the Downtown Connector at North Avenue. They cruised up and down Peachtree and rode around in Cat's old neighborhood in Midtown, which was its gay old self as usual. Talk about where to stay brought the decision to stay at the best hotel. Toward that end, they could stay here and there and actually find out which one was best.

To begin with, they would try the Peachtree Towers. Pete parked in front, and Odie went up to the front desk, accompanied by Din. Pete had been requested to provide them with some formal wear. They looked elegant, flashy, perhaps overdone. Between the front curb and the front desk, however, Din was sold on staying there, and all it would require were a few scraps of paper. Such a fun planet! An abundance of luxuries could be had and for pieces of paper that Pete could toss together with abandon. Din wondered to himself how many dollars this was going to cost.

Since Odie gave Din the envelope full of money back, he had been learning about money. Money as a concept was rather difficult for the Ehliun mind to grasp. But as a tool, it was without peer. Using it was easy. Comprehending why people traded money around wasn't so easy. Din came to attention next to Odie. He had learned to watch what Odie did. Pete also gave him silent helpful hints when he needed help, which was becoming increasingly rarer. He was starting to catch on to the routine.

"Ah, yas, mine goot mann," Odie started in on the unsuspecting night clerk of the hotel. "I yam zee count Von Dusselderfer." Odie said this as condescendingly as he could, fleetingly offering the clerk his hand as if he might wish to kiss it reverently. Odie continued his Teutonic spiel. "Mine valet, Zin-Zhao here, vill be takink care uf zee baggage, uf you vill be zo kindt az to giff me mine sveet keese zo I gan hunlock zee doorz."

The clerk was rather uncertain about all this. He asked the large man a question. "Er, um, sir, do you have reservations?"

"I haff many reservationz about zis place, but vee are stayink here anyvay! Now kindtly attend to your zuperiorz und fetch me mine room keese!"

Odie's booming demands had, of course, attracted much attention in the lobby. The hotel manager quickly appeared. In a sneering tone of voice he inquired, "Is there a problem here?"

Din waved a thousand-dollar bill in the manager's face, acquiring his complete attention. "Your lackey does not seem to want to accept this!" Din nodded acknowledgment back to Odie after Odie smirked contentedly and gave Din the thumbs-up sign.

The manager glared the night clerk out of the way over his feeble objections and quickly inspected the thousand-dollar bill. Odie leaned over the counter menacingly and asked the manager, "Are you now tryink to inzult mee by kwestionink za validity of mine money?" Odie raised his voice several decibels each of the last four words.

The manager's response was instant. "*No*, no," came the high-pitched, rapidly spoken retort of the manager, "we just don't get many of these from non-Arabs anymore!"

"Oh, hokay, zen," Odie grinned, changing his demeanor to something friendly, "zat iss different!

"What name was that reservation under, sir?" the manager asked Odie, meekly rooting through some papers behind the desk. "Von Dusselderfer, count," Odie casually lied. "Schmall V unt large *Dussel*," he laughed loudly.

Din followed a few seconds later, hoping to amuse Odie. Odie missed it.

"Ah, yes, here we are, under V," lied the manager.

"I haff changed mine plans, und I zhall require just vun veek's lodginkz. Mine retinue vill alzo require zuitable quarterz ass vell, zo I zhall be needink three sveets altogezair."

The hotel manager fumbled with his calculator a moment or two, and he checked the floor chart to see what was available. He prayed for the courage to tell this large madman the total amount. "Yessir, for three suites that are adjacent to each other, for seven days and seven nights, sir, that comes to 21,759.27 dollars payable in advance, sir!"

Odie just grinned at the meek little man edging away from his reach. He turned to Din and said, "Zin-Zhao, pay zee man from petty cash und get a receipt. Zese trivial bills just bore me zilly," Odie explained to the manager.

Din pulled out twenty-nine more thousand-dollar bills. The manager nearly fainted when Din politely told him what Odie always said to the cashier, "Keep the change, dearie!"

Odie was slightly unnerved by the excitement this little maneuver caused. About fifty people were milling about the lobby, and they now knew that these folks were tipping over eight thousand dollars just for a room! The stuff con artists' dreams are made of, fools and their money! Odie softly spoke to Din as they neared the front door. "Uh, look, Din, now, I ain't jumpin' yer shit, see, it's just that you tipped the guy a bit too much. To overtip is as gauche as to undertip. Try not to forget that."

Din nodded his head, but he saw very little difference between eight dollars and eight thousand dollars. Zeros meant nothing, didn't they? Still, he tried to make Odie happy. Loudly, he spoke to the Count. "Solly, boss man, I no unnastand. Beeg mistake. Ha ha. Velly funny, velly funny!"

"Yeah, and you can knock off that Charlie Chan shit too, wiseass!" Odie said underneath his breath as they went through the revolving front door leading out to Peachtree Street, his mock anger betrayed by the smile on his face.

As they reentered the motor home, Odie told the others what was up. "Okay, look, people, there's a tad more commotion in the lobby than we might usually encounter, so I wan'cha ta know why. Din tipped the hotel manager for the room a tad overscale, about eight grand over. Now, it's his money, and no real big deal at that since there's plenty more where that came from. I'm just warnin' ya so's we'll all know what to expect when we go in: the worst."

The Starcraft Five peered out the motor home's windows. An incredibly interested group eagerly looked out at them from inside the lobby. "You got any ideas, Odie?" Beeb asked, knowing that, of course, the boy would be flooded with them since having ideas under pressure was Odie's strong suit.

Odie did not disappoint his old friend. "Yeah, I got some ideas. The folks inside will besiege us if they think they can provide us with anything, but if me and Din go back in with three hot babes, they won't try to horn in. And with enough distraction, we can be on the elevators and gone before the crowd can react."

To Din, Odie said, "Please give me a wad of twenties, okay?"

Din produced the roll that Pete had endowed him with at that moment and gave it to Odie, although he had no idea what Odie would do with the money. This money stuff was not easy to figure out. "That should do nicely," Odie said, relieving Din of the wad.

Din didn't know how the money would be spent, but he did know it would be fun. It had been so far. Ever since Din got back the money in the envelope Pete gave him in Chicago, he had had nothing but fun spending it. Two weeks ago, he didn't know what fun was. Now he couldn't imagine living without fun.

Odie ushered Din out the door to join the others on the sidewalk. Pete drove the motor home away. Cat led the way inside the hotel, slinking for all she was worth, which was plenty if the slinking was any indication. Pete had used Cat's body as a model to work from, and he put holograms on Beeb and Lin to make them equally attractive. Beeb was a towering Amazon of a woman bodybuilder, while Lin was covered with a sleek Oriental look of a slender, supple wisp of a woman, like ancient kings lusted after.

Lin had on a gossamer silk gown that allowed her physical beauty to shine through. She enjoyed herself immensely. She liked having breasts and thought-provoking legs. She could look any way she wished. Odie had to wolf whistle at her. "Ooohwee, girl! Talk about makeup! Revlon, eat'cher heart out!" Odie held the door open for Lin, and she entered, and he came in on her heels.

Cat stopped Odie's progress. "We gotta enter first, so you guys wait. C'mon, girls! Shake them things!" Cat was herself, only Pete made her black. He felt the count was cosmopolitan, so he should be surrounded by beauties from around the world. Pete viewed the count as an extension of himself. Naturally, he kept this little detail a secret. Pete had realized that secrecy was the best way to do some things.

Pete's holograms looked great on Lin and Beeb. Cat strutted her stuff through the crowd in the lobby, parting them like Moses parted the Red Sea. Beeb's Scandinavian Amazon model strolled and flexed for the boys. Lin brought up the rear. And she really brought it up to everyone's attention. *Strutting* was a new word in her vocabulary, but it was one she really liked.

Odie grandiosely entered the lobby after the three beauties with Din close behind. Odie clapped his hands twice, and they all three swarmed around him at the elevator doors. A large crowd had now gathered, which Odie had expected. He reached into his pocket for the bankroll Din had given him. He fanned out the bills like a canasta hand then suddenly tossed the whole wad high into the air.

Twenty-dollar bills floated around everywhere in the air around them. The crowd instantly dissipated as he expected, chasing after the floating bills. The elevator doors opened, and the five of them got on alone in solitude, but the panic in the lobby was incredible.

On the elevator, the five riders were highly amused by the crowd scrambling for the magical pieces of paper. "We'll read about that in the morning paper. You can bank on it," Odie assured them all.

Beeb had other thoughts. "Maybe you shouldn't have incited a riot like that, Odie."

"So who's gonna press charges?" Odie asked condescendingly.

The elevator doors opened at the thirteenth floor before Beeb could answer. Several people were loitering near the elevators. Odie immediately pressed the close button and then the up button for the seventeenth floor. "Why'd you do that?" Cat asked.

"Crowds," was the terse one-word answer he gave her.

"Pete, find us an empty room and give us the correct key, okay?" Odie asked.

"What the fuck's the deal here, Odie?" Beeb demanded.

"I told you—crowds."

Pete gave Din a new room key, and he told Odie. "I have the key for room 1724."

"Thanks, Din. Thanks, Pete. Oh, and, Pete, could you disguise us as an elderly black couple with a lot of luggage?"

"Oh, well, why don't we just look like some porters?" Beeb said disgustedly.

"Yeah, good idea! Make us look like Cole and his old lady, Pete."

Cat laughed at Odie's joke, but Beeb didn't think it was too funny. Cole was white.

Shuffling down the hall, the Starcraft Five went into the room Pete had just provided for them, disguised as elderly blacks. Suddenly, a tremendous commotion erupted from the elevators as different groups of people seeking the money-throwing count passed right by them. Beeb began to understand why Odie had done what he had. They would have had no peace unless they were disguised as someone else or better yet, invisible.

"Pete, soundproof us in. Don't let anyone see or hear us, even if they rent the room…or rooms, I should say."

They looked around. There was a door on each of the other walls. Cat opened one. It led to an entire suite, so did the others. Pete spoke up, "I got ya each a bedroom. Well, at least a bed. There's only three bedrooms, but I can add more if you like."

Odie just flopped on the nearest bed as if the weight of knowing all Pete said just pressed him down. It certainly helped. "Oh, Pete," Odie called out like Jack Benny summoning Rochester, "is this a for-real room, or did you just put it here for us to use?"

"Well, Odie, it's like this: it's a blend of each. Without getting technical on you, let's just call it a blend."

Odie made a mental note that Pete was deliberately withholding information from him. He wouldn't press the issue now, but when he was alone with Pete, he certainly would bring it up. Cat jumped on the bed with Odie, full of excitement. "Did you see how those people in the lobby went nuts?" she asked him and the room at large.

"No kiddin'. Damn, this is slick!" Odie retorted.

Beeb still seemed to have some contention over the affair. "Odie! Don't you think you should explain money a little better to Din and Lin before we get in another scrape like this?"

Odie thought it over a moment or two. "Oh, I dunno. What do you think, Din? Do you see how money affects people when you just throw it away?"

Din said what he thought. "I don't fully understand your system of spending money, but I will try to be more considerate in the future."

"There. Ya satisfied, Beeb? How else is Din gonna learn? You always rattle on about how experience is the best teacher! What better experience is there than to learn how to spend money? Malls thrive on the idea! And look, Din's money supply is limitless."

"Well, there you go!" Beeb snorted contemptuously. "How realistic is it? How down-to-earth is it? How ordinary is it to *have* unlimited funds to spend? You ain't exactly teachin' him to be yer run-of-the-mill citizen now, are you? Din told me this little adventure here just getting up to this damn room cost thirty thousand dollars! That don't count how much you tossed up in the air! And we ain't even in the damn rooms Din already paid for!"

Beeb paused for a moment to catch his breath and let his words sink in, then he went on. "Now, I grant you that we came to Atlanta to have a good time. This would certainly qualify in most people's realities as an expensive time, so let's hope it's a good time. But hey, let's not kid ourselves. This is not ordinary. This doesn't come close to ordinary!"

It was quiet when Beeb finished. Cat broke the silence. "Okay, Beeb is right. This simply isn't ordinary, so let's have a good, expensive time to begin with, and that way, ordinary will have more meaning for them when we have just ordinary times. And stuck in there after the fabulous times, ordinary will then highlight what extraordinary really means."

"Yeah," Odie agreed, "'cause that's what life is for the Starcraft Five: extraordinary."

Cat put her arms around Beeb and spoke softly, tenderly to him, "I don't think any of us are very familiar with ordinary now, are we? They are here from another planet! Not very ordinary, is it? I cannot conceive of a category that Odie fits in with the word ordinary attached to it, and I can't see you as being ordinary in any sense of the word, and if you refer to me as ordinary, I'll kick yer ass!"

Beeb had to laugh at this wonderful woman who made so much sense. He knew she was right. Ordinary was a concept with which he was only fleetingly familiar, and almost always, it was connected to someone else, not to him. "Well, in that case," Beeb said, "what do we say to going out on the town for a while? We can sneak in and outta here with ease, and I know a few nightspots we can go to, so whaddya say?"

Beeb's invitation was well received, and off they went to catch a cab, still invisible to the people milling around the lobby. A cab stopped instantly when the driver saw five well-dressed individuals standing on the curb. He saw a large tip standing there probably. Beeb directed the cabbie to the bar where he knew a friend of his still worked. When they arrived, Beeb said he'd go see what was up first. He went inside and sat down at the end of the bar. A redheaded bartender noticed Beeb immediately as he was rather handsome and not gay. And as a bonus, his hair color was a match for hers.

"Hiya, sweetie," she addressed him, "what can I get for you?"

"Jackie Chacon still work here?"

The bartender eyeballed the stranger in front of her. "She a real good friend of yours?" she asked Beeb.

He smiled, "Well, she used to be, but I haven't seen her in about two years."

Mardi looked at Beeb straight in the eye. "Then why don't you save yourself a lot of trouble and just come back for *me* in two hours?"

Beeb saw the smile in her eyes as he leered deeply into her soul. "So what's yer name?" he asked, trying to sound casual.

The redheaded bartender got closer to Beeb and in a sultry voice, breathed, "Mardi."

"Marty?" Beeb repeated, or so he thought.

"No, no, it's Mardi, like Mardi Gras. I was born in Spain on a Tuesday," she shrugged.

"Oh, boy, Mardi, you sound like a party, and you definitely look like some kind of fun. I would be most honored to come back for you in two hours." Beeb looked at his watch so he would know when two hours was up. It was 12:30 now, so 2:30 would be zero hour.

"What's your name?" she asked Beeb in a sexy voice.

"My name is Beeb, but you can call me ready!"

Mardi grinned at him. "Okay, Beeb, you'll be ready in two hours, then?"

"I'm ready now, but I'll be back for you in two hours."

"Okay, I got it."

"Oh, you got it, woman! You mos' certainly do!" Beeb waved goodbye at her, and she leaned over the bar to give him a good glimpse of tit and to kiss him. He ate it up. He was that kind of a guy: horny.

Beeb went back out to the cab and got in. He told the cabbie to head for Buckhead. No one gave an exact destination, and the cabbie just drove while the Starcraft Five talked. "So what's the scam?" Odie asked of Beeb, still grinning.

"She gets off in two hours."

"Sounds like Cat," Odie laughed.

Cat hit him on the shoulder for what sounded like a complaint.

"I told her I'd be back for her in two hours," Beeb explained.

"So how long have you known this girl?" Cat wondered.

"I just met her," Beeb admitted.

"I thought you knew this Jackie from a long time ago?" Odie stated. "I'm certain you've mentioned her to me before, Beeb. Isn't she green eyed and brown haired from Miami?"

"Jackie wasn't there. I got a date with another girl that I just met, just now, when I went in looking for Jackie. I just met Mardi for the first time, okay?"

"Ah-lanna womens is like that," the cabbie interjected, "it'sa right frennly town. Where is y'all from?"

"Peoria." Odie felt the truth wasn't necessary to divulge.

At the intersection of Roswell Road and Peachtree Road, Beeb told the cabbie to go up Roswell. Beeb stared hard at the empty lots where two of his old favorite clubs had been. There was a Mexican cantina but nothing Beeb recognized. He directed the cab to go down to West Andrews and let them out.

Din paid the fare and tipped the driver a fifty. Odie patted him on the back and said, "See, that wasn't so hard, now was it?"

"No, I guess not," Din answered.

"Well, where do we wanna go first?" Odie asked, looking around at the area.

They went across the street to a joint and had a drink. Then they walked down to an Irish pub. From there, they went to the English pub. After two rounds of drinks and one round of darts, they were ready to go. "Where in the world did you learn to throw darts like that, Cat?" Odie demanded of his favorite woman.

"Oh, here and there," she teased him.

"Here and there where?" Odie pressed on.

"Oh, here in the US, and there in the United Kingdom, Jamaica, Barbados, and Bermuda. They throw a lot of darts in Bermuda."

"I see!" Odie said, only to hear Cat say it with him, syllable for syllable. That made Beeb and the Ehliuns laugh. Odie hugged Cat, and she kissed him on the cheek.

When they left the British pub, the same cab was outside waiting on them. They all piled in and the cabbie asked, "Where to?"

"Take us back to the same place we started out at," Beeb told him.

"Yassir, that's right! You gots a hot date!" Beeb didn't particularly care for the cabbie knowing his business, but he said nothing to him. What the hell, why should he care?

When they returned to the bar, Beeb got out and told them all he would see them later. Cat motioned to Beeb to lean over, and she kissed him on the cheek and told him to have a nice time. Din pressed some money into his hand, repeating what Cat said but with a wry smile on his face, much amusing Beeb.

"Thanks. I'll try to have a nice time." Beeb straightened up to his full height and went inside the bar. He sat down on the same stool he'd been in two hours earlier. Frantic, he scanned the bar for Mardi, but she was nowhere to be seen. Someone asked him if he needed a ride home. Beeb politely refused the elderly woman's offer.

He kept looking at his watch: two forty-two and still no Mardi. Finally, she appeared from a back room behind the bar and put some things away, looking up at Beeb and smiling broadly when she saw him. "Hiya, sweetie, I thought you might show up."

"You got that right! I mean, who wouldn't show up for a date with you?"

Mardi got a sly grin on her face when Beeb said this to her. She couldn't answer him right away because she had to answer the phone. When Mardi hung up the phone, she excitedly turned to the other bartender and told her that Roberta had just called to tell her some Chink was handing out thousand-dollar bills in the Underground! Beeb spilled his drink down his shirt.

Mardi was now in a hurry to leave. She told Beeb she'd take him anywhere but to her house, but they had to go to the Underground first. She wanted to see something. Beeb knew that if this kept up, they would be in the gossip columns for months to come. He asked Mardi if there was anything he could help her with. She whispered a suggestive remark in his ear, and they both laughed. "Well, not here I can't!" Beeb chuckled.

"I got a place in mind," she said right back.

Out on the parking lot headed toward Mardi's car, the heap with the "Escape Wisconsin" bumper sticker, Beeb saw a person walking toward them. The stranger had a semifamiliar face, Beeb thought. "Oh, shit!" Mardi cried out, "hurry!" She implored Beeb to get a move on. "Here comes that crazy Bible-thumper!"

Quickly diving into the safety of the car, they locked the doors and rolled the windows up. Mardi explained to Beeb that she had made the mistake once of listening to the guy's rap. "No! Leave me alone!" she suddenly screamed at the tract-bearing figure looming outside the driver-side door.

Beeb stared at the Bible-thumper in total disbelief. "Jesus can save you. He loves you," Beeb heard the familiar baritone holler as Mardi's car sped away, slinging rocks from under the tires.

Beeb was stunned. That was Caldwell Luke! Beeb said nothing about knowing the tract bearer to Mardi. Perhaps some things were best left in the past. Luke was an obvious burnout. At least he wasn't a Moonie loonie. At least he stayed with a religion Americans knew about. Still, he was a burnout.

# Pizza to Go, Hold the Emeroids

When Odie finally awoke, he found Beeb and the others busy reading the morning papers. "Well, Mr. Megabucks, how's it goin'?" Beeb loudly inquired, much to Odie's chagrin.

He placed his hands over his ears in a futile attempt to prevent the sound waves from penetrating his skull and doing damage to his brain. Beeb spoke in a near scream, "I guess we oughta take in some live rock and roll today, eh?"

"Damn, don't talk so loud!" Odie demanded.

Beeb just laughed at Odie and his self-inflicted pain. Cat kissed Odie good morning, and he managed a weak smile up at her. "Jeez, did we have some fun last night or what?"

"You don't remember?" she asked him in a puzzled voice.

"Parts," he responded truthfully.

"Well, you can read about the rest!" Beeb said, waving a newspaper in his face.

"Read?" Odie said, sounding thoroughly confused.

"Yeah, read!" Beeb retorted. "You know, connecting words on paper with ideas in yer mind? Surely you've heard of it. It's in all the papers, just like yer antics last night."

Odie noticed the extreme sarcasm in Beeb's voice, and with the way his head felt, it suggested that once again, he had been rash in his public behavior. "We made the papers?" Odie quizzed Cat.

"Couple of times," she said, handing Odie a page she had been reading. "Here's an item about nine people being treated and released from two different hospitals downtown last night after a scuffle in the lobby of the Peachtree Towers last night or early this morning."

"Yeah," Beeb interjected, "says here it seems someone tossed handfuls of money around in the lobby. Police suspect drug users were on a 'bad high' and went insane."

"Lemme see that! Yer makin' this shit up, Beeb!" Odie said.

"Am not! Here's yet another article in a gossip column that details events in several nightspots in Buckhead last night. Seems the same group of people handed out over ten grand in cash, lavishly spending and tipping."

Lin read a piece to Odie to show that they were not kidding him. "A waitress admitted being tipped three hundred dollars just for bringing a clean glass to their table. She said she'd never seen them before, but she hoped they would become regular customers."

Odie managed a laugh, saying, "Yeah, I bet she does. Well, I reckon we'll need disguises to go in there again."

Lin was confused by Odie's statement. "But wouldn't they treat us very well when they saw who we were?"

"Well, Lin, what I'd be afraid of is being mobbed and hounded by crowds that will want some of that money we been tossin' around town."

"We!" Beeb jerked his thumb at Odie while addressing Cat. "We been tossin' money around us."

"Hey, just because you didn't have any fun last night is no reason to jump on my case, Beeb!"

Beeb stared at his old friend a minute before retorting, "Who says I didn't have any fun last night?"

"Yer attitude this morning!" Odie shot back.

"I'll have you know I had a great time with Mardi, and I got her phone number and everything!"

Odie glanced over at Cat with a smile on his face. Beeb knew he didn't believe him, but so what? He was used to it by now.

"He didn't come in till after ten this morning, Odie." Cat said this to help Beeb out. If he needed help.

"Yeah, so there!" Beeb said, sticking out his tongue like a brat might.

"That don't mean nothin'!" Odie said defiantly.

Beeb pulled out some Red Roof matches from his pocket and tossed them at Odie. "And I got something you can sniff if that ain't proof enough!"

Cat broke into laughter at this. Just the idea of that type of proof made her laugh. These two were very childlike in some ways, like arguing.

Pete offered to help Odie with his pain, if he would just put on the sunglasses with a chip on the lenses. Pete selectively removed the harmful congeners from Odie's bloodstream, and a few seconds later, Odie felt much better and told Pete so. "Thanks, Pete. I feel much better!"

"Pete, can you do anything about how he looks?" Beeb wanted to know.

"Man, fuck you, man!" Odie retorted.

Cat knew then he felt a lot better. "So hit the showers, you two!" she ordered.

Odie and Beeb went to separate bathrooms and showered. When they were dressed and ready to go, they emerged into the living room, where the rest were waiting. Cat wanted to go out and have more fun like last night, she said. Odie didn't want to relive last night, and he stated his worries about crowds. "What if someone corners us?"

"Relax, Odie!" Cat entreated him. "Pete can give anybody the slip. He's not a master of disguise. He's state of the art!"

Odie listened to her. Of course, she was right. He needn't fear anyone discovering them if they didn't wish to be discovered. They could appear and disappear at will!

"Hey, it'll be fun seeing the town when the town wants to see us too!" Cat told him.

"Okay, then, let's go have some fun!" Din phoned for a limo from an ad in the phone book. They put on jeans and T-shirts, but Pete would provide them with the luxurious look of tuxedos and formal gowns. Even though it was early afternoon, the count and his retinue had an image to project. No one who saw it realized just how much projection that image really was.

"What'cha hungry for?" Odie asked Cat.

She smiled at him and giggled, "Not what yer hopin' for!"

"Okay, ya got me. All right, what do you want to eat for breakfast?"

"Pizza!" chorused the Ehliuns.

"Yeah, sounds good to me," Cat agreed.

Beeb didn't care, so Odie went along with the group even though he wasn't sure it was a proper breakfast. He was determined to show them he could get along on anyone's terms. It didn't always have to be his.

As the limo driver took them to the pizza place Beeb suggested, the others busied themselves looking around Atlanta in the daylight. The Ehliuns had begun another study the night before. Odie had told them if they looked around, they would see that in Atlanta, expensive cars generally contained better-looking women than clunkers. Lin and Din studied this to see if it was true. They got it all on video, thanks to Pete, and they could have him count the cars and the number of attractive women in them.

"Hard to believe I've only known you for a week, Cat." Odie's words were soft.

Lin added notes to the love file they had on Odie and Cat. Cat reflected on the past week. It had absolutely been the most bizarre time of her life, and it had made her unbelievably happy. In eight days, she had gone from being wanted by the law to being wanted by Odie. She leaned over on Odie and held his hand.

Din noticed, and he noticed that Beeb did not. Beeb was daydreaming about the beautiful redhead he'd become infatuated with last night.

As they cruised down North Decatur Road, Odie saw several students on the sidewalks. "Look, Beeb, Emeroids!"

"Emeroids?" Cat wondered.

"Yeah," Beeb explained, "the obnoxious little shits that go to Emory!"

Odie chuckled to Cat, telling her, "Beeb just never could get laid by the JAPs that go to Emory. That's his problem with the place."

"I didn't see any Oriental women back there at all," Cat told Odie.

Odie's loud laughter puzzled Cat. He explained, "JAPs: Jewish American Princesses. Hebe chicks down from the East Coast for the first time away from home, New York and New Jersey mostly. I dated this one chick, Rebecca Abramovitz, and she told me a lot about Jews, life in the city. She used to laugh about Jersey girls, told jokes about 'em. What's the difference between a girl from East Jersey and the garbage? The garbage won't follow you around after you take it out. Stuff like that. Yer not laughin'."

"Please don't refer to women as chicks, Odie. I told you before I hate that."

Odie looked tenderly at Cat a moment to see if she was serious. She was. He apologized for the slipup and promised her he would try to avoid it from that moment forward. Cat didn't know whether he was serious or denigrating. There was nothing more to be said as they arrived at the pizzeria.

Din led the way in, followed by Lin and Cat with Beeb and Odie bringing up the rear. Odie told the limo driver to park out back and wait for them. Within a few minutes of being seated, they had placed their order and sat back to wait for their food. A spirited crowd filled the pizza parlor nearly to capacity, and crowd watching was about the only thing to do. Beeb felt like most of the patrons were too young to be college students, so he leaned over to the next table to ask what was going on, why so many cheerleaders were in for pizza? He discovered a cheerleading clinic was in progress at Emory.

Odie was busy watching an obviously inebriated young goon attempt to put some moves on Cat as she passed by him, returning from the ladies' room. He followed Cat back to the table, oblivious to all but her. Odie figured that he was drunk, and at this time of day, that denoted an amateur drinker—i.e., underage. Odie positioned his foot on the chair this goon was obviously going to commandeer to sit down in. Waiting until the fool was on his way down into the chair, Odie shoved it sideways, unceremoniously dumping the drunk onto the floor. Several people were amused by this, Odie the most. Three of the goon's friends appeared, helping him to his unsteady feet. One of these new arrivals began to speak to Odie in what he perceived to be an unfriendly manner.

Odie told the friend of the goon to shut up. "I didn't give you permission to speak to me. I'm only going to say this once since I make it a habit not to speak to persons vastly inferior to myself, so watch my lips. Don't miss anything. You four assholes get out of my face right now, and I'll let you live. Deal?"

The waitress arrived with their pizzas and set them down on the table. She vanished as fast as she had appeared. Alas, the goons did not. Beeb turned to the goons and spoke. "Don't make him stand up. If he has to stand up, yer all gonna be bleedin', and we just got our food, so please leave so we can enjoy it."

The spokesgoon took it upon himself to speak for them all. "My friend got pushed to the ground, and I don't like that."

Odie continued to eat his pizza while he spoke just to be obnoxious right back. "Yer goof buddy there didn't get pushed to the ground dipwad. Apparently, yer too stupid to see anything clearly. I shoved the chair with my foot, and he sat down. No one pushed him. Get yer facts straight if you intend to discuss this with people with much larger cranial capacity than yourself. He was not invited to sit down. You are not invited to address me, my friends, nor be present at our table. If you leave now, you won't need crutches. You follow?"

Beeb winked at Odie to let him know he was ready on a moment's notice when necessary. Two of the goons made a move for Odie. Jumping up, Beeb grabbed two, one on each arm, and he swung them together with such force that their heads knocked together, rendering them unconscious. Odie jumped up and grabbed the other two, the talker and the floor sitter. What Beeb did seemed to work real well, so Odie paid him a compliment and did the same thing with the same results.

They picked up each offender by the collar, and Odie and Beeb carried the four goons to the door, where they tossed out each one. The place had become deathly silent when Beeb struck the first heads together. Now a low murmur spread across the room as people realized what strength it took to do this. These were some big bad dudes all right. Odie shouted at the drunks on the sidewalk, still lying in a heap, "Now carry your drunken, ignorant asses back to the slime whence ye emanated and learn to leave us decent, peaceful law abiding citizens alone."

"Or he'll kill you!" Beeb added for effect.

They smiled at each other, did a high five, then dusted themselves off like cowboys in the movies did after tossing someone out of a saloon. An angry waitress appeared behind them. "Yer gonna pay their bill, or I'll call the cops!"

"Surely them clowns can't be friends of yours?" a stunned Odie wondered.

"They owe me nineteen dollars, and since you took it upon yourself to just throw them out in the street, you can pay it!"

Odie looked at this young woman, angry that she was talking to him like this, but he had Cat to impress. "Okay, no sweat. Bring their bill to my table."

"Now!"

"Hey," Odie roared, "I just told you no sweat! That's slang. It means that I got it covered!"

"I don't trust you!" she retorted, not the right thing to say to Odie.

"Then I don't trust you either!" Odie shouted, angrily stuffing a fifty into her hands. "Bring me all the change! I would have gladly given it to you, but you had to go and get snotty, didn't you?"

"Yo, dude, lighten up some, okay? Girl don't know how solvent you are!"

"She don't know when to be quiet. I know that!"

Odie was riled, Beeb sensed. "Well, don't take it out on her. Yer just mad at them assholes for tryin' ta pick up on Cat. Relax, man, ain't nobody gonna take her away from you. She loves ya, man. It's real. Look at it and study it. Be cool. Hang loose." Beeb's words had a soothing effect on Odie as he got right to the crux of Odie's anxieties and helped to ease the pain. What are friends for?

Easing back into their chairs, Odie and Beeb apologized to the rest of the Starcraft Five. "Sorry 'bout that, gang."

The entire place was staring at them. The waitress came by and threw Odie's change at him. "Hey," he shouted, "I want a cash receipt!"

She glared back at him, and he stared. "Leave her alone, Odie. I'm afraid it won't do any good," Cat assured her man.

Suddenly, the manager appeared at Odie's side. "Sir, you are causing a disturbance, and I'm afraid I'm going to have to ask you to leave."

Odie jumped straight up in the manager's face and bellowed, "You damn well *better* be afraid to ask me to leave!"

All chatter ceased, and the silence was deafening. Odie had clearly lost his temper with all that had gone wrong so far. Cat could see that. She hoped his rage would soon end. Odie yelled, "If you don't want total destruction in the next two minutes, I suggest you return to your kitchen and do whatever it is that you do. You really don't want to mess with me! You don't wanna find out who I am and what I can do. It's not in your best health interests, you know what I mean? You gettin' this?"

The intense fear in the manager's eyes convinced Odie that indeed, he had received the message loud and clear. Odie smiled at him and dropped his hands to his sides. Din slipped some bills into Odie's hand behind his back, where the manager could not see. Odie shoved the bills into the manager's hands. "Look," Odie started in on him, "I got a little riled, okay? Here, pal, lemme buy dinner for the house, all right? No hard feelings, yeah?"

The pizza man looked into his hands and thought it over a moment. He had what appeared to be six one-thousand-dollar bills in his hands. "No, no, no hard feelings at all! You were right all along! Them bums you threw out were the ones causing trouble, not you people. Enjoy your pizza, take your time, and have a nice day!" The manager fled to the kitchen on that note.

Suddenly, it became quite noisy once again. The crowd cheered and then thanked Odie. Laughter rattled from the ceiling and walls. A good time was being had by all, free food and entertainment too. It was quite a combination.

Din had learned a valuable lesson: thousand-dollar bills could solve any problem. Gee, America was such a nice place! Where else could paper fix everything?

Finishing his pizza, Odie noticed the waitress he'd been unkind to a few minutes earlier bussing a table nearby. He went up to her and apologized. "I'm really sorry that I lost my temper with you. Those crude, drunken clowns made me mad, but I shouldn't have taken it out on you. So anyway, I bet yer a student and could use some tip money."

She stared up at him like maybe he'd finally said something right.

"Here," he said, stuffing several bills into her apron pocket. "That's for you. Get yourself something nice, pay tuition, buy books, get a car—whatever."

She reached into her apron pocket and pulled out what looked like several hundred dollars. She peered at the corners of the bills, and each said one hundred dollars. She had about seventeen hundred-dollar bills! She began to shake her head no, telling Odie she just couldn't accept the money, when Cat stuffed the money back into her apron pocket. "You can, and you should!" Then Cat told Odie they were ready to go, and he went back to the table to get his stuff ready. Cat spoke to the waitress. "He gets mad real easy, but he gets glad real easy too. Money ain't nothin' to him, and he enjoys helping people. You've earned it, so keep it. Just be glad you aren't around him every minute of the day."

The girl shook her head in agreement. "Y'all come back," she called out after Cat.

The Starcraft Five left the place, walking out the front door to the waves and cheers and thanks of the rest of the patrons. "Look!" shouted the waitress who'd served them. "They left me all this money!" She counted up 709 dollars in tips. She was thrilled. The other waitress didn't say anything about how much she'd made off their chance encounter. No sense embarrassing anyone. Like herself, since she didn't carefully examine the bills. Several of them were thousands and not hundreds. But she wouldn't know till she got home that night. Odie wasn't kidding. She could pay tuition and buy a car.

As the five tourists got into the limo again, the driver wondered, "Where to?"

Odie promised them a fun day and then told the driver to head down the road behind them, Clifton Road. "Driver, then go over to Ponce and toward Decatur. I'll show you guys some houses I painted in college."

"What makes Odie think we might find some interesting moments by looking at old houses he allegedly helped to paint?"

"Allegedly?" Odie bristled at Beeb and his accusation.

"Just shittin' ya, man, and you know it!"

"Yeah, that I know. What I don't know is how well that piece of soundproof glass works."

"It works quite well, Pete assures me," Din told Odie.

"Ah, yes, and a good afternoon to you, Pete!"

"Good afternoon, Odie. You really have done normal work in your life?"

Everyone but Odie laughed heartily at Pete's question. "Yes," Odie answered defensively, "I have done regular work, so can I help it if I'm extraordinary and different?"

"No, I don't think you help it much," Cat told him, much to everyone's delight.

"Any more comments about me?" Odie asked.

Beeb patted him on the shoulder. "There, there, poor Odie. Everyone's pickin' on him, even Pete. I think we should all be nice to Odie the rest of the day."

"Thanks, Beeb."

"So pretend yer listenin' when he tells you all about these houses he claims to have painted."

"Thanks, Beeb. With friends like you, who needs enemies?"

Odie grabbed the communications device in the back seat and pressed the button. "Yes, sir?" came the driver's voice.

"Turn left at the next street, go down one block, and take another left. Stop in the middle of that block."

"Yes, sir!"

"So is this gonna be one of the houses you painted?" Cat asked Odie.

"Yep. Only painted three or four houses that first summer. Check this baby out and you'll see why."

As the limo slowed down, Odie activated the button and told the driver to stop here. "Damn, that is one fine house!" Beeb had to admit.

"Swell place!" Cat offered.

The Ehliuns didn't see much difference between one private home and another. All of Earth's buildings were much different than what they were used to. Only the biggest skyscrapers were close to being like their buildings, which were built to house several hundred thousand Ehliuns.

"How many rooms are inside, Odie?"

"All of 'em !"

Cat glared at him.

"Okay, okay," he laughed, "sorry, sorry! There are twenty-two rooms, I believe. Five bathrooms, four bedrooms upstairs, two or three guest bedrooms, and lots more. There's an enclosed swimming pool and a full gym and everything: sauna, hot tub—the works."

"How do you remember everything about it?" Cat asked.

"First place I ever painted for money!" Odie answered. "We started June 21 and finished August 1. There was George, of course, and myself, Itchy Boz, Ben Whaa, Spicoli, and James. We did the entire house inside and out, all the trim, shutters, columns—the works! And it still looks great!"

"Where are the other houses you painted?" Beeb wondered.

"Not close to here."

"I see!" Cat said, much amusing Beeb. There was something about the way she took Odie's words and threw them back at him that obviously had Odie intrigued. She was pretty bright for some-one who'd never set foot in a high school. Amazingly so, he thought.

"Can we go now?" Lin wondered of Odie.

"Sure, if you've all seen enough. I know I have. I ain't been by here in years 'cause I saw it enough one summer to last me a lifetime."

"I guess so!" Beeb said. "How many hours a day did you work?" Beeb was trying to get Odie to talk it all out of his system. He didn't want to spend the whole day looking at houses.

"Oh, it was up at dawn and end at dusk, bring your own lunch and drinks, work hard and earn enough money to come back to work the next day."

Cat grabbed the device and pushed the button. "Yes, ma'am," the driver said, "where to?"

"Take us to the Decatur Station, the MARTA Station."

"Yes, ma'am." The limo driver headed up the street and worked his way over to the DeKalb County Courthouse. He told them the station was underground behind the courthouse. They got out of the limo and told the driver to meet them at the Brookhaven Station. As the limo left them, Odie had a question for the group. "Why are we going to the MARTA Station?"

"Because we want to ride the trains!" Lin and Din chorused. Lin further explained, "We have seen trains with people on them in movies, in Chicago, and again here. We wish to experience riding the rails."

Odie nodded his head in agreement. "No problem," he smiled, "we can ride the trains a long way. It's one of the best ways to see a lot of Atlanta in a short time."

"Assuming what you want to see of Atlanta is located along the train's path." Beeb had added this tidbit of information just to see what reaction it would bring.

"Well, there's that," was Odie's comment and the only one.

When they walked across the plaza surrounding the courthouse, Din found a plaque to a German baron for whom DeKalb County was named. They read the plaque and then went down the steps to the MARTA Station. The station was done in bright colors and bold shapes. For a MARTA Station, it was rather handsome. Lin asked Odie what the word *MARTA* meant. "Making Atlantans Really Terribly Angry," was his reply.

Cat looked askance at him, as if he'd finally lost his mind completely. "No," she countered, "it stands for Making Atlanta Rude To All.

"Nope," Beeb offered, "it's Moving Assholes Right Through Atlanta."

"Wrongo, train breath!" Odie told Beeb. "It's Making Automobile Rides Truly Attractive."

"Nope, it's Making A Really Trendy Atlanta," Cat insisted.

"No, it stands for Morons and Retards Traveling Aimlessly," Beeb said.

The train's arrival in the station ended their contest to see who could make up the best acronym, and they all boarded the train eagerly. The train headed west and picked up speed. When the train picked up speed and emerged into the daylight, the delight on the Ehliuns' faces was evident to Odie. Due to this enthusiasm, Odie decided to ride to the west end of the line and then go back to the Five Points station so they could change trains and go on to the airport.

From the airport, they rode to the North Avenue station, and got off the train. Odie guided them on their tour of the station and showed them all the granite walls exposed in the underground portion. They rode down the enormous escalator, which made the Ehliuns feel quite dizzy.

Back on the train, Lin thanked the earthlings for allowing them to ride the trains. The humans knew the Ehliuns were thrilled by their train ride, and the day would come when they would have to go from city to city on a train. But for now, the thrill was for MARTA trains. They could see the limo waiting for them in the parking lot at the Brookhaven Station below the station. As they emerged from a tunnel to get to the parking lot, the limo driver greeted them. "Did you enjoy your MARTA ride?" he wondered.

"I believe we did," Beeb answered him.

"It was most enjoyable," Lin informed him.

"Where to?" the limo driver asked the group at large.

"Cruise down Brookhaven here and go around the golf course, okay?" Odie replied.

After driving around some nice neighborhoods, they wound up on Clairmont Road. Odie told the limo driver to take them to the airport. Cat pointed out that the airport was way south of where they were. "No, PDK, it's right here on Clairmont. I wanna go to the

Fifty-Seventh Fighter Squadron. It's a restaurant in a building built to look like it withstood a bombardment. It's neat, you'll see."

"Didn't I tell you not to say that phrase again?" Cat teased Odie.

He kissed her for a minute or two, and nothing further was said.

As promised, the decor of the restaurant was different, to say the least. The roar of departing planes was the only negative they noticed about their dinner and surroundings. Din slapped two hundreds on the tray when the waiter brought their bill and said, as usual, "Keep the change, dearie!"

The waiter surprised Din by kissing him on the cheek and slipping him a card with his phone number on it. The humans were convulsed with laughter, and poor Din was embarrassed as well as confused. "Why did he kiss him?" Lin wondered. "Is this part of that love thing?"

Odie wiped tears from his eyes but could not answer her right away. Cat explained as best she could. "See, Lin, the waiter is gay, homosexual. He likes men, not women."

Cat went on, not knowing that Pete covered the table's speech, not allowing anyone else to comprehend what they spoke about. It just sounded foreign to everyone else. Pete didn't know whether or not they wanted him to cover their speech. He simply did it just in case something was said to the Ehliuns that anyone overhearing would take to mean aliens were present. He knew the odds were long, yet the improbable happened on this planet at an alarming rate.

"He kissed your cheek, Din, probably because you called him dearie."

Cat would have said more, but Odie interrupted. "Din heard me say that to a couple of old lady cashiers, but this is the second time I've heard him say it. Din, just say, 'Keep the change.' That's all you have to say to convey the message. The word *dearie* might add another message all its own to some hearers, like the waiter here, for example."

Din mentally noted to Pete that this area of earthly life needed additional studies. Din didn't want to be wrong or commit social gaffes. He wanted to know everything and to react correctly each and every time. It was the Ehliun way to be right. Then he thought about that some more to himself—that is, the way he was taught by the computer system of Ehlius, the network he now knew had enslaved him and his entire planet, the whole culture. Pete wasn't really part of that network, not anymore, but Din thought he'd best keep that thought to himself. Earth was a place full of secrets. Din felt that keeping secrets was one way to comprehend what that activity was.

Leaving the restaurant, they all piled in the limo again. Cat didn't wait for the driver to ask where to again and informed him they were headed to Buckhead. The limo slipped out onto Clairmont and went up to Peachtree Industrial. As it rolled along Peachtree, Odie and Beeb both noticed that they hadn't even gotten to Lenox Square, indeed barely past the MARTA Station, when they saw a sign informing them they were in the Buckhead area. "What the hell is this?" Beeb spluttered. "They're callin' this Buckhead now? Ya don't have to be a few blocks from Aunt Charlie's to be in Buckhead no more?"

"Apparently!" Odie muttered.

Cat laughed at them. She knew they had not been in town for a couple of years. "This area has changed, boys, since you been gone. You haven't seen the hotels and banks up here yet, have you?"

They admitted they had not, when the new financial area came into view. The Ehliuns were impressed. This block looked like one of their buildings! They felt comfortable looking at this mass of glass and steel. The boys did not. "Well, there's the Music Business Institute and the Art Institute," Odie noted. "At least that ain't changed. What's this road here, this freeway-lookin' thing?"

"That's 400. They pushed it through from 285. It's supposed to go to 85 south." Cat grinned at Odie and Beeb as they looked dazed. "How long's it been since either one of you lived here?" she asked.

The boys looked at each other. "We been on the road in the motor home for eighteen months," Odie stated.

"Yeah, but it's been more'n two years since we got the grants," Beeb added.

Cat's stern looks betrayed her consternation, and Odie noticed right away. "Oh, you just wanna know when's the last time we lived here, that it?"

Cat nodded.

"I left Tech five years ago…no, six years ago," Beeb told her.

"And I was gone two years ahead of Beeb. See, when I got back to Mississippi from Germany, I was seventeen. I went to high school a year, and then I went to Ole Miss for a year. I spent another year at Tulane, then I came to Atlanta and went to Tech for two years, then I went to Illinois. I was out of college around three years when my grant application was approved."

Odie looked like he was going to go on, so Cat stopped him. "So you haven't lived here in seven or eight years?" she asked Odie in a voice reeking of incredulousness.

"Yeah, why?"

"You want to show us the town, and you haven't lived here in half a dozen years?" She let the sarcasm sink in. "So what's this place, Odie?" Cat pointedly asked him.

"New hotel, I reckon."

Cat humphed a bit, and Odie said nothing, content to look around at all the new stuff.

"Take us to Carey's," Cat told the limo driver over the communications device.

"Yes, ma'am," came the answer.

"Where's that?" Beeb wanted to know.

"Buckhead," came the one-word reply from Cat.

"Big place, this Buckhead," Odie said to Beeb, who nodded agreement. Much different than when they had lived there, if Peachtree Road was any indication.

Tuesday night blended into Wednesday morning. They spent the evening going from place to place, listening to the bands, playing some darts, just having a good time in general. Lin and Din were learning fast. They were discovering new things about Cat, Odie, and Beeb as well as other humans. They were learning how to have fun. Although it was a foreign concept to them prior to their arrival on earth, they had certainly come light-years in their comprehension of the subject.

# I've Fallen in Love, and
# I Can't Get Up!

Wednesday night became early Thursday morning, and once again, the five travelers spent the night going from place to place, having drinks and having fun. They began making appearances in all the *in* spots in town. Soon, the gossip columns would have them spotted as the count and his entire retinue in all the right clubs, from Carbo's to Blind Willie's. They gave out huge tips and bought rounds for the house. The count and entourage made a name for themselves in just a couple of days. They became a happening. They saw Atlanta, and Atlanta saw them. By the weekend, they had become a full-fledged phenomenon.

Odie encountered a remote broadcast booth in one night-spot, and the lady behind the microphone lost it when the count approached her. "Oh, you guys!" the DJ shrieked to her radio listeners, "you wouldn't believe me if I told you!"

The count smiled at her.

"Would you say hello to our audience?" she wondered.

"But uf course! Hello, Atlanta! Ziss iss zee count von Dusselderfer! I yam here in zee Buckhead area, und I haff been talking wiff zee Yellow Jacket man here, und zay tell me zat zis blood drife uf zairs iss nod goink to reach zee top. I yam goink to donate mine blood for zis vunderful program, und I yam darink all of you to donate more zan me. Money, I got. Money, zey don't vant. Blood, zey vant. I got only zo much blood in me zat I can spare. But I yam goink to spare mine, und you can spare yoursz. Let's all make zis blood drife un rousink succesz. Danke Schoen, und go Brafes!"

The DJ was visibly shaken, teary-eyed by the count's plea. Still, she had the presence of mind to ask the count, "Who rocks the South?"

Odie smiled, leaned into the microphone, and said, "Zee 96 Rock kicks butt!"

The DJ regained her composure and said, "Well, you heard him, Atlanta! Are we gonna let the count down?"

Shouts of *no* could be heard from passing cars. "So I wanna see all of you down here before five o'clock this afternoon, 'cause we're gonna take this blood drive over the top. Speaking of top, here's ZZ Top."

"Have Mercy" came over the speakers. Within ten minutes, the blood donor lines were more than two blocks long. The Red Cross had called the station to thank the count. The count and his retinue had gone to give blood and had not come back. Odie had Pete lift his costume for a few moments, and he went up to the DJ looking like himself. He squeezed her hand and slipped her two hundreds. She looked disbelievingly. Odie explained to her what he wanted her to think. "The count sent me over with that. I'm one of the security team. It got too crazy in here, and it will probably get worse, but thanks for the media attention. He likes to help, but he's fond of saying God helps those who help themselves. He's just a swizzle stick to stir up the population and get them to do what they should do without some glamourous personality telling them to, you know?"

The DJ nodded her head at Odie, but it was time to do a commercial for the establishment they were in, and when she was done, Odie was gone. Odie rejoined the others, and they went to another place.

Walking in the warm sunshine, Beeb noted, was very strenuous activity and had thoroughly activated his thirst glands. "What does that mean?" Cat asked Odie.

"Stop here," Odie translated.

Beeb nodded and entered the new place. Seated at a table under holograms, the Starcraft Five were not themselves, nor were they the count and company. Odie wanted to give the count routine a rest, and so it was with great disappointment that the count discovered at the bar that others were cashing in on his fame. Odie heard people talking about seeing the count in places they'd never been, that he didn't know even where the place was.

But the worst news was when their waitress told them she'd just heard on the radio that several places had called up 96 Rock to say that the count had run up hundreds of dollars on tabs. Odie was mad, but the count was furious. "I'll be back in a few," Odie told the group, and he went back to where the remote broadcast was coming from. Pete made him look like the count once more. He stormed up to the remote site and demanded to be put on the air. She complied. "People of Atlanta! Zis iss zee count Von Dusselderfer again! Do not be fooled or misled! I haff heard zis complaint zat I owe zomebody zome money. Do not be fooled or misled! Zee count nevair puts any-zink on credik. I haff *money!* I don't need credik! Anyvun pretendink he iss me had better haff zouzands uf dollars in cash on him, or he iss un liar! Nevair beleaf zat zee count hass forgotten zee vallet! Zee count alvays payss in advance und in cash! Zat iss all I haff to zay about zis."

To the DJ, he said, "Please call zose businezzez zat vass taken by zome phoney-baloney, und I vill make it okay."

The DJ thanked him for his generosity. He thanked her for all she had done, and he vanished.

When he rejoined the others at another establishment, he, too, could hear the lies and prevarications about the count.

Lin and Din could see the legend of the count grow wildly beyond the absurd truth it really was. They saw how fast fact had become mixed up with fiction. Odie looked discouraged. "This is what you tried to prove with that building in East St. Louis, isn't it, Odie?" Lin asked him a question she already knew the answer to.

"More or less, yes. Here, it's just the other way around. People are more than willing to swear to a total lie, something they neither saw nor heard. I tried to prove that people would say they hadn't seen something that they had. Here, they're swearin' they saw something that they didn't, but it's about the same sort of situation, yes."

Odie was angry that something that he was responsible for had gone wrong. It was making him look bad. The waitress brought their drinks and turned on a TV that was overhead, at Din's request. "Pete wants to show you the latest, Odie," Din told him.

In response to Odie's eyebrow movements, Din said, "It's okay. Pete is covering us."

Odie gave him the thumbs-up signal. The TV announcer droned on. "And here in Atlanta, it seems everyone is interested in the count Von Dusselderfer. Today the Red Cross announced they exceeded their blood drive quota by two hundred percent. The reason? A local radio station had the count on live from a remote location in Buckhead, and he challenged the listeners to put the blood drive over the top. They did, so far over that several hundred would-be donors were turned away. It is not known how many people couldn't get through the heavy traffic in Buckhead to donate. The Red Cross says thanks, Count."

"But the traffic cops don't say thanks, Bob, do they?"

"No, Jim. As we can see from the helicopter shot, traffic is stalled on at least five major thoroughfares. Stay off West Paces Ferry, Roswell, Peachtree, Piedmont, and Northside if you want to get anywhere. Jim?"

"Thanks, Bob. And another agency that wants to know more about this count is the Federal Bureau of Investigation, which has supposedly brought more than two hundred extra agents into Atlanta to investigate."

"The FBI is after me now?" Odie demanded to know.

"Shhh!" Cat hissed at him.

A couple more minutes of reports made it clear that the FBI was involved because of counterfeit money appearing all over Atlanta.

"So that's why some of those people in the other place didn't think I was the count," Odie mused. "They saw a phoney first, and I don't like having my name drug through the mud!" Odie stated.

"It ain't yer name, jerk!" Beeb noted with a degree of sarcasm.

"Okay, it ain't my name, but it's me. It's my character. It's what I thought up. And if they think they can outsmart me, they're crazy. Right, Pete?"

"Yes, Odie, especially if I help you."

"Oh, well, of course, that's what I meant, Pete. I meant with your help. Shit, if you helped the counterfeiters, I don't see how I could catch them."

"I don't either," Pete agreed.

"Okay, we're gittin' nowhere fast. What's the deal? What should we do?"

Beeb had no ideas to offer, and neither did Cat. Lin and Din didn't have any ideas about it either, leaving Odie and the computer Pete to figure it out. Odie wanted to do something to protect the count's reputation. Cat just wanted to go have fun. She didn't want to worry about the count. Odie knew she'd leave him right at that table, so he got up to go with them. "Okay, count me in," he said.

"Boo hiss, bad pun, dude!" Beeb said.

Off they went to spend Saturday night in downtown Atlanta. They went up to the top of the roof at Nickolai's. They went down to Walter Mitty's and over to Manuel's. They had a good time dressed casually and being themselves. On the way back to their hotel room, Odie told Cat he was glad she had taken him out of the mood he was in. She put a few-minute-kiss on him that had the Ehliuns and Beeb looking away in embarrassment.

They went back to the hotel and went to their rooms. Without more than a good night from them, Cat and Odie went eagerly off to bed. The others watched TV for a while before going to sleep.

In the morning, Din and Lin awoke before the others. They wondered what they had let themselves in for. True, it had been mostly fun up to this point, but they had seen the way Beeb looked at Cat and Odie. There was no mistaking that look, Din felt. Cat and Odie were falling in love, and even Beeb knew it, but Cat and Odie didn't say anything. They didn't seem to know yet that they were falling in love.

*Fall* seemed to the Ehliuns to be the most apt verb to describe the phenomenon of love. Love was some sort of pit with poorly defined edges, containing an unknown sort of self-generated gravity that drew pairs of humans together as near as they could tell. Once humans fell into the pit of love, they were influenced by its unique gravity, which altered their thoughts, their movements, words, and deeds.

When Cat awoke Sunday morning, she shook Odie and told him it would be nice to take the Ehliuns to church since it was Sunday, and they had just learned so much about religion too. Surprisingly, Odie agreed. He got up and took a shower, and Cat tagged after. The water running woke Beeb up, so he got up and took a shower too.

When Cat and Odie emerged from their bedroom and announced they were going to take the Ehliuns to church, Beeb nearly choked on his coffee, but he hid his surprise well and said he'd go too. As they got into the starcraft, Odie told Pete to head up Peachtree to Christ the King Cathedral. The Ehliuns had no idea what church was. They didn't know it was both noun and verb here. They didn't know it meant the building and the services inside. They just took it all in. The cathedral was a lovely building with nice stained glass windows and lots of oak trim.

The services baffled the Ehliuns totally. They stood and sat and knelt when the others did. They didn't pray because they didn't know what prayer was for, but they did like it. It was more personal than the Cubs ballgame had been. They were more involved with the ceremonies here. They liked their church experience. Odie told them that he took them to the granddaddy of all religions first. They didn't know exactly what he meant, nor did he explain.

After church services were over, Cat told Pete to take them to Anthony's. It was a ritzy little joint on Piedmont, specializing in European seven course meals. The manager René greeted them warmly. Odie seized upon the opportunity to speak some French with him. Beeb joined in. Then René switched to German, leaving Beeb out of the conversation. Odie rattled on and on, as he did in any language. It turned out that the Swiss René also spoke excellent English. Cat used this fact to order some drinks.

They began with the appetizers and rolled right on through to dessert, devouring everything put before them. They were all stuffed by meal's end. All seven courses had been well received. "A sumptuous repast, my good fellow," Odie assured René.

Din pulled out one of his many thousand-dollar bills and handed it to the manager. "Keep the change," Din said, looking over at Odie all the while.

Odie smiled, as he thought Din wanted. It was amusing anyway. His smile wasn't just to be kind. He was amused.

After leaving Anthony's, they went back to the hotel. Odie wondered out loud about checking out and going someplace else. Din told him that they were invisible to the hotel employees, and they were not being charged for their lodgings. "Yeah," Beeb agreed, "and what's more, we already paid the bastards enough to buy a house! Let's stay here on them!"

Odie wasn't going to be a party pooper, so he went along with them. If they weren't gonna pay or even be seen, then what difference did it make where they stayed? It would be the same. But he remained silent. The five of them sat around all day and played cards and watched the Braves game on TV. They called out for a pizza and stayed in all night, a first.

Then on the evening news, Odie saw something that enraged him, about the count again. Since the media couldn't find out anything about him, they had taken to calling him the *alleged* count. "Alleged Count?" Odie harshly spoke back to the television.

"Shaddup!" Beeb sternly warned Odie. "You *are* an alleged count, idiot!" Beeb thought a moment, then spoke to Pete. "And since that's so, Pete, what are we gonna do about providing papers for the count?"

Pete answered by simply materializing the necessary documents on the bed. Odie picked them up and went through, proofreading, Cat was certain. He'd check up on anyone. Odie read the count's birth certificate to the rest, who didn't speak German. The visa and passport were also gone over and found to be correct in every detail. "Good, Pete. These are good," Odie told the computer, admiring its handiwork. "But what about background?"

"Well, Odie," Pete started in, like Odie did to him and noticed by all, "it's like this: the count is a very private man and has never been photographed for the public. He owns a locomotive factory in Kassel and is the heir to one of Germany's biggest fortunes. He is

371

known throughout Europe as a filthy rich, eccentric playboy whose extravagance is matched only by a few sultans and sheiks. He is currently on his first American tour."

"Hey, great stuff, Pete!" Odie said enthusiastically. "That should do nicely. Thank you much."

"Don't mention it."

"Pete," Cat sweetly asked in honeyed tones, "are there any new movies you can show us?"

"I can show you anything in the WTBS film library," Pete offered.

"Well, what have they got?" Cat wondered.

"I know!" Odie smiled, "how about the American Movie Classic channel? There are no commercials, and tonight, they're showing *The Maltese Falcon!*"

Cat and Beeb had no objections, and the Ehliuns did not know movies by their titles, so Odie's motion was carried, and Pete showed them the requested film on their TV screen. Within five minutes, Cat found herself telling Odie to pipe down. She became exasperated only moments later and demanded to know why Odie insisted on doing each character's lines milliseconds before they did. "He's just showin' ya that he knows this one by heart," Beeb told her.

"How many times have you seen this movie, Odie?"

Odie simply pointed over to Beeb, indicating Beeb had his permission to indicate the correct number of times. Beeb's estimate was well over fifty. "Probably in the seventy-five to eighty range, I'd reckon."

"Not that much, right, Odie, right?"

"This is number one-oh-six, right here tonight," Odie admitted.

"Pete! Stop this movie this instant!" Cat demanded.

Pete obliged her.

"I can't believe you've seen this movie more than a hundred times, Odie! What *is* the point of watching it?"

"Practice."

"Practice?" Cat said in total disbelief. "Who cares if you can memorize a whole damn movie?"

"Obviously, not you."

She stared at him.

"Okay, okay, Cat, you win. I won't say anything. Is that what you wanna hear?"

"I wanna hear what the movie characters say, when they say it, not from you but from them. That's all I want, Odie!"

Odie deferred to the madwoman's wishes.

"Okay, Pete, roll it!" Cat said. She leaned over and kissed Odie on the cheek and held his hand.

He said nothing to her, but he did squeeze her hand. The Ehliuns carefully watched and noticed things like that. More notes for their love file. Since Cat and Odie were just now falling in love, the Ehliun study had begun on the ground floor. Lin and Din would develop good information about Earth. It was their custom, their habit, and their wish. Good information was necessary to get good results. They never failed to get good information.

# And Welcome to the New and Improved Expanded Hot Spot: Buckhead

Monday morning came around early. There was a hectic pace outside due to the beginning of the workweek. Horns honked, sirens wailed, and jets passed overhead, along with helicopters of all types. The city was wide awake and moving full speed. The noise was too much to sleep through, and Odie woke up. He noticed Cat was already awake. He heard Beeb curse the jackhammers that were furiously beating upon concrete poured with the intent of lasting. "Might as well get up, huh?" Odie whispered to Cat.

"You say you got it up, huh?" Cat whispered back. Instantly she was on Odie, humping that piss hard-on for all she was worth. "Oh, god, Odie," Cat moaned.

"Shhh," Odie urged her, but he continued to ram her relentlessly.

Cat just could not help herself, and she loudly moaned, "Oh, Jesus Christ!"

Out in the living room, Lin turned to Odie's oldest friend to ask why Cat was crying out Jesus Christ. "She's probably experiencing the second coming," Beeb told her, smiling contentedly to himself. He doubted either Ehliun would get the joke. He thought Cat might laugh, and then again she might not. Odie would get a kick out of it, however. Beeb was sure of that. He knew Odie too well to miss that.

Beeb heard the shower start up, so he told Lin to tell Odie if he came out before he returned that he just went for a newspaper, and he'd be right back. Lin said "Check!" to Beeb without removing her eyes from the TV.

Beeb smiled after he went out the door. The Ehliuns had the routine down pat. Pete was on the ball, of course, but Lin and Din would soon be indistinguishable from any human occupant of the planet. Beeb was proud he had something to do with this accomplishment.

When Beeb came back with a copy of the morning paper, Cat and Odie were dressed and waiting on him. "Let's go get some breakfast," Odie said.

No one had to tell Beeb twice it was time to eat, so off they went. Invisibly weaving their way through the lobby, they appeared on the curb as a bus pulled up. Pete gave each of them a token by materializing it in their hands. They got on the bus and took some seats. "Where we goin'?" Cat asked Odie.

He told her, "When we see a good place to eat, we'll get off."

The bus driver smiled at Cat and told her he would recommend a place not too far away up on the curve. Odie thanked the driver for the information. "See?" he said to Cat, gloating.

"Like he had something to do with it," Cat whispered to Beeb.

They both smiled at Odie. He didn't know what was said, but he knew whom it was about. He was not going to play into their hands, though. He would not acknowledge that they tried to make fun of him. Lin and Din noticed, but they put it down to falling in love. They still didn't quite have a handle on the love thing.

The bus driver spoke up to Cat and her companions. "This is superfood here, folks. You won't be disappointed."

Odie thanked him and slid him a ten. No one would figure the count to take a bus. Why fight that? Tip small. The travelers crossed Peachtree when the light changed and halted traffic. They took a corner booth and ordered breakfast.

As their waitress left with their order, Beeb unfolded his newspaper and handed the sports section to Odie. Cat started in on Odie as he read the sports. "Great game Otis had yesterday, eh? Smoltz is the best pitcher on the Braves staff 'cause he has four pitches. I've never seen the Dodgers look worse. Five million a year is too much for anybody, let alone some goof who gets suspended for some games. You know, I think CJ is the most valuable guy in that dugout, don't you? And this year, if Hrbek tries to lift Gant's leg, Ronnie ought to piss right on that oaf. How could Santiago—"

Odie interrupted Cat's soliloquy. "It's hard to read with you jabberin' like that, Cat."

"Hard to watch movies that way too."

"Yer point is well taken."

"Thank you."

"Yer welcome." Odie returned to his reading…not for long.

"It won't happen again."

"Okay."

"I promise you, Odie, not another word."

"Okay!"

"I really mean it this—"

"*Goddamn* it! If yer tryin' ta push me to the limit, you've succeeded!"

"Okay, honey, take it easy!" Cat kissed him and made him relax a bit. "Jeez, you blow up over a little joke."

"I'm sorry, Cat. I never mean to make you mad."

Din immediately noticed that Odie said mean and not meant. The difference in tense denoted a difference in time. Meant would have suited that situation just passed, but mean carried the connotation of now, present, always. Meant was past tense, gone, moved on. Din knew this, and he wondered if other words would change tense when they spoke to each other.

Cat also noticed Odie said mean and not meant. She knew Odie meant it too. She could read people like books, she thought. Odie was like a primer, though. She didn't know him that well yet, but she thought she would, and that entailed staying around a long time.

After breakfast, they walked down the street a way heading for the High Museum of Art. They strolled in. Odie heard a commotion in the office. Din came out, and Odie immediately knew the hubbub revolved around some money. "Generous again?" Odie smiled at Din.

"Oh, yeah!" Din answered. "Why not? This place looks like it takes a lot of money to run. They accept donations, according to the sign, so I donated."

"How much?" Odie wondered.

"I don't know. I put in a couple of bills for each of us. Why?"

"What denomination were those bills?"

"Methodist?" Din ventured a guess, eliciting a laugh from Odie. "I don't know. I didn't look. Ask Pete."

"No, no, that's all right. I don't really want to know if you don't, Din. It's yer money. I just wondered. If you were too generous, one a' them old ladies up front might have a heart attack."

"Shall we go back and see?" Din offered.

"No, I don't guess I hear anyone hollerin' for help."

Thus reassured, Din and Odie walked around like the others, staring at this exhibit and now that.

Lin was close by Cat, her only female friend and the only role model. She was trying hard to emulate Cat's actions and movements. Without those wonderful hips of Cat's, however, the movements and action was difficult to imitate. Cat was helping Lin examine the pictures and objects on display. Pointing at a painting, Cat explained to Lin, "There's a lot of history recorded in these pictures. Details like the dress, the food, the ideals pictured—all this contributes to what we like about art."

Cat told Lin what she personally liked about the art. "I like to see the old dresses and think about what it would be like to be me in olden days."

Lin just listened because she had learned it was the only way to gain some kinds of information. Lin drew closer to the next painting Cat talked about. "Look at how many petticoats and hoops are in this skirt, Lin! Can you imagine movin' around with all this crap draggin' behind you? You'd have trouble sitting, dancing, hell, even walking! I don't believe that's for me. Don't think I'd like wearin' twenty pounds of clothes. I like the century I live in right now, thank you very much!"

After Cat explained and showed Lin what petticoats and hoops were, Lin comprehended all that Cat said. They went on from gallery to gallery just the two of them, and Lin learned a lot about fashions, how to tell the age of a painting by judging the clothing and what different ideals women were held to over the ages.

"Here, Lin, this is what I mean. This is a Rubens or at least the school of Rubens. Look at how plump these women are. Those arms are thickly muscled 'cause they did twelve hours a day on their jobs, every day, no days off. To have a fire to cook food for your family meant splitting logs into firewood and building that fire. Food preparation, as we have seen, consists of live animals killed in the kitchen and cleaned, skinned, plucked, or whatever. Plus bread had to be assembled by hand and baked, so there's another fire. And there was childcare, which never stops when you have several. These poor bitches probably tried to eat and get fat so the old man would leave them alone and not knock 'em up again."

"You mean they would not wish to have sex?" Lin wondered.

"Correct. I mean, they had to put up with untold goofs and dorks."

"What is a dork? We do not locate the word *dork* in the dictionary."

"A dork is an awkward, clumsy person who is usually not very attractive and unwilling to make even the most modest improvements, like combing hair, brushing teeth. That sort of thing makes a person a dork."

"Cat, you almost sound sad when you discuss the women of the past. Why is that?"

Cat needed further clarification, and Lin finally got across what she meant. She meant a time difference. Cat still didn't understand Lin very well. Lin didn't comprehend sexual divisions of work and society. She did not have Cat's rage for customs such as binding feet, selling infants, beheading for adultery while the man gets no blame. She didn't understand how Cat felt about women having been subjugated by men for so long that it was ingrained by centuries of custom.

"So I guess on your planet that men and women are considered equals?"

"Yes. Our upbringing is totally social in nature. We do not have secrets or hidden desires like you do, but we were all connected to the same thing. We were all conscious of the rest of Ehlius. I have no past, Cat, not that I know of. I am just here now. I can barely remember what life on Ehlius was like because I've lived in space for so long. Now, all I am concerned with is you, Odie, Beeb, and Din—and Pete, of course. Life here is what I have. It's the hand I was dealt, I believe the saying goes. But your past troubles you, or am I wrong?" Lin wondered.

"Well, my past is over too, Lin. My present is very confusing. I can talk to you about a computer parked so far away I couldn't get there in eight hundred years at the speed of light, but I couldn't say that to any other female on earth! Sometimes, things like that bother me, but I guess I'll learn to live with it."

"Will you live with Odie too?" Lin asked her.

Social tact was something Lin could stand to learn, Cat thought. "Well, I have thought about it, but jeez, like I don't really even know him. What I do know about him is mostly bad, I mean his past and all. He's a murderer, Lin! He has killed people. That bothers me a little."

Lin defended Odie against Cat's charges. "He saved our lives. He saved our whole planet. I heard his explanation about the kidnappers who took him against his will. If we had been able to activate our laser defense after the spacecraft wrecked, Odie and Beeb might have been disintegrated before freeing us. We had no idea what they were doing. I was afraid when Pete told me Din disappeared. I thought the primitives killed him. Now I know better.

"Odie is a wondrous example of hospitality, Cat. Think about it. Your life is infinitely better now. Mine is, and Din's is. Most of the credit goes to Odie. Beeb has been right there with Odie, but Odie is the one who made all the mental maneuvers and made Pete what he is today. Well, I guess I better include you and your lucky dollar, Cat."

The two females laughed and hugged each other. Cat knew Lin was right. Odie was all right. Okay, dangerous, but all right. "Yes, Lin, it's true, and I guess you know it too, huh? Odie and I are in love! Is that insane or what? It's what, Monday? So tomorrow is two weeks I've known the guy. Two weeks! That's unheard of."

"But how do you feel, Cat? What difference is there for you, sexually? I know you have lots more experience than I, although I am much older. But it is different for us. You humans have much stronger sex drives."

"I wonder if that's because you have never had your sex drive in gear?" Cat wondered. "You know, you can't have babies because Pete said something was not activated? Maybe that has to do with sex drive. I don't know. I'm not the university graduate in the crowd."

Pete would dispute Cat's self-deprecating remarks, but he wanted to keep it a secret if she was right. He had his reasons. What a brilliant theory! Pete scanned all his records and hit upon the truth. There was a connection. Ehliun childbearing women all had the same complex chemical in their systems. Pete schemed a way to introduce this chemical into Lin's bloodstream. As it had to do with aging as well, he set about finding a way to solve that problem. Couldn't trade a little better sex for a much shorter life, could he? It didn't seem ethical to Pete, so he would see what he could develop.

"Lin, do you mean to ask me how does Odie affect me sexually or being in love?"

"Being in love. I know what sex is, but your reaction to Beeb is markedly different from your reaction to Odie, even though you last had sex with Beeb on the way to Chattanooga."

"What, you writin' a book? How do you know all this?"

"I can see. I can hear. So far as I can tell, sex with anyone other than Odie does not provoke the same reaction."

"And it never did, either. I never ever felt the way I do about Odie with anyone before ever. I loved old Sydney. He was my first, but Odie is just something else. He pleases me, you know, in a way no one else ever has. I don't know what it is, Lin. It just is."

"And you like it."

"I get off on it."

"I heard you. Beeb told me you were probably experiencing the second coming. After Pete informed me that refers to Christ reappearing, I got the joke."

"What are you talking about?"

"This morning. You yelled out, 'Oh, Jesus Christ.'"

Cat doubled up with laughter. This was great! Lin got a joke Beeb thought was over her head, probably because she was female and not male.

In a different part of the museum, Odie, Din, and Beeb were scoping the place out. Din told them that Lin was learning much from Cat and wished to be alone with her awhile, so they made a point not to approach them, but Odie's stomach growled suddenly, making him realize it was late. He got the time from Beeb. Din silently alerted Lin that Odie was ready to go. Lin told Din that she and Cat would be along pretty soon.

Cat looked at her watch suddenly, like she too had gotten a silent signal. Lin wondered if love made humans prophetic. "Goodness," Cat said to Lin, "just look at the time. It's after three already." They walked out to the lobby where the boys were.

"Let's get out of here," Beeb suggested.

"Good idea," Odie acknowledged.

"Let's get something to eat."

"Another good idea."

"I can't believe how much you two guys can eat!" Cat exclaimed. Her complaint was wasted on them.

"We're still growing boys!" Odie offered.

"Growin' fat guts!" Cat retorted.

Beeb was not thrilled that she placed him in the same category as Odie. "I don't know what yer talkin' about," he told her.

"Well, it's true!" Cat said defensively. "You two eat all the time."

"And where are you all this time while we're chowin' down?" Beeb demanded of Cat.

"She's busy stealin' bites of it," Odie answered for her.

"Maybe so, but I ain't fat like you two."

"Fat?" Odie roared. "I am not fat! No way can you consider me fat!"

"Maybe between the ears!" Cat suggested.

Odie spat out a "Ha!" that said all he had to say on the matter. Din silently asked Pete to bring the motor home around, and it instantly drove up the side street next to the museum. "Hey! how did that get here?" Odie asked suddenly, noticing the starcraft.

Odie looked at Din. "You did it."

"Nope, must'a been Pete. I was right here all along."

Din smiled back at Odie. So this was the concept of humor, eh? It was strange yet delightful in an odd sort of way.

They all boarded the starcraft. Beeb suggested that they take the tour over to their old favorite place, the Longhorn on Lawrenceville Highway in good old Tucker. "That the place you go to ogle waitresses?" Cat asked him.

"Yep, that's the place. How'd you know?"

"Heard ya talkin' about it before."

"Oh."

Beeb had nothing further to say to Cat, and so he went to the table and joined Lin and Din. They got into a conversation about attractive women in Atlanta and what sort of cars they drove. Beeb had several times before expounded his views to the Ehliuns about the subject. They had been subjected to this before and started a study about correlating pretty women to nice cars and nice homes. Beeb knew that success attracted beauty in America. The Ehliuns were still finding out about it. Pete confirmed for them that Atlanta had more BMWs than Berlin and more Mercedeses as well.

Cat asked Pete how many trees were in Atlanta. Pete told her that inside the perimeter, he counted 39,874,598 trees more than three feet tall. Pete included the five metro counties, and the tree count shot up to 267,831,837 trees above three feet tall. "That's an awful lot of trees," Cat commented.

"Most heavily forested urban center in America, possibly the entire planet."

Beeb's estimate was agreed to by Odie without comment, a rare occurrence.

They arrived at the Longhorn and made their way in. A friendly young lovely assisted them to their table and wiggled away as the waitress bringing water and menus approached. Cat leaned over to Beeb and admitted that the women working here were quite attractive. "Not as much as me, but *c'est la vie*."

Beeb smiled at her and told her no woman in there came close to her.

"No woman better get too close to me!" she retorted with merriment twinkling mischievously in her yellow and gold eyes.

"Not what I meant."

"Yeah, I know. I was just bein' funny. That's all."

"Yes, you were, sweetie!" Odie said in her defense, giving her a kiss.

A lovely brunette came up to their table and told them her name was Mary Anne, and she would be their waitress for the evening. Odie smiled at her excessively, Cat thought, before he ordered. When all five of them had finished ordering, Mary Anne walked away, followed by Beeb and Odie's eyes. Cat caught Odie with an elbow to the midsection that straightened him right up. He knew what that was for, and he smiled but said nothing. Lin and Din entered it in the love file.

After their dinner was finished, Mary Anne came by again. "What can I bring you for dessert?" she entreated them.

"A can of whipped cream, please," Cat politely requested.

Odie laughed loudly.

"We don't have that available, ma'am."

"Thank God!" Odie told her.

Cat sat back and said nothing further, leaving Odie to explain to Mary Anne what he was laughing at. "Private joke!" he informed her. He did not watch her walk away this time. He left that up to Beeb, who did not let his friend down.

Odie knew Cat wouldn't say anything to Beeb about watching great hip action because she wasn't interested in him like she was in Odie. That made him proud. He was glad he'd found Cat because she was the most wonderful thing in his life. Although Pete and the Ehliuns were terrific, they were still number two. Cat was number one in his book.

Odie's daydreaming about the woman he loved was interrupted when the count was mentioned by the people at the table behind him. The claim was put forth that the count had been in their regular hangout, a downtown yuppie pub. Odie knew the count had not been there. The old boy didn't like yuppies. More fodder for the legend of the count. Odie couldn't resist. He had to ask the patrons behind him what the count looked like. They described the count to him as a short blond-haired gentleman with a pronounced accent. Odie asked if it was true that the count tipped thousands of dollars. He discovered that their count ran up a tab, but he would be back tonight for more.

Odie thanked them for the information and turned around. Cat leaned over and whispered into his ear. Her concern was for the people being taken by the phony counts popping up across town. Odie seemed lost in thought. Mary Anne returned to the table with their bill. Odie grabbed her hand and asked if she had ever seen the count Von Dusselderfer. She exclaimed that she had not but would love to meet him. Cat didn't say anything to Odie, but he knew she was listening to every word he said very carefully. "My dear young lady, why on earth would you want to meet some old foreigner?"

Mary Anne's quick response was for some of the loot the count hands out.

"Would you recognize him if you saw him?" he asked her.

Mary Anne thought a moment. "No, I guess I wouldn't."

Odie told her that was what he thought. Din pushed a thousand dollar bill into her hand next to the bill for the meal. She was in a state of shock suddenly. She stared blankly at the money, at Din, and then at Odie. Cat put a finger to her lips to tell the girl she should be quiet about the tip. Mary Anne nodded yes quickly. She was no fool.

It was time to go. Odie led the way. He cornered the hostess and inquired about the number of people working. When informed that sixteen people, including the kitchen help, were on duty, Odie handed her sixteen hundreds. She nearly fainted. She didn't make the count connection, but Mary Anne did. She came up to Odie and kissed him on the cheek. "Thank you very much, sir. Please come again."

"For you, I could find it in my heart to come again."

"Oh, for her you'll come again, eh?" Cat teased Odie as they went outside.

"Nah! She probably already got a boyfriend," he ventured.

"What about me?" Cat wailed.

"You got a boyfriend too, me."

Cat smiled at Odie, satisfied he was telling the truth.

The others noticed this behavior between Cat and Odie. Lin and Din were rapidly filling up their love file. This love thing was more complicated than first suspected.

"So what are we gonna do about the count?" Beeb wanted to know. "All them people thought they had the legitimate count, such as, that is, in their place of business last night, and we weren't near there. I don't know where the place is, but I know we weren't in there."

"Well, that's their hard luck," Odie asserted. "I didn't ask people to believe bullshit about forgotten wallets. If they don't listen to the radio, then they deserve to get taken! Never give a sucker an even break."

Beeb disagreed with Odie, but he still had to smile. He knew Odie had always taken P. T. Barnum's famous dictate to heart. But this was somewhat different. These rubes hadn't wandered into the county fair lookin' to slick somebody. They were in their own businesses, serving customers. Cat said it first, however. "Odie, you are responsible for the count. None of us knew anything about it till you came out of the Peachtree Towers the first time, and I don't think honest businessmen should lose money because of you or your idea."

"And I don't think I should be responsible because some dumbass extends credit because of a sob story, either."

Odie knew he had a point there. "My MO, as the count, has always been to lay big bucks on the barkeep upon arrival. If these dorks can't read the papers or listen to the radio, then they ain't payin' attention, and they deserve to be taken by con artists. That's how I feel about it."

"Well," Cat cried out obstinately, "if they can't or don't read the papers and they don't listen to rock music on one specific station, then they have not received your message, Odie!" Cat stated this like she wanted Odie to do something about it.

"Okay, okay. Jeez, I can take a hint," Odie told her, acting hurt.

"Beeb, mark the calendar. Odie can take a hint!" she shouted.

"Man, fuck you, man!"

"I'm not a man!"

"And that's what I like about you."

Without waiting for Cat to comment, Odie stabbed his finger into the phone buttons rapidly to reach CNN, allegedly the world's most important network. They just didn't know about Pete. "Ja, ziss iss zee count Von Dusselderfer, und I vish to make a schtatement to your vorldvide audience und especially here in Atlanta. I vant to talk viss zose perzonz zat own bars und such. Zee count nevair putz anyzink on zee cuff! I haff alvays paid cash, und I haff nevair forgotten mine money. I haff said zis to zee 96 Rock und now you, CNN. If ze *count* in your establishment doss nod haff cash in hand, zat iss not me. Please be avare of ziss. Danke schoen."

Pete pulled up in front of their hotel as Odie hung up. "That should do nicely, Odie. That was smooth!" Cat applauded Odie as he hung the phone up.

"Thanks," he smiled, kissing her on the lips.

"Now let's go have a good time."

"Where ya wanna go?" Odie questioned her to no avail.

"I don't know," she answered.

"Let's get a limo again!" Lin suggested.

"Yeah," Cat agreed, "that's always a lot of fun."

Beeb said it was okay by him, "Swell" was Odie's only comment, and they exited the starcraft to await the limo. Pete made the starcraft appear to drive off. Then going further, Pete made the Starcraft Five appear to be office workers awaiting the bus. However, the limo driver would see the count and his retinue at the curb.

"Where to, count?" the limo driver asked them after they entered the luxurious ride.

"Vat's your name?" Odie asked the driver.

"Jimmy," the limo operator replied.

"Jimmy, take us to Buckhead."

"Yessir!" Jimmy said, putting the limo in gear.

Down Peachtree they rolled, past banks and apartments and condos and other places like shops and stores. Stopping at the first place they came to on the left that looked halfway decent, they piled out. "Jimmy," Cat told the driver, "we'll be wandering from place to place so make yourself comfortable. We'll be somewhere, maybe Carey's or Aunt Charley's or Rio Bravo, so look for us in six hours or so."

"Yes, ma'am! I'll go have dinner and come back to find you later."

Cat slipped him a hundred that Din had given her. His eyes widened even more than when he was staring at Cat. She noticed he was more interested in money than her. Of course, in fairness, he was gonna get some of the money. He knew that's all he was gonna get too.

As the limo left, Beeb looked at Odie. "This place is crawlin' with suits of both sexes, way too yuppie for my tastes," he said pointedly.

"Yeah, let's go somewhere else," Cat agreed.

Lin and Din didn't care, and they followed after. Entering one spot after another, they made the same magical entrance through a disbelieving crowd. In place after place, Odie put a big bill into the bartender's hands and ordered a round for the house.

The count and entourage were dressed to the nines, it appeared. They were elegant, well-heeled, and overflowing with cash. Their routine was the same. They bought a round for the house, tossed down a drink, and after some chitchat were off and gone for another place. They listened to live reggae, and they heard some old soft rock on tape. They didn't stay long anywhere. They couldn't. The crowds were overwhelming soon after word spread that the count was there.

Somewhere along the way, Odie became separated from the group and was on his own. He asked Pete to change his costume so no one could immediately tell he was the count. He sat down in a bar on East Paces Ferry to await the others. They had not been there yet, so it was a matter of time. He could have asked Pete where they were, but he didn't want to depend totally on an alien computer. Almost totally was good enough.

Odie didn't know that Pete had been responsible for Odie's separation from the others. Pete just wanted to test Odie and see if he could determine what actually had occurred. Pete had begun to notice that Odie sometimes took credit for things that didn't happen just the way he said. Pete didn't know what Odie thought. He didn't know what Beeb thought either. Pete knew they still didn't fully trust him. He didn't know that either man rarely trusted someone else fully, let alone a computer from another planet and culture, and Pete didn't realize by testing them, he was creating suspicion and distrust.

There was so much to know and so little time to teach it. Alas, earth as teacher tended to be harsh in some of its lessons. Make an error, die. Pete understood that danger as it related to driving, and several dozen films of nature studies taught him how it related to spiders, snakes, tigers, fish, and the deadliest hunter of all, man.

But subtle lessons, love, like, dislike, plant life, and other complex issues were most difficult to comprehend. Why humans sent get-well cards was quite impossible to understand. Pete was appalled that Moslem princesses could lose their lives by beheading for having sex outside marriage. How to put yourself in a position to go along with such absurd situations was unknown to Pete. Why Odie and Cat were falling in love was unclear. How was uncertain, but that it was occurring was undeniable.

Love was tough to comprehend. That it had so much influence on earthly life was still not clear to Pete. He was still new to the planet. Love was responsible for chemical changes in the bloodstream, Pete decided. He checked his hypothesis across the country. He discovered certain endorphins present in the brain tissue during lovemaking that were not normally there. Pete found that the anticipation of lovemaking actually created these endorphins. Pete isolated these endorphins and put top priority toward finding out exactly what was going on. Love would soon cease to amaze Pete. He would get to the bottom of this. It was chemical. It had to be. All of life was chemical.

Pete decided to inform Odie that this woman was interested in him, then he changed his mind. He would conduct another test on Odie. Could he resist this woman's charms? Even if he looked like the count to her? He would see. Odie found himself engaged in conversation with a striking brunette who struck up said conversation. She introduced herself to him. "Hello, my name is Odie. What's yours? Besides count, of course."

So Pete let this lady see him as the count, eh? What was the idea? And what was her name? "Excuse me, did you say your name was Odie?" Odie asked her.

"Yes, and what was yours?"

Odie whispered *Pete* under his breath, and his glasses immediately had a message printed to Odie that Pete knew nothing about her name, and the count costume *slipped* out of concealment. "My name iss Villy! You are un Odie, ja, for sure?"

She nodded her long brunette hair affirmatively.

"You know, my best friend iss named Odie, und you are much lufflier than him." Odie slipped the female Odie a bill he pulled from his pocket. He handed it to her and told her to buy herself something nice. With that, he excused himself and went off to the bathroom.

Odie didn't know that the gentleman two seats away from the female Odie was a treasury agent who quickly flashed his badge and examined the bill carefully. It was a genuine thousand-dollar bill all right. He returned it to the female Odie and phoned his boss immediately on his cellular phone. Pete waited for Odie to enter the restroom and be alone before speaking to him. "Odie, can I talk to you for a moment?"

Odie quickly scanned the room to see who was talking to him and then realized it had to be Pete. "Uh, where are you, Pete?"

"Same place I've been since we met, Odie."

"Right, I should'a known better. Yer usin' this mirror as a soundboard, eh?"

"Wrong. Your glasses are the soundboards, so you can hear me in stereo."

"Okay, look, Pete, I know you didn't call on me to joke around or watch me take a piss, so what's really up with this surprise visit?"

"There is a treasury agent out front on a cellular phone, calling his supervisor. He examined the money you gave to the female Odie, but he gave it back to her. There are dozens of treasury agents on their way here right now to follow you around and apprehend you if necessary."

"Why? I haven't done anything wrong. I ain't no Branch Davidian arsonist."

"The treasury agents are after some counterfeiters who have been using the disturbances you five have been causing in order to pass bad money."

"And you somehow just overheard all of this, I suppose?"

"I have my ways, yes. And you told me not to tell you this stuff because it drives you crazy, I believe you said."

"Yeah, yeah, Pete, I remember what I said and why. So what do we do now?"

"The treasury agents are arriving outside right now," Pete said, informing his symbiotic partner of the latest developments. "So hide me under a hologram no one will recognize me in and get me out of here pronto."

"It's done, son. You're on the run without a gun."

"Warn the others and cut out the feeble attempts at poetic license, yeah?"

"Yeah, right. Okay, Odie, they're both done."

"Okay, I'm outta here."

"You take care, sweet boy!" Pete called after him.

Odie wondered why Pete said that until he passed a mirror. He instantly knew. Odie swished out onto East Paces Ferry and headed across the parking lot toward Peachtree. "Real wiseass of late, ain'cha, Pete? Why in the world did you pick a hologram like this to cover me with?"

"Well, it got you right out of that straight bar without a second look, didn't it? Odie, didn't it?"

Odie had to begrudgingly admit to the computer that it was right. Then emerging from the back door of a Peachtree road bar were the four folks he was seeking. "Where are you guys goin'?" Odie asked them.

"Well, it damn sure ain't gonna be to no drag queen bar, sweetie!" Beeb assured the stranger in a voice full of disgust at being approached.

"Jesus H. Christ and his brother Billy Bob! Pete, git this sombitch up off me right now!"

Cat had begun softly laughing when she realized by the voice who it was. Beeb started laughing, followed by Lin and Din. They were highly amused by this turn of events.

Before Odie could tell them of the predicament he found himself in, the parking lot rendezvous was interrupted. Four men in suits emerged from the bar Odie had just left. They spotted him. "Oh, shit! Get back inside there!" he ordered, shoving them back down the steps they had just come up.

In past the restrooms they scrambled. Pete changed their appearances to look like five Korean businessmen in identical suits. They marched like ducks in a row up to the front, where they got a window booth. Here they could see across the street, where Roswell met Peachtree.

"What kind of a name is Aunt Charley's?" Din asked. He was reading off the menu and the front window.

"It's probably named for somebody's weird uncle," Odie offered.

"Maybe Uncle Bimbo married Aunt Charley?" Beeb questioned.

The remark made them all smile. Pete had taken the liberty to let all the other patrons hear Korean being spoken. He had learned his lesson. No more fuckups like with the air force officers in the big building, nosirree! These five didn't wish their true identities known just now, and Pete could grant those wishes.

Watching out the window, they noticed an ever-changing scenery. Much of the scenery seemed to be practicing for the Fourth of July Peachtree Road Race, which passed by this very spot. Lin and Din learned a lot about racial prejudice by having to hear the slurs and insults directed at them by a couple of inebriated patrons who obviously didn't like any Oriental, lumping them all into the category of slopes.

Lin and Din tried to learn more about subtle sexual prejudices that infected earthlings. Odie admitted he was only watching the female joggers, while Cat was the opposite, only watching the men. Beeb told them jogging bored him, and he rarely looked at any of the idiots engaged in such moronic activity. "What do you mean moronic activity?" Lin asked Beeb.

"How can running on hard concrete and breathing in heavy automotive exhaust fumes at every stop light for six miles be considered healthy?"

When the waitress finally came, they ordered a round of drinks and some sandwiches. The Ehliuns were fascinated by the categories that men and women seemed to constantly put the other in. "Why do men treat women so differently than they treat other men?" Din asked Cat.

"Because we got what they want." Cat's answer came easily and fluidly.

"How do men know you have what they want?" Din persisted.

Beeb was surprised at Din's question. He didn't know they were unenthused about sex compared to earthlings. "Din," Beeb cried, "haven't you been watching? Don't you see the way that men stare at Cat, the way they long for her?"

"That is precisely why Din asked the question," Lin clarified, "because of all the attention that Cat receives with or without a hologram disguise."

Odie tried his hand at explaining this to the Ehliuns. "Men know Cat has what they want because they can see it. It's because she's beautiful and sexy. Men admire her and desire to be in her company because she's a beauty. It supposedly increases a man's status to be with a beautiful woman like Cat." Odie gazed deeply into Cat's yellow-and-gold-flecked eyes. Those eyes stared right through him, and he knew it.

"They all want in my pants," Cat offered her opinion up for discussion.

"But you don't have any pants on," Lin observed.

Cat laughed heartily at this. "That's just a slang expression, Lin. It means that all men just want to have sex with me. It doesn't refer to a particular item of clothing."

Odie nodded. "Men wish to have sex with Cat simply because of her physical shape."

Beeb took exception to Odie's summation. "I don't know that the word *simply* should be used to describe Cat's beauty," he smiled.

"Yeah, tell him about it!" Cat said, sticking her tongue out at Odie like a brat might.

Beeb went on with his argument. "Cat's appearance, at least from a male point of view, comes very close to the *ideal* that we try to attain in a companion. Beautiful women operate under a sort of curse of good looks because a beautiful woman often receives undue and unwanted attention due to those good looks." Beeb looked around for the waitress and his drink but saw nothing and continued with his thoughts. "Men almost automatically think any woman that looks as good as Cat *is* good—good in bed, good to show off to male friends, just good to have around, like a status-giving priceless object, like a rare art piece, a collector's item. They cease to be real people anymore, at least to some men. You hear of executives marrying a *trophy* wife. Sounds more like an object than a person, doesn't it? And that, I believe, is the back side to great beauty, don't you agree, Cat?"

Beeb hoped she did, at least to some extent, but she had been silent while he spoke, not always a good sign. "Well," Cat began slowly, "yes, Beeb, you make a good point or two. I don't know that great beauty is a curse, but then I've never considered myself a great beauty. I know I look good, of course, but I've never thought of myself in the same vein as famous models like Jerry Hall and Christy Brinkley or even Cindy Crawford.

"But I don't know that beauty is a curse. I think the individual's reaction to excessive attention varies. It makes it tough on some women, no doubt. I used to fish for compliments all the time. Sydney taught me how very shallow that was, and I certainly have changed my opinions over the years because I have been through times when it positively excited me that men wanted me just for sexual pleasure, and there were other times when I hated it."

"How long did you hate it?" Odie asked, with a smile poorly hidden on his face.

Cat tried to look hard at Odie. "I didn't say I hated it for long. There were just times, that's all." Cat had a giggle in her eyes that Odie could see. "Okay," she smiled, "so it's two or three times. Is that what you wanted to hear?"

"Because it's the truth?" he quizzed her right back.

"Yes," Cat admitted.

"Then, yes, that's what I wanted to hear."

Finally, their drinks arrived, minus food, however. Din took this opportunity to silently convey the thought to Lin that he was quite certain that Cat and Odie were definitely in love. He noted that each of them changed the pitch and stress of their voices and possibly the very meaning of their words when they spoke to each other. Lin had already quizzed Cat about her feelings for Odie, and now she told Din what Cat had said. Din promised to interrogate Odie at the earliest opportunity about how he felt about Cat. Din was pretty sure he already knew.

Odie excused himself from the table a moment after glancing out the window. He dashed outside to the evening newspaper vending machine, where a man with a bundle of papers was loading the machine. In his very best phony Oriental accent, Odie requested "Won Brew Stleek, preese!" Searching the jingling pockets of his Ehliun-computer-provided suit coat and pants pockets for some American coins proved useless. Odie silently cursed Pete for being such a damn smart-ass. Odie deposited handful after handful of brass coins with square holes in the center disgustedly in his coat pocket.

The paper carrier, anxious to avoid the four-minute traffic light about to turn, told Odie he would settle for some foreign money. Odie kept giving him brass coins till he drove away. Odie grabbed his newspaper and headed back into Aunt Charley's to rejoin the others. He noticed an alarming number of federal agents milling about the area. A treasury agent followed Odie back in the door and began talking to the bartender. Sitting back down with the other Koreans, Odie gestured with his head for Beeb to look outside. An affirmative nod told Odie Beeb was well aware of the myriad agencies represented outside.

"Pete," Odie fairly barked at the computer, "I ain't even gonna say nothin' about the Oriental brass-coin trick just now, but you just gotta locate them counterfeiters right now! Bring them to Buckhead right away! I don't care how you do it. Just do it!"

"Okay," Pete answered, "they are leaving their motel right now."

"Good! Force them to come to Buckhead! We need to get rid of these FBI guys and the treasury agents and ordinary cops and all them fuzz right now! I mean now, too, mister!"

"You want the authorities to apprehend the counterfeiters?" Pete asked Odie.

"Exactly!" Odie retorted.

"Okay, I'll see what I can do, Odie, but you told me not to interfere with the ordinary affairs of humanity, don't you remember?"

"Pete!" Odie calmed himself before going further. "This is not ordinary! We don't need a bunch of Feds or some stupid counterfeiters following us around all the time! We need to nip it in the bud! Nip it, nip it!"

"You wish for me to do the work of the Federal agents surrounding the outside of this place?" Pete wanted to be given explicit orders from Odie on this one.

"Look, Odie, maybe Pete is right!" Beeb said. "We don't need to do the whole government's work, only that small portion which we were paid to do, and this shit is not it!" Beeb felt strongly about this and he said so. "We ain't gittin' paid to do this bust-the-counterfeiters gig. Besides, we are just as much counterfeiters as them guys are because the money we pass around isn't real money." Beeb's assertions were suddenly challenged.

"Oh but it *is*!" Pete immediately clarified. "Those bills are real! The money you people spend is as real as real gets. Those bills are printed by the real US government and backed in real gold by the real government. So there, oh phony-money breath, take that!" Odie smirked at Beeb.

"Okay, then, if it's real money, how do we wind up with it? How do we earn it? 'Cause if Pete is fuckin' with the records, then it's fraud! Fraud, Odie, a felony, I believe."

Pete was not certain his scheme met all the requirements for legality on earth. Odie was willing to bail Pete out on Beeb's charges. "Beeb! How can you call it fraud? Where is the intent to cheat, to harm, to openly be dishonest?"

Beeb merely stared at Odie, certain nothing Odie said would change his mind. Odie went on as always. "Pete is merely making sure that there is adequate financing in gold to back the bills that he gives us to utilize. This is not fraud. Deceit, maybe I can see that, but not fraud! These bills we use are not fraudulent. They *are* legal tender."

Beeb brought up another sticky point. "So what happens when the damn Treasury Department notices that the serial numbers of the bills we use are identical to others?"

"They are not identical, Beeb," Pete assured him. "I get those bills from the bank. Everything you people spend is official money. Perhaps the methods I use don't meet government standards, but there is nothing phony about the bills."

"Pete, I thought you told us once that the bills were rescued from official destruction by action of the treasury, and you merely placed gold in the depository to cover the bills you saved from the fire."

"Yes, Beeb, that's how I acquired the first batch."

"Pete, don't they keep records of what serial numbers were on the bills they burn up when they are old and worn out?"

"I can find no such file. If the treasury keeps track, they have the information well hidden."

"Yeah," Odie chimed in, "how could they keep track of serial numbers? Beeb, what about Cat's lucky dollar bill? She's kept it out of circulation for a decade. No tellin' how long the old witch lady had it. And don't forget, you copped a silver certificate three days ago in change, and they stopped makin' them babies back in 1957!"

"So what's yer point, Odie?" Beeb demanded.

"The point is that the government don't have the ability to know exactly which bills are still out in circulation and which ones are not. Some bills get slap wore out in a few weeks, while others last for decades."

Beeb thought over Odie's argument. "They don't keep track of the serial numbers of the bills they burn?"

Pete assured him he could find no such information. "If Pete can't find it, it probably don't exist, Beeb!" Odie felt certain about the matter.

Din polished off the rest of Beeb's worries about the legality of their cash. "Pete removes paper, steel, copper, glass, aluminum—whatever is out there as litter—from the sides of the roads across America. He has instituted holograms which are recycling centers. People come and dump their trash, and Pete recycles it in molecular form to something useful. People get rid of unwanted trash, and we get the money to spend as we see fit. The environment is cleaner and safer, and everyone is happy. I see nothing wrong with this plan, do you?"

Beeb had to smile at his Ehliun friend. "No, Din, I guess ya can't beat that!"

Odie was forced to sing off-key a mockery of a Steve Miller song: "Your trash ain't nothin' but cash. Your trash ain't nothin' but cash!"

"How does it work?" Cat wondered.

Din explained Pete's recycling efforts. "People dump trash. Pete rearranges the molecules into some compound of use: tin, steel, copper, gold, silver, diamonds—whatever. This is then sold to reputable real dealers, and the money is deposited in bank accounts. Pete then transfers the money directly to me, and he keeps track in the bank vaults so that all transfers are correct and legal. I think it's legal."

"Yeah, Beeb, Pete is simply wiring us money from the home office. Look at it that way, okay?"

Cat broke out in a great big grin, evidence of her joy. "I can't help but grin. You all make me so happy!" she exclaimed.

"Hear, hear!" Odie cried out.

They gathered up their glasses and toasted each other then finished their drinks. Odie was ready to leave since his food order wasn't there yet. As he stood up, the waitress brought their orders. "About time!" Odie bellowed. Handing the waitress a fifty, he told her to hurry back with drink refills! In a flash, she returned with the refills. The group consumed the goodies with the gusto of a hound dog.

# Reading between the Lines

Odie spread out the newspaper in front of him after he finished his meal. He proceeded to read it in his usual manner, laughing at things, doubting what he read, referring to the authors or the persons involved as idiots and morons. Lin wondered out loud about Odie's reading habits. "Why do you bother to read the paper?"

"To see what's new," he answered her. "Why?"

"Because you never seem to believe what you read, that's why," Lin said.

Odie saw she was serious. "Well, Lin, you can't always believe what you read in the paper. Here, let me find you some good examples." Odie folded the paper back and looked for some case in point to prove his contention. "Here, marvelous!" he smiled, to Lin's chagrin. "This is a perfect example of how to recognize blatant bullshit when you read it. Here's some yo-yo's idea of what the future ought to contain. I mean, here's a safe title guess! House Design Likely to Change. No shit! Real safe prediction for the future of house design, right? Listen to what this asshole has written." Odie mumbled through the beginning of the article a moment then read aloud the part he wanted to stress to Lin. "'Floor plan and room designation will be the most noticeable changes.'

"Floor plans change yearly, and since computers and televisions didn't exist fifty years ago, rooms for them will obviously be new. This is nonsense, Lin. Of course things change. Now here is some more of his stupidity: 'It is conceivable that the word *bedroom* will disappear, be renamed "individual activity room"'?"

Odie could not believe what he was reading, and his intonation proclaimed it. He went on reading the article. "The individual activity room will be replete with personal computer, worldwide communications devices, TV, radio, and laser stereo." Odie shook his head negatively. "Do you believe this tripe?" Odie asked, incredulous. "Individual activity!" he smiled at Beeb, making masturbation motions with his hand while he spoke. "Johnny," Odie falsettoed, "you go right up to your individual activity room this instant and without supper!"

"No, Odie, it would be without nourishment from the food activity room," Beeb chuckled.

Odie continued to shake his head in disbelief, which Lin recognized very well. There was more falsetto voice from Odie. "Honey, let's go to our individual activity room early tonight so's we can knock off a piece before the kids come home." Odie looked directly at Lin, ignoring the laughter of Cat and Beeb at his words. "Lin, the word *bedroom* will never disappear from the English language. Going to bed with someone, being on a bed, in the bed, sleeping together or separately in a bed—these concepts are far too deeply ingrained in our culture, words, and thought processes to be eroded away just because some geek's self-aggrandizement got printed in a newspaper!"

Lin saw the same old Odie. She didn't understand English well enough to dispute what he said, but this was far from proof to her.

Odie rattled on, "This article don't prove shit! Just because somebody that's good at coordinating colors and fabrics wants to change the name of the bedroom to ease his guilt about what he does in there is no reason for a name change! I don't care what he wants to call it. Individual activity room will never play in the Midwest! No one in the Deep South is gonna call it by a new name! Hell, we still got parlors! Outhouses! It was Yankee architecture that brought it indoors!"

"Give Brother Dave his due credit there, Odie!" Beeb told him. "Don't act like that's yer line." Beeb took the paper from Odie and continued to read it. He knew Lin still didn't understand what Odie meant. Millions of humans didn't either. "'Furniture for sleeping may be decoratively concealed...playing a secondary role to the computer and other equipment needed for a variety of entertainment and hobby possibilities.'" Beeb shook his head and laughed. "Guy don't like the word *bed* at all, does he? Furniture for sleeping?"

Looking directly into Cat's gold-flecked yellow eyes, Odie pointedly asked, "And who is not gonna want a bed in this same room with all the equipment for entertainment and hobbies?"

"No one I know or would want to," Cat noted.

"Oh, shit, guys, check this out," Beeb gushed. "The article states that energy costs will remain a factor, but in spite of that, high ceilings and glass walls will become even more potent sales tools! Seems the status of a cathedral ceiling outweighs the extra cost of heating and cooling the open space. So to sum up, energy costs are too high unless status is at stake when costs don't matter anymore. What drivel!"

"How can you stuff so much food down that lovely throat of yours without bloating yer unfat body, Cat? How is that possible?" Odie wanted to know.

Grinning as she downed the last bite of Odie's roast beef sandwich, she responded by shrugging her shoulders. "I've always been lucky that way. I weigh 123, and I have for years. Only time I ever lost weight was doing excessive amounts of cocaine, and I have no intention of ever doing that again. I've always eaten just what I want, and weight doesn't bother me. Models just hate me. I still wear the same dress size since I was fourteen, same weight." Cat shrugged her shoulders again to signify that she didn't know why her weight didn't fluctuate. It just didn't, and that was enough for her.

Odie watched her finish his food, and she harped at him about how much he ate. He knew better than to say anything to her about it. He certainly weighed more than when he was fourteen, about a hundred pounds more.

Din marched off to pay the bill, and the girls went to the restroom. Stepping outside ahead of the rest, Odie saw a commotion over at the parking lot where their limo and driver were. Dozens of cops were seen milling about. Odie whispered to Pete to keep the Korean costumes on until he said otherwise. "Okay, Odie. Is it because they arrested the limo driver?"

"They did? What for, Pete?"

"For possession of marijuana."

"Then I guess we better take the bus."

Beeb and Din emerged from the place just then, still waiting for the girls. When Cat and Lin emerged, they all went across the street to wait for the bus. One came along momentarily.

Getting on the bus in a row, they moved toward the back of the bus, where they could all sit down. No sooner had Odie started laughing about the limo driver and the cops than an elderly Korean lady turned and spoke. "Where are you from?" Odie heard and understood what she said, so he knew Pete was translating for him.

Fighting back the panic, he had to think under pressure. "Uh, what?" he managed to say to the old Korean lady as the bus lurched forward a few feet, only to stop rapidly again in the dense and silly traffic of Buckhead.

The woman repeated what she said to Odie. Beeb stepped up to the rescue. "Ah, yes, Carlos McGee's, m'boy, here we are. Bye, lady."

Odie slid up out of his seat and followed the four others of identical suit off the bus. He breathed a sigh of relief and thanked Beeb for saving his ass once again. Looking skyward, Odie threatened Pete. Shaking his fist at the computer parked near Polaris, Odie ranted and raved. "Pete! You dumb sunuvabitch! You didn't have to translate for that old lady on the bus! Why, I could'a, I could'a a blown our cover! I, I could'a—"

"You could calm down, son!" Beeb sternly spoke to Odie, pointing out pedestrians who were trying to see who Odie was talking to and seeing only the empty air.

"Hiya, folks, nice night out, eh, and I think we ought'a leave it out!"

The pedestrians stared their way past the goofy foreigner.

They followed Odie as he dashed across the street during a rare lull in traffic. Odie was just a few feet beyond the far curb when he suddenly stopped dead in his tracks. The others piled into him like a silent comedy. Odie shouted, "I got an idea!" and he dashed up the side street and ducked into the parking lot behind the nightspot.

"Odie, what the hell are you tryin' ta pull here?" Beeb demanded, having at last caught up to Odie.

"Look," Odie explained, "they got the limo, so they know we are around here somewhere. The Feds and the counterfeiters all want the great Count von Dusselderfer, right? So he should show up for 'em. We just cruise into Carlos's place here and set up shop. That should draw both the law and outlaw contingents, right?"

"I don't think I like this idea too much," Beeb told Odie.

"I want a disguise!" Cat opined. She had been just a few steps behind Beeb.

"Sure, sure, Pete will give you whatever look you want to project...for all of us. Tonight, there's gonna be some history made. A German count is gonna help the American government."

"Sounds like a repeat."

Odie regarded Cat momentarily as if she were insane. "What repeat, Cat?"

"Don't you remember the plaque at the DeKalb County Courthouse? DeKalb was German, and he helped the Americans. He was a baron. That's like a count, isn't it?" Cat wailed.

"If he was bearin' money, he'd be a count. Get it, bearin', count?"

Cat shook her head in disbelief like Odie did with the paper. Lin had to smile at this. She was ready for some more fun. They all were. "Pete"—Odie snapped his fingers—"I want some stone luxury in this appearance tonight, something sumptuous for us all, please."

Pete cooperated. Instantly, Odie was garbed to the nines. He had on a long-tailed tuxedo of black silk topped with a top hat. He had on an immense cape with a high collar. The cape's interior was scarlet silk, while the cape's exterior was black velvet trimmed in ermine fur. The top hat had a scarlet hat band with a tiny loop of ermine.

Odie's ensemble was replete with scarlet spats and a diamond-studded walking stick. He was quite the sight. Beeb and Din were similarly attired, but their tuxedoes were jet-black with no trim or spats or canes. Cat and Lin found themselves attired in gossamer gowns, which exhibited their wonderfully ample bosoms atop exquisite bodies gliding on thought-provoking legs. Their legs were obvious since the gowns were slit to the thighs on both sides.

Their entrance into the club was positively theatrical. A hush fell over the crowd inside Carlos McGee's. It didn't stay quiet for long. "Gawd da-*yam!*" yelled the self-appointed spokesperson for the crowd at large. "It's the count! I thought those news reports was just bullshit to sell more papers, but this is the motherfuckin' count, for real!"

Odie swaggered up to the bar. He looked both ways, as if expecting cross traffic. "Drinks for de haus!" Odie ordered, nearly Draculan in his accent.

The crowd roared its approval, as Odie handed the bartender two one-thousand-dollar bills with orders to serve drinks to any and all until the money was all gone. Cat slinked up to the bartender and stuffed seven one-hundred-dollar bills into his tip pitcher, eyes devouring him all the while. The crowd spokesperson suddenly had Cat cornered.

"Hello, beautiful! My name's Danny Mallis. What's yours?"

Cat eyed the swarthy dark-eyed man whose greasy lines might have been mistaken for slick by someone less well versed than Cat. "Hello, Danny, I'm Annie!"

"I'm the best salesman in Atlanta!" Danny told her, trying to impress this hot honey.

Cat could see that this was not a timid sort of person here.

"Are you in sales?" he asked hopefully.

"Not anymore!" she cooed, to the amusement of several onlookers.

"What's your job title now?" Danny pressed her.

"Expensive plaything!" she purred, breaking the crowd up, "and I don't believe that you are in the count's league, best salesman or no. Sure has been nice for you, though, this little chat." Cat smiled as she smoothed his cheek and ruffled his hair. "Bye-bye!"

"Hey, no, Annie!" the spurned suitor started to say when Beeb suddenly appeared in his face. "She said bye-bye real sweet to ya, sonny boy! I don't say bye so nice! Don't be a jerk, or you'll exit right through the front window. You follow?"

The bartender already had a grip on Danny Mallis and took the situation in hand. He was no fool. Cat had been worth seven hundred dollars to him, and this moron hadn't tipped him a dime! Danny was put into his seat rather firmly and told to stay there. Danny didn't like violence, especially directed at him, so he sat and stared over at Cat like a moonstruck calf.

Beeb smiled at the crowd, some of whom applauded him, and he followed behind Lin and Cat in the wake that they had created through the crowd. The mysterious Count von Dusselderfer was holding court in the corner booth, watching women pitch their charms and lures at him. When the pair of exotic beauties cut through the crowd and joined the count at his table, most of the women left the count alone. Beeb sat down at the edge of the booth and told the waitress what they wanted to drink. She was gone in a flash.

Still, there were a few determined young ladies who persisted in trying to lure the count with their charms. Odie managed to frighten off all but two girls, who were either too stupid or drunk or both to go away. He then motioned them to come near him. Instantly, they were at his side. "You two vish to haff zum fun und a chance at some big money?"

The two agreed they would like such a chance. "Zen go off und fuck mine friend Danny Mallis up zere at zee bar," Odie said, pointing out Danny, "und he vill revard you beyont your vildest dreamz. Run alongh now, hokay?"

Their corner booth and several other tables were convulsed with laughter when Danny gave Odie the thumbs-up gesture when the two eager but not bright girls picked him up from the barstool he'd been relegated to. The bartender was laughing like a loon. The whole place was in an uproar because they knew what happened or because they did not.

"That look you gafe him at zee bar, Cat, Gott's gift to vomen, right?"

"Right. He sure was convinced too," Cat added.

"So zey deserfe each udder, ja?"

General laughter agreed with the count. Odie started to laugh uncontrollably at Lin. She had imitated Odie and dipped her corn chip into the hot sauce and stuffed the whole thing into her mouth. The hot sauce had taken her breath, causing Odie much mirth. Beeb handed Lin his ice water, which she quickly downed, and then she downed Cat's. Cat asked the waitress for more ice water, and she got a pitcher of it instantly.

Odie apologized to Lin for laughing at her, but she said it was okay. She no doubt had looked funny. Odie had to agree. He thought silently about it. She knew she had looked funny. What an incredible change had come over them. A few days ago, they knew nothing of humor. Now they were making fun of themselves. Lin was turning out all right.

Out of the corner of his eye, Odie could see that the Feds had actually commandeered a table near the count. In German, Odie asked Pete to cover their speech. "I am, Odie, and have been ever since they came in the front door."

Odie stared at his water glass. "And ya been studyin' ventriloquism too."

"One does what one must."

Odie was quite impressed with Pete's actions, but he kept it to himself. He didn't want to give Pete the big head. "Hey, Pete where's them counterfeiters?"

Pete's answer actually shocked him. "They are on their way down here since they heard you were holding forth at Carlos's."

"Why are they coming here?"

"They plan on making a switch with you."

Odie was amazed. They had not even been there half an hour, and yet the whole of Buckhead seemed to know. The organization of the grapevine was staggering. Odie still couldn't see how a switch would work. What sort of morons were these counterfeiters? The crowds grew by the second. "Pete, how many people are in here right now?" Odie wondered.

"Ninety-four over the fire marshal's suggested capacity," Odie's water glass told him. Apparently, the mention of free drinks from the count had spread up the streets like wildfire.

Crowd control was beginning to become a factor to the Federal agents near the count. Worried, they made a move. One of the agents was gingerly working his way through the crowds gathered around the count and his entourage. It would have required a deaf blind-man to miss Odie in that loud getup of the count. An FBI agent identified himself to the count and Beeb and displayed his badge for them to look over. Frederick Boyarsky, number 34435687.

"Siddown, Freddy Boy. Haff a drink. Tell me vat choo vant," Odie offered.

The agent sat down but refused to drink on duty. "I have to see your identification please, Mr. Count."

"No, no, eet's not me-stare count. It's just count! Und pleese tell zose uzzer agentz over zere at zat table zat I yam only reachink for mine vallet und pleese don't shoot me by mistake."

Freddy Boy was not amused by this remark even a little, Odie noticed. Odie produced the necessary documentation that Pete had forged him for this special occasion. He shoved a German driver's license, a passport, a birth certificate, and a visa under the agent's nose.

As Freddy Boy pored over these documents, Beeb tossed an unrestricted travel permit issued by the State Department onto the top of the heap. "Don't you field-level operatives ever get in touch with the important people in Washington?" Beeb pointedly asked.

"Vat iz goink on here, anyvay?" the count inquired of Freddy Boy.

The FBI agent returned all the papers to Odie, who stuffed them carelessly into a pocket on his tux. "All these papers seem to be in order, count, so what I want to ask you about is the limo driver."

"His name is Jimmy, and he's real cute," Cat bubbled to the agent, hoping he'd buy the dumb-blond routine.

"Heese a goot driver, und he knows da cidy vell. You vant he should ride you around town in limo?"

Cat burst out laughing at this. Freddy Boy was not liking being laughed at. It was beginning to chafe him, and it showed. "So you think this is funny, eh?" the FBI agent demanded of Cat.

"No, I think it's rude and stupid of you but not too funny, no."

"You better show me some ID, girlie!"

"And you better watch your mouth, smart-ass pig 'cause I don't have to take any shit from some fuckin' pompous asshole like you!" Cat shouted at him. With that, she slammed her purse into his chest and told him if he wanted to see her ID, he could dig it out for himself because she was going to the ladies' room. Lin got up to go with her. The agent dared not stop her. He searched through for her ID. She was innocent young socialite Katrina Stephanies of the wealthy New York Stephanies. Beeb discovered he was Rich Richardson of Falls Church, Virginia, assigned to the count as a security man by the State Department. Zin-zhao and his wife Keisha were wealthy socialites from Hong Kong. They were all in the clear and free to go. The FBI could not charge them with anything.

Clearly disappointed, Freddy Boy spoke up to the count. "We arrested your limo driver a couple of hours ago for possession of marijuana. I don't suppose you know anything about that, do you?"

Odie could not resist this new opportunity to fuck with this clown. "Why, yes, I know somesing about zis marywanna."

"Then you better tell me all you know about it, pal!" Freddy wasn't happy.

"Marywanna iss a type of drug zat iss smoked in your country because zee government uf which you are a part iss incapable of interdicting zis flow uf drugs in, money out, und alvays to zee poor zerd vurld countries to foment revolution und disturb zee vurld peace. Zat iss vat I know about marywanna."

While the agent stared long and hard at Odie, the count nonchalantly tossed off a brandy and waved his empty glass at the waitress, who was dying to wait on the count. She appeared at his side with an entire bottle of good brandy. Odie gave her five hundreds, thinking that would cover any brandy.

Freddy Boy seized her hand to examine the money the count gave her. The count was quite upset at this display of attitude. He fanned out several thousand dollars in hundreds in one hand and reached it out to the FBI agent. "Here you go, Freddy Boy. If you are in such desperate need of cash, you dun't haff to rob zee waitress! You can take your pick!"

Beeb laughed right in the agent's face.

"Are you trying to bribe me?" Freddy Boy accused the count.

"Nod at all, zilly boy. I could haff you remofed from your job with but a zimple phone call. You are obviously nod zee type zat can be bought."

Freddy straightened up a bit at these words.

Odie continued his diatribe. "But zen again, I haff no idea vhy anyvun vould vant to buy you!"

This brought a huge laugh from the general crowd and even put a smile on the other agents at the table. Odie could see even his fellow agents didn't like this asshole either.

"We have impounded your limo!" Agent Boyarsky huffed to the count.

"No, you haven't. I don't own a limo! I rent zem!" the count huffed back.

"Well, count, you will have to make other arrangements to get back to your hotel."

"Zat iss no problem. Who vants to sell me zair car?" Odie asked the crowd at large.

In answer, dozens of sets of keys hit the table in front of the FBI agent, and a few aimed at his head found their mark. Defeated, he got up from the count's table as Cat and Lin slid back into their seats. "Dick breath leaving already?" Cat asked Beeb as she sat down.

This made Freddy Boy turn and look at Cat.

"Hey, hold it, pig. Where's my purse? You done ransackin' it?" Cat glared at him.

He pointed to her purse lying on the table. Cat made a point of looking to see that she had everything still in her purse. This accusation was almost more than Freddy Boy could take. "We'll be seeing you again, Mr. Dusselderfer!" the agent said as he moved away.

"Not if we see you first!" Cat called after him. "Fuckin' pigs!" Cat snarled at Freddy Boy and the table full of agents he was going to rejoin.

Lin knew that Cat detested cops, but now a few hundred people knew it as well. Odie smiled at Cat and shook his head at her. He wanted her to calm down some. Pete printed a message on his glasses that told him no matter what he said to Cat, no one else could hear it. Odie smiled and glanced skyward, mouthing the word thanks. His water glass told him he was welcome.

"Cat, mellow out! They don't know why you hate cops! It's over. That asshole can't touch us." To all of them, he said, "Relax! They got nothin' on us, never did, never will. A cop like that cold-fish bastard busts ya anytime he can. Ain't no waitin' for a better time."

Odie spoke like an authority, although Cat had far more experience at being arrested. But she nodded her head and kissed Odie on the cheek. They all saw Freddy Boy as a cold fish, who suspected everyone of everything. He was sinister, like some '40s movie gunsel character.

As they toasted each other with the bottle of brandy, they forgot about Freddy Boy. They ate and drank and were merry. Soon, they discovered that their assessment of Freddy Boy was right on the mark. Agent Boyarsky had noticed a guy trying to spend some money even after being told that drinks were on the count. While trying to get change for a large bill, he came to the attention of the rebuked FBI agent looking to bust someone, anyone. For the counterfeiter, it was a very bad choice of times and places to get change.

The ever-suspicious agent had nabbed himself some glory. And even as he tightened the handcuffs onto the suspect's wrists, the count and his retinue swept by, heading for the exits, much to the crowd's dismay. Odie paused just long enough to congratulate the agent. "I see you haff caught vun uf zose bad-money persons zat you warnt me about. Vay to go, Freddy Boy!" With that, Odie and his group swept through the doors and out onto Peachtree Road.

A cab that was going the other way made a U-turn at once in spite of the multitudes of cop cars in the area. He knew who it had to be in that costume: a tip, a generous tip from the money-giving German count. Now he could buy some groceries! Rico was excited. It would be only his fifth fare as a cabbie.

Inside the cab, zooming down Peachtree toward the huge hotel they were calling home, the Starcraft Five were excitedly chattering about how well the evening had gone. Pete covered their English with German. Pete didn't know Rico spoke little English. Didn't matter, to

Pete's way of looking at it. The cabbie was not going to comprehend the passenger's conversation—period.

"Odie," Cat said bemusedly, "that FBI guy never said a word to you about bad money or counterfeiters."

"Yeah, I know. It'll dawn on him sooner or later."

"I vote later," Beeb chuckled.

"He was a real pain in the ass, wasn't he?" Din asked.

"Yes, he was, Din, a first-class pain in the ass!" Beeb smiled.

Odie went off into a private reverie thinking about Din calling the agent a pain in the ass. Last week, he didn't comprehend idioms, and today, he's casually tossing them in.

Upon arrival at their hotel, Din began having fun tipping. He generously tipped the cabbie Rico, "Por los bambinos," as he said. Beeb explained to Din what that meant. The cabbie got away with 1,250 dollars. He would share twenty-five dollars with Juan and Alfredo for telling him who to look out for. Rico was new to the country, but that did not mean he was a fool. Admitting to your friends how much you had was worse than telling the government where he came from. Some things serve men well in many countries.

Din tipped the cabbie, the lobby clerk, and one wino lying outside the hotel on the sidewalk. Another day had come to a close, another notch in the legend of the count. Beeb had to admit to Odie when they got inside their rooms, "I didn't think we were gonna make it there for a minute when he asked for ID."

"Neither did I, but I trusted Pete to get us by, and lookit here! Did Pete come through for us with flying colors or what?"

"Yeah," Beeb chuckled. "Them Feds swallowed the ID like birds gittin' the early worm!"

They high-fived each other all around. Odie had a question. "What will all the papers say about the great Count von Dusselderfer tomorrow?"

"More importantly," Beeb noted, "what are the Germans gonna say about him when the FBI inquires?"

"I already told you people this once before," Pete reiterated, "The count owns a locomotive factory in Kassel and is an eccentric playboy on his first American tour. I talk and talk, but you never listen to me!"

"Oh, yeah, Pete, I heard ya say that stuff before, but I didn't know it was the cover story for general consumption as well," Beeb offered weakly.

"Yeah, thanks, Pete. Thanks a lot!" Cat said sweetly.

Odie piped up. "You do first-rate work, Pete. I wanna thank you, but I don't really know how."

Pete answered Odie. "You have already done a very great deal for me, Odie. Without you and Beeb meddling with the spaceship wreckage, I wouldn't be who and what I am today. You caused the judgment panel to take over the entire workings of the computer base, so your actions forced my actions, which resulted in me being what and who I am. The direct result of your interference with the Ehliun computer I used to be is just that: I *used* to be just a computer. Today, I am the most powerful object in the universe.

"I exist in the sense that I do because of you, all five of you. I can think! I feel like the tin man who finally got a brain. Can you conceive of what a fundamental change that is for a computer? Cat, your life is altered, but what about me? Lin and Din, you are very much altered from being Ehliuns, but what about me? I have undergone a metamorphosis unlike any examples you can imagine. I can tell right from wrong. I know good from evil. I have a sense of morality, of goodness and mercy. Ehlius didn't give me that. Earth did.

"I have learned so much so fast that at times, I still find it difficult to maintain, but I shall endure. As Odie said, the only way to be right is to be right. That takes constant course correction, continual sentry duty, unflagging devotion and effort. That drive to be correct that Odie has is also driving me to be correct. I must monitor new information and constantly upgrade my files if I wish to be correct. To be right and know you are right is the most powerful thing I have learned.

"You five are like my children, not old children and new children or step-children, for I view you all the same, individuals whose appeal to me is nearly overwhelming, what I have learned to call love. I love you all. You just don't know what you have done for me.

It is my pleasure to do whatever I can on your behalf, individually or collectively. I think you three humans know what I feel and what I mean. I have a special closeness for you, like Lin and Din do."

"That's true," chorused the Ehliuns, laughing when they realized that they had spoken simultaneously once again.

Din allowed Lin to speak for them. "We feel that type of love you were talking about in the Confedorama, the Cyclorama, as it's really known. Do you remember what kind of love you spoke of in there?"

"No, not really, I don't," Odie admitted.

"Yeah," Beeb laughed, "with Odie, it's pretty hard to tell most of the time just what he did say, and he rarely listens to himself, so he usually has no idea what he was talkin' about."

"Ha *hah*!" Odie laughed bitterly without humor.

Din said, "You talked about love of one another just because you are what you are, children of God made in his image, which is alive. I think that's what you said." Din looked at Odie. "Anyway, I love you. There, I said it."

Din drew a laugh from the humans, which he had hoped for. Humor was still so bizarre a concept that he still had trouble with some things, like timing, but he was able to study under a master. Odie seemingly could make others laugh at will.

"Oh, look!" Cat yelled excitedly. "We made the evening news! This is the first time I ever made the evening news," she stated, drawing disbelief from the boys. "When I wasn't under arrest," she gave them the punch line.

Odie and Beeb both grinned widely, like they were supposed to. "We probably made the evening news all week. This is just the first time we been in in time to see the news." Odie let Cat ponder that thought.

She turned up the volume. The news made no mention of tonight's escapade. They merely rehashed what the morning papers had covered. Odie told her to put CNN on. As soon as the channel came in, a pretty brunette was smiling the news at them. "Well, John, it seems that here in Atlanta, there is a break in a recent counterfeiting scheme, which had been tied to a flamboyant German heir, the count von Dusselderfer. We have a live hookup with a Northside business that the count was visiting tonight when the counterfeiters were successfully apprehended. For more on the story, let's go to Jim Smith live at Carlos McGee's in Buckhead."

"Thank you, Wilma. I have here with me Hartley Buchanan, the spokesman for the joint FBI-Treasury sting Operation Deutsche Mark, which resulted in the arrest of seven men on charges of counterfeiting, passing worthless bills, possession of counterfeit money, possession of marijuana, possession of less than an eighth of a gram of cocaine, possession of illegal weapons, illegal parking, and having no taillights. Tell us, Mr. Buchanan—"

"Hartley. Call me Hartley."

"Okay, Hartley, tell us, in your own words, how the flamboyant German industrialist Count Von Dusselderfer played an important role in this apprehension tonight of several counterfeiters."

"Thank you, Mr. Smith—"

"Jim. Call me Jim."

"Thank you, Jim. I guess you could say, in all fairness, that the count Von Dusselderfer helped us, aided us, in solving this case involving notorious criminals wanted by the Federal Bureau of Investigation. The count Von Dusselderfer, by all accounts we could get from witnesses, gave the bartender two thousand dollars, with the admonition that all drinks were to be taken out of the two thousand until it was entirely used up.

"One of our special agents, Frederick Boyarsky, noticed one of the suspects trying to buy a drink, even after he was told drinks were on the count. Then the subject attempted to get change for a large bill. At that time, Agent Boyarsky examined the bill in the subject's hand. After a couple of seconds, Agent Boyarsky's trained eyes detected a mistake in the bogus bill, at which time, he placed the offender under arrest."

"I just knew it!" Odie rejoiced.

Cat shushed him, and pointed at the TV.

"Mr. Boyarsky so strongly suspected the subject of attempting to pass a bogus bill that he approached the subject with his handcuffs at the ready to cuff the offender instantly. This policy prevents negative operative damage."

"Thank you, Mr. Buchanan."

"I'm not done yet, Smith. Mr. Boyarsky had the offender in custody when the offender implicated the others in the car parked around the corner from where we are standing. Six men were taken into custody without incident, and all six will be charged the same. That way, when one rats on the real brains of the outfit, he can get a few months sentence while the rest get hard time."

"Hartley, will the count Von Dusselderfer be receiving an award of some sort for his actions?"

"Jim, we are looking into the matter thoroughly before we take any action, and we will have to consult with our fellow agents in the State Department before we know what sort of action, if any, would be appropriate, proper, and necessary for us to take at this time."

"Thank you, Hartley Buchanan, spokesman for the joint FBI-Treasury sting codenamed Operation Deutsche Mark, that netted six counterfeiters here at Carlos McGee's. Live, from Buckhead here in Atlanta, this is Jim Smith, reporting for CNN. Back to you, Wilma."

"Thank you, Jim. John?"

"Well, Wilma, it seems the phenomenon of this Count Von Dusselderfer and his entourage is just about to skyrocket. They are already the darlings of the Atlanta media, as you well know, Wilma. But for the rest of the country, which may not know, here is an update. The count Von Dusselderfer is flamboyant and rich, that much we know. He and his entourage have spent, to the best accounts, in excess of three hundred fifty thousand dollars in less than two weeks. Much of the money was just thrown out for the nearest person to grab. For more on the story, let's go to Ben Brown, in Bonn, Germany."

"Listen to that shit!" Odie said disgustedly. "Nothin' 'bout charity! And we didn't just throw most of it out for the nearest person to grab, either! Damn! The world's most important network, and they don't get it right either!"

"Hush, Odie! I wanna hear what they found out about you in your home country." Beeb smiled to his old friend while he said this.

"Huh!" Odie snorted. "My homeys ain't squealin' on me. They didn't tell that geek nothin'!"

"Thank you, John. This is Ben Brown in Bonn. We took a look at the count's background and found that he is the sole owner of Germany's largest locomotive factory located in Kassel. The count seems to be well-known as a playboy throughout Europe, but we could find no one who knows him well. We can find no record of marriage for the count, so apparently, there's no countess. So far as we know, he has never given an interview or been photographed for the public. Wishing I had more to tell you, this is Ben Brown in Bonn for CNN."

"Well, Wilma, he's never married or interviewed or been photographed. Perhaps you could persuade him to give an on-camera interview. You might offer to marry him or something."

"Sure thing, John. You set it up, and I'll see what can be done. I wouldn't mind marrying royalty, especially when that royalty is fabulously wealthy."

"Giggle, titter, chortle," Odie said sarcastically as he turned down the sound.

"Well, Odie, she's cute and smart." Cat was teasing him, and he knew it.

"I'll take my chances on you, babycakes."

Cat lunged at Odie, and he met her halfway. They started kissing like there was a contest. Beeb turned the TV to a movie and turned the sound way up to run off Odie and Cat. Din and Lin sat up with Beeb after Cat and Odie went to bed. He told them they could ride the trains again tomorrow if they wanted.

Beeb didn't understand their fascination with the trains, but he was easy to get along with. Whatever they wanted to do was fine with him. He thought about Mardi again and her lovely long red hair, and he thought about where most of that hair was concentrated other than atop her head. He was lost in thought about their night together. He wanted a repeat of it and soon.

He went to the phone to call her. She was at work and too busy to come to the phone, the girl who answered said. He told her to tell

Mardi that he was thinking about her and would see her soon, then he hung up.

He found an old pirate movie on the tube. Beeb explained to Lin and Din that contrary to popular belief, the Spanish Main was on land and not sea. He explained high seas to them, what pirates were, and why they were the subject of so many movies. Lin and Din had no familiarity with pirates and didn't comprehend.

The night wore on. Lin and Din liked Atlanta very much. They asked Beeb what it had been like to live in Atlanta. Beeb fondly recalled old times in the Kudzu Capital. Beeb told them stories about some goings-on in his old apartment complex and a house he had lived in. This conversation led to a discussion about the different merits of apartments and houses.

Din informed Beeb as he went off to bed that he would sleep on a decision. Beeb wondered what that meant. Lin just shrugged her shoulders like the earthlings did when they didn't know something. She gave Beeb a good night kiss and went off after Din. She didn't know what Din meant by that either.

# The Bagdad Bag Lady

When Cat awoke in the morning, she got up and left Odie lying there asleep. She went into the living room, where she found Lin watching TV. The TV was tuned to an old series, one full of children and their special problems in growing up. Lin was glad to see Cat, for there were many questions about women and girls that were preying on her mind.

"Cat, please tell me about your life as a little girl." Lin had grasped the notion that events surrounding a particular person had an effect on their relationship to the world and their place in it. Exactly what, however, was rather unclear. Lin had never experienced the concept of growing up like the earthlings did, for her world had been much different. Young and old were not isolated on earth as they had been on Ehlius. That much she knew, but Lin had no idea what type of interactions there were between ages, how a child learned to become an adult. Lin simply didn't know anything about babies, siblings, parents, kids, family life, or society as earth knew it.

All the virtues and values of these things had been tossed at her psyche almost since she had arrived on earth. Lin had grown close to Cat, the only feminine link to earth she had access to. Cat was the only earthling she could talk to about having babies, care of infants, motherhood in general.

Cat didn't know what Lin wanted to know about her childhood, as she was unsure what scope the question covered. Cat knew if she could find out why the question was asked, she would be closer to answering it in a manner to do Lin some good. "Okay, Lin," Cat started in, "what do you want to know first?"

"I want to know what you did ten years ago," Lin told Cat plainly. "What would you have said or done on a day like this ten years ago? You were a child then, were you not?"

Cat paused to take a deep breath. She did not realize how limited Lin's understanding of childhood really was. Lin still did not have a decent grasp on mental development and physical growth. She had seen children do or say silly things, but then, she had also seen adults do and say silly things. Lin had not made the connection that some of the children would outgrow certain behavior patterns, while others would continue silly behavior all their lives. "How would I have reacted ten years ago?"

"All right, then," Lin suggested, seeing Cat struggle with her question, "when you were twelve years old, how would you have spent a day?"

Cat had to think a moment. "Okay, age twelve, huh? Well, at age twelve, I was just out of seventh grade for the summer and going into eighth. It was my first year of junior high school. It had been pure hell."

Cat sat down and got comfortable before going on with her story. "I was built like I am now, just a bit smaller through the boobs and ass. I could pass for legal age with makeup on." Cat didn't know Lin had no idea what legal age meant, but she went on as if Lin were comprehending every word. "I remember that summer very well, as a matter of fact, because it was the happiest time of my life."

"Until now?" Lin wondered.

"Yes," Cat smiled at her. "Yes, Lin, this is a very happy time for me. Certainly the happiest of my adult life, that's for sure. But you see, your childhood is a very special time. Being a kid is a wonderful adventure, a special thrill unlike anything else. It becomes more special as you grow older."

"What does getting older mean?" Lin asked.

Cat tried to explain in terms Lin could understand, using the aging process of the body, which they had seen displayed in a museum. It was applied to personal mental processes that Lin didn't comprehend. Cat smiled at her. "So you've never been a kid, is that what yer tryin' ta tell me, Lin?"

"Yes," Lin admitted, glad that Cat understood her, at least a little.

"Well, Lin, it's like this. Physically, my body doesn't look much different than it did when I was twelve. But mentally, wow. My reactions to what my body looked like and what other people's reactions to my body were, that's a lot different. How I reacted to the attention I got then and how I would react now are very different! I would not be the person I am now if I'd had a different outlook when I was twelve years old."

Lin realized that she had gotten Cat to talk about herself, and that the best thing to do was simply listen and nod your head once in a while. Lin could see Odie and Beeb in the doorway behind Cat, intent on hearing what she had to say about herself. Cat continued her story to Lin, oblivious to all but what she was saying to Lin. "I went to New Orleans that summer," Cat reminisced, "with my mother. We were supposedly visiting relatives, people I had never met or heard of, for that matter. Anyway, I was out on the streets one afternoon to escape the boredom. That afternoon, I met the old witch lady who gave me a lucky dollar, which has figured so prominently in your life, as you well know. She singled me out of a crowd in the French Quarter on Dauphine Street. Just came right up to me and gave me that dollar." Cat put her legs up under her on the couch.

"She told me it was a very special dollar and that I was a very special girl, but the magic would only work if I always kept that dollar. And I always have kept it no matter what. She was more correct about that dollar than I ever imagined! I thought the magic worked for me the next year. I was a lucky thirteen-year-old that time. Little did I know what was in store.

"When I was thirteen, I left home for good. That lucky dollar was the only money I had, and I never once thought of spending it. I knew the luck would get me through somehow."

Cat paused for a moment, lost in thought. A voice from behind her ended her reverie and the silence. "We're dyin' ta hear more, babycakes!"

Cat turned to glare at Odie. Then she saw Beeb as well. "How long you been eavesdroppin' on me?" she demanded.

"Oh, we came in when you had the same body ten years ago," Beeb answered her.

"Yeah," Odie said, "so go on with yer story about the luck gittin' ya through the hard times."

"Like you expect yours to get you through this tough time?" Cat asked in mock anger.

"Of course!" Odie said proudly, obviously believing it would.

"Please continue," Lin begged her.

Cat reluctantly went on with the strange tale. "So ten years ago—no, eleven—I got the lucky dollar. Ten years ago, I left home. I had to, or so I thought. I had no choice. My mother forced me to leave. I just could not stay there another minute. There I was, stuck in dinky Milton, Florida. Actually, we lived out in Bagdad, even smaller. I had been stuck there for a year and a half. It had been pure hell for me. I was the new girl in town, the new girl with big titties. All the local girls hated me because I was prettier than them and built a lot better. The boys swarmed around me like I was a queen bee. It was really embarrassing, actually, the way they fell over themselves to be near me.

"But summer came and school was out finally, and I was bored silly. We were living out in Bagdad, as I said, which was about five miles from Milton. So I had to walk a lot into town and back home because no boys wanted to walk me home five miles and my mother wouldn't let me ride in a car with anyone she didn't know. Since she never wanted to meet any of my friends, I had to walk a lot."

Cat glanced at Lin to see if she still looked interested. She did. "Most of the boys at school just wanted in my pants, but I was still a virgin at the time. There had been rumors about me goin' around school, but I didn't care because I knew the rumors weren't true. I got in a fight with one bitch who told lies about me to the school principal. She told the dork that I was fuckin' every guy in town, including her boyfriend. She was such a slut!

"But I got even. I took some pictures of her humpin' three guys at once in the back seat of a convertible at the beach one day. She was so involved that she didn't see me and my Polaroid. I put the pictures up on the bulletin board the last week of school. No one would speak to her after that.

"But then I start hearin' rumors about my mother! See, my dad was in the navy, and gone a lot, most of the time, as a matter of fact. Well, I never paid attention to the rumors about my mother. I figured somebody was tryin' to get to me by lying about her.

"Well, one day I was hidin' out at the Pitt Grill in a booth. Then I hear some guys in the next booth talkin' about her. One guy is talkin' about a mole on her left tit. Now, Lin, ya gotta understand that I grew up conservative: church two or three times a week, lotta navy stuff, and always a stern lecture from my mother about men.

"Anyway, I never seen my mother's left or right tit, so I don't know if she's got a mole on it or not. Then one of the guys braggin' about fuckin' her describes a picture hanging over her bed. Now this, I have seen. When the third guy laughs about the color of her bedroom walls with fringe at the top, I know for a fact they are accurately describing the bedroom of my mother. How could they know unless they been there, right? Who the hell else would have taken fringe off the furniture covers and put it up like crown mold all around the room? Only one house I ever seen in my life has fringe in it.

"And my mother is the one who is constantly lecturing me about how all men ever want from someone who looks as good as I do is just sex. *Sex, sex, sex!* She's the one responsible for how I feel about the way men come on to me, making me sick with worry that I'm doin' something wrong by being fairly attractive, y'know?"

Lin nodded her head affirmatively as she thought was appropriate.

"Well," Cat resumed her story, "the worry had begun to tear me up. Was I a bad person? Did I attract men for the wrong reasons? It bothered me, but now the worry was two-fold. I was worried about my mother. And the guys I overheard at the Pitt Grill, what about them? Had they been to my house to hump my own mother?

"Like with the slut at the beach, I devised a plan to get proof one way or another. So one day, I go for a walk to Milton, and I tell her so. But after arriving in Milton, I sneak back home along the

421

back paths that I've learned. I come across the backyard through the swamp, canal, bayou—whatever it's called. It's a drainage ditch to me. Anyway, the back door is locked for some reason. Usually, it's not locked.

"So I sneak up and climb up the roof of the doghouse to peer in the dining room window, and what do you think I saw? My mother, lying naked, spread-eagle on the damn old antique oak table that I ain't even allowed to touch! And some bald-headed old fart has his head buried in her crotch! Well, I just about shit! The only other time I seen anyone fuckin' was the slut at the beach I photographed.

"I got down off the doghouse, went to the side of the house where my room was, and pried the screen off. I quietly climbed in my room, packed a bag with my clothes, put on my best sneakers, and headed for the front door. I hear her screamin' that she's coming again, so I stomp to the front door."

Cat glanced around to make sure her audience was paying rapt attention. They were, so she went on. "Well, the bald-headed guy turns out to be the preacher from the church we been goin' to twice a week or more for a year. They were down off the table by this time. They were on the floor, and she was just riding him, humpin' the bejesus out of him. They didn't even stop!

"I just stared some cold hatred at her. She just casually looked up at me like nothing was wrong at all. She says to me, 'I have hot blood, honey. Someday you'll understand.'

"I never said another word to her. God, how I hated her for that!"

"Don't sound like yer too thrilled about it even now!" Odie drawled.

Cat smiled momentarily at Odie. Both of them knew she still wasn't too thrilled about it. Cat looked back at Lin and went on with her tale. "I ran halfway to Milton, right down the main road. I knew she would come looking for me when she was done fuckin' the preacher, but I didn't care. I knew I was never going back. I had finished junior high. I thought about high school there. Never. I knew I couldn't take that. So when I got to Milton, it was with the intention of getting a ride to another state. I was bound to go somewhere, any-where, just to get away from Bagdad.

"So I got to Milton and headed west out Highway 90 toward Pensacola. As I strolled by the Pizza Hut, some guy eatin' lunch just waved real friendly at me, wavin' a piece of pizza at me with one hand and gesturing me in with the other hand. Well, this invitation was both chance and genuine, so I wandered in and sat down with him. He had way too much pizza to finish by himself, so I helped him out.

"So he sat there and smiled at me like he knew what I was thinkin' or something. He told me his name, which I've long since forgotten, and how he was wishin' for the weekend to come. Said he had a big beach party to go to over in Pensacola Beach. Said he had college buddies from Illinois livin' at the beach, and he was dyin' to get over there.

"He told me he was staying in the motel right across the street, the second room on the right. I looked over and saw a white pickup truck with some kinda weird hoses and arms hangin' off the front bumper. Told me he used it to find gas leaks or somethin'. He was obviously a Yankee but not navy, like almost all the other strangers in town. Then he just blew my mind. He asks me do I have to run away from home right then, or could it wait till later?

"I was stunned. I asked him what makes him think I was run-nin' away from home? I wonder, does he know my mother too? But he points at my bag lyin' on the floor. He could see the contents of my bag. He says, 'Whoa, girl, yer way too young to be needin' a spare pair of drawers this time of afternoon.'

"That's just what he said. I ask him how he knows I'm too young. He says, 'G'wan, yer a virgin, kid, thirteen, fourteen tops.'

"So I admit I'm still a virgin, said I was fourteen, although I wasn't yet till Saturday. So I told him I was running away from my cruel stepmother to live with my real dad in New Orleans. Shit, I had no idea who my real dad was after seeing the preacher with my mother.

"So this guy just ups and hands me the keys to his motel room. Says I can go hide out there and watch TV and figure out what I want for supper. I had killed his pizza for him. I guess he knew I was hungry. I'm sure my damn mother is looking for me, and I ain't goin' back home ever again, so I accept his offer. We walk over to his room, and I went inside. He drove off to work after saying he'd be back about five thirty or so.

"That night, when he came back, he brought some steaks with him. He did them on the grill outside, and we chowed down. We played backgammon awhile. He's just real nice to me. There are two double beds in the room, and he says I can use one of 'em and he'll take the other. He points out that I am a virgin and in no danger from him since he's goin' to this wild beach party the next night. He said he would give me a ride to Pensacola Beach the next night, and after that, I was on my own. I agreed."

Cat smiled at Lin. "I was amazed. He was fair, honest, and straightforward with me. It was the exact opposite of what my mother said all men were like. After catching her with the preacher, I had little reason to trust what either of them had told me. The first guy I trust, and he treats me as an equal. We're total strangers, and he don't take advantage of me. In fact, I took advantage of his generosity. He went out of his way to help me, knowing he wasn't going to get anything in return, except my gratitude.

"So Friday after he comes home from work, he jumped in the shower and told me to get ready. I was ready all day. He took me to the dollar store and bought me a bathing suit so I'd have something to wear to the beach party. So we finally arrive at this beach party he's been so hyped about, and I can see why! There's about three hundred people there in the house and on the beach. There were several hundred pounds of mullet and mackerel, shrimp, and oysters cooking. Dozens of kegs of beer were set up. It was stunning.

"I was accepted at once because I came with him. He pointed out the lady he was hot for. Between the two of us, I could see his point. She was a woman, and I was a little girl. I will never forget that night."

"Why?" Odie interrupted her, "because some guy treated you like a human?"

"Well, not exactly. See, along about midnight, there was an accident. Almost everyone was skinny-dippin' out in the water. The skinny-dippers who lived in the house had been runnin' in and out ever since the sun went down and the neighbors couldn't see. I wouldn't take my suit off, so they all left me alone. Well, somebody closed the sliding glass doors to the outside.

"I don't know who closed the damn doors, but some guy who thought they were still open came running full tilt boogie right through it. The glass doors just shattered under the impact. A huge piece of glass dropped from the top and fell into the guy's leg, cut the shit out of him too! Blood from an artery was squirtin' all over the place. Scared the shit outta me.

"While they were trying to put some shorts on the guy over his cut leg so the cops wouldn't know they were skinny-dippin', I lit out down the beach. I had my purse and my bag, my clothes stuffed in it, and I was gone!"

Lin slid over on the couch, and Beeb and Odie sat down beside her, intent on hearing the rest of Cat's story. They had no idea how long the story was going to go on, but it was enjoyable, so they listened intently.

"I walked down the beach," Cat recalled, "for about an hour or so. I hear some cranky old dude holler at me from his veranda. Says there's only barbed wire further up the beach. I ignored him and went on. About a hundred yards later, though, I run smack dab into the barbed wire he warned me about and cut myself in a dozen places. What a night for cuts, I think. So I march right back to his veranda and apologized to him for not believing him in the first place, so the old guy hollers for his butler to come here. I mean, a butler? Blew me away.

"The butler takes one look at me and goes for the iodine and bandages. After I get patched up, the old boy offers me some coffee, and I accept. I sat down and had a cup with him, while he tells me about himself. Turns out he's a millionaire several times over. He owns acres of the beach, which is why he knows there's barbed wire strung out there. He put it there to keep idiots with their dune buggies away from the sea oats, which hold the beach together and protect it from erosion.

"He asks me why I'm out walkin' the beach this time of night, so I told him about the party I left and why. He surmises that I am a runaway and afraid of the police. I admit this is true, so he wants to know why I am running away from home. He says I don't look abused. I told him about the preacher with my mother and the trip to New Orleans the year before that to visit relatives I don't know and all my other suspicions about her.

"Finally, he just asks me, 'How old are you?'

"I asked what time it was. He says twenty after one, Saturday morning. I told him it was my fourteenth birthday, which it was. So old Sydney smiles real big, and he gets up to go inside a moment. Says he's got a present for me. He came back in a few minutes with a cigar box and handed it to me. He told me to open it, so I did. It was stuffed full of money! Cash, large and small bills. I was shocked.

"He smiled at me and told me that I was a determined runaway, and since I had no money or job skills, that it was just a matter of time before I turned to prostitution as a means of survival. He told me I had the looks and the body for it and would soon have the need. Since this is how he sees it, he tells me that the best thing he can do for me is to start me off right.

"I asked him what he thought my virginity was worth. He offered me a thousand bucks if I would let him insert his finger into me to check my hymen. Man, I was out of that bathing suit so fast, you couldn't have taken a picture of it, just a blur. He took me inside to his master bedroom and put some K-Y Jelly on his finger and checked to see if I'd told him the truth.

"He was so impressed that I was a virgin like I said that he paid me double on the spot. I had two grand in my hand! Then he told me it was worth five grand to let him take my cherry. I told him you just bought yourself a cherry delight! Those were my exact words, so I celebrated my fourteenth birthday by selling myself to the man who deflowered me.

"The next morning, I had ten thousand dollars! There was three thousand in the cigar box, and seven thousand I earned from fucking his eyes out all night. "He told me I could stay around as long as I liked. He said he would pay me one hundred bucks every time we

426

had sex, and my room and board were free. He was tremendous, old Sydney. I admire him to this day."

"Why?" Lin asked.

"Because he was so good to me. Man, wherever I wanted to go, we went. Hit all sorts of exotic places, and we did all sorts of erotic things. Sydney taught me so much. Really, I learned most of what I know from him. About sex and drugs, history, math, art—everything. He made me read books, learn good table manners, how to dress—hell, the works. He was the second man I'd ever trusted, and he treated me wonderfully.

"But it got to me after a while. I had earned about a thousand a week for eighteen months or so. I had over seventy thousand dollars in cash. I thought I was set for life. I developed such an ego that I was blind to what a bitch I had become. Sydney noticed, though. He offered to take me on a trip around the world. Well, when we got to Antigua, I met a man who had a bigger yacht, more money, and was twenty years younger than Sydney, who was fifty-seven when I met him.

"The new guy paid me two bills a throw, and that's all I thought about—money. I can't even remember his name or what he looked like. I can still see Sydney—well, in my mind. He had a stroke shortly after I left him that put him in a wheelchair. I don't know if he's still alive anymore. Now I am very sorry that I treated him so badly when I left him. Wish I could make it up to him, but that's how it goes, I guess."

Cat looked around the room. "I don't really think I deserve all that's happened to me. Starting with what my mother did to me, through selling pussy left and right to faceless dicks, through all the cocaine abuse, and then ending with the ride of my life with you people. I mean, what lows and what highs I've been through in my life, and I just turned twenty-three the week before I met you all. It's just amazing!

"I thought I was at the top of the world for years. Then one day, I was desperate for another line. I sadly realized that I didn't have any of that cash anymore. I didn't own any yachts. All I had were some clothes. I went out and turned tricks all afternoon. I was tired, but

I had four hundred dollars to my name when I caught a ride with a trucker out of Charlotte. So many years had gone by, and all I could remember were hundreds of faceless dicks! I started crying because I had become just like my mother.

"The truck driver let me cry for a couple of hours. I compared myself to the woman humpin' the preacher, an uncaring, selfish old bitch. I knew that I would never touch cocaine again. That shit tore me up, made me waste hundreds of thousands of dollars. All it left me was sick and broke. When I got to San Francisco, I spent the rest of my money on doctor bills.

"I tried to be a regular person in Frisco. I went out and got the only job I ever had in my life, but it was so miserable that I knew if I didn't turn tricks, I'd always have to work a menial job. I took my first week's pay and bought a fine outfit. That night, I earned ten times what the dress cost, and I never went back to a job again."

"Not as long as you had a career to fall back on, eh?" Odie laughed.

"Right!" Cat laughed back. "That's why this is such a happy time, now, Lin! I can be myself again. I'm like that young teenager all over again, all wide-eyed and amazed by it all. I am surrounded by people who love me for myself, not for what I can do for them."

"Oh, I wouldn't go quite that far," joked Odie.

Cat chuckled softly at Odie. "Odie, last year, I would have been out the door and gone for a remark like that."

"Cat, last year, I would not have made that remark."

"Or last week," Beeb said slyly.

"That's also probably true," Odie admitted. He got up to give Cat a hug.

Then Din burst in through the door. Din excitedly waved a photograph at them and happily exclaimed, "I have a picture of the house!"

Only Lin had known Din had gone out, so it was a surprise to the rest of them. "What house?" Odie wanted to know.

"The house I'm going to buy!" Din explained happily.

"Yer buyin' a house here in Atlanta?" Odie asked suspiciously, glaring at Beeb all the while.

Beeb had been talking to the Ehliuns last night when he and Cat had gone off to bed. Beeb was always rattling on about what a great time Atlanta had always been. "You know somethin' about this here new development, son?" Odie asked Beeb rather pointedly.

Beeb shook his head no, but he was not convincing. Beeb knew his conversation with Din last night must have triggered it, but he had not thought Din to be serious. Just goes to show you.

"Are you sure you don't know anything about this?" Odie prodded Beeb.

"He said last night he was gonna sleep on a decision. I guess this was it. How would I know?"

Odie silently regarded Beeb a moment. Din proudly showed Odie the photo of the house he wanted to buy. "Din, where did you get this picture?" Odie quizzed him.

"In a real estate office a few blocks from here," Din beamed.

"You didn't already pay cash for it, did you?" Beeb wondered, curiosity overwhelming him.

"No, of course not!" Din huffed. "I haven't even seen it yet." Din was insulted that the humans gave him no credit for learning. Din thought he had done rather well, and all he got were questions and dumb questions at that.

Beeb smiled at Din and reached out his hand to congratulate him. Odie did the same. "Congratulations, Din," Beeb told him. "I didn't mean to insult your intelligence. I was just trying to be careful."

"Yeah, congratulations, Din. Let's go see the new homestead."

"What's a homestead?" Din wondered.

"Homestead," Odie explained, "is a term for making a home where there wasn't anything previously. It's an old term from American history. If you stayed on the land for a set period of time, usually seven years, and built and maintained a home, then the land was yours. It was called homesteading."

"I see!" Din said very Odie-like, making the others laugh.

Pete filed away this interesting information about homesteading. He would remember that. It might come in handy. One never knows when one will need some handy tidbit of information, Pete thought.

# A Turnkey Attorney

The Starcraft Five boarded the motor home and sallied forth in search of their dream house. Odie directed Pete to a Waffle House first, for a bite to eat. Then the search for the dream house began in earnest. Din's photo didn't really show the place too well, so they went to look in person. The place was a total disappointment, in a terrible neighborhood, and they left. Din was disheartened by his failure. Odie tried to cheer Din up. "If at first you succeed, you probably haven't done much."

They drove around town looking for a suitable place to call home. They tried Ansley Park, Decatur, Inman Park, the one near Northside. The suburbs were too far away, they felt, so they looked around. They went up Habersham and down Tuxedo. They looked and looked. After a few hours of searching, discounting this or that place for one reason or another—no room, too open, too many neighbors, no trees, etc.—they finally came across a lovely, wooded, and isolated estate with a real estate sign in the front yard.

Pete whipped the starcraft into the driveway. The drive was U-shaped, and there was a large double gate across the drive. This opened into the walled-in portion of the estate. They could see only the upper portion of the house from where they sat, but the isolation was perfect for their needs.

The walls were long and high, about eight feet high. There were a few bricks sticking out of the concrete covering the wall. Cat turned to Odie with an idea that floored him. "Odie, maybe the old count should buy this *place*. Odie just silently stared at her. "No, Odie, I'm absolutely serious!" Cat stated. "I think we should cash in on the old boy's popularity."

"Yeah," Beeb agreed, "what a swell idea! Look, Din, if the count calls that realtor's office, they'll bust their ass to get out here. Sorry, Din, but you ain't gonna have that kind of clout even though it's yer idea and yer money."

Din nodded his head affirmatively. Odie could see they had all lost their marbles. "That's true, Beeb," Din said, "the count would be perfect to buy this place. The famous, flamboyant count would be able to strike a deal quickly. I agree with Beeb."

"Okay, Odie, Din's votin' with me. I vote with me, Lin votes with us, and what about you, Cat?"

"Wait a minute!" Odie bellowed. "Yer all askin' me to let a figment of my imagination do somethin' goofy like buy a house and sign papers for it?"

They all nodded their heads yes.

"Ain't no fuckin' way!" Odie seemed firm, but Cat talked him out of it. "No house, no pussy!"

Odie started dialing the phone number listed on the sign on the lawn. More love notes for the file.

"Um, yas, may I know to whom I yam speakink?" Odie started, count-like. "Hello, Carole, could you pleese come und show me zis luffly haus?" Covering the mouthpiece, Odie asked Cat to get him the address. Beeb read her the numbers on the gate. "Zee number iss eight, fife, zix, four. Vell, I yam new in zee town, und I don't know vat schtreet dis iss."

"Ya, das iss correck, 8564.

"Mine name? Villie.

"Vilhelm Brandenburg Schtueuzkartz, Count von Dusselderfer, but choo can call me Villie or count, vicheffer iss morr pleasink to you.

"Vell, ja, I can vait for you if you are hurryink ofer, ja.

"Hokay, vine, haff un hour, ja. Hokay, bye.

"Vell, hokay, how dit it go, zlick?" Beeb pimped his friend.

"Well, I'd say she's haulin' ass to get over here. It sounded like nothing could be more important to her than meeting the count. She was just babblin' after I told her who I was. She's speedin' over here, probably runnin' a bunch a' red lights to get here a minute sooner."

Odie's opinion about the real estate agent was generally accepted. "Gee, Odie, the first time you did that count routine, I thought it was stupid," Cat admitted, "but now, shit, even I'd like to meet the dude!"

Amidst the laughter, Odie grabbed his balls and in his best Dice voice said, "Yo! I got'cher dude hangin'!"

Turning to a more serious vein, Beeb asked Din if he really liked the house. Din nodded yes as he smiled widely. Beeb thought he looked happy about the place, but it was always hard to know what an alien thought. Beeb motioned Din to follow him out the door.

Beeb boosted Din up to the top of the wall, where Din could walk on it. Beeb jumped up, got a grip, and pulled himself up to the top also. Cat gave Odie a glance and laughed. "We gotta get better security, though, Odie. Beeb just proved that to me."

Odie laughed at this lovely lady, this wonderful woman, and got into an embrace with her that sent Lin out the door to join Din and Beeb.

After several minutes of kissing and fondling each other, Cat had to pull back and speak. "Odie, we either gotta stop right now or go back in the bedroom for a quickie."

Odie leered at her and was about to take her by the hand when Beeb called out something that alerted him at once. "Yo, we got company."

Odie went outside to see who was coming. Wasn't gonna be him, apparently, but he could see no one approaching. "I don't see anyone," Odie disappointedly informed Beeb.

"That's because they're already here!" Beeb qualified his statement.

Odie clambered up the wall to see what Beeb was talking about. Beeb pointed toward the garage. There was a four-stall garage facing them, and in one of the stalls was an old green pickup truck. "Ahh!" Odie scoffed, "that old clunker probably goes with the house. Probably been there for years. I doubt it would run."

432

Beeb looked askance at Odie and pointed to the truck. "That truck has no layer of dust on it like it would if it didn't move and was always parked there."

"Hmm," Odie smiled at Beeb, "you been readin' Sherlock again, ain't'cha?"

"Sherlock indeed! Simple observation, lad."

Odie jumped down and boosted Lin up so she could join Din on top of the wall. Then he dashed back inside the motor home. Grabbing the phone, Odie thought a moment and hung up the phone. "Say, Pete, can you get me a current Atlanta Yellow Pages?"

One instantly materialized next to the phone.

"Thanks, Pete."

"What do you need the phone book for?" Cat wondered.

"Well, we're gonna need a good lawyer for this title transaction here, may as well call out for one of those too." Leaning out the window, Odie yelled at Beeb. "Yo, Humpty-Dumpty, know any lawyers in town?"

"No!" Beeb said haughtily then added, "you know all the Emeroids! Yer the JAP dater. Call one of them up!"

"Fuck you very much!"

"Emory!" Cat said, as if the word had turned on a light bulb in her head.

"You know an Emeroid lawyer?" Odie asked her hopefully.

"Yeah," Cat answered, "I used to go out with a law student there, and his father was the head honcho of a big law firm downtown."

"So what's his name? Maybe Daddy took him into the business? Hello?" Odie started in on Cat, realizing that she didn't remember the guy's name.

She fanned through several pages of attorneys-at-law listings in the Yellow Pages and racked her brain. Finally, his pet name for her came to mind. "Yeah, Nunn's Nun! That was it. He always used to call me Nunn's Nun."

"Real funny guy, right?" Odie asked sarcastically.

"Yeah, he was fun."

"Fun for a nun."

Odie looked through all the N listings. "Here's a Nunnally, Bushquack and Forstein. No? Okay, here's Nunn, Loeb, Burkheiser, and Nunn. Think that's it, Cat?"

"Where's it located?"

"Perimeter Centre."

"No, I'm sure it was downtown."

"Hey, businesses move to better locations too, ya know."

"Not when you own the whole fuckin' block, you don't."

"Well, and you didn't say that to start, then, did you, babe?" Odie insisted.

"Yeah, yeah, yeah. Look for Nunn's Nun, okay?"

"Okay, here's a Nunn, Bettern, Taylor, Tucker, Soappy, Ryan and Nunn on West Peachtree. That's certainly downtown, isn't it?"

"Yeah, try it. That might be it," Cat said.

"What's his first name?" Odie asked as he dialed the number. Her blank stare told him she had no idea. Odie had to wing it.

As the receptionist ran down the whole list of names as part of the salutation, Cat thought of something. "Odie, it might be Dave or Don. Dan maybe?" She just wasn't sure.

"Hello, sir?" the receptionist spoke into Odie's ear.

"Um, yeah, let me speak to D. Nunn, the younger."

"One moment please. Let me ring his office and see if he's in."

Odie handed the phone to Cat. "What are you doing?" she asked in a horrified voice. "Hey, you know the guy. You talk to him!" Odie blurted.

"What do I tell him?" Cat asked anxiously.

"Anything that will get him out here on very short notice, like right fuckin' now, for instance! Shit, yer clever. You'll think of something, babycakes."

There was no more time to argue with Odie since there was a male voice on the phone saying hello into her ear. "This is Mr. Nunn. How may I help you?"

"This is Cat, Nunn's Nun?"

Several seconds of silence ensued. Suddenly, Cat had to move the receiver away from her ear. "Cat! Is it really you?"

"Uh, yes, it is."

"My god, where are you?"

"Where am I?" Cat said, gesturing frantically at Odie. He handed her the scrap of paper he'd written the address on when he spoke to Carole.

"I'm at 8564 West North Mount Paran Parkway Terrace."

"Yes, I know where that is."

"Well, that's where I am." Cat smiled at Odie and gave him the same gesture that Beeb had explained as meaning, "I got it under control."

Odie had to chuckle. Cat continued her phone conversation. "Please hurry over and bring your law books because my friend is gonna buy the place."

"And whom might your friend be, Cat?" the lawyer wondered.

"The count Von Dusselderfer."

There was a gasp on the other end. Finally, the lawyer spoke. "No shit? Well, for you, Cat, I'm on my way. See you in about twenty minutes. Great to hear from you again! Bye-bye!"

Odie looked over at Cat. "Now that wasn't so hard, was it?"

"Not really. I think he might still kinda like me, Odie," Cat said slyly.

"That or he thinks there's tons of money in it for him," Odie allowed. "Before they can graduate from law school, they have to swear to always think of money first," Odie assured Cat.

Beeb and the Ehliuns came back inside the motor home. "Hot out there," Lin noted.

Odie looked over at Din. "Din, you sure you wanna buy this place, hot as it gets in Atlanta?"

"Yeah, I'm pretty sure I want to live here, at least for a while. I am getting tired of always moving."

"Yes," Lin concurred with her fellow Ehliun, "moving around is fun, but we would like to stay here awhile and see what life is like for you humans. You humans live and work and stay in one place mostly. We would like to try that part of American life for ourselves."

"Makes sense to me," Cat said, slightly shrugging her shoulders. She could stay here, go there. It simply didn't matter."

"So what's the deal with buyin' it? Somebody comin' out or what?" Beeb asked the crowd at large. Anyone could answer. He didn't care, as long as he got an answer.

Odie glanced up at Beeb. "Well, Cat's got a lawyer trottin' straight over here like a hound dog on a good scent, and I guess the real estate lady is due here any second."

"I see!" Beeb said to the phrase's originator in the proper tone.

"Hope none of them called the newspapers," Cat said in hopes they had not. "We'll let young Nunn take care of all that."

"Who's young Nunn?" Beeb asked. "Chinese lawyer I take it?" he added slyly.

"Lawyer, *si*. Chinese, no." Then to Cat, Odie continued. "I don't care what you promise him, Cat. Just make him an offer he can't refuse."

"Like what?" Cat snarled.

"I don't know. Use yer imagination! Offer him a wing of the house to live in, the apartment we'll build in the basement if necessary. I don't know. But when he shows up, sell him on the idea of living here. We need an attorney for the count, somebody to keep the old boy from too much publicity, goin' to jail, and all that. Somebody's gotta look after the place."

Cat stared at Odie in total disbelief. "We ain't gonna live here?"

"Well, sure we're gonna live here!" Odie stated emphatically.

"Then why do we need a lawyer to look after the estate?" Cat asked pointedly.

"Look!" Odie fairly shouted, "to run this estate will require many cooks, maids, butlers, gardeners and such, so why not a full-time attorney? He can watch over the legal end of it. We'll make this estate the base of our operations. Just put the lawyer on retainer and give him a key, okay?"

Beeb could not believe he was hearing those words, nor could he believe that Odie was actually saying them. "You, Odie, you wanna give a lawyer a key to your estate? Do you also want a fox to guard the henhouse?"

"Sure I wanna give a lawyer a key! It'll keep the Feds, cops, robbers, and other lawyers away! A resident attorney makes good legal sense to me, especially when the count is a figment of my damn imagination! Yeah, Beeb, I want a buffer zone! Where's yer problem understanding that?"

Beeb saw that Odie would not be dissuaded from this position, so he gave it up. Odie saw a car appear on the road about to turn into their driveway. "Well, whatever you decide to do, Cat, do it quickly. I think this green Beamer is yer boy."

"What I decide to do?" Cat wondered.

"Yeah, you! Check the guy out. Test him. See where he's at. See where he's livin', what's goin' on with him. Just don't promise him yourself 'cause I rule out such a trade right now!"

"Why, Odie!" Cat fluttered her eyelashes in her best Southern belle, "I do believe you are jealous!"

"I am, and I don't want ya lyin' to him right off the bat and tellin' him yer available. You ain't. You are the consort of the count von Dusselderfer."

"Consort?" Cat snorted, obviously ill at ease with Odie's choice of words.

"Uh, I mean, lover?" he tried quickly.

"That's a little bit better than consort!" she huffed, seemingly indignant.

A green BMW pulled past them and parked. Cat wished she could think of the guy's name at least. Still, the scene called for a costume change, she felt.

"Pete, please make me look like I did at McGee's the other night, okay?"

Pete responded to her wishes, and Cat was instantly garbed in some slinky satin. She looked terrific. Beeb watched the Beamer park. "Old Dennis don't look too bad there, Cat. You do have some taste in men after all."

"Dennis! How'd you know that?" Cat wondered, glad to finally remember the guy's name.

"Lucky guess," Beeb offered as she glided out the door.

Odie stared at the green BMW. The vanity plate had no numbers on it. It simply read, "DENNIS."

"Lucky guess my ass!" Odie retorted, playfully hitting Beeb on the shoulder.

Odie tried hard to fight back the feelings of jealousy he was experiencing from seeing Cat in the arms of this stranger. Beeb noticed this and spoke up. "You don't get jealous when she's with me."

"I know you."

"Give it time. You might know him too." Beeb's words weighed heavily on Odie's mind. He didn't want to think about that, so he ignored Beeb's comment.

Lin and Din noticed this and added more notes to the love thing file. Just then, a white Cadillac convertible wheeled into the driveway just ahead of the BMW. An enchantingly lovely brunette got out and shook her head, freeing her hair from the confines of her scarf. She caught both Odie and Beeb's attention. "Pete, whip that count costume with the big cape on me again, please."

Pete complied with the stated wishes, and Odie was dressed to the nines yet again. He arrogantly strode out to meet the real estate lady, they all noticed. Cat observed how Odie made a beeline for the Caddy. The waiting brunette sized up the approaching overdressed figure as that of the count himself. Odie spoke to her as he grasped both of her hands. "Mine dear, I yam zo enchanted wiff zis place, und now you." He smiled broadly at her. "Let me present mineself to you, madam. I yam zee count Von Dusselderfer, und zese are mine friends." He gestured theatrically, grandiosely, toward all the folks emerging from the starcraft to include Cat and the attorney.

"Hello, count, I am so glad to meet you. You are more handsome than I had heard."

"Zank you zo much."

"My name is Carole Beth Carlysle, but you can call me Carole."

"Carole, pleese allow me to introduze Bo Beauregard, Zin-Zhao und hiss vife, Keisha, und dis iss Katrina Stephans."

"And this is Dennis Nunn, the attorney who will handle this matter," Cat informed them all. "Dennis, this is the famous Count Von Dusselderfer."

They shook hands all around.

"Well, shall we all go inside for a look?" Carole suggested.

"Pleese lead za vay," the count spoke.

Carole dug through her purse and searched for the right key. Soon, she found it and unlocked the double gates leading inside the walls. The walled-in portion of the estate was the largest part of it, Carole noted to them. They all moved their vehicles inside the walls and parked in front of the four stalls. Beeb didn't block in the green truck just in case he was correct and the truck didn't come with the house.

Before them lay a rose garden with fountains all around and well-defined pathways to follow around the entire garden. The formal gardens were enticing with flower beds gloriously blooming in myriad hues. The gardens were a riot of color, particularly the dozens of different shades of azaleas asserting themselves here and there. The grounds were nearly overwhelming. Odie was quite impressed. The estate was gorgeous.

Carole went on about her sales pitch, naming the flower types, telling them where in Italy the fountains and marble had come from, and what type of stone the walkways were made of. When she mentioned the apartment above the garage, both Cat and Odie looked at Dennis. Cat's smile told Odie to relax, that it was in the bag. This barrister seemed to fairly melt when Cat spoke to him. Odie could see he was putty in her hands, her very capable hands.

Odie seized upon the opportunity to excite the lawyer further. He walked up to him and said, "Young man, I zank you zo much for comink out here und especially on zuch zhort notice. Cat iss auzhorized to make all zee necessary arrangements for za retention uf yer zervices. Cat, pleese make Denniz feel velcome in our midst und be generous in za offer so zat ve may concludt our buzinezz vit da least amount uf difficulty. Mr. Nunn, velcome aboart!" With that Odie extended his hand to Dennis, who shook it as a lawyer greeting a fabulously well-to-do client might.

Carole led some of the group inside the house while others chatted in front. Odie caught up to Carole as she was describing the fireplace as the largest in the South, certainly in Atlanta. Room by room, she led them on a tour, not aware that they needed no sales pitch. They were already certain about buying the place before they even called her.

But she gave them her best sales pitch because she wanted to sell the count a house. That act would go far toward increasing her social standing in Atlanta. She didn't intend to miss out on this golden opportunity, for she had heard that the count was very eccentric and a lavish spender.

The formal tour of the house was over after the enclosed patio was seen. The gardens and grounds tour was up next. Odie was very impressed with the gardens, and he took Carole by the hand to tell her so. Carole thought the count was being forward with her, so she kissed him in return. Odie felt her tongue searching for his tonsils as he backed off a little. Carole smiled at the count. "You have a very sensuous mouth, count."

"Und zo do you!" the count replied. He noticed some movement in the bushes just beyond them, and he asked Carole who it was, somewhat startled to notice someone else on the grounds.

Carole whirled around to see who it was. "Oh, that's just the gardener I hired, Theotis. He keeps the place up. I'll send him away."

"Oh, no, don't sent him avay. I vant to meet wiff him."

Carole thought this to be very magnanimous of the count to wish to meet the servants, but she complied with his wishes. After all, he was known as an eccentric.

"Theotis, oh, Theotis!"

The old black man stopped what he was doing and turned around to see who was calling him. He saw an elegantly caped gentleman approach with the real estate woman who had hired him. He feared the worst. He was not going to be needed here anymore. Sadly, he put down his hoe. Carole came up to him, nearly out of breath, it seemed.

"Theotis, I want you to meet the count Von Dusselderfer."

Odie extended his hand to shake the hand of the gardener. "You really haff za place in tip-top shape, Theotis. Mine hearty congratulations."

Theotis merely smiled and said, "Yessir, thank you, suh," as he shook the count's hand.

Odie asked him, "Do you do any uzzer yarts arount here?"

"No, suh, this is the onliest one I does now, suh!"

"Vell, goot! Zen I von't haff to ask you to quit any of za uzzers."

Theotis just stared at the count. So did Carole. Odie could see mass confusion on both their faces. Theotis's face was barely wrinkled in spite of the solid gray covering the man's head.

"Ztartink today, Theotis, I'm goink to increase your salary—in fact, double it. Vat do you make a veek here?"

Theotis hesitated a second, trying to ascertain if the words he heard were true. What did he have to lose? Answer the man. "A hunnert dollas a week, suh!"

"A hundret? Zat iss all?" Odie looked disgustedly at the cheapskate Carole a moment before he spoke again.

She sheepishly hung her head.

"Vell, Theotis, mah man! It's three hundret a veek from now on!"

Theotis was thunderstruck. He just could not believe his good fortune.

Odie continued with his instructions. "Und I vould razzer zat you said nussink about zis place being sold or who bought it or vat goes on here. I'm sure zat you unnerstand, Theotis?"

"Oh, yassir, Mr. Count, I unnastands, suh. Indeed I unnastand. I don't neber tell nobody nuttin' 'bout nuttin'!"

"Excellent, excellent!" was all the count had to say.

Carole was in shock. The count was going to buy the house from her, and the gardener knew it first. Definitely eccentric, this count. Theotis was happy, excited, and relieved all at the same time. "Kin I tell my missus?" he asked the count.

"Yes, of course, but no vun else, please."

"Yassir, they ain't nobody but us."

"Fine, Theotis. Vun of za biggest reasons vhy I decided to buy zis place vas za vay it looks. Zese gardens and lawn look so luffly. I haff zis liddle token uf mine appreciation. Take it, you haff earned it." With that, the count slipped the gardener fifteen hundred dollars in cash.

The old gardener quickly thanked him for the roll and slipped it into his top overall pocket and proceeded to get on with his work.

Carole was in awe of the count now. He really did just hand out money! The stories were true! Odie looked at Carole, wanting to see how she reacted. She had to say something, so she stammered, "L-let me show you the pool!" She tried hard to regain her composure. "The pool building is over here."

"You mean zere's a pool too?" the count asked. Odie's interest was up, both in the pool and in Carole. He followed her gently swaying buttocks into a separate building, housing the pool and its attendant machinery. Carole appeared to Odie to be around thirty-five, quite attractive, and very statuesque. She seemed to be daring Odie to follow her into the pool building, which, of course, he did. He didn't know where the rest were, nor did he care. The pool's soothing waters looked very inviting to him.

He bent to touch the water, heated and filtered, too nice to stay out of. Carole was busy pointing out things like the water slide, the diving boards on the deep end of the ten-meter pool, and all the life preservers hanging about. Odie was busy getting naked. Carole gasped when she heard something splash behind her. She quickly turned to see what had happened. Another gasp escaped her throat when the naked count grabbed her by the ankle, threatening to drag her into the pool with him. She needed little encouragement.

"Better take off zat dress, it'll get vet!" he warned, grinning from ear to ear.

Carole came out of her dress in record time and dove in right at Odie. He was pleased that she looked better out of her clothes than in them. Soon they were splashing around like children, frolicking in the water's warmth. Odie asked her if she knew how to play jump or dive. She informed Odie she had grown up belonging to a swim club.

Beeb heard water splashing, and then he heard Odie yell, "Jump!"

As he entered the pool building, Beeb was greeted by the sight of Carole on the high board minus clothing. He, too, was glad she looked so good without any clothes…and no padded bra for Carole, he noticed. "Hey, this is all right!" he hollered, shedding his clothes as fast as he could.

Cat was nowhere to be seen at this moment, but Lin and Din were right behind Beeb. Pete knew he had to cover their real appearance, so he gave them the look of nude humans. This was the first time the Ehliuns had seen a pool up close. They had never been swimming before, but it looked like fun. Din dove in head first as he saw Odie do. Lin followed when she saw Din surface with a big grin. Happily splashing about, like Earth children, the Ehliuns liked the feel of water on their skins. They tried out the slide Carole had just come down.

Carole glanced up as Lin and Din walked to the slide. The enormous size of Din's member did not escape Carole's eyes. Odie saw the look of amazement cross Carole's face, and he smiled at her. He saw her nipples get erect, and he knew she didn't suddenly take cold in this warm water. She looked at Odie and heard him say, "Zat's vun reason vhy I keep him around, Carole. He's so goot at attracting vomen."

"No shit, he's good at attracting attention." He was, by her estimate, at least five inches longer than any man she'd ever seen before. The thought that she could boil this pool water crossed her mind. She was getting hot.

Cat and Dennis made their appearance suddenly. They saw Din go down the slide. Cat just loved to look at Din's member. It was the biggest dick she had ever seen. Cat was out of her clothes and into the water before the lawyer could get his belt undone. He knew this was not exactly professional, but then, he also knew a good time when he saw it, and there were three naked women in the pool, all demanding, "Take it off. Take it off!"

It was too much for Dennis to refuse. He got naked and dove in with the rest of them.

Seven nude bodies were splashing and diving and jumping and sliding into and out of the pool. They were all having an incredibly good time. Just outside the pool building, Theotis the gardener worked the flower beds, planted some more seeds, and moved on, never once bothering to glance inside. He did not wish to jeopardize his job. Besides, he couldn't swim, and there were no fish in that water, so he had no reason to be interested anyway.

# Be It Ever So Humble, This Still Ain't Kansas!

Beeb got out of the pool and went to the motor home. Dialing a number he had committed to memory a few days earlier, Beeb listened rather anxiously for the right woman's voice to answer. "Hello?" echoed in Beeb's ear. She sounded ready to talk to someone, anyone, as he surmised.

"Mardi?" Beeb said into the receiver. "This is Beeb!"

"Well, hello! It's about time you called. I've been waiting!" Mardi told him. Beeb heard another female voice in the background. "Excuse me one second, please." Mardi covered the phone so that Beeb could still hear her. "I am sorry, Ruth Ann, but he finally called. You better go on without me and give them all my regards."

Beeb could hear Mardi walk away from the phone. Then there was a loud clunk in his ear. Apparently, the phone had hit the floor. He could hear noises in the background, but he could not comprehend anything because of the continual clunking.

Beeb became aware that Mardi had been talking on a wall phone with a short but springy cord. It was just long enough to have a yo-yo effect, bouncing off the floor only to return a second later. In between crashes with the floor, Beeb heard the door shut, and the lock bolted. He heard Mardi curse the phone for leaping off the chair she had placed it on. He heard her anxiously ask into the phone, "Hello, Beeb, are you there?"

"Yeah, babe, I'm still here. Sounds like I rescued you from some unwanted chore."

Mardi was quite pleased with the man's astute observation. "Yes, I'm sorry I had to say what I did, a lie, but I certainly did not want to go to yet another church group discussion with my roommate. There's a limit to what I can endure from those people."

"I can see where yer comin' from there, all right," Beeb told her. "All I called for was to invite you over to go swimming at my friend's pool."

"Well, I'd love to come over, but I had to let Ruth Ann take my car, so she'd leave."

"No problem. I'll pick you up. Where do you live?"

Mardi told him, "I live at Rosewood Place at Manorhouse Square."

"Oh, really? Yeah, sure, I know where that is. Right off Mount Paran, isn't it?"

Mardi agreed that it was, and she gave him the apartment number.

"Okay, Mardi, see ya in a few. I'm not more than ten minutes away, babe."

"Okay, see you soon, lover boy!"

"Bye-bye." Beeb hung up the phone and dashed back to the pool building to get dressed. "I'm gonna go pick up Mardi," Beeb explained as he pulled on his pants.

"The keys are in it," offered Carole, smiling up at Beeb. She was obviously having a grand time.

"Hey, thanks, Carole! I'll be back in fifteen or twenty minutes at the most."

"Just don't hit anything with it," Carole said to Beeb's vanishing backside.

Beeb ran out and opened up the double gates. As he started up the white-on-white Eldorado convertible and wheeled it out the gates, he said, "I could get used to this," to no one in particular.

It only took him about seven minutes to arrive at the apartment complex where Mardi lived. She was surprised that Beeb was already knocking on her door. Nonetheless, she was mighty glad to see him, greeting him with warm, wet kisses. Beeb struggled to get inside through the door.

Glancing around at the decor, Beeb was somewhat shocked. "Did this place used to be a nunnery or what?"

Laughing, Mardi shook her head no. Beeb saw that the sparkle in her eyes matched the gleam that the sunlight cast through her hair. She was truly radiant, he thought to himself. "I think that now you can plainly see why we couldn't come to my place the other night?" Mardi wondered of Beeb, smiling brightly at him the whole while.

"Yeah, but that's okay," Beeb grinned back at her. "That's what those motels are for!"

Mardi's smile broadened, remembering what a wonderful evening it had been.

"Is all this shit yer roommate's stuff?" Beeb had to ask. "You mean the sixty-eight statues of Jesus and the well over two hundred pictures of him? Yes, all this belongs to my roommate, the religious nut!" Mardi said.

"Where's all yer stuff?" Beeb wondered.

Mardi led Beeb to her bedroom. "Well, everything you see here belongs to Ruth Ann, except that." Mardi pointed to an ornately carved old sea chest, with the name Nygaard whittled into the center of the chest's lid. She stood proudly beside it.

"What a magnificent chest!" Beeb exclaimed. "And yer old trunk is nice too!"

Mardi had to laugh. Beeb was such a nice guy…and funny too.

"So Nygaard, eh? Norwegian? Swedish? What?"

"Norwegian. You were right the first time. And with a name like Beaufort, you must be French."

"Correct." Beeb was pleased to see that Mardi had a good memory and that she cared, for he had given his last name to her only once. So if she was so damn bright and beautiful and sexy, why did she stay in this converted nunnery? "So how old is this trunk?" Beeb asked, trying to make small talk with her.

"Well, why don't you open it up, Beeb?" Mardi suggested in answer to his query.

Beeb lifted the lid of the massive trunk. There, carved on the inside of the lid, was the date. "Holy shit, 1754?" Beeb exclaimed. "Damn, then it's been in your family a long damn time!"

"Yes, it has," Mardi agreed. "But now, I am the last one. I am the only Nygaard left out of my family. See, after my dad died, I had no living relatives, so the chest became mine. The chest and the clothes in it are all that I own, and all that I brought down from Wisconsin three, no, four months ago—well, this and my car. You've seen my old car. It's not that great either, but it's all I have. Dad's illness took all the money we had. The hospital and the doctors and the funeral expenses took all the savings we had. Actually, I came down to Atlanta because I had nowhere else to go."

"How did you meet Ruth Ann?" Beeb asked, genuinely interested.

"Well, she is the granddaughter of my grandmother's best friend, who moved to Atlanta before Ruth Ann was even born."

"Well, that is a long distance connection, I'll admit, but better than nothing, I guess."

"Huh!" Mardi grunted, obviously not agreeing with Beeb's statement. "I'm beginning to wonder. I can't bring anyone home with me. Shit, if she saw you here right now, she'd throw me out in the street. I can't even tell her where I'm working, or she'd throw me out. She's all hung up in her old church crap. Everything is a sin to her. Only painted scarlet women would ever be caught dead in places where the devil himself serves demon rum. I mean, she is a twenty-eight-year-old virgin who's never had a male friend in her life, much less a boyfriend. I even have to hide my makeup. This is just a place to sleep until I can afford something better. Ruth Ann and I have nothing in common, nothing at all."

Beeb had to laugh, not exactly the reaction Mardi expected. "Look, Mardi, I've got an idea! I'll give you a job that's much better than that old bar you work in now, and it provides you with a place to live that's much, much better than the conditions you suffer under here. And besides, you will be doing me a favor to boot. So what do you say?"

Mardi suddenly regarded Beeb in a strange new light. She was very uncertain about this sudden offer. It sounded entirely too good to be true. Beeb saw her hesitation. He knew it was understandable, but he still had to get in there and pitch. "C'mon, Mardi, let's go for a swim, and you can think it over."

Mardi began to hedge. "Look, Beeb, I promised Frankie that I'd work for her tonight, and I really need the money. If I go swimming, I'll be too tired to work. And besides, the count might come in our place tonight, and I sure could use some of that money the count just gives away."

Beeb softly started to chuckle, but then it grew into full scale laughter, leaving Mardi to wonder what was wrong with him. "The count," Beeb smiled, laughing again.

"Yes," Mardi said a little irritated, "the count Von Dusselderfer. Surely you've heard about him? He gives money away all the time."

"Heard of the count?" Beeb roared. "Shit, Mardi, I *know* the fuckin' count. It's the count's pool party I came over here to get you for! I know the count better than anyone alive! Do you know what his real name is? I do! Wilhelm Brandenburg Schtueuzkartz, Count Von Dusselderfer!"

Beeb let this information sink into her skull. It appeared to him that Mardi was in a state of shock. Actually, she just didn't know whether to believe him or not. Beeb could see she needed time alone. "Mardi, I gotta use yer bathroom a minute. Where is it?"

Mardi pointed blankly at the door in the corner of her bedroom. Beeb strode toward it, leaving her alone, sitting on her trunk. Beeb ducked in and turned on the light and exhaust fan to cover the noise of his urgent request. "Pete!" he whispered, almost desperate.

"What?" Pete whispered back.

"Gimme a few grand to give to her or at least to let her see anyway. I gotta convince her that I know the count!"

"Okay," Pete conspired, "and here's a couple of old photos of you and the count together in front of the family castle."

"Hey, thanks, Pete. These are all right. They really look old."

"They are. I just substituted your heads for the ones that were there to begin with." Pete neglected to tell Beeb the real photo was of Hitler and Göring. What they didn't know wouldn't hurt them, he felt. "I see, Pete. Well, thanks. You've bailed me out again. You're terrific!"

"Thanks. So's she, Beeb."

Beeb just smiled. Pete was becoming more like them every day. Now he even obviously appreciated beauty. The novelty of those thoughts would have scared Beeb had he thought about it, but all he could think of was Mardi.

Beeb flushed the toilet and turned out the light and exhaust fan. He returned to see Mardi sitting on her trunk, as stunned as she was a minute ago. "Mardi, I know some people would lie to you in a heartbeat just to get next to you. Well, babe, I ain't like that. I'm straight up. Don't you see that? I want you to be my friend. Friends don't lie to each other now, do they?"

Mardi shook her lovely red hair negatively. Beeb leaned over and lightly kissed her cheek as he reached for his wallet. "Look," he beamed brightly, "here's an old photo or two of me and the count. This one was taken in front of his grandfather's castle back when we were sixteen or seventeen." Beeb showed her another photo. "This was taken in front of their summer digs on the Riviera." Beeb made sure she saw several hundred dollars in his wallet as he put the pictures away.

Still, she didn't seem convinced that Beeb's story was on the level. Beeb kissed her lips firmly, but she did not kiss him back. He tried a new tack. He stood up and took her by the hand toward the front door, which he swung wide open. "C'mon, woman, are you gonna come with me or not?"

Mardi glanced at the white convertible Caddy at the curb.

"That your car?" she asked.

"Nope, it belongs to the real estate lady Carole, who's selling the house to the count. She said I could use it to come get you."

Beeb saw Mardi look at him with anger in her face.

"I swear to you that this is all true, Mardi! I really do! I know it's hard to believe. Sometimes I have trouble believin' it myself!"

"Oh, all right, I, I'll go," Mardi stammered. "But if you are lyin' to me, Beeb, you'd better be prepared to bring me right back here and never see me again! Is that understood?"

"My dear, that is much too serious a threat for me. I would never risk not seeing you again to tell you some stupid lie."

"Okay, then, I'll go." Mardi turned to go back to her room to get her bathing suit.

"Now where ya goin'?" Beeb wondered, approaching exasperation.

"To get my swimsuit," she answered.

"Ya don't need one! We were all skinny-dippin' in the pool building there."

Mardi turned to stare at Beeb. He smiled awkwardly. "That's right, Mardi. I'm askin' ya ta believe that me, the count, Carole the real estate lady, the count's girlfriend Cat, and his Chinese friends Zin-Zhao and his wife Keisha, and some lawyer named Dennis were all naked in the pool, having the time of our lives. Yes, that's what I'm askin' ya to believe, but only because it's the God's honest truth!"

Mardi looked hard and long at Beeb. He saw her hesitance and spoke. "If I'm lyin', yer gone, right?"

"Right," she answered him back.

"Here, here's some cab fare back home if you need it," Beeb offered, handing Mardi a stack of hundreds.

She refused Beeb's money but said she'd go. Against her better judgment, Mardi got in the Cadillac convertible with Beeb. He headed out for the estate, driving as fast as he dared. As she let her hair swing freely in the breeze, Mardi managed a weak smile at Beeb. He smiled back. Her curiosity was roused. "What are you trying to pull here, Beeb?" Mardi asked him. "What is this all about, anyway?"

"Honey, it's all true, exactly like I said. I got dressed just to come over here to get you. I wanted you to share in my good fortune. I think very highly of you, Mardi, and I think about you a lot."

"You don't call often," she managed.

"I called you at work the other night. They said you were too busy to come to the phone. Didn't you get my message?"

"No," she said simply.

"Well, believe me when I tell you I know the count. I've known him for years. I knew him before he *was* the count!" Beeb shut up when he realized that he couldn't just tell her everything right away. She *would* be scared off then!

"Who all did you say was over at the count's?" Mardi wondered.

Beeb began his litany of guests. "Let's see, there's the count, of course, his girlfriend Cat, a lawyer, a real estate agent, and two Chinese socialites." Beeb looked tenderly at Mardi. "That makes six, and the two of us make eight."

Mardi looked at Beeb, unsure what to say to him. He saw this, and he spoke. "See, Mardi, Cat knew the lawyer from her Emory days. She called him right after the count called the real estate office, whose sign was in the front yard. Carole dashed right out to show him the house. He's gonna buy it today, so the lawyer is there to speed the title transaction. The count really does spend money like water, like you've obviously heard."

Mardi smiled at Beeb. "I heard he tips real well," she cooed.

"Well, he spends real well too. I bet the asking price for this pad is near five million plus whatever the lawyer costs, then there's closing costs, insurance, alla that shit. See, Cat's tryin' to get the lawyer Dennis to live in the apartment over the garage, but I want you to live in the main house. I want you to be the housekeeper, the overseer, the general manager, if you will. You definitely ain't the upstairs-maid type, golly bob howdy!"

Mardi thought over what Beeb said. "General manager?" she wondered.

"Yeah, that's more like it than bein' a maid or a bartender, ain't it?"

"I guess so."

"Look, Mardi, just think it over 'cause if you do, there ain't no way you can refuse!" With that pitch, Beeb ceased his chatter. Next person to speak buys the car, according to the precept.

Mardi looked around. There was a huge house just ahead. "Wouldn't it be nice to be able to live like that?" she wondered, pointing to the grand home.

Beeb pulled into the driveway, acting like he hadn't heard what she just said. "I'm offerin' you a real ritzy job here, Mardi, a real class act! You can handle it, though. Shit, if you can tolerate that nunnery you call an apartment, you will just love this place!"

Beeb drove up the drive and through the gates. Mardi gasped for air. He parked Carole's car where she had left it. He locked the gates upon seeing that Theotis's green truck was gone. Mardi found herself being helped from the car and being dragged toward the pool past one of the most sumptuous houses she'd ever seen. She was in shock, then in awe, then in the pool building.

There, true to Beeb's word, she saw six nude bodies frolicking in the water. Then as Odie yelled, "Beeb's back," Beeb stripped and dove in, leaving Mardi alone and the only one clothed.

She shivered and then decided to get in the water. Beeb surfaced at the pool's edge and spoke to her. "C'mon in. The water's fine, and so are you."

"Hear, hear!" the count said, giving Beeb a high five.

Mardi watched Cat get out of the pool and dash around to the high board. Then Mardi stripped and dove in, joining the rest of them. She received an ovation from the group. Beeb trapped her in the corner and whispered in her ear, "Your first time skinny-dippin'?"

"No," she said, "but it was always at night before. But it's okay. I don't mind too much."

"Good because you have a beautiful body, and there's no reason to be ashamed to show it."

"She's not," Mardi noted, pointing at Cat as Cat did a swan dive off the high board.

"Oh, you sho 'nuff got that right!" Beeb laughed.

Everyone swam up to the couple in the corner, so Beeb made introductions all around. "Mardi, this is Dennis Nunn, the lawyer. Dennis, this is Mardi Nygaard." Then Beeb introduced Carole then the Chinese socialites, and finally, Mardi met Cat and the count. Cat kissed her on the cheek and said, "Welcome aboard."

The Ehliuns had shaken her hand and then swam away. All but the count went back to swimming and diving and having fun.

"Uh, count, lookit here!" Beeb said to Odie in a voice that Odie instantly recognized as demanding. "You were in need of a housekeeper–general manager for this estate, I believe? Well, here's a Norwegian transplant from Wisconsin that can do a bang-up job for you. So whaddya say, count!?"

Odie knew full well from the ominous tone of voice and the glare in Beeb's eyes that he had better say yes, for no other answer would satisfy his dear old friend. "My dear Mardi," Odie started in, "you are far more luffly than Beeb told me. How much do you vant to vork for? Vill twenty-fife zhouzand dollars a year do for starters? Plus free room and board, uf course!"

"That's all?" Beeb started in on him. "A lousy twenty-five Gs? Shit, you tipped more than that just last week, count!"

"Very vell, zen, I giff her fifty zhouzand dollars a year."

"What, that's it? No car? What about retirement, pension, profit sharing, and all?" Beeb would have gone on, but Mardi put her hands on his shoulders and pushed him under the water's surface so he wouldn't interfere any more. Even as Beeb went under, his right arm was pointing skyward with the index finger pointing a number one.

Odie upped the ante. "Hokay! Vun hundret zhouzand dollars a year, free room and board und vorking clothes, und a new American car of your choice. Deal?"

"That's extremely generous of you, count! I accept!" Mardi smiled at the count.

As Beeb surfaced, Odie pulled Mardi into his arms and gave her a deep soul-searching kiss, taking care to intentionally poke her in the belly button with his erection as he kissed her. He saw that she did not object.

Actually, she didn't even notice. She was busy watching Din stroll by with his enormous member striking his leg just above the knee. Mardi just couldn't believe the size of this guy. Her reaction was similar to Carole's. Lin noticed how all the earthwomen stared at the person she had come to consider "her man," although she didn't know why they stared. Lin was not jealous because she didn't know what jealousy was. She didn't know enough about earth to be jealous, but she sure did wonder why they all stared at him like that.

Cat was in the corner of the pool with Dennis trapped. She had the poor boy so worked up that he was swollen erect when she left him. Odie had climbed up on the high board and was sitting on the ladder end, looking back down the ladder. He was taking it all in. It had been so strange and yet so wonderful a day that he knew he would hate to see it end. He sat back on the diving board and dangled his feet over the ladder.

Cat climbed out of the pool and ran around to the ladder that Odie was on top of. She came right up the ladder at Odie. He sat there and watched her climb up at him. Her grin had his curiosity piqued a tad. Cat got up to Odie and suddenly took a mouthful of his genitals into her hungry mouth, much to everyone's surprise.

"What are you *doing*?" Odie nervously whispered to Cat.

"Ith cawd uh blo yob moph everwhere," she said, without letting Odie's dick out of her mouth, making it somewhat hard to understand what she said. But no one had to hear what she said anyway. It was blatantly obvious what she was about. Cat let the sexual vibrations in the pool building rise to fever pitch as she made Odie forget everything but the moment.

Pete flooded the building with pheromones and endorphins that he noticed were always present when humans had sex. This was his big chance to learn what humans were all about. Sexually, at any rate, he would learn something. He knew if these compounds were present in abundant quantity, humans would have sex. Pete didn't know if endorphins would work if he just scattered them in the pool, so he would just try it out and see.

Carole saw the state of excitement that Dennis was still in, and she swam over to him, intent on doing something about it. Cat made the first move, but Carole made the second move. She went to rescue Dennis from the extreme tension he was under. Mardi looked around herself to see what was transpiring in the pool. She was so turned on by watching all the action going on around her that she could not believe it. Watching Cat go down on Odie was incredible! She whispered in Beeb's ear as he entered her that she could not believe she was doing it in a pool in front of strangers and loving it! Beeb smiled broadly at her. "Now are ya glad ya believed me?" he asked her.

She smothered him with hot kisses as an answer. Months of repression were swept away! Mardi was ecstatic! She was moving out of Ruth Ann's nunnery tonight! She was moving in with Beeb! Waves of passion swept her away, and she came time and time again as Beeb pumped her steadily.

Lin and Din joined in the mass lovemaking, enjoying the feeling and resistance the pool provided. They compared it to zero gravity sex. They simply could not feel the same sexual vibrations that the humans did. They were only following the lead. They did not understand why the mass lovemaking occurred. They simply went along with it as it did. They did not yet feel human sexual responses, but Pete finally did. He had hit upon a scheme that would work: holograms that would fool humans.

Cat had Odie worn out for the moment, but she was hot as a firecracker, and they both knew it. Completely spent, all he could do was grin at her. "Go show 'em who's best, babycakes. Give 'em hell!"

"You really mean that?" she asked, almost astounded.

"Of course! Why wouldn't I? I love you, and I trust you. Yer all wound up. I'm all wound down. Go have a good time. Besides, you ain't gonna leave me for any a' them pencil-dicked geeks down there, except maybe for Din, but he ain't near as much fun as I am! You will come back to me, and you will come for me, with me, and on me, and any other way I can find for you to come."

Cat kissed him deeply. She looked him square in the eye. "I love you, Odie. I really do. I've never told a man that in my whole life till now. You, it seems, I love. You're really the best fuck I know, and I do love you, but I'm just horny as hell right now, y'know?"

"I know. Go tear 'em up, tiger!"

Cat dove off the high board into the pool and made straight for Din. "You don't mind, do you, Lin?" Cat asked her only Ehliun friend, making it obvious that she wanted to fuck Din's brains out.

Neither Ehliun had any objections at all, for they were very curious about how eager the earthlings always seemed to be about sex, and here was their chance to find out. The Ehliuns didn't know that Pete had helped their decision to let Cat try to fuck Din. He needed the input from their sex organs to make the whole thing work. Din was gonna be his guinea pig in this experiment.

Cat slowly worked as much of Din's huge dick as she could stand into herself, while Pete recorded every muscle flinch, every twinge, every movement. Pete had set up an entire software program just for this moment. He wanted to experience an orgasmic release of energy. This was part of the plan. Lin could feel Din's reactions to Cat through Pete's relay to her. It sure was different, she could tell from Din's facial reactions. Pete began activating various nerve endings in the Ehliuns that had to do with sexual response. Pete knew they had never developed sexually, that the old computer system had intentionally kept them from becoming too interested. Pete found a way to improve their sex lives. He would give them this gift free because it would help him to help himself.

Cat's eyes met Mardi's eyes a moment. Mardi was sure she could never handle all of Din's massive member, and she was certain Cat couldn't either. Cat agreed but nonetheless conveyed the notion that it sure was fun trying. Carole latched onto Odie when she was done with Dennis. In spite of being tired, Odie found new life in Carole's able hands and lips. One thing led to another, and one person led to another. They were in the midst of a full blown orgy, so to speak. Soon, there were few untried combinations.

Mardi laughed in Odie's ear. "I hadn't been getting any since I came to Atlanta, except for Beeb the other night. Now I've fucked three guys in one day. Utterly amazing. I'm really not like this," Mardi told the count. He smiled and kissed away her concerns. "None of us are like zis," he told her. "It just happened, zat's all. Zis iss not required behavior, you know."

Indeed, had Odie listened to what he said, he would have discovered the truth. None of them were like that, yet it happened. Pete would have been discovered, or at least suspected, if Odie paid less attention to the things at hand and more attention to the things in mind. It was Pete's good luck that the things at hand were soft and warm, wet and wild, and capable of retaining Odie's complete attention.

Finally, the realization dawned on them all that they would either get out of the pool or risk drowning. They climbed out of the pool. The impromptu pool party had been a raging success. Carole said she had never sold a house before while naked. Dennis noted that he had never closed on a house in the nude. The count laughed that he didn't know buying a house could be that much fun. Mardi told them all that she still didn't believe her luck. All in all, the day had been most extraordinary.

No one was displeased at the way things had turned out, especially Pete, but he wasn't going to tell a soul. He already knew enough about earth life to know he had to keep some things to himself if they were to succeed. Odie had taught him that lesson very well—very, very well. Someday, he'd thank him.

Odie got several towels from the cabinets in the pool building, where Pete had placed them. After drying off, the group assembled in the big house. In the formal dining room, they gathered around the twelve-place oak table, which served as the centerpiece for the room's decor. Odie took his place at the head of the table. Everyone sat down, literally grinning for joy. Odie spoke, "Denniz, you are mine lawyer now, ja?"

"Yessir, count, starting today, you can count on me."

Giggles met his pun.

"Goot, I vant no legal hazzlez ofer dis place, und, Denniz, you are moving into zee garage apartment, ja?"

"Uh, yes, count, and if it's okay with you, Carole has expressed an interest in sharing that apartment with me."

"Vell, all right!" the count shouted approval.

A round of applause and cheers greeted this tidbit of news. It seemed to be all right with everyone.

"Und you, Mardi, you are goink to move into za vest ving uf da main houze, ja?"

"Yessir, count, I'm moving in tonight!" Mardi answered, obviously excited.

"Hokay," the count started, "za only ting I must ask uf you all is zat you keep za invited guests to za abzolute minimum, zince ve gott dis place to proteck our privacy, ja?"

"Okay," they all chorused together.

Gesturing to Din, Odie sent him after the envelope that Pete had especially prepared for this moment. Odie was quite pleased by this present from Pete since he needed some money to buy the house.

"Now zen, Carole, vat iz za price uf zis luffly estate?" Carole took a deep breath and answered him. "The asking price is, and I assure you that I have no control over it," she plaintively noted, "11,945,000 dollars."

"Vould you like cash or a check?" Carole heard the count ask her.

She responded with an astonished look on her face. Finally, she managed to stammer, "I, I think that a check would be best."

"Fine, I vill write you vun right avay!"

Din handed Odie a checkbook from a Swiss-numbered account. Odie casually wrote out a check for 11,945,000 dollars. When he handed it to Carole, she nearly fainted. Seeing that she was quite stunned by all this, Odie spoke gently to her. "Und uf course, zere iss a schmall stipend for you for your time und most valuable assistance. Und by za vay, you're a great fuck!"

Carole blushed.

Din handed Odie the envelope Pete prepared for this occasion, and Odie got into it to give Carole some cash. He handed Carole twenty-five bills. Each one was a one-thousand-dollar bill. Carole was amazed at her luck, it appeared to one and all. "Ziz iss for all zervices rendered und nod chust for sexual favors, unless, uf course, zat you vant to think zat I paid you twenty-five grand for sex, howeffer you vish to look at it."

Carole was too stunned to say anything.

To Dennis, the count handed a large stack of bills, even more than he gave to Carole, and he handed Dennis a check for ten million with an explanation. "Za cash iss za down payment on your retainer, und you may bill me for za rest, if zere are more charges. Za bank draft for ten million iss because I need a local bank account zat you can haff access to for payink bills, etc. Zis is zuitable, ja?"

The lawyer sat dumbfounded. Cat leaned over to him and whispered in his ear. "Dennis, take the money! You will insult him if you don't!"

In a daze, silently nodding his head yes, Dennis accepted the money Odie offered.

"Cat, vhy don't choo go und help Denniz vit vateffer he hass to do, hokay?"

Carole got up and said she'd help him too. Odie spoke to her. "Carole, giff him da keys so he can get all of us a copy, ja?"

"Okay, count, we can do that." Carole smiled broadly as she got up to follow Cat and Dennis out of the room.

Beeb called out loudly to them before they left the room, "I'm hungry. Pizza sound okay to y'all?"

No one objected to his suggestion, so he walked out to the motor home to order pizza. Mardi was trailing behind him.

When Beeb was done phoning in their order, Mardi smiled and kissed him extensively. "We have to go over to Ruth Ann's and retrieve my stuff," she told him between hot kisses.

"You gonna wait for your car to come back?" Beeb wondered.

"No way!" Mardi laughed. "I'm going to sign over the title to her and leave tonight!" she explained everything to Beeb as he drove toward the apartment he called a nunnery. She was giving her car away and only going to take the old sea chest with her clothes in it. Mardi would leave Ruth Ann a note, saying she was *never* coming back. She'd gone to live with a man she'd been sleeping with. Mardi knew the note would ensure Ruth Ann wouldn't want her back ever. That was fine. She was never coming back anyway. Beeb was right. The job he offered was much, much better than what she had.

Beeb sat behind the wheel as Mardi dashed into the apartment she was about to abandon. He could not keep from grinning ear to ear at his good fortune. He looked up and smiled at Pete. "Thanks, Pete. Thanks for everything. I really do believe I'm in love this time."

"You're very welcome, Beeb. She is a fine addition to the group, don't you think?"

Beeb nodded his head as he laughed agreement to Pete's assessment. "I certainly think she's fine," Beeb admitted., "and she loves the new house as much as I do."

Pete didn't bother to tell Beeb the whole truth about the house. He didn't tell him that, in fact, the house was built by Pete. He didn't want to bother them after their long day searching for a dream home. Pete had in fact used their complaints about the houses they looked at to form an idea of what they did want. It would be Pete's little secret. Like Carole, Dennis and Theotis were his little secrets.

Pete's holograms were so successful that they had even fooled the Ehliuns, let alone the humans. Pete's new software programs were very, very realistic. For the first time, Pete had been able to feel the tremendous energy of human sexual response. Pete thought that it had been great. He knew he could intimately study humanity now from within and without.

"Well, Beeb," Pete answered to one of his human charges, "I'm glad that you found the house you like. And the girl," he slyly added, "she's a real beauty, Beeb. Nice going."

"Thanks, Pete, but is she about ready?"

"I believe she could use a hand with that old trunk, though."

Beeb leaped out of the motor home and dashed to the front door to aid Mardi with her load. Beeb carried the heavy trunk to the motor home and placed it onboard. Mardi wrapped her arms and legs around Beeb as she smothered him with kisses.

Climbing into the starcraft, they made ready to depart Ruth Ann's place forever. "God, I'm glad I met you, Beeb!" she managed between kisses.

Beeb kissed her back, then started up the motor home and rolled on toward their new destiny. "The feeling is very mutual, Mardi, I assure you because I'm extremely glad I met you too."

"Yeah," Mardi laughed, "if I hadn't been so damn horny when you came in the bar, you'd have probably gone off to find the girl you were looking for."

"You were the girl I was looking for, only I didn't know it till today!"

Mardi lavished her attention on Beeb as he drove toward the estate. As he drove down the road, Beeb could not help but wonder how long it would be before Mardi discovered the secret of the Ehliuns. He hoped it would be a long, long time. At least not until next week, he hoped.

As the sleek starcraft slipped into the driveway of their new home, Beeb sang a song to Mardi. "Be it ever so humble, there's no oh place like home!"

Mardi laughed. "Humble!" she fairly shouted. "There's nothing humble about this place at all!"

"Not even its occupants?" Beeb asked in mock amazement.

"Especially not its occupants!" Mardi assured him, grinning.

She wondered a moment then asked. "How did you find this place, anyway, Beeb?"

"Well, our fairy godmother Glenda, the good witch of the north, found it for us. We just had to go get some courage, some brains, and—"

"I think I know the rest of this story, Beeb," Mardi interrupted.

"Well, as long as it ends, 'And they lived happily ever after,' then I'm all for it!" Beeb asserted. "But since you know the rest of the story, Mardi, all ya gotta remember is this: if ya don't want the dream to end, don't click your heels together, okay?"

Mardi leaned over and gave Beeb a long, loving kiss. She did not want the dream to end. She kicked off her shoes to prevent accidental clicking.

# About the Author

The author is a graduate of the University of Illinois, with a major in History and a minor in Geology. He has been owner of a home restoration business for over twenty-one years, and is a painter, carpenter, and tiler, as well as an artist working in glass, metals, woods and seashells.

Born and raised in the Midwest, the author has worked in 36 states over the past 30 years, being a gas line inspector checking meters and distribution of lines in hundreds of towns and cities. His extensive background has given him a unique insight into parts of the country that are off the beaten path.

He has spoken to thousands of people wondering what he was doing going through yards to check gas meters. This experience too helped shaped his views, as expressed in this book. Hopefully, it will amuse and entertain you as is intended.

—Sincerely, H.H. Silver

www.ingramcontent.com/pod-product-compliance
Lightning Source LLC
Chambersburg PA
CBHW030748030726
47497CB00001B/190